FIRING BLANCS

Peter Stafford-Bow

Santé !

[signature]

May 2020

Cover design by Patrick Latimer Illustration
www.PatrickLatimer.co.za

www.PeterStaffordBow.com
@PonceDuVin

Acorn Independent Press Ltd
82 Southwark Bridge Road
London
SEI 0AS

To Curly, with love. I'm the customer!

Chapter 1

The Festive Forum

There I stood, an executive at the top of my game.

A master of the universe.

Well, a middle manager of the universe, perhaps. But is it a sin to dream, to aspire to greatness? Sadly, too often, the answer is yes, for we live in petty, jealous times. If you're a confident type, cantering towards the sunlit uplands, you'd better damn-well watch your back. For this world is but a bucket of crabs, elbowing, clacking and pinching; a thicket of beady eyes on stalks, checking those who might dream of upward mobility, grabbing the legs of any who dare bid for freedom, dragging them down into the fisherman's pail. Down, back down, into the sea of mediocrity.

So, mark me as a sinner. Brand me as a heretic. Press the white-hot iron to my flesh, if your quivering arms have the strength! I shall not flinch.

I glanced around the boardroom and took another mouthful of Burgundy. It was barely eleven in the morning, and I really should have been spitting, but the wine was showing magnificently. I'm a well-built chap, in good shape too, so I doubted a few small sips would impair my judgement. And today, of all days, I had to be on top form. For everyone in the business, from executive director to plughole scrubber, knew an event of the most momentous importance was upon us. And I was no mere spectator. I had a speaking part! Not a starring role – I'm a humble sergeant, not a five-star general – but an appreciable one, nevertheless. An opportunity to shine, you might say.

I surveyed the colleagues scampering around me, each a tiny cog in a vast, global mechanism of buying and selling.

The boardroom, usually a desert of sterile grey, had been transformed. The great, glass-topped desk and padded chairs were gone, replaced by a dozen long trestle tables, draped in white linen. Before my eyes, every square inch was filling with platters of food, as though a famished army had descended and were hammering at the doors, demanding replenishment on pain of death.

"They're coming!" whispered a voice.

The feast grew, aproned colleagues nudging and coaxing the crockery to make space for just one more dish, one more tureen. Before me lay a table choked with cakes, glistening with jewelled fruit and brandy. The next heaved with steaming beast and fowl; haunches of beef, plump turkeys and crusted pies. Others were laden with puddings; chocolate-slathered sponges, sugary igloos and mighty bowls of trifle. Yet more groaned under mounds of nuts, heaps of biscuits and great wheels of cheese.

What occasion had brought forth this bounty, you might ask? To what end had this smorgasbord of cholesterol and carbohydrate been conjured? The answer screamed in block capitals from the diary of every colleague present. For today was that monstrous day of reckoning known, to the employees of Gatesave Supermarkets, as the Festive Forum.

Yes, the Festive Forum! That majestic milestone, casting its terrifying shadow over the path to Christmas Eve, holiest of days in the retail calendar. It was barely July and simple folk, unfamiliar with the ways of retail, might throw their hands to the heavens, aghast at the thought of consuming mince pies, yule logs and sprouts in high summer. But my fellow supermarket legionnaires, marching to the beat of the festive drum, will nod grimly. For they know the truth, which is that Christmas is to a retailer what war, famine and pestilence are to the medieval peasant – always just around the corner, and only survivable through suffering, courage and bitter sacrifice.

A guard of honour flanked each food-choked table; a crack team of buyers, product developers and technologists. All were tensed in anticipation, all primed to sing the praises of their lovingly curated festive range. As the Head of Wine, Beer and Spirits, my own table was festooned with bottles from the four corners of the alcoholic world; magnums of Champagne and Prosecco, growlers of Kentish ale and Cornish cider, gift tins of Scotch embossed with magnificently antlered stags, and, of course, wines from the finest slopes in Christendom, from the plains of Patagonia to the hills of Tuscany.

A pert assistant popped her head around the door. "Sorry, false alarm. They're still running a little late. Bear with us, please."

The room sighed. I took a dozen silent steps across the carpet, drawn to the floor-to-ceiling windows despite the overcast sky. Slowly, hands in pockets, I leaned forward until my forehead met the glass. Frigid air played from the grille beneath my feet, chilling my ankles. I gazed down at the world, nine storeys below.

As mid-summer days went, this was a pretty miserable effort, even by England's clammy standards. Perhaps the weather, mindful of the Festive Forum, was attempting its best impression of a damp, dismal December. Below me lay the Thames, an immense sleeping snake, offering no clue to its direction of flow, its leaden surface studded with peaks whipped up by the wind. A line of black trees guarded the far bank and, above them, the sky matched the water's shade, an endless, featureless sea of grey. Drizzle played silently against the inch-thick glass. I imagined floating through the window and out over the river, the rain against my face, then onwards over the plains of Kent, the English Channel, and south, further south, to warmer climes, red wines and exotic, sultry nights.

"They're here!"

I strode back to my station. The door flew open and a six-strong group of directors filed into the room, eyes widening at the feast laid before them. They were led by Donald Parker, the Chief Executive, a cruel and startlingly ugly man known informally, and out of earshot, as Sweaty Parker. His face and head carried a perpetual wet sheen and, when agitated, he had a habit of breathing through his mouth in a strange panting manner, giving the impression of a man who'd just fought his way out of damp undergrowth after a strenuous act of foulness. The remaining directors cowered behind him in a submissive knot.

He sneered triumphantly at the assembled crowd. It may have been mid-July but there was no doubt about it: for Sweaty Parker, Christmas had arrived.

"Sorry I'm late," he lied.

Parker was, indeed, nearly an hour overdue. In the warm boardroom, some of the frozen desserts were showing signs of structural distress and the room was filled with the aroma of ripe meat and over-relaxed cheese.

Now, a naïve onlooker could be forgiven for thinking a pleasant, even joyous event was about to unfold. Some kind of Olympic nibble-a-thon, perhaps, the participants waltzing around the room, nuzzling moist turkey breast one second and pigs-in-blankets the next, skipping between the tables of party food, scooping up fistfuls of honey-glazed pecans with one paw and salted caramels with the other. One might imagine the assembled suits sucking the innards from luxury mince pies, eyes rolling back in delirious pleasure, lowing their approval like engorged oxen, before washing down the crumbs with fine, aged Cognac.

But nothing could be further from the truth.

For the Festive Forum was, in fact, a deeply traumatic experience, best described as one third Gestapo interrogation, one third Stalinist show trial and one third Zulu coming-of-age ceremony, the type where you line up stark naked while a wizened holy man saws at your private parts with a half-sharpened gazelle hoof.

The main event involved the buying teams standing to attention beside their Christmas ranges, while the Chief Executive and his minions sniffed, prodded and gnawed each festive proffering. Every item had to be accompanied by a small card, detailing its name, selling price and profit margin, and woe betide the buyer who didn't know the percentage of cocoa solids in their frozen tiramisu, or the maturation period of the prosciutto enveloping their oven-ready canapés. If Sweaty Parker objected to the price, taste, smell or appearance of a particular item, it was game over for the offending product. And, if that ended up jeopardising Christmas sales, it would be game over for your Gatesave career too.

"Good afternoon, Donald! Welcome, everyone!" said the Head of Seasonal Products, a jolly, round woman dressed in chefs' whites. "We're really looking forward to sharing our inspirational festive ranges with you! We have some incredible new—"

"Two-point-one percent," barked Sweaty Parker. His fellow directors remained huddled behind him, heads bowed.

"Er... pardon?" said the Head of Seasonal Products, smile frozen.

"Two. Point. One. Percent." Parker stared at the woman. "Do you understand?"

The poor woman didn't, of course. And Sweaty Parker would have known that. The role of the Head of Seasonal Products was to travel the world researching exotic nibbles and desserts, and, once suitably inspired, to invent wonderful new party snacks to delight the British public. Her role was not to regurgitate percentages and decimal points – that was the job of Buyers and Heads of Department, like yours truly. I, of course, knew the significance of that dismal number. Two-point-one percent was the amount by which Gatesave's market share had declined last Christmas. This was, as even the most mathematically disinclined infant could have told you, a very bad thing. I weighed up whether to insert myself into the conversation but quickly decided against it. Much as I liked the Head of Seasonal Products, Sweaty Parker was making a point, namely that he despised the colleagues assembled before him and that he would be making their lives a misery over the next five hours. It would have been inappropriate, and possibly career-limiting, to spoil his moment.

"Let me elucidate," sneered Parker, his face growing slightly moister. "It's the amount by which you need to *improve* Gatesave's market share, this Christmas, if you all want to keep your jobs."

He surveyed the silent crowd before him. As he caught my eye, I nodded and put on my grittiest Napoleon-marching-on-Moscow face.

"I can assure you, we're all completely committed to doing that," said the Head of Seasonal Products, her smile now looking slightly desperate.

"What are we tasting first?" demanded Parker. "Where's the Head of Festive Direction?"

"Here I am, Donald," called a chic, young woman, emerging from the scrum of marketing executives at the side of the room. "Now, before we start sampling, there's someone I'd like you all to meet. Yes, it gives me great pleasure to introduce this year's Christmas Champion!"

"I hope it's an improvement on last year's," said Parker.

"Yes, we've gathered a lot of learnings since Eric the Elf. He didn't play as well as we expected with our core demographic."

"You don't say," snapped Parker. "There were children in tears in our stores!"

"Yes, the communication didn't quite execute the way we wanted, particularly on the in-store décor. We've gathered a lot of learnings from that."

"He looked like a baby murderer!"

"Yes, with hindsight, Eric the Elf's features were too angular. And his teeth were, perhaps, too sharp. But we've learned from that."

"I hope so. Who's this year's Christmas Champion then? Please tell me he's a robin. Or a reindeer?"

"Actually, we wanted to move on from conventional, stereotyped Christmas characters. These days, for many communities, robins and reindeers don't carry emotional resonance."

Oblivious to the slick of moisture forming over Parker's face, the Head of Festive Direction clicked a remote control, and the ceiling-mounted projector flickered to life.

"Colleagues, please put your hands together for this year's Christmas Champion!"

A white furry slug, with whiskers and tusks, appeared on the wall. The marketing team applauded, loudly, and one over-excited man even let out a little whoop. The rest of the room stared, slack-jawed.

"It's Willis the baby Walrus!" declared the Head of Festive Direction.

"What the hell is that?" said Parker.

"It's our Willis! Willis the Walrus! Isn't he cute?"

"A walrus?" Parker was scowling and his face had become very sweaty indeed.

"He focus-grouped very well!" said the woman, a note of anxiety creeping into her voice. "Everyone else did a penguin last year and we wanted to move things on."

"But *we* didn't do a penguin last year, did we?" snarled Parker. He was panting now. "We did a terrifying elf that made children cry. We plastered it on our in-store decorations, iced it on our Christmas cakes, printed it on our festive tablecloths, and, of course, featured it in glorious Technicolour on our multi-million-pound TV advert. And then we lost two-point-one percentage points of market share! And now… now… we're doing a *walrus*?"

Parker's face dripped with rage. "A bloody *WALRUS*?"

"Everyone loves walruses," blurted the woman. "They're cuddly, they tick the environmental boxes, they—"

"It's Christmas, for the love of God! Who ever heard of a festive walrus?"

"They're from the Arctic, the same as Santa," pleaded the woman. "We can put Willis on cakes and chocolates—"

"And who in God's name decided to call him *Willis*?" shouted Parker. He wiped a sleeve across his sopping face. "Who ever heard of *anyone* being called Willis?"

"There's Bruce Willis," said one of the directors, stroking his chin.

"And Willis from *Diff'rent Strokes*," said another.

"Oh, I used to love that show!" said the first man. "Whatchu talkin' 'bout, Willis?"

Parker turned on his colleagues, teeth bared. The directors looked at their shoes.

"The focus groups liked it," the woman whimpered.

Parker began to vibrate with anger.

"Get out!" he spat. "Take your bloody walrus and get out! I want to see the entire marketing team, tomorrow morning, in my office, where you will unveil a new Christmas Champion. And God help you if you show me anything other than a robin, a reindeer or a man in a red suit with an effing white fur trim."

The marketing team filed silently from the room. Parker surveyed the remaining crowd.

"Somebody reassure me that no-one has gone and designed a range of products covered in walruses."

"Ahhh," quavered the Head of Seasonal Products, wiping her palms on her chef's whites, "there may be one or two things but there's nothing we can't redesign. Though the Christmas toilet tissue has a long lead-time, so that might be tricky…"

"Show me."

A young buyer, presumably in charge of the festive hygiene range, approached Parker with a toilet roll. Shaking, he held it out with both hands, like a peasant offering his lord a weevil-infested bushel of corn. Parker snatched it from him and stared at it. Even from a distance, I could see it was liberally decorated with images of Willis, the ex-festive walrus.

"How many of these have you printed?" asked Parker.

"T-t-two million," stammered the buyer.

"Cancel the order," he whispered, shaking with rage, "and redo it with pictures of robins. Got it?"

"Y-y-yes sir," said the buyer, backing away.

"Er, sorry to raise an awkward point," said a man near the back, hand half-raised. It was Bill, one of the senior technical managers responsible for product safety.

Parker glared at him.

"I'm afraid we can't really print robins on toilet paper. Brown and red, you see. Not… best practice. People might think they have a… medical complaint." Bill gave an apologetic smile.

Parker gritted his teeth and a droplet of sweat fell from his chin. "Put a bloody reindeer on it then!"

"Well… they're brown too," Bill tailed off.

"And red, if it's Rudolph…" added the young buyer, grimacing as it dawned on him that silence might have been the better policy.

Parker's eyes bulged. "Put something green on it then!" he shouted.

"Like an elf?" suggested the buyer, remembering the previous year's Christmas Champion just a split-second too late.

Parker's head turned so red, I thought it might explode.

"Or a frog," called Bill, from the back. "We could make it a Christmas frog?"

A few seconds passed, while Parker, panting with rage, removed a handkerchief and mopped his face.

"Shall we try some food?" said the Head of Seasonal Products, with frantic jollity, as Parker rubbed the sopping fabric around his head. "Why don't we start with savoury nibbles? These were inspired by my trip to—"

"I do hope we've executed the actions from last year's Post-Implementation Review," said Parker, tucking the sodden handkerchief away.

"I… yes, I'm sure we have," she replied.

"Show me the review then. Show me what you've implemented." Parker stared at her, his re-moistening face gleaming under the boardroom lights.

The woman looked to her colleagues for inspiration, but all stayed silent, eyes focussed on the carpet. She lifted a wad of papers from the table and began rifling through it, but the paperwork too refused to give up its secrets. Parker tutted, angrily.

"I'm sure it's here," she mumbled, a dozen papers between her teeth. The lower half of the bundle liberated itself from her grasp and spilled over the floor, some particularly aerodynamic sheets gliding beneath a table.

"Let me refresh your memory," said Parker, as the Head of Seasonal Products dropped to her knees. "It said too much of our party food was small, brown and round."

"Oh yes, I remember now," she said, gathering the scattered sheets into a pile.

Parker turned to the Savoury Party Food Buyer, a tall youth with ginger hair. "With that in mind, please show us your range." Parker lifted a breadcrumb-coated nugget from a pile of similarly shaped morsels. "This is frustratingly small, brown and round," he said, inspecting the snack as if it were a disease-ridden sheep dropping. "What is it?"

"Er… a premium sausage-meat nibble, sir," quavered the buyer.

Parker took a bite and scowled. "What's premium about it?"

"It… it… contains a higher meat content and a richer—"

"How much more meat?" demanded Parker, expelling a spray of premium breadcrumbs.

"It's forty percent meat, as opposed to thirty percent for the standard nibble," called the Head of Seasonal Products from beneath the table.

"Well, what do we think?" asked Parker, turning on the knot of directors huddled behind him.

Each crept forward and lifted a premium sausage-meat nibble from the platter.

"What's the cost differential between the tiers of nibbles?" muttered the Director of Finance, a furtive little man with bitten-down fingernails. "Do we need a premium *and* a standard nibble?" He sniffed the nugget. "Is the nibble category sufficiently elastic?"

"It's… er… thirty pence more, no, sorry, twenty pence…" the buyer looked down at a sheet of figures and reddened.

"You don't know!" shouted Parker, sweatily.

"Yes, twenty pence more. I apologise, I was confusing it with the premium tikka bites."

"Where are the tikka bites?"

"On the next platter, sir." The youth gestured at a pile of similarly shaped breadcrumb-coated nuggets.

Sweaty Parker lifted a premium tikka bite, smelt it, and held it aloft.

"I made the observation, last year, that our party food range was largely small, brown and round. The same observation was made the year before. And yet, every Christmas, our Product Development team insist on creating yet another range of small, brown and very round party snacks."

He threw the premium tikka bite back on to the platter, where it sat, anonymous once more among its brothers and sisters. Parker raised his voice.

"Well? Any response? Because I'll be making some permanent changes, right now, to the Party Food team, if I'm shown anything else small, brown and round!"

The Head of Seasonal Products clambered to her feet, clutching a wad of paperwork to her chest. Parker thrust his head at her.

"What's the matter with you people?" he snarled. "I want to be inspired! Inspire me!"

"The prawn and crab bites are new," she said, miserably, nodding at a platter of flattened, beige disks. I winced.

"They're *small, brown and round*!" shouted Parker, taking hold of one and shaking it at her.

"Well… they're flat, not spherical," she said, in a small voice.

"A disk is round, damn it! Do you think I'm stupid?"

The woman looked frantically from platter to platter, but all were piled high with small, tawny, spherical foodstuffs of slightly varying diameter.

"Do you have anything vegetarian, Cathy?" asked the Director of Human Resources, a thin woman in a dark suit.

"Yes!" cried the Head of Seasonal Products, dropping her papers and clasping her hands to the side of her head. She scurried to the next table and returned with a platter piled high with little bundles of folded lettuce leaves.

"Finally!" declared Parker. "And what do you call these?"

"Premium veggie party bites," said the woman. She held out the platter and each of the directors took one. Parker raised the lettuce parcel to his lips then paused. He placed the snack on the table and unfolded the leaf. A small brown sphere rolled out, trundled to the edge of the table, and dropped to the floor. It bounced once then lay still, surrounded by a halo of breadcrumbs.

"What is that?" he whispered. The room was deathly quiet.

"It's… the centre of the veggie party bite..." said the Head of Seasonal Products. She tailed off and a tear ran down her cheek.

"Please leave."

The Head of Seasonal Products ran from the room, hands over her face.

"I want to see this entire range reworked for next week. If any of our Christmas party food remains capable of transporting itself down a shallow incline, unaided, you can all find yourselves another job. Understand?"

The Party Food team nodded, miserably.

"Who's next?" he barked.

With the Head of Seasonal Products now absent, the chain of command had been broken. I suspected Sweaty Parker's mood was on a fierce, downward trajectory, so I decided to step up before things degenerated further.

"Christmas drinks, sir?" I called.

"Yes! I need a drink, the way this forum's going!" Parker turned to his fellow directors, who smiled and nodded at his wit. He strode to my table.

"Ah yes, Felix Hart. Winner of the prize for biggest departmental travel budget overspend, I recall. How are you intending to remedy your profit-diluting, operational incompetence this year?"

"I apologise for the slight expenses variance, sir. But you'll have noticed the improved margins on this year's products, I'm sure. That's all down to my team getting out to our suppliers and negotiating, face to face."

I swept my hand over the little tent-cards displaying my festive range's profit margins. In a moment of artistic genius, I had written the improvement on last year's profit in thick, green felt-tip. The numbers were complete fiction, of course, but there was no way anyone would know the truth until Christmas was well under way. And by then, hopefully, I'd have hammered out a decent deal with my suppliers.

The Director of Finance peered at my ludicrously optimistic figures. His eyes narrowed.

"How have you achieved a four percentage-point improvement in Sherry profitability, Hart?" he scowled. "The Euro exchange rate has depreciated significantly since last year."

"It certainly has. But I was able to convince our supplier to lower his prices, on my trip to Jerez last month. That's why it's so important to travel. You can't negotiate in earnest without seeing the whites of their eyes." I smiled, brightly.

It had been a superb trip to Jerez. I had planned my visit to coincide with the annual *Feria del Caballo*, one of the great spectacles of Andalucía. Beautiful Spanish girls trotting around on horseback, salted almonds and jamón ibérico washed down with ice-cold glasses of Fino dispensed straight from the cask, then dancing, all night, to live, wild flamenco, until the Andalusian sun had risen high into the morning sky.

"Hart! I said a few thousand bottles of Sherry aren't going to turn around our deplorable market share performance!" I snapped out of my reverie to find Parker's damp face just inches from my own.

"Apologies, sir. I was just calculating how much profit we're going to make this year on Buck's Fizz. Over a million pounds more!"

"Buck's Fizz isn't going to save you any more than Sherry is. The market for those products is in decline. What's *new*? It had better be good, Hart. I have a feeling you're taking us for a ride."

"Of course, sir, you're right. Growth can only come from innovation."

I nodded to my assistant. She lifted a bottle from the table and presented it to Sweaty Parker.

"Our hero product this year... is *glögg*!" I declared.

There was a Willis-the-Walrus-style silence. But I was prepared.

"Of course, this beverage is currently little-known to the drinkers of Britain. But, this Christmas, *glögg* will be on everyone's lips!"

"What the hell is *glögg*?" sneered Parker, his moist face still uncomfortably close to my own. He snatched the bottle and scowled at it.

"It's the Swedish version of mulled wine, sir. But this is a hundred times more delicious than a stewed saucepan of plonk with a half an orange floating in it."

My assistant lifted a tray of small glasses, each filled to the brim with a steaming, cloudy, red liqueur.

"I don't like mulled wine," said Parker, banging the bottle down on the table. "And I don't like your idea either. If this is the best you've got, we'll be looking for a new Head of Wine, very shortly."

"I promise you, once you've tried *glögg*, you'll never look back! The wine is infused with Madagascan vanilla, Indian cardamom and Jamaican ginger, and blended with juice from the plumpest Californian raisins. It's bursting full of flavour!"

"I think *you're* bursting full of it, Hart," said Parker, arms folded.

Oh Christ, I thought. This is going badly. Come on you sods, Christmas is coming! Get some bloody festive spirit inside you. I nudged my assistant and she approached the other directors with the tray.

"Try it!" I ordered, fixing the Director of Finance with gleaming eyes. "Close your eyes and think of mistletoe!" Perhaps I *had* sampled a couple too many wines earlier, I mused.

The Director of Finance squinted at the little tent-card boasting a sixty percent profit margin, complete with exclamation mark, and raised a glass to his nose.

"It does smell of Christmas, I suppose," he muttered.

"Smell the fruit and taste the margin!" I said, feeling slightly unhinged.

The other directors lifted their glasses, but Parker remained unmoved. "I'm still halving your travel budget," he said.

"Mmmmm," declared the Director of Supply Chain, a large, ruddy-faced man with a vast belly. "That *is* nice! I might have another."

"I don't like the name," said Parker. "*Glögg*. It sounds too foreign. *Glögg*," he repeated, scowling.

"Everything Swedish is very fashionable right now," I said. "I checked with the home accessories buyer, and *glögg*-scented candles are the market's fastest-growing aroma."

Genius. That got his attention. Christ, I was good. Parker unfolded his arms, hesitated, then took a glass of the gently steaming beverage.

"If I don't like it, we're not selling it," he said, and poured the liquid into his mouth.

"You'll love it!" I said, praying to Bacchus for divine intervention.

"What are all those bits in the bottom?" sniffed the Director of Human Resources, screwing up her face.

"Oh, that's a Swedish tradition," said my assistant. "You add nuts, raisins and spices to the glass then pour the *glögg* on top."

"Sounds like a choking hazard," she said, poking at the stray nuts with her finger. "I hope there are no bits in the bottled product?"

"No, don't worry! I don't think Bill would allow us to add fragments of nuts and cinnamon to a bottle of wine, would you, Bill?" I gave the Senior Technical Manager a wave.

"No, I definitely wouldn't!" called Bill, cheerfully.

"So, does everyone like it?" I asked, watching Parker's face. He was sweating quite assertively, little rivulets of moisture tracing paths down his cheeks, and he appeared to be concentrating intensely on the flavour, eyes wide and head tilted back.

There was a somewhat unsettling period of silence. All eyes were on Sweaty Parker. Would *glögg* be the Christmas Hero line or would I be stripped of my rank and put in charge of festive toilet tissue? Come on, you sweaty bastard, I prayed, give us a sign!

"Donald?" said the Director of Human Resources.

"Arrghh," croaked Parker. He raised a hand to his throat and attempted to insert the other into his mouth.

"Oh my God, he's choking!" she screamed. "Somebody, help him!"

No-one moved. Perhaps it was the heady aroma of mulled wine, mince pies and brandy butter, but everyone appeared rooted to the spot, as if drugged by the booze-laden air.

Parker made several more distressed noises and attempted to push his hand further into his mouth.

"Pat him on the back!" someone shouted.

The Director of Supply Chain discarded his empty glasses of *glögg* and positioned himself behind Parker. Then he balled his huge fist and thumped him between the shoulder blades. Parker flew forward and sprawled across the party food table, his face pressing into a pile of mini samosas. Several dozen festive nibbles catapulted themselves high into the air, raining down on neighbouring tables like a breadcrumb-coated air strike. Parker was making horrific wheezing noises now, his groans punctuated by the tinkle of crockery and the patter of spherical party bites dropping to the carpet.

"Again!" I shouted.

The Director of Supply Chain raised his huge fist once more.

"No! You're hitting him too hard!" screamed the Director of Human Resources.

"Once more, just in case!" called another voice.

"Who's first-aid trained?"

"Find Cathy! She's trained!"

"Where is she? Where did she go?"

"I think she's in the toilet, crying."

A couple of people ran to find the Head of Seasonal Products.

I could no longer see Parker; he was surrounded by a crowd of helpers shouting at each other to give him more space. I could still hear him over the hubbub, however, making horrendous gargling noises.

"Try the Heimlich manoeuvre!"

"I can't lift him! We need someone stronger."

"Felix! Where's Felix?"

The crowd parted and all eyes turned to me. Parker lay on his back, on a carpet of mangled party food, his face coated by a foam of *glögg*. He was juddering like a scarecrow on a cattle prod, limbs flailing in all directions.

"But I've never done the Heimlich manoeuvre!" I yelped.

"Improvise!" someone shouted.

Christ, I wished I'd knocked back a couple more glasses of *glögg* when I'd had the chance. I stepped forward, grabbed Parker's lapels and wrestled him off the table, receiving a couple of elbows in the face for my trouble. I managed to turn him round and wrap my arms around his stomach from behind, but his legs had gone floppy and he began to slide to the floor. I sank to my knees and paused, rather out of breath.

"Do it!" someone shouted. "Squeeze him!"

I joined my hands around his front and hugged Sweaty Parker as hard as I could. He made a half-hearted wheeze, like a depressed accordion. I tried again and again, but his wheezes became weaker each time. His stubbly, wet head lolled back against my face and I grimaced.

"I'm not sure it's working," I panted.

"Cathy's here!"

The crowd parted once more. The puffy, tear-streaked face of the Head of Seasonal Products looked down at me clinging to Parker's unhelpfully relaxed body.

"Thank God you're here!" I said, exhausted. "Am I doing it right?"

"No," she said, sniffing. "You're doing it very wrong."

Chapter 2

Modern Slavery

The Heimlich manoeuvre, I now know, is an extremely tricky procedure, which should only be carried out by a competent and well-trained medical professional. Thankfully, my intervention was placed in the well-meaning-but-misjudged category, and the coroner decided I had only played a minor role in the Chief Executive's demise. My unfortunate assistant received the main portion of blame, of course, for the negligent concealment of a jagged star anise in the bottom of Parker's glass of *glögg*. The Director of Supply Chain didn't escape censure either. The post-mortem revealed that his over-enthusiastic thump to Parker's back had dislodged a vertebra, which had probably contributed to him losing consciousness.

Bill, the technical manager, dropped by my desk the day after Parker's funeral.

"The Head of Compliance has asked to see you right away, Felix. I'm afraid it sounds rather serious."

My heart sank. I'd thought I was in the clear. How the hell had I allowed myself to be talked into administering a violent medical procedure to the Chief Executive? That's what you get for being too eager to please, I mused. Well, too late now. My time was up. I wondered if they'd let me clear my desk before I was escorted from the premises. I had a couple of good bottles locked in my bottom drawer and it would have been a pity to lose them.

"Bill, it's been good working with you. I suppose I'd better get it over with."

Bill gave me a brief, sympathetic smile, and I made my way to the corner office.

There, behind a paper-strewn desk, sat the Head of Compliance, fingers drumming on the tabletop. Upon seeing me, his anxious face fell a little further, as it often did when we met. Our interactions to date, thank goodness, had been relatively infrequent. Not because I didn't like the man, though he wouldn't have been my first choice of drinking companion, what with him being a rather depressive type. It was simply that a meeting with the Head of Compliance usually implied trouble. And not mild, inconvenient trouble, like being caught in light rain without an umbrella. I mean proper, buttock-clenching trouble, like finding yourself locked in a toilet cubicle with a live cobra.

For the Head of Compliance's job was to manage every calamity that might, and frequently did, befall any of the thirty thousand products stocked on Gatesave's shelves. This could be anything from a corporate catastrophe, such as the discovery of zebra meat in Gatesave's Moroccan-style sausages, to more small-scale concerns; an alarmingly hairy spider creeping from a box of mangoes, perhaps, or a stray toenail emerging from a jar of pesto sauce.

He was accompanied by the Head of Message, a fierce-looking woman festooned with chunky bangles, who perched on the corner of his desk like an eagle scouting for slow-witted rabbits. Her role was to manage issues erupting on social media, or likely to be of interest to the press. The fact that the two of them were in the room together suggested an incident at the more vigorous end of the Richter scale.

I slid the frosted door closed.

"Listen, Felix. We have a problem," said the Head of Compliance, his fingers still drumming.

"Yes, so I understand."

The Head of Message rose from the corner of the table.

"Before we begin, you're required to sign a non-disclosure agreement." Her bangles clunked as she thrust an official-looking piece of paper at me.

Of course, I thought. Standard practice when they want to boot someone out of the door with the minimum of fuss. Hopefully, they'd lubricate my exit with a generous lump of cash. I quite fancied a break, to be honest. Perhaps I'd head to Argentina, for a little southern hemisphere sun. Hook up with Valentina, my gorgeous winemaking friend, and spend the season swimming in the beautiful lake district of Salta.

I signed the paperwork and the Head of Message placed it in a file.

"Now then," said the Head of Compliance, pointing to a seat. "An ethical issue has arisen."

"Ethical?" I said, sitting down. "I don't understand."

"No, that doesn't surprise us in the slightest," sighed the Head of Message. "You are, after all, the man who choked to death our Chief Executive."

"I was only trying to help. It was traumatic for me as well."

"Yes," she said, glaring at me, "so traumatic that the following week, you shipped half-a-million bottles of the offending liquor into our warehouse, ready for sale to the British public."

"Well, we had a contract with the supplier. It would have been rather awkward to renege on it. And the profit margin is excellent."

The Head of Message closed her eyes and a pained expression passed across her face. "Can you imagine, just for one second, what the press would say if word got out that we were profiting from the very product that caused the death of our Chief Executive?"

"It was a rogue star anise that did the damage. Not the *glögg*. Besides—"

"The *glögg* was the main feature of the coroner's report, man!" wailed the Head of Compliance, slapping his hands against the desk. "The *glögg* appeared in headlines from here to Sydney! 'Hashtag *glögg*' was trending on Twitter for an entire fortnight. The Oxford English Dictionary will probably nominate *glögg* as their word of the bloody year!" He sighed and rubbed his eyes. "I prayed I would never hear that dreadful sound ever again. And now, I find out there's half a million bottles of the stuff about to flood into our stores."

I remained silent. The Head of Compliance was now scratching his head with both hands, quite vigorously, and I didn't want to agitate him any further.

"You'll have to return the stock," said the Head of Message. "We cannot have *glögg* on our shelves. We'll be a laughing stock!"

"Ah, but I've thought of that," I replied. "I asked the supplier to relabel the bottles with a different name."

"You mean it's no longer called *glögg*?"

"Exactly!"

"What's it called then?"

"*Hygge*," I replied.

"Hugger?" said the Head of Compliance, aghast. "You squeezed a man to death with your bare arms as he choked on mulled wine and you're calling the drink that killed him *hugger*? What kind of sick bastard are you?"

"Not hugger. *Hygge*," I said. "It means cosy, in Danish."

"Oh, Jesus wept," said the Head of Compliance, putting his head in his hands.

"Well, I'm sorry for all the trouble. I was only trying to do my best. Will I be marched off the premises or can I collect my belongings first?"

"No-one's marching anywhere, Felix," said the Head of Message. "We've got far bigger problems than your mulled wine misadventures." She lifted a report from the desk and tossed it into my lap. "Take a look at that."

Highly Confidential. For the CEO and Business Continuity Secretariat only.

I scanned the front page. It was a red audit from Gatesave's Safety & Compliance team, a summary of a failed inspection at one of our suppliers. And a pretty shabby story it looked too, with the front page bathed in red ink highlighting no fewer than fourteen instances of non-compliance with Gatesave policy. At the bottom, in a box marked 'Head of Compliance comments', a handwritten scrawl read: *Hard stop! Brand damaging! Business critical!* The name of the unfortunate supplier was printed beneath the box in bold red type: Blanchkopf Wine Growers.

25

Bugger, I thought. Blanchkopf Wine Growers was my largest supplier of South African wine.

"Oh dear," I said. "What did the inspector find? Mice on the bottling line?"

"It's a lot worse than mice," said the Head of Compliance.

"Leopards?"

"It's not funny, Felix," snapped the Head of Message, making me jump. "And it's not a safety failure either. This is *ethical* non-compliance. That's what we meant when we said we have an ethical problem."

"So... you're not firing me?"

"We're very tempted, but no. This issue rather supersedes your negligent dispensing of spiced wine." The Head of Message paused and fiddled with her bangles. "A Scandinavian NGO contacted us last month. They claim employees of Blanchkopf Wine Growers are complaining of poor working conditions at the winery. They want to ask us some questions regarding our sourcing practices in developing countries."

"Sourcing practices?"

"Yes, Felix. Specifically, what due diligence we carry out to ensure a supplier is treating their workforce fairly. Paying a living wage, allowing trade union recognition, that type of thing."

"Oh, I see. Well, we insist our suppliers all adhere to the highest possible standards, as you know." I looked from the Head of Message to the Head of Compliance, expecting some kind of acknowledgement. But both remained stony-faced. "We audit our suppliers to check up on that kind of thing. Don't we...?" I tailed off.

"We audit wine suppliers to monitor product safety issues on bottling lines," said the Head of Compliance. "Not to investigate ethical issues." He peered down at a report. "The last person to visit Blanchkopf Wine Growers was you, Felix. Eighteen months ago."

I racked my brains to remember the visit. It would have been one of dozens of wineries, all crammed into a busy fortnight tearing around the Cape winelands. Blanchkopf himself was a grumpy old Afrikaner, always complaining he wasn't being paid enough. He supplied Gatesave with a good value Pinotage and a cheap white, a mixture of Riesling and Chenin Blanc. I vaguely recalled tasting the new vintage wines, which were perfectly adequate plonk for the bottom end of our range. Not the sort of thing I'd drink, but fine for a certain segment of the British public that isn't particularly bothered about the finer points of wine quality. Most of the population, in other words.

"Yes, I recall the visit. Nothing seemed untoward."

"Nothing untoward?" said the Head of Compliance. "Did you ask any questions about workplace conditions?"

"I tend to concentrate on tasting wine and discussing prices, really."

"Sounds a real hardship," he said. "You do realise you're responsible for the entire business relationship, don't you? You're not there to just gargle the product over a good dinner and ignore everything else."

"Well, like I said, nothing seemed untoward. I gave the vineyard workers a wave as we toured the site. They seemed cheerful enough."

The Head of Compliance closed his eyes and sighed. I tried to recall whether anyone waved back. One vineyard full of toiling Africans looks pretty much like another, particularly when you're on your twentieth visit of the week, and hung-over as hell.

"We sent an audit team to visit Blanchkopf Wine Growers, last week," said the Head of Compliance, leaning forward. "To see if there was anything that could be interpreted as a cause for concern."

I looked down at the report in my lap.

"Yes, Felix," said the Head of Message. "It's fair to say they found several issues that gave us very great cause for concern."

"Let me explain the seriousness of this situation," said the Head of Compliance. "In the past six months, we've already had two instances of a red ethical audit. One was that Chinese factory making toys for Gatesave's Christmas crackers, the workforce of which was composed entirely of children kidnapped from the local primary school. The other involved our Pakistani talcum powder manufacturer, who was buying his raw material directly from the Taliban."

"The trouble is we're always on the back bloody foot," said the Head of Message. "The issue has usually leaked into the public domain, along with all the negative publicity, by the time we get to the bottom of it. The BBC are even making a documentary highlighting our recent ethical hiccups, with the working title '*Sorry, We've Sold Out!*'"

"Yes, that doesn't sound ideal," I said.

"Indeed. And neither is that." The Head of Compliance pointed to the report. "I'll cut to the chase. We suspect Blanchkopf Wine Growers may be using slave labour in their vineyards."

"Blimey!" I said. "Isn't that illegal?"

"Yes, of course it's bloody illegal! They're slaves! It doesn't *get* any more illegal."

"Right. So, what did the auditor find? Was everybody chained up?"

"It's called indentured labour. They don't need to chain people up. They're probably in debt, obliged to work for no pay."

"How unpleasant," I said.

"Quite," said the Head of Message, snatching the report from my hands. "We cannot afford yet another brand-damaging disaster. We need you to put a stop to this, immediately."

"What? You want me to go and rescue them?"

"No, you bloody idiot! We want you to end Gatesave's trading relationship with Blanchkopf Wine Growers. As quickly as possible. Before anyone finds out!"

"Ah, I see. Of course."

The Head of Message rapped her fingernails against the desk. "This has the potential to be very embarrassing for Gatesave, Felix. Critically embarrassing. Our customer trust scores are already the worst in the industry. Do you understand?"

Oh dear, I thought. Sounds like it's squeaky bottom time in the Corporate Comms department. I nodded, sympathetically. "Yes, I understand."

28

Head of Message raised her eyes to the ceiling. "That bloody palm oil stunt was bad enough, but this would be a different league of brand damage. The media would crucify us."

I suppressed a smirk. Just last month, an environmental charity had decided to draw attention to Gatesave's laissez-faire approach to palm oil procurement. A dozen activists, dressed in surprisingly life-like orangutan suits, had abseiled on to the stage at the shareholders' annual general meeting, in front of the national press. Footage of the Chairman wrestling a long-haired, orange ape, while other primates leapt around the auditorium, hooting and hurling bananas into the crowd of bemused shareholders, had made the nine o'clock news. It was fair to say the business considered the episode a sub-optimal piece of corporate communication.

"We'll reconvene tomorrow, at eight a.m.," said the Head of Compliance, scratching his head vigorously, "when we look forward to hearing how you've extricated Gatesave from your abysmally managed wine supply chain."

"And may I remind you that you're under an NDA," said the Head of Message, tapping the sheet I'd signed. "Breathe one word of this and you really are out. Without compensation."

"I know nothing," I said, gravely.

The Head of Compliance closed his eyes, placed his fingers against the sides of his head and began to move them in slow circles. Poor chap, I thought. Beats me why anyone would want such a stressful job.

Chapter 3

A Gathering Storm

Gatesave Supermarkets Ltd are delighted to announce the appointment of Herbert Marris as Group Chief Executive. Herbert, of course, needs no introduction. He is a retail legend, beginning his career in 1965 with the Tadcaster Grocery Company, where he grew a small market stall into Yorkshire's largest supermarket chain. Herbert went on to make his name as a world-renowned turnaround expert for under-performing retailers, earning plaudits from institutional investors across the globe. For the past three years, Herbert has been CEO of Goedkoper, the Dutch hypermarket chain, and Gatesave are delighted to have tempted Herbert back to these shores to take on the challenge of leading Britain's largest grocer. Herbert fills the vacancy left by Donald Parker, who died in service, so tragically, last July.

"Yes, he's a complete arsehole," said Elmo, taking a large swig of Burgundy.

"Can't be as bad as Sweaty Parker," I replied.

Elmo smiled, grimly, and sucked air through his wine. Elmo was Head Drinks Buyer for Goedkoper, an Amsterdam-based supermarket chain, whose outgoing Chief Executive was one Herbert Marris, the man soon to be taking over the leadership of my own dear employer. Elmo was in London overnight, en route to Scotland for a whisky conference, and I'd jumped at the opportunity to interrogate him on my new head honcho.

"Felix, I assure you, the man is a gold-plated sphincter. A king-sized colon."

"Right. I think I get the idea."

We were sitting at the bar of the Salon de Dijon, my favourite of the many watering holes dotted around Minstrels Hall, the headquarters of the Worshipful Institute of the Minstrels of Wine. The barman pulled the bottle from its ice bucket and refreshed our glasses.

"You're going to regret killing your last CEO, Felix."

"Regret it? I'm gutted, Elmo. It's brought me nothing but grief."

"Listen. This man, Herbert Marris, he's obsessed with discipline. Purity of mind, body and soul. He's a bloody Nazi. Even worse, he's stingy. I thought we Dutch were penny-pinchers but, by God, that Yorkshireman redefines the word! Redundancies, recruitment freezes, head office canteen closed, staff discount cancelled, travel budgets slashed..." Elmo tailed off, shaking his head.

"I suppose that's why he's called the Terror of Tadcaster."

"Oh yes – and he disapproves of alcohol too. No more taking home free samples. He stopped us tasting wine on company premises completely. We had to go to our suppliers' offices to make our selections. It was like working for al-Qaeda. If it weren't for the fact that we sell a billion Euros of liquor each year, I swear the guy would have closed the beverage department completely."

"Hell's bells. And is it true he tests his employees for drugs?"

"You don't know the half of it! Compulsory, random drug tests, every month. One minute you're on your way to a meeting to discuss Champagne forecasts, the next you're caught in a pincer movement between an HR manager and a nurse, and it's 'pee in here please, Elmo', todger out, tinkle tinkle, then 'you'll hear from us in forty-eight hours, here's a moist towelette, don't forget to wipe your fingers.'"

"Christ on a bike. You must be delighted to see the back of him."

"I tell you, Felix, when we heard that bastard was off, the whole team headed straight to the red-light district, stoked a row of bongs with pure sinsemilla, and sucked that smoke down like drowning sailors. Three whole years I worked under that fascist, without a single day of toot. We made up for it that evening, though. By the end of the night I was snorting cocaine off a dwarf's buttocks."

"Sounds like a red-letter day."

"You can say that again. Sorry to hear our loss is your gain, though. My advice is to keep your head down. Maybe even find another job. As a fellow Minstrel of Wine, you'd be welcome to come and work for us in Amsterdam."

"Sounds quite tempting, Elmo, thank you." I glanced at the empty bottle of Marsannay and nodded to the barman. "Yes please, I think we could do with another."

***

"No, you listen to *me*, Mr Hart," shouted Blanchkopf. "If you don't like how much I'm paying my workers, you can damn well pay me more for your wine!"

I moved the receiver another couple of inches from my ear. Blanchkopf had taken the news of his problematic audit rather badly and was now conducting the conversation at a volume more appropriate for a Bondi Beach lifeguard informing a group of half-deaf, paddling pensioners of the proximity of a family of Great Whites.

"We don't really want to pay you anything anymore, Mr Blanchkopf. I'm afraid your business practices are incompatible with those of my employer. I'm calling to inform you that our trading relationship is at an end."

"Oh no you don't, you arrogant British shit!" shouted Blanchkopf. I raised my eyebrows. Blanchkopf may have been the eighth generation of a family of intrepid grape growers, whose forefathers had valiantly chased the natives off their land with nothing more than a well-armed militia and a dose of syphilis, but that didn't mean he had the right to subject a VIP customer to his potty-mouthed rantings.

"Can I remind you that you're speaking to a client, Mr Blanchkopf? I would appreciate it if you toned down your cursing."

"You are not a client! You are a conceited, over-entitled colonist! A slave driver!"

Takes one to know one, I thought. But I suspected that accusing Blanchkopf of slave ownership at that moment might not improve his temper.

"Well, Mr Blanchkopf, it appears you're unhappy with us as a customer. And frankly, we're more than a little disappointed in you as a supplier. So, I'm proposing we take a mutual break from the partnership. A conscious uncoupling, you might call it."

"I am not uncoupling anything, Hart! You think you can treat me like an oily rag? Wipe your arse with me then toss me in the crapper?"

"It's really not a matter for discussion, Mr Blanchkopf. It takes two to tango and your dancing partner is leaving the ballroom. We will, of course, pay all outstanding—"

"It will be embarrassing when the press finds out about your complicity in slavery, Mr Hart."

My bowels gave a twitch of alarm.

"I beg your pardon?"

"You are a hypocrite, Mr Hart. You forced me to give you the cheapest wine price in the whole of South Africa, even though you knew the effect it would have on my poor workforce."

"I don't know what you're talking about."

"I have an email from you, Mr Hart, following last year's harvest. I asked you for a small price increase, just to cover the cost of living for my workers. Do you remember your reply?"

I didn't, though I suspected it had been along the lines of 'stick your price increase up your arse, sunshine, or you're out'. That is, after all, what I'm employed for.

"I have your email here, Mr Hart," continued Blanchkopf. "You said *'the cost of living is very low in South Africa, so I suggest you find ways to economise. Our customers cannot be expected to subsidise the inefficiencies in your supply chain.*' Do you remember saying that?"

"Not really. But, so what if I did? It's a perfectly reasonable reaction to an unwarranted price increase."

"And then, Mr Hart, I pleaded with you, asking you to think of the poor workers. I said I would have to cut their wages if you didn't give me the increase I needed. Do you remember your reply to that?"

I had a feeling that I might have responded with a sarcastic barb. Given that Blanchkopf owned a boutique hotel in Franschhoek, I felt sarcastic barbs were generally a reasonable response to his claims of poverty.

"You said, Mr Hart, '*What you pay your workers is your business, it doesn't interest me in the slightest.*' And now, here you are, claiming to be outraged. I think you are more worried about that nosy NGO that has been poking about. I think you care nothing for me and my poor workers, all you care about is your supermarket's precious reputation."

"There are certain standards, Mr Blanchkopf, clearly laid out in Gatesave's supplier bible—"

"Ah yes, the Gospel according to St. Gatesave! Listen to you, taking the Lord's Book in vain, you arrogant, two-faced heathen!"

"I have a nasty feeling you're attempting to blackmail me, Mr Blanchkopf. I'm sure that NGO will be as outraged as we are with your behaviour."

"Oh, I do not think so, Mr Hart. How about I show the NGO your emails and some nice pictures of you in the vineyards last year with my workers? And then I will tell them that you knew full well about whatever is in that damn audit of yours. You are our biggest customer by far and I think we both know that they are much more interested in dragging Gatesave through the *kak* than some poor old *boer*."

My bowels were twitching rather assertively now. The sly old sod had me over a barrel.

"I see. What do you want, Mr Blanchkopf?"

"I want you to behave like a decent customer, rather than a stuck-up little emperor, giving orders to his subjects overseas."

"And how, in your book, does a decent customer behave, exactly?"

"He comes to South Africa, to my winery in Aasvoëlsfontein, and signs a contract giving me the price I deserve. A fifty percent increase and guaranteed supply for the next five years."

Oh bollocks, I thought. I suspected the Heads of Message and Compliance would consider this a sub-optimal development.

***

"Sounds like you cocked it up, Felix."

The Head of Message stood over me, hands on hips, while the Head of Compliance sat behind his desk, tugging at his hair.

"Yes, I'm afraid Mr Blanchkopf was rather intransigent. He knows there's an NGO sniffing about and he's threatening to tell them Gatesave are aware of his regressive approach to employee relations."

"Regressive approach?" wailed the Head of Compliance, grasping the edge of his desk. "The man's a bloody slave-owner! Our report says he boasts about setting his dogs on vineyard workers who don't pick fast enough!" He put his head in his hands. "Oh God, we're screwed. We'll be the first out of the door when Herbert Marris takes over."

"Oh, is he quite strict about stuff like that?"

"Yes, Felix, you nincompoop," said the Head of Message. "I think he's probably very strict about slavery. It's the kind of thing people tend to be strict about."

"I see. But look, Blanchkopf still wants to supply Gatesave. He's asked that I visit him to sign a new contract. If we give him a price increase, perhaps I can persuade him to clean up his act."

"Is that likely? How long would it take?"

"I don't know. A few months? We could send an audit team in every week to check on progress."

"No way." The Head of Message stabbed a finger at me, bangles clanking. "This has to remain confidential. These audit companies talk to each other and the NGO probably uses the same people. It's your mess, so you can clear it up. We'll send you out there on a sabbatical." She turned to the Head of Compliance. "We can assign Felix to a development charity working in the Cape, can't we? Let's make a donation and tell them we want to sponsor something, like a school or a clinic, preferably with some nice, bold Gatesave branding over the entrance. Generate some decent PR for a change."

"Yes, I suppose," he sighed. "I'll make a few calls."

"Good. And no-one outside this room knows about the real reason for your trip, Felix, understood? I want you to turn this fiasco into a positive story."

"Positive? That might be a bit tricky."

"How many Fairly Trod wines do we sell?"

The Fairly Trod Foundation was an international body that recognised wineries working to a higher level of social responsibility in developing countries. Those wishing to obtain Fairly Trod certification were obliged to pay their workers above the legal minimum, allow one day off each week, and provide accommodation fit for human habitation. Wineries achieving this enlightened standard were permitted, in exchange for a modest licence fee, to place the Fairly Trod logo, a foot with a smiling face, upon their wine bottles, thus assuaging any guilt suffered by the liberal-minded plonk-swillers of the West.

"We have two Fairly Trod wines in the range."

"Not enough. Source a few more, so we can tell a compelling story about our commitment to disadvantaged stakeholders. Better still, find a black-owned winery, so we can talk about empowering people of colour." The Head of Message was rubbing her hands now, her bangles clanking in agreement. "The BBC might even do a feature on us. A nice one, this time."

"Right. Fairly Trod wines and black empowerment."

She narrowed her eyes. "And you might think we're in this together, Felix, but don't forget that this whole shambles is your fault. If the slightest sniff of this story leaks, I'll make damn sure your name's attached to all the negative publicity. And good luck finding another job if that happens."

Chapter 4

Tears of Pity

Troy Frittersley sandwiched my outstretched hand between his moist, meaty palms, and jostled it up and down, before grasping my upper arm and pulling me to him in a manly hug. He was a large, round man, with an earnest face, his globular frame enveloped in a suit of crumpled linen. The ends of his trousers were piled, in a ruck of material, upon a pair of white sneakers the size of small rowing boats.

"Felix, Felix. Such a pleasure," he said, in a New England accent. "So, you're the man giving up a life of wine and luxury to live among the wretched of the earth."

If you think I'm giving up wine, sunshine, you've been poorly briefed, I thought. And I'm not sure about living among the wretched either. I can tolerate living within commuting distance of the wretched, but I have no intention of bunking up with them.

"Yes, that's me," I said, extricating myself from Frittersley's ham-like arms.

"Wonderful, wonderful," he said, stepping back to consider me from head to toe. "You are the best of us, Felix. The very best."

"Well, one tries to do one's bit."

Troy Frittersley was the CEO of Tears of Pity, a charity dedicated to the alleviation of world poverty and the upliftment of the unfortunate. I was standing in Frittersley's London home, a smart townhouse just off Marylebone High Street, which doubled as Tears of Pity's European headquarters. I had been dispatched there by the Head of Compliance, who'd briefed me that Frittersley was recruiting for a role to spearhead his new southern African project. He'd made it clear that I should ingratiate myself with the man, so I'd promised to be on my best behaviour.

Frittersley was a multi-millionaire, umpteen times over, having made his fortune through the marketing of adult colouring books. I had assumed adult colouring books were filled with line drawings of buff young men and women, going at it hammer-and-tongs, but it turned out adult colouring books are similar to children's colouring books, except the lines are closer together, presumably rendering the process of colouring-in more tedious. I was glad I'd taken the time to check, otherwise I might have committed a buttock-clenching *faux pas*. Frittersley, perhaps embarrassed by his obscene wealth, had now embarked on a second career as a philanthropist.

Frittersley patted me on the shoulder and presented his business card. But, as I tucked it into my pocket, he held up a hand.

"No, read the card, Felix."

I withdrew it and peered at the fussy calligraphy.

Troy Frittersley, Chief Empathy Officer

"Oh, yes. CEO. How clever," I said, feeling mildly nauseated.

"Thank you," smiled Frittersley. "Empathy is what makes the world go round, Felix. The ability to feel the pain of others. The ability to weep, not for oneself, but on behalf of one's fellow man."

"Well, there's a lot to weep about, Mr Frittersley."

"There is, Felix, there is indeed. And call me Troy, please. Here, sit down." Frittersley manoeuvred himself into a large office chair and tapped the neighbouring seat. "Now, you have been to Africa, have you not?"

"Yes, Troy, I have. An enchanting continent."

"Tell me more."

I suspected I shouldn't mention the week I'd spent at my school friend Abdul's *riad* in Marrakech, tearing through the medina on mopeds and getting bladdered every night on Moroccan Cabernet. Nor the surfing holiday on Namibia's Skeleton Coast, hosted by the diamond mining division of Paris-

Blois, a luxury goods conglomerate who happened to supply Gatesave with fine wine. And I don't think he'd have appreciated tales of debauched cruises round Zanzibar on my old pal Tariq's floating gin palace either.

"Oh, there's the open skies, the wildlife, the ancient landscape, of course. But for me it's the people that make Africa special. Their courage. Their knowledge. And, most of all, their dignity."

Frittersley nodded, vigorously. "That's just what I hoped you'd say, Felix. Have you seen the townships of South Africa?"

I had. Anyone driving from Cape Town to the winelands couldn't miss the mile upon mile of tin shacks, glittering beneath their tangled skeins of electric cable. The townships covered the entirety of the Cape Flats, its shifting sands unsuitable for building anything over a single storey. Millions of families, from the poor to the utterly destitute, suffocating in summer under the African sun, flooded in winter as the Cape storms raged.

"Yes, a wretched sight."

"But have you visited the townships?"

Now, it wasn't my choice, but as a matter of fact, I had. One of my wine suppliers, in a fit of charity, had sponsored a community centre in the middle of Khayelitsha, the largest and roughest township of all. Despite my attempts to avoid the excursion, they had insisted I view the new facility, so I was driven, at speed, in a blacked-out people carrier, into the centre of the neighbourhood. I'd expected my arrival to be met with bloodcurdling screams and a hail of automatic gunfire, but the locals seemed pretty relaxed and the community centre was a jolly enough place, with children singing and groups of older women manufacturing trinkets for tourists. I left with a cute model ostrich, fashioned from discarded electrical flex wrapped around a punctured football, and absolutely no bullet wounds at all.

"I have, Troy, on several occasions," I said. "I've persuaded many of our South African suppliers to contribute funds to local community projects, so I spend time in the townships whenever I'm out there. After all, what's the point in wielding power if you can't use it to forge a better world?"

"Good for you, Felix," he said. "I knew you were made of the right stuff." Frittersley appeared lost in reverie for a moment. "I too have visited the townships. My experience was… alas… less amicable than yours."

"Oh?"

"I was rather foolish, you see. I hired a car and visited the township alone. I was scouting for charitable opportunities and had arranged to meet a local fixer, by the name of Chopper."

"That sounds ill-advised."

"Indeed. I was naïve. I lost my bearings and soon became completely lost in the informal settlements. Then the road petered out and my car became stuck in the sand. I tried to call Chopper, but he didn't answer. Then… I was accosted, by some young men."

"Oh dear."

"Yes, they took my phone and wallet. I implored them to let me call my hotel but… they set about me, Felix. They beat me. I tried to explain that I was there to help them. But they just laughed."

"They sound like a very unpleasant bunch."

"No, Felix. I believe they were angels."

This was, by some degree, the most idiotic thing I'd heard for a long time. I nodded and smiled, wondering whether Frittersley had incurred brain damage during his unfortunate encounter with the township ruffians.

"You see, it was as they rained their blows down upon me, in the dirt of that township alley, that I had an epiphany. I realised it was my duty to help these people."

"That's very generous of you. A weaker man might have taken the first flight home."

"Do you know what really brought it home to me? It was the kicking. Oh, they kicked my ass, Felix. Don't get me wrong, they kicked my sides, my back, my front, my head. It hurt, a lot. If that had happened on the streets of New York or London, I'd probably be dead. But, those poor, dear boys were wearing flip-flops. They were so disadvantaged, they couldn't even afford the footwear to injure me properly. Do you know what that's called, Felix?"

It's called a stroke of bloody luck, I thought. But I knew I had to humour the soft-headed lunatic. I shook my head.

"It's called white privilege, my friend."

"I see," I said, not really seeing at all. "So, you escaped without serious injury?"

"Well, no, not really. As I had my epiphany, I was overcome with a kind of rapture. I called out to those poor boys, half-crying, half-laughing, trying to share my joy with them."

"Were they receptive?"

"Angels aren't our friends, Felix. They are here to guide us, to teach us. No, they didn't take it well. They stopped kicking me and began beating me with pieces of metal torn from my car. One youth even attempted to insert the tailpipe into my... well, you get the idea. I lost consciousness and woke up in hospital in Cape Town two days later. I still have the scars. Look, right here."

Frittersley lowered his head and pointed to a rather alarming crease, clearly visible through his thinning hair.

"Ouch," I said, making a mental note to never venture into a township again.

"But these things happen for a reason. Ever since my epiphany, I've been waiting for the right person to enter my life and let me realise my vision. When your Head of Compliance phoned me, yesterday, and said he knew a young man with passionate, humanitarian instincts, looking for an opportunity to help the needy, I felt a prickle pass down my neck."

Probably your brains seeping out of that wound, I thought.

"You come very highly recommended. Your credentials are impeccable. The light shines from you, Felix. It shines."

Frittersley took my hand and stared into my eyes, like a half-sharp puppy.

"Well, I'd be delighted to help," I said. "What's the plan?"

"Your employer has made a generous donation to our cause. We intend to use those funds to establish a place of pilgrimage."

"What, like a church? I'm not sure I'm really qualified for that."

"No, not a traditional religious institution. A humanist sanctuary. A place where our tears of pity can irrigate the soil and bring forth a harvest of empathy. We're working with the South African Ministry of Development, right now, to identify a suitable project. Most excitingly of all, Felix, you'll have the chance to stay in the township and live alongside the beneficiaries of your aid."

Harvest of empathy or not, I'll be staying on a luxury wine farm in Stellenbosch, I thought. You won't catch me in a township after dark, not without an assault rifle and close air support.

"Do you think that's wise, after your experience?" I said.

Frittersley placed his hand on my shoulder.

"I understand your concern, Felix, but you can't truly empathise until you've shed your white privilege. It may be an uncomfortable process, but I have no doubt that a man with your degree of humility will soon find a way to unpack that invisible knapsack."

Chapter 5

The Terror of Tadcaster

"What is the truest measure of a man's worth? Or a woman's, for that matter?"

Herbert Marris's thick, Yorkshire vowels hung in the air-conditioned chill of the boardroom. He surveyed the room through his gold-rimmed spectacles. The Terror of Tadcaster may have been short in stature, but he was a titan of retail. He placed his hands on the great glass table and leaned towards us. The fifty or so executives, crowded at the other end of the room, shrank back.

"Integrity!"

My heart sank a little.

Day One: Start As We Mean to Go On! the email invitation had declared, together with an order to assemble in the ninth-floor boardroom. And it was quite clear by now that Marris intended to go on, and on, and on.

"You are guilty. All of you!" said Marris, looking from executive to executive. "You!" he said, pointing at a hapless supply chain manager at the edge of our huddle. "Of what are you guilty?"

"Erm… of not thinking about the customer enough?" offered the man.

"Conspiracy!" said Marris, with a grim little smile. "Conspiracy against the shareholder!" He moved his stare to a marketing executive standing in front of me. "Do you understand?"

"Er, ah… I think so…" she stammered.

"What is for dinner?" demanded Marris.

"Er... I'm not sure," said the woman, bewildered. "I usually have fish on Wednesdays."

"I'm talking about dinner, not supper, madam!" said Marris. "Dinner in the staff canteen. I took a little look, earlier. Chicken Kiev. Beef Stroganoff. Very fancy. What are the shareholders having for dinner? Are they invited?"

"I… don't know," said the woman, quietly.

"You don't know. Why should you have free dinner when the shareholders do not?"

"I don't know," said the woman.

"No. You don't know much, do you, madam? Let me tell you something then. There'll be no more breakfast, no more dinner and no more tea in Gatesave Head Office. Because free breakfast, dinner and tea are a conspiracy. A conspiracy against… what?"

"The shareholder?" said the woman.

"You see! You do know something. You're learning. You're all going to learn a lot over the next few days and weeks. You're going to learn what it means to work. To work honestly, and with integrity, for the owners of this business."

Oh Jesus, I thought. It's worse than I could have imagined. No more bacon and black pudding sandwiches for breakfast. What a bloody disgrace.

"Who is Hart?"

My blood froze.

"Er, I think that's me, sir," I said, half-raising my arm.

"You think it's you? The man doesn't even know his own name! Well? Are you Hart or are you not Hart?"

"Oh, definitely Hart."

"Well, Definitely Hart. You have a problem, don't you?"

"Er… I dare say, sir."

"You dare say? I dare say you do, lad. Eh?"

"Is it a conspiracy, sir?"

A flutter of titters rippled across the assembled crowd and a light rouge flushed Marris's cheeks. I grimaced, inwardly. Why the hell hadn't I kept my mouth shut?

"It's not just a conspiracy, lad," shouted Marris. "It's a bloody disgrace, is what it is. Do you know what the first thing is that I do when I join a new business?"

"No, sir."

"No, I know you don't, lad. The first thing I do is check the travel expenditure of every department and every employee. Because I can tell, at a glance, who is taking advantage of the shareholder. And who do you think has the worst travel expenditure of anyone in Gatesave?"

"Well, I run the wine team, you see. We have lots of suppliers in far-flung places."

"I didn't ask what you run, lad. You run a racket, so far as I can see."

There was no tittering now. I looked as grave as I could. I wondered if I was about to be fired.

"I'm told you're off to South Africa. On a sabbatical, whatever that is."

"Yes, sir."

"Sounds like another racket to me. You're going to work for a charity, I've been told."

"That's right, sir. I'm working on upliftment of the impoverished."

"Well, that's laudable. Very laudable. But it sounds like it's the shareholder who's been impoverished on your watch, lad. So, you'll be flying economy class. And I have specified that you should stay in a township for the duration of your trip, not some fancy hotel. That way you can learn what impoverishment is all about."

"Very good, sir."

"And when you are back, you will not be travelling abroad again at the expense of our shareholders. Because we have suppliers who can do that for us."

I nodded, miserably.

"To fly around the world, in first class, at the expense of our shareholders, is bad enough. But flying around, first class, to visit vineyards and drink wine is decadence. I will be frank. I do not like alcohol. If I had my way, we would not sell it. I permit it because we live in a licentious society and selling liquor adds value for the shareholder. But I will not tolerate consumption of alcohol in my offices. Any bottles of wine or liquor on the premises will be surrendered to the personnel department, today, whereupon they will be destroyed. From tomorrow morning, anyone found in possession of liquor in my offices will be dismissed. Is that understood?"

Marris scanned the crestfallen group before him. I slid my phone from my pocket and, barely daring to glance down, sent a text to Foyley, my most capable buying assistant.

Go to storeroom and remove all expensive bottles from premises. Use unmarked crates. You have 15 minutes. Failure not an option.

"Good," said Marris. "I will enlighten you to other changes to policy as they are implemented."

The meeting was over. As we filed out in silence, my phone vibrated.

Sorry. Maintenance already changing locks on storeroom door.

By God, I thought, this is horrific. It was time to leave the country.

***

"Felix! Felix!" A savage whisper from the corner of the room. I turned to see the Head of Compliance and Head of Message gesturing to me. "Get in here!"

I did as I was told. The Head of Message slid the door shut. "We've got a problem," she said, with a look suggesting I might be partially to blame.

"Another one?"

"Yes. I've just finished a very uncomfortable phone call with that Scandinavian NGO. They've expanded their investigation into working conditions in South African wineries and they intend to name and shame those who, in their opinion, fall short of civilised wage and labour standards. They also intend to name and shame the major customers of those wineries. They're drawing up a report contrasting the pay of retail chief executives with the pay of their suppliers' grape pickers."

"Oh dear, that sounds awkward."

"Yes, it is rather. Herbert Marris is the highest-paid retail executive in the country, and they intend to headline their report with a comparison of his salary against one of Blanchkopf's vineyard workers."

"Ah. Having met Mr Marris, I don't think he'll take that very well."

"No Felix, he won't," said the Head of Message. "He'll take it very badly indeed. I expect he'll want to know exactly who has put him in such an embarrassing position, so early in his new role."

"Yes, I see. How did Blanchkopf fare in the NGO's investigation?"

"Blanchkopf wouldn't allow them on the premises."

"Sensible chap. Thank God for that."

"Sensible?" wailed the Head of Compliance. "He set his dogs on the NGO's investigators! Your supplier's a bloody psychopath, man!"

"Oh, gosh," I said. "I suppose that set alarm bells ringing for the NGO?"

"Yes Felix," said the Head of Message. "Being chased down the winery driveway by two half-rabid German Shepherds does tend to set alarm bells ringing."

"But the NGO hasn't actually visited Blanchkopf's winery?"

"No. That's why they called me. They're insisting we share our own audit with them."

"We don't have to do that, do we?"

"We don't have to, but it makes us look rather dodgy if we refuse. It'll confirm their suspicions that there's a problem."

"It won't take them long to send an undercover investigator into the vineyard or interview some of the workers and their families," said the Head of Compliance, shaking his head. "Then we'll be for it."

"We're going to release an edited version of our audit to the NGO, suggesting we identified some minor non-conformities," said the Head of Message. "That should buy us a couple of weeks. During which time you," at this, she jabbed my chest with her finger, her bangles clunking angrily, "need to be out there, on the ground, sorting things out."

"I can assure you, I have no desire to remain in this building a minute longer."

***

"Here are your tickets to Cape Town, Felix," said Foyley. "I'm afraid you're flying Ethiopian Airlines, via Addis Ababa and Johannesburg. Had to book the cheapest possible ticket. New company policy."

"Thank you, Foyley. So long as they're serving unlimited wine, I'm sure I can tolerate it." I zipped the tickets into my hand luggage.

"And there's a couple of mixed cases waiting for you at Minstrels Hall on your return. A little overflow from the wine storeroom."

"I thought you said they'd changed the locks?"

"They were in the process of changing them. But the maintenance team's attention was diverted by a flood in the disabled toilet just long enough to liberate a few of the finer samples."

"Showing excellent initiative, as usual, Foyley. I'm going to miss your proactive approach to problem solving."

I sat and scrolled through my unread emails. A very recent one, sent just ten minutes ago, caught my eye. It was from the People & Wellbeing team, a shadowy department within Human Resources. I clicked on the message.

Hello Felix. Before you depart on your sabbatical, you're required to drop into the People & Wellbeing office today for a mandatory briefing. Keep well, P&W team.

"Oh, there were two blokes looking for you first thing this morning," said Foyley. "One was from HR, didn't recognise the other. They were muttering about samples. I told them we'd handed in all our booze, as ordered. One of them said he wasn't talking about wine samples, but the other guy nudged him to be quiet. Struck me as a bit suspicious."

A shiver ran down my spine. I recalled Elmo's warning about Marris's enthusiasm for urine ambushes. Now, I'm no drug-addled crack fiend, but I suspected my bloodstream wasn't as pure as an imam at Ramadan, if you know what I mean. I wondered whether Marris had singled me out for the first batch of employee drug tests, the self-righteous swine.

No problem, I typed. *See you in the P&W office this afternoon.*

"Foyley!" I whispered. "Get over here."

Foyley crouched next to my chair. "What's up, boss?"

"What's Durange's password? I need to check some of his wine prices on the Masterdata system."

"It's *I love Debbie*. Lower case, no spaces."

"Thanks, Foyley."

There would come a time, I mused, when Gatesave would be forced to take IT security seriously. No doubt some enterprising thirteen-year-old, sitting in his underpants in his parents' house, was already working on a method to download Gatesave's database of customer credit cards and sell them to the Russian mafia. But that time, thank God, was not yet upon us. I opened Facebook and typed in Durange's email address. Then, checking no-one was overlooking my screen, I typed *ilovedebbie* into the password field and hit enter.

Timmy Durange was a dependable, if somewhat wet, member of my buying team. In my early days at Gatesave, as junior wine buyer, he'd been rather mean to me, though I'm not one to take these things to heart. A few years later, when I'd been promoted to Head of Department, and Durange found himself reporting to me, a lesser man might have chosen the path of revenge and made Durange's life a misery. But I'm a generous chap and above that kind of thing. In fact, given our difficult early history, I felt there was an unspoken understanding between the two of us. He worked loyally and uncomplainingly, and I resisted the occasional impulse to squash the snivelling little urchin like a cockroach.

I'd overheard Durange whinging last month about the multitude of different systems we were expected to use, and the number of different passwords one was obliged to remember. He'd declared, quite openly, that he used the same password for everything, which struck me at the time as an unwise boast. And, sure enough, Timmy Durange's Facebook timeline opened up before me, detailing the wholesome adventures of himself, the lovely Debbie, and his wider circle of pale, unworldly friends and family.

I ate lunch at a local trattoria, to avoid any HR personnel who might be patrolling the canteen with paper cups and moist wipes. After an excellent ox cheek ragu and a carafe of Dolcetto, I strolled back to the office. Spotting Durange at his desk, I tapped him on the shoulder. "A word please, Timmy."

Durange followed me to a meeting room. I locked the door and sat down. As Timmy frowned in confusion at the absence of any other chairs, I opened my laptop.

"I've just received a disturbing phone call from HR, Timmy," I said.

"What about?" said Durange. He gave a nervous half-smile, half-grimace, as he always did when things weren't quite going his way.

"I'm sure you're aware that the HR department monitor the social media profiles of Gatesave employees," I said.

"Oh, er… yes?" said Durange.

"Well, I'm sorry to say that something rather unfortunate has been brought to my attention."

I turned the laptop and pointed to Durange's most recent Facebook post.

Boss is away for six months from tonight. Going to enjoy a few wines – maybe a few lines too!

Durange's post had already received two likes and a comment from someone called Moira Durange, asking: *Lines of what, Timmy?*

Durange's face turned white. He stared at the screen, goggle-eyed. "That's not me!" he yelped. "That's not me!"

"Timmy, so far as I'm concerned, what you get up to in your own time is your own business."

"But that's not me!" Durange gibbered, looking frantically from the screen to me and back again. "I didn't write that!" Durange stabbed at the screen. "It's not me!"

"Look Timmy," I said. "Don't worry. You've not broken any laws. I'm sure it was just a joke. But our new CEO is quite hot on this kind of thing."

"It's… it's not me! I would never! I have never!"

"You're required to pee into this bottle," I said, placing an empty mineral water bottle and a wet wipe on the table. "New rules, from the very top. You have to do it right here, I'm afraid."

Durange stared at the bottle and wet wipe, his mouth opening and closing. I swivelled my chair and faced the wall.

"Use the wet wipe if you spill down the sides," I said. "I have to take the sample to HR myself, so I'd rather everything was lemon-fresh."

I heard Durange remove the cap from the bottle and unzip his flies. Then there was silence.

"In your own time," I said.

"I only went half an hour ago," Durange croaked.

"Would you like a cup of tea to get things going?"

"No thanks."

After what seemed an eternity, I heard a series of little squirts against the inside of the water bottle.

"All done?" I asked when the tinkling had stopped.

"Yes."

"Excellent," I said, spinning my chair back round.

The bottle was a third-full of deep amber liquid.

"Good God, look at the colour of that!" I exclaimed. "Are you sure you're keeping hydrated, Timmy?"

Durange sniffed unhappily and shrugged.

"If you wouldn't mind polishing the bottle with the wet wipe before you go, I'd be ever so grateful. Germs and sneezes cause diseases, as they say."

Durange did as I asked and turned to the door.

"Oh, and you might want to change your Facebook privacy settings."

Durange nodded and left the office, used wet wipe in hand. I waited a few seconds, then leapt up and re-locked the door. I checked the mineral water bottle was properly sealed and slid the foul receptacle under my shirt, gripping it snugly under my armpit. I tucked my shirt into my trousers and adjusted my jacket, before heading up to the People & Wellbeing office.

I knocked and entered. Two women and a man sat behind a table, a row of glass beakers and a box of wet wipes before them. In the corner of the room stood a hospital privacy screen on wheels.

"Goodness me!" I said, eyeing the beakers. "I hope you're not conducting an illicit wine tasting!"

"Ah, hello Felix," said one of the women. "I'm afraid we have a rather unusual request."

"Ask away, my dear colleagues," I replied. "My conscience is clear."

Chapter 6

Crossed Wires

Ethiopian Airlines were indeed generous with their on-board beverage service. I managed to doze, in a pleasant, wine-fuelled haze, most of the way from London to Addis Ababa, and from there on to Johannesburg. I alighted from the final leg to Cape Town, had my working visa stamped by immigration, and stood before the baggage carousel, awaiting my luggage. One by one, my fellow passengers retrieved their cases until I was the last person left. Then, the carousel stopped.

"All finish," called a voice, and the overhead lights went out.

I have no idea whether a Londoner, an Ethiopian, a Johannesburger or a Capetonian stole my luggage, or whether it was mislabelled and still lies in the lost property office of some provincial airport in Utter Pradesh, but that was the last I saw of my clothes, washbag and machete. I was sorry to have lost that last item, I'd felt it might have come in handy. It was a souvenir from a trip to the Selous some years ago and had served me well in my early career running London liquor stores, requiring only the briefest of flourishes to discourage shoplifters, aggressive drunks and other ne'er-do-wells.

Tomorrow, I decided, I would visit a mall and pick up some new clothes. Today, though, I had an appointment. I collected my hire car and nosed out of the shade of the multi-storey car park, squinting as I joined the highway. It was only early spring, but the midday glare was dazzling. I slipped on my sunglasses, thanking my lucky stars that I'd packed them in my hand luggage.

My destination was the vast township of Khayelitsha, for Tears of Pity had arranged a meeting with Mr Maduma, head of the local bureau of the Ministry of Development. Now, it is not generally advised for non-locals to drive, merrily, into the townships, especially not Khayelitsha, which has a somewhat troubled reputation. But, according to my directions, the Ministry of Development was located just a few hundred yards from the N2 highway, and I wasn't intending to conduct any freelance sightseeing further inside the neighbourhood. I patted the money belt strapped to my stomach, in which I had secreted a few crisp twenty-pound notes. It was already itchy and moist with sweat, but better safe than sorry.

The tarmac petered out a hundred yards from the highway and I bumped, slowly, along a treeless road lined with single-storey, prefabricated houses festooned with satellite dishes. Every few yards, I passed a post supporting a gob of electrical cables, from which a fan of wires emerged, touching every dwelling, as though a great spider had ensnared the entire settlement. This was the formal part of the township, where the inhabitants enjoyed an intermittent power and water supply. But the majority, living deeper inside, had few such comforts.

Several times, as I crawled my way along the unsurfaced road, I was overtaken by a minibus taxi, which sprayed my car with grit and left a blinding cloud of dust in its wake. As each vehicle sped past, I could see it crammed with township residents on their return from cleaning and gardening jobs in Cape Town's wealthy suburbs. After another ten minutes of careful bumping, I was worried I'd taken the wrong road, but Tears of Pity's directions were sound and half a mile later I pulled up outside a single-storey, concrete building with a tin roof. Several of the letters over the door had vanished, leaving the office with the cryptic title: *Mini try of elopment*. I locked the car and approached the entrance, which was barred by a metal gate. A security guard sat just inside, on a plastic chair, eating a packet of macadamia nuts.

"Hello, I'm Felix Hart," I said, brightly, through the bars. "I have an appointment with Mr Maduma, the Head of Sustainable Development for Khayelitsha."

The security guard extracted a nut from his bag and examined it, silently.

"I'm here for Mr Maduma," I repeated. I tested the metal gate, but it was locked. I smiled, encouragingly. "Can I come in?"

The guard replaced the nut in the bag and extracted another.

"*Molo. Unjani?*" I said, calling upon my somewhat limited knowledge of Xhosa.

The man lifted the nut up to his left eye, frowned, and observed me with the right, as if comparing my head, unfavourably, to the macadamia.

"Look," I said, "I'm here to see Mr Maduma. Is he here?" I lifted my shades, pressed my head against the gate's bars and tried to peer into the room. The office was bathed in a gloomy, brown light; the single window, caked with grime, doing its upmost to exclude the African sun from the room's interior. A bookcase, crammed with dried, curling magazines, leant against the rear wall, while a sack barrow, missing a wheel, lay on the floor beside it. The floor appeared to be strewn with flattened cereal boxes.

"No," said the guard, moving the nut further from his eye.

I spotted an office door in the far corner. I could just make out a sign hanging on it, saying *Head of Sustainable Development*.

"Is that Mr Maduma's office, there?" I said, pointing through the bars.

The guard placed the nut in his mouth and crunched it. "No," he said, through fragments of macadamia.

I stepped back from the door, replaced my shades and walked round the back of the building. A window, lined with anti-burglar bars, stood open just above head height. Spotting an empty twenty-litre drum of cooking oil lying in the weeds, I placed it beneath the window and stepped on top, using the burglar bars to steady myself. I peered through the window and down into the office of the Head of Sustainable Development.

A bald African man lay snoring, peacefully, in a padded chair dotted with escaping bulges of sponge. His shoeless feet were propped upon the desk before him, which was empty except for an old-fashioned mobile phone and a box of tissues. The tip of a big toe peeped out from a hole at the end of his sock.

"Mr Maduma?" I called, through the window.

The man awoke with a start, removed his feet from the desk and grabbed his mobile.

"Yes, hello?" he shouted, into the phone.

"Hello, Mr Maduma," I called, my face pressed against the metal grille.

"Yes! Who is this?" shouted Maduma, into the phone.

"I'm up here, Mr Maduma. At the window."

Maduma looked up and his eyes widened in shock. I gave a little wave, while clinging tightly to the burglar bars with my other hand. Maduma looked at his phone, slapped it on the desk and covered it with his hand, before turning back to me.

"What are you doing?" he said.

"I'm Felix Hart, from Tears of Pity in London. I think we have an appointment, Mr Maduma."

"Appointment?" Maduma considered the empty desk before him for a few seconds, tapping his fingers against the top, then opened a drawer. He removed a large office diary, opened it and leafed through a few pages, all of which, so far as I could tell from my outdoor perch, were completely blank.

"Yes," he said, finally, replacing the diary in the drawer. "How can I help?"

"Can I come in, Mr Maduma?"

"Yes, yes. You should come to the front. Charles will let you in."

"Jolly good," I called. I stepped off the wobbling oil canister and lowered myself to the ground.

I returned to the front, to find the security gate open and no sign of the guard. I crossed the cardboard-strewn floor and knocked on the office door. There was no reply, so I knocked again, harder.

"Who is it?" called Maduma, from the other side.

"It's me, Mr Maduma. Felix Hart. The man from the window."

"The man from what?"

"The man from the window, Mr Maduma," I shouted, moving my lips to within a couple of inches of the door frame. "Can I come in please?"

"What do you want?"

"We have an appointment. To discuss the money for the development project. From Tears of Pity."

The door suddenly opened and Maduma stood before me. He was quite a short man, though I noticed he was now wearing black leather shoes, polished to a brilliant shine.

"Money?" he said.

"Yes, the money from Tears of Pity. For the development project. Troy Frittersley said the funding would be funnelled through your department. Can I come in?"

Maduma looked past me into the decrepit reception room. "Where is Charles?"

"I have no idea, I'm afraid. He was here earlier."

"Charles?" shouted Maduma, over my shoulder, making me jump.

There was no reply.

"*Charles!*" shouted Maduma, even louder. I placed a finger in my left ear, by way of protection.

"Perhaps he's gone to buy some nuts."

"*Charles! Charles! Charles!*" screamed Maduma.

There was a clumping of boots against the dirt outside and the guard hurled himself, wild-eyed, through the front door. Spotting me, he raced across the floor towards us, arms outstretched.

"I'm not a burglar!" I shouted, raising my hands.

"Sit down!" shouted Maduma, and the confused guard, arms wheeling, attempted to execute an emergency stop. Unfortunately, the carpet of cereal boxes had other ideas, and the man's feet slid from under him, depositing him on his behind, his considerable momentum propelling him feet-first into the bookshelves, which collapsed on top of him in a chaos of paper.

Maduma waved his hand in front of his face, as a cloud of dust enveloped the room.

"Shall we… continue this in your office?" I suggested.

"Yes, yes, ok," said Maduma.

"Thank you," I said, following Maduma through the door. His office was slightly more attractively decorated than the reception area, the window at least performing its basic function of permitting the ingress of light. A church pew stood on one side of the room, completely covered by mouldering box files, while the other was lined with filing cabinets, a couple of which appeared to have been beaten by an enraged elephant armed with a fence post.

I held out my hand, which startled Maduma for a second. Then, he grasped it, grinned and pumped it up and down. "Yes, very good to meet you, Mr…?"

"Mr Hart."

"Yes! Very good. Please, please, sit down."

Maduma waved me towards a plastic chair on which someone had written *Do Not* in black marker pen. As the seat took my weight, it began to subside backwards, and I was forced to place a hand on the ground to prevent myself toppling over. A quick check confirmed that one of the rear legs was missing.

"Ah yes, sorry, sorry. I forgot," said Maduma, jumping to his feet and waving both hands. "That chair is no good. Sorry, sorry."

"Not a problem," I replied, climbing to my feet. I righted the chair and perched on the front edge.

"So, yes," said Maduma. "What can I do for you?"

"Well, I understand you have one million rand in your development account, donated by Tears of Pity International," I said, placing the charity's bank transfer receipt on the desk. "I'm here to supervise the investment of that money in the township."

Maduma drew the receipt towards him and peered at it. "No, no, I don't have that kind of money!" he chuckled.

"No, I don't mean your own money, Mr Maduma. This is Tears of Pity's money. They transferred it to you. I understand the money has to pass through the Ministry of Development, to ensure it is spent in line with government policy. The account details are right there."

"One million rand! No, I would have noticed that," said Maduma. "That is a lot of money!"

"Yes, it is rather a lot. Which is why I'm quite anxious to find out where it is."

"Well, it is not here, Mr Hat."

"Hart."

"Harrot?"

"Hart, Mr Maduma. My name is Mr Hart." I took a deep breath. "Never mind. Look, I do need you to help me find the money. It must be in one of your department's bank accounts."

"Maybe it is still in England?"

"No, they definitely transferred it here. They have finance people and lawyers to make sure this kind of thing happens properly."

"Lawyers! They are very expensive. They probably spent it all!"

"Mr Maduma. Do you have a manager, please, someone with whom I can escalate this? Someone at the Ministry Headquarters in Cape Town, perhaps?"

"Yes, yes! Of course!"

"Thank you."

I waited for Maduma to suggest a name, but he just sat there, smiling.

"So… can I have a contact name please?"

"They are closed now. They close at four p.m."

"Then I'll visit them in the morning."

"Oh! You are staying more than one day?"

"Yes, Mr Maduma, I'm here for several months. I'm supervising a long-term development project, right here, in the township!"

"Oh, ok. Very good, yes. But we are closed now. We also close at four p.m."

"Can you just give me a contact name and number, please?"

"No, I do not have that. I will have to phone them tomorrow."

59

"You have to phone them to get the phone number?"

"Yes, yes. Exactly. I have to phone them."

"Right. I see. You've been moderately helpful, Mr Maduma, thank you very much. I will see you first thing in the morning. When does this office open?"

"At nine o'clock."

"See you at nine then."

"Or ten o'clock, sometimes."

I retrieved the bank transfer receipt, shook Maduma's hand and returned to the reception area, closing the office door behind me. The guard was nowhere to be seen and the front grille was locked. I returned to the office and knocked on the door. There was no reply, so I opened it. Maduma was sitting in his chair, his feet up and his eyes closed. I cleared my throat. Maduma opened his eyes and leapt up.

"Mr Harrut!"

"Yes, sorry to disturb you, I appear to be locked in. Can you let me out please?"

Maduma stared at me for a second. "Where is Charles?"

"I don't know where Charles is. Perhaps he's buying a new cupboard. I don't know. Please can you let me out?"

"Shout for Charles. He should be there."

"You want me to shout for Charles? Don't you have a key?"

"No, sorry."

I strode back to the front grille and gave it a vigorous shake. The lock rattled angrily in the mortice.

"Charles!" I shouted, through the bars. "Charles, you useless bastard, where are you?"

There was no reply. I looked through the bars and realised something was wrong. My car was missing.

"Mr Maduma, call the police – my car has been stolen!" I shouted, striding back into the office.

"Oh! That is very bad!"

"Yes, I know it is. Please, call the police. They can't have gone far." With a sinking feeling, I realised I'd left my hand luggage in the boot, including my passport.

60

"The police station is closed now. They close at—"

"Call the emergency number! Forget it, I'll do it." I pulled out my phone, but the battery was flat. "Jesus Christ!" I shouted, recalling that my charger was in the car. "Can you just let me out of this bloody building please?"

"Oh. Yes. Where is Charles?"

"I don't know where bloody Charles is!" I shouted. "Probably half-way to KwaZulu in my hire car!"

I stalked back to the front door and, to my astonishment, there was Charles, unlocking the gate.

"My car's been stolen!" I said, dashing past him and looking up and down the dirt road. "Did you see who took it?"

"Criminals," said Maduma, following me outside.

"Yes, Mr Maduma," I said, putting my head in my hands, "I think you're probably right. God almighty, I don't even know where I'm staying. My accommodation details were in the car."

"You could stay at Mama Bisha's," suggested Maduma.

"Mama Bisha's?"

"It's a very nice place. Not too far away. Come, I will take you there."

Chapter 7

Mama Bisha's

Maduma waved down an approaching minibus, which swerved enthusiastically from the centre of the road and drew up alongside us, around six inches from my nose. I was saved serious injury by the absence of any protruding accessories, such as wing mirrors, indicators or door handles, all of which appeared to have been shorn from the body of the vehicle in a series of abrasive incidents earlier in its career. The sliding door, operated by a bobble hat-wearing youth in the front passenger seat, was flung open well before the vehicle had come to a stop.

"Quick, quick, get in, *mlungu!*" shouted the driver's mate over the deafening *kwaito* hip-hop.

Maduma pushed me inside and leapt in, sandwiching me against a large woman with two grocery bags on her lap. The driver accelerated away – in fact, I'm not sure the vehicle was ever truly stationary at any point during our boarding – and proceeded to fly over the potholed road as if he were destruction-testing the suspension. Every two seconds, I was hurled in turn against Maduma's elbow, the ceiling of the minibus, and the woman's shopping, which appeared to be packed with viciously shaped pieces of scrap metal.

Luckily, my whimpers of pain were drowned out by the stereo, the volume of which was making my bladder vibrate. It was clear the taxi's owner had chosen to prioritise investment in the audio system over more superficial elements, such as the vehicle's bodywork, windscreen or chassis, and the amplifier would have done credit to a medium-sized concert venue. The windows hummed, my neighbour's shrapnel-filled shopping bags vibrated, and the entire fabric of the vehicle buzzed in sympathetic resonance.

After what seemed like an age, Maduma beat his palm against the front passenger headrest and the taxi slowed to a fast walking speed. He handed a few coins to the driver's mate, who slid the door open, and Maduma jumped out. I interpreted the driver's shout of "Let's go, *mlungu*, let's go!" as advice that there was little chance of the taxi slowing any further, and followed Maduma out of the vehicle. I'd barely lifted my rear from the seat before the driver stamped on the gas, the open door glancing my arm as I leapt clear.

The dust settled and I realised we were in a much poorer section of the township, the houses little more than shacks, self-built from scrap timber and corrugated metal. The only sign of commerce was a tiny *spaza*, a township convenience store, painted red to match the Coca-Cola advert above the serving window. Behind the glass, ribbons of lottery tickets curled in the sun. Another taxi drew up and disgorged a handful of passengers; men in overalls, women with bags of laundry, youths in school uniform. They observed me with mild interest, before disappearing into the alleyways between the shacks.

"Come, I take you to Mama Bisha," said Maduma, disappearing down a passage between the *spaza* and a shed constructed from planks lashed together with nylon rope. I followed and after a minute the passage met a broader road, busy with pedestrians, some carrying bags of fabric or lengths of timber, others standing in groups, apparently engaged in a competition as to who could speak the loudest. Smoke rose into the sky from a multitude of points behind the mass of shacks, and the air was filled with the aroma of burning wood punctuated, every so often, with the sharper smell of rotting trash.

We passed two young children, merrily beating an upturned plastic tub with sticks, watched by a tiny, barefoot child, wearing only a dust-caked nappy. When they saw me, they stopped their percussion and grinned. "*Mlungu! Mlungu!*" they shouted, in near-unison. "*Mlungu*," I replied, and all three screamed in delight.

"*Mlungu*," chuckled an elderly man, sitting in the doorway of his shack, and held out his hand. I shook it. It was as dry and rough as sandpaper. The man chuckled again.

Half a dozen more stick-wielding children appeared from the myriad passageways between the dwellings and they followed us down the street, thrashing items of rubbish and the occasional stunted tree as they danced around us, all the while shouting, "*Mlungu*! *Mlungu*!"

"Yes, you are *mlungu*," said Maduma.

"So it would seem," I replied. "What does it mean?"

"White person," he shrugged.

We arrived at a larger, single-storey building. Unlike the neighbouring shacks, it was made of concrete, though the walls were scarred with cracks, and the roof was a patchwork of mismatched corrugated metal.

"Mama Bisha's," he said, pointing at the door, which appeared to have once been the front entrance to a suburban house but had now, rather surreally, been mounted on two large gatepost hinges, despite being several inches too short and narrow to fit the doorway. It creaked to and fro in the wind, as if unsure whether it was the entrance to a family home or a Wild West saloon.

Maduma pushed at the door and I followed, stepping over a line of grubby sandbags, one layer high, lying just inside the entrance. I turned to give my little fan club a friendly wave goodbye. "Cheerio," I called.

"*Mlungu* bastard!" shouted one of the larger children, gleefully, at which the crowd of infants screamed with laughter. Slightly taken aback, I released the door. It swung back and forth on its hinges, giving me a series of shorter and shorter glimpses of the hooting children. I saw the tiny child in nappies bent over double, hands on his thighs, wheezing with laughter like an old man who'd just been told the joke of his life.

"Welcome! Welcome!" said a voice. A young man wearing a pair of expensive headphones leapt to his feet, a broad smile on his face.

"I have brought you a guest," said Maduma.

"Wonderful!" grinned the man, pulling the headphones down around his neck. "Welcome to Mama Bisha's. The finest hotel in Khayelitsha!" He swept his arm across the room, inviting me to admire the furnishings. The room was rather lighter than Maduma's office, bathed in a yellow glow courtesy of the afternoon sun streaming through a plastic skylight. Against the wall lay a metal bunk bed, the top of which was piled with cardboard boxes branded Iwisa Super Maize Meal, while the lower bunk's mattress had been replaced by a sheet of plywood, on which stood a partially dismantled television. A table football game, missing several spindles, stood pride of place in the centre of the room.

"My name is Shooter," continued the man, holding out his hand. "Do you like football?"

"Hello Shooter," I said, shaking his hand. "I'm Felix. How much is a bed for the night?"

"One hundred dollars!" said Shooter, brightly, continuing to shake my hand. "Ok, no, fifty dollars. Ten dollars."

"Right. Unfortunately, I don't have any dollars. I'm not American."

"Oh. Where are you from?"

Before I could reply, Shooter glanced over my shoulder. *"Sala kakuhle umhlobo!"*

I turned to see Maduma already half-way out of the door. "Goodbye Mister Harrut," he called, waving cheerily. "Nice to meet you. Hope you have a nice night. Maybe we meet again one day, maybe not."

I shook myself free of Shooter's hand and span around. "Wait, Mr Maduma! We're meeting in the morning, remember? Nine o'clock?"

"Yes, very good, see you later," called Maduma over his shoulder, as the front door swung back and forth on its saloon bar hinges.

I turned back to Shooter. "Do you take credit cards?"

"Yes, we take American Express. All credit cards. But our machine is broken. So, only cash."

I realised I'd forgotten to withdraw any rand from the ATM at the airport. "I only have British pounds. Can you wait until tomorrow when I can get to a cash machine?"

"The room is thirty pounds." From a doorway in the corner, a tall, slim woman stepped into the room. "All payment in advance, please."

Whether it was her tone or her bearing, it was indisputably clear that this woman was in charge. Her face was stern with no hint of a smile. She wore a long, dark dress that reached her feet, revealing not even a glimpse of ankle, and rose high at the neck, with a simple ring of lace around the collar. Her skin was dark and her features fine, you might even say handsome. But it was her eyes that caught my attention. They were a deep, dark brown, and the centre of each appeared to shine with a pinpoint of light. Just a reflection from the window, perhaps, but so vivid that it seemed a pair of ice-cold spotlights were trained upon me.

"Shooter here just quoted me ten dollars," I said.

"And I am quoting you thirty pounds."

The whites of her eyes were bright too, in contrast with the dark of the iris. And right in the centre of each, that cold needle of light.

She turned to Shooter. "Check that our best room is ready for the gentleman." Shooter darted out of the room.

"That's quite expensive. For a…" I looked around, suddenly embarrassed, trying to conjure a polite word for this particular category of accommodation.

"For a what?" Her voice was soft but there was steel behind it.

"Well, you can stay on a wine farm in Stellenbosch for the same amount."

"Then why didn't you stay on a wine farm?"

"Well, I'm a bit stuck, to be honest."

"Perhaps you don't like the neighbourhood."

Her eyes were most disconcerting.

"No, it's not that…"

"Perhaps you don't like the people. You would rather stay on a wine farm with just white people."

"No, no, no! Not at all!"

"Then, the price is thirty pounds."

"Fine." I didn't want to reveal the money belt beneath my shirt, so I pulled out my wallet. To my dismay, I saw I had no small denomination notes, just twenties. I fished two out. "I don't suppose you have any change?"

The woman took the notes and folded them into her pocket. "Thank you. Dinner will be ten pounds." The icy points at the centre of her eyes sparkled. I decided not to haggle any further.

"Wonderful. I look forward to perusing the wine list."

Shooter reappeared in the doorway.

"Shooter will show you to your room. Dinner will be served at seven o'clock."

"Thank you. Sorry, I didn't catch your name."

"You may call me Mama Bisha." She returned to the doorway in the corner, from where she had appeared. I glimpsed a small, tidy office, a net curtain drawn across a barred window, then she closed the door behind her.

Shooter led me into a large, rather dim back room containing half a dozen mismatched tables and a long bench along the far wall, on which sat an elderly, unhappy-looking African man, nursing a bottle of beer. A Chinese-branded refrigerator stood in the opposite corner, growling like a lion with catarrh.

"This is the restaurant," said Shooter.

"It's lovely," I said.

"The rooms are through here." I followed him into a short passageway, which ended in a rear entrance blocked by a barred security gate.

"You are in room one," said Shooter, tapping on the numeral scrawled on a door in black marker pen. "This is room two," he continued, pointing at another door, which was unadorned, presumably in the interests of saving ink. "This is not your room. It is occupied."

"Room one it is," I said. "May I take a look?"

Shooter turned the handle and encouraged the door assertively with his shoulder. It scraped open against the concrete floor and a skin-corroding wave of bleach rolled out to meet us. I staggered backwards, choking.

"Good Lord!" I wheezed. "Did something die in there? That's strong enough to turn your hair white."

"Yes. It is very clean now," said Shooter, breathing into the crook of his arm.

Pulling my shirt over my mouth, I stepped inside. The windowless room contained a metal-framed bed, a clothes rail and a small side table supporting a lamp and a glass vase full of crispy-looking rose petals. A mildewed poster advertising Three Ships whisky had been pasted to the bare wall, providing the only splash of colour. I peered, apprehensively, at the bed linen. It appeared clean, but before I could examine it more closely, my eyes filled with bleach-induced tears and I was forced to retreat.

"Very good," I gasped, "but could we leave the door open, please? I'm not sure I'll last the night otherwise."

"No problem," said Shooter, into his arm.

"And where's the bathroom?"

"Outside. You need toilet?"

"Yes, I do."

Shooter approached the security gate and knocked against the bars.

"What you want?" called a deep voice.

"Toilet," said Shooter.

The voice gave a short reply, in Xhosa. I'm not a confident speaker of Southern African tribal languages, but it was clear that the owner of the voice was unimpressed with Shooter's request.

"No, it's for the guest. *Mlungu* guest," said Shooter, looking back at me and flashing a smile.

A figure appeared on the other side of the gate, a heavily built man with a shaved head. "Yes, I'd like a pee please," I said, stepping up behind Shooter. "I'm a bit desperate actually."

The large man looked at me through the bars, astonished. "Who are you?" he demanded.

"I'm a guest. I'm staying the night," I said.

"Yes! He is a guest," said Shooter, triumphantly. "This is McGregor," he added, pointing at the large man.

"Hello, McGregor," I said, extending a hand through the bars.

McGregor considered my hand for a second, then took it in his huge paw and shook it. "Why you staying here?" he said, looking appalled.

"It was recommended on Trip Advisor," I said, "though you'll be losing a star if I end up wetting myself."

McGregor looked at Shooter and back to me, then shook his head, fished a key out of his pocket and unlocked the security gate. "*Mshengu*," he said, gesturing across the waste ground before me.

"Much obliged," I replied.

I stepped over another line of sandbags into the outside air and shaded my eyes against the low sun. In front of me lay a litter-strewn area of dirty sand, about the size of a football field. The left-hand side and the far end were bordered by shacks of corrugated iron, punctuated by alleyways knee-deep in rubbish, while the right-hand side was lined by a gully filled with reeds tall enough to obscure the view of the township beyond. A simple bridge with no guard rails, just wide enough for a motor vehicle, provided the only way across. It was blocked by a tangle of barbed wire and old car tyres. Beyond the bridge, I glimpsed a rough track lined by shacks as far as the eye could see.

I crossed the sand, skirting the broken glass and rusted metal hiding among the tufts of grass. A pair of tall concrete posts straddled the far end of the waste ground, supporting a thicket of electricity cables. A washing line had been strung between the posts and a row of bed linen flapped in the late afternoon sun. Just beyond, I glimpsed the top of a blue portable toilet cubicle.

I was obliged to duck between the sheets to reach it and, as I did so, I heard the sound of gushing water.

A few yards beyond the portable toilet, a line of township women queued before a gushing standpipe. A youth sat on a plastic chair nearby. At the head of the line stood a barefoot girl in dirty clothes, holding a battered, five-litre mineral water bottle. She crouched and placed the bottle beneath the stream. She watched it fill, slowly, most of the water missing the vessel's mouth and bouncing off its exterior, where it snaked away in a darkening stream to collect in a large, muddy puddle around the toilet cubicle's door. I gave the girl a friendly wave, but she didn't respond, just watched me pick my way through the pool of grubby water, tug open the door and step into the cubicle.

The facility, unsurprisingly, was in a fairly distressed state. Someone had recently hosed down the interior, though it was unclear whether this was the action of a cleaning operative or that of a drunken patron. The fug of generously applied fly repellent suggested a recent, possibly hysterical battle against a regiment of assertive invertebrates, a battle which, going by the number of beady eyes peering from the danker corners of the cubicle, had been comprehensively lost.

As I re-emerged into the sunshine, I saw the little girl's bottle was now full. She lifted it and hugged it to her chest, leaning backwards to balance the weight. She stared at me for a few seconds, unsmiling, a smear of mud on one cheek. Then, as I rinsed my hands at the standpipe, she turned, made her unsteady way towards an alleyway between the shacks, and vanished. The next woman in line gave a coin to the seated youth and placed a large cooking pot beneath the stream of water.

I ducked back under the line of washing and returned to the gate at the back of Mama Bisha's.

"Your dinner. It will be ready soon," grinned Shooter, waving me inside. "Very good, very special. We will eat with you."

"Jolly good," I said, stepping over the line of sandbags. "What's on the menu?"

"Smiley!" declared Shooter.

Chapter 8

The Rubicon

It was unclear whether Shooter's reply was a hint for me to cheer up, or a declaration of his own carefree mood. My attempt to gain clarification was interrupted by the arrival of two washerwomen, carrying a tub piled high with laundry, who launched into a loud negotiation with McGregor, in stereo.

"Come, have some beer," said Shooter, which was by some distance the best offer I'd had all day.

We returned to the dining room, holding our breath as we passed through the eye-watering fog of cleaning fluid. Shooter gestured to a table and opened the growling fridge, returning with two bottles of Castle lager, slightly above room temperature. The old African man watched us from the bench, his own bottle empty beside him.

"You like beer?" asked Shooter, aligning the bottle tops with the edge of the table and removing them simultaneously with a swift downward slap.

"I do, Shooter, thank you. Though I prefer wine."

"Ah, wine! Yes, the *mlungu* love wine."

"Well, you don't have to be *mlungu* to like wine. Lots of African people drink wine, I'm sure." I took a swig of warm beer, which foamed aggressively up the back of my throat.

"Yes!" agreed Shooter. "When African people become *mlungu*, then they drink wine!"

"When they become *mlungu*? I thought *mlungu* meant white person, doesn't it?"

"Yes, when they become white person, then they drink wine," agreed Shooter, taking a long swig of beer.

71

I suspected I might be straying into a tricky area of racial politics, so I decided to change course.

"So you like football? Is that why you're called Shooter?"

"Yes, exactly, that is why. I played five times for Cape Town All Stars. First Division."

"That sounds pretty good. Do you still play?"

"No, I had to retire. They stole my club."

"They what? They stole your football club?"

"Yes. They stole it, they took it to Mpumalanga."

"On the other side of the country, near Johannesburg? One thousand miles away?"

"Yes, they stole it."

"That's a very ambitious burglary. Didn't anyone spot them doing it?"

"Rich people did it. Everybody saw them do it. With money, you don't even need to hide."

"Well, yes, it helps, I suppose."

"I will become rich and own a football club." Shooter took a swig of beer. "You are rich. What is your job?"

"I'm not really that rich. I work in the wine industry, in England."

"Ah, in England! You have wine in England?"

"Yes, a little bit. But mainly I import wine. In fact, I could write you a wine list, if you like. For your restaurant."

Shooter frowned. "You will bring us English wine?"

"I could, but no… I just meant I could recommend some local wines. Look, never mind."

"We do not have many requests for wine here, Mr Hart," said Mama Bisha. She'd entered silently. I wondered how long she'd been standing there. "Beer, brandy, whisky, but rarely wine. But Shooter will find some wine for you."

"I can get anything," said Shooter, grinning.

"I'm sure you can, but I don't want to put you to any trouble."

"I insist," replied Mama Bisha. "Shooter, go and see Jikela and bring his best wine here." Shooter leapt to his feet and disappeared.

"Well, that's very kind," I said.

Mama Bisha gave a thin smile and left me to finish my beer. I realised the sad African man was staring at me. I smiled and raised my bottle.

"Cheers," I said, remembering just too late that the man's bottle was empty.

The man glanced at the beer-less bottle beside him and looked back at me, sadness in his eyes.

"Have one on me," I said, feeling rather sorry for him. I wondered if he'd had his car stolen too. The man continued to stare.

"Have a beer," I urged, pointing at the growling fridge and raising my own bottle.

The man suddenly smiled, revealing a mass of huge, largely intact teeth.

"Yes," he said, nodding.

"Yes," I said, pointing at the fridge.

The man leaned forward on to his toes and lifted his rear from the bench. But, instead of straightening up, he remained bent at a right-angle, his eyes fixed on a point just in front of his toes. He tottered forward briefly then grasped the seat behind him with both hands.

"Are you all right?" I half-rose to my feet, wondering if I should help.

The old man held the edge of the bench until he was steady. Then, he released his grip and with a high-pitched "Wheeee!" launched himself across the room.

"Good Lord!" I exclaimed, leaping to my feet as the man hurtled past, head down and arms trailing behind him. He covered the distance to the fridge in around two seconds, then flung his arms forward and embraced the appliance as he collided with it. The unit rocked backwards, rather alarmingly, then righted itself.

"Christ on a bike! Are you all right?" I said, taking a couple of steps towards him.

The man lifted his chin from the top of the unit, shuffled around, and opened the door.

"Two?" he said, addressing the floor.

"Yes, why not?" I replied, after I'd got over my shock at the man's astonishing method of perambulation. "I've nearly finished mine."

The man rummaged in the fridge, removed two bottles and shut the door. He then lined himself up for the return journey, head down, this time with a beer in each hand. He swayed a little and steadied himself by pressing his rear against the fridge door.

"Are you *quite* sure you don't want a hand?" I asked, taking a token half-step towards him.

The man tilted forwards. Then, just at the moment when he seemed certain to topple onto his head, he hurled himself across the floor once more, emitting another "Wheeee!" all the way.

"Bloody Hell!" I said, leaping backwards to avoid a collision.

I winced, anticipating a painful meeting between the man's skull and the rapidly approaching wall but, a split-second before disaster, he twisted his body to one side and tucked in his head. Keeping the beers hugged to his chest, he rolled onto the bench, the momentum rotating his legs upwards to a twelve o'clock position.

"Are you hurt?" I said, rushing over. The man's feet were now pointing at the ceiling and his head hung backwards, rather sickeningly, off the end of the bench. "Do you need any help reorienting?"

The man didn't answer, just jiggled himself around for a few seconds, until he was back in an upright position. He placed the two bottles beside him.

"Well, you've earned that," I said, reaching for one of the beers.

The man snatched both bottles and held them to his chest. He glared at me.

"Right, I see. Both for you, are they?"

"I am sick," he said.

"Oh. I'm sorry. I hope the beers help with your recovery. Don't worry, I'll get my own."

I approached the refrigerator, which was now silent, presumably out of astonishment at the proceedings, and withdrew another lukewarm beer. As I closed the door, it made a farting sound and began growling again.

Shooter reappeared, grinning and out of breath.

"I have wine!" he declared, placing a bottle on the table before me.

To my surprise, the label was none other than Meerlust Rubicon, a rather fine and aristocratic red. Someone, however, had already extracted the cork, then part-way re-inserted it, upside-down.

"That's a very good wine," I said.

"Yes! Very good wine," agreed Shooter. "To go with the food." He placed a highball glass next to the bottle.

"But I see it's already been opened," I said, suspecting that the contents might not be entirely as advertised.

"Yes, we don't have a wine opener. Jikela opened it in the shop."

"Did he indeed?" I replied. "I'd like to try it first." I removed the cork and poured an inch into the glass.

Shooter's face fell. "Oh. But this is very good wine," he protested.

"I know this wine well," I said. "I'm just checking it first."

"It is very good wine," repeated Shooter, sounding rather offended.

"I'll be the judge of that," I replied.

I wondered what gut-rot they'd decanted into the bottle. Some cheap plonk from the Breede River Valley, no doubt. I gave the wine a sniff and, to my surprise, was met by a rich bouquet of cassis and cigar box. A small sip confirmed that the wine was a very fine blend of Cabernet Sauvignon and Merlot. Meerlust Rubicon, in fact, unless Shooter had gone to the trouble of replacing the contents with another super-premium Bordeaux blend, which seemed unlikely.

"Very good," I said.

"I told you," said Shooter. "You don't trust me. You think I changed the wine!"

"No, I didn't!" I said, my cheeks reddening. "One must always taste the wine first."

"You think I changed the wine," Shooter insisted.

"Look, Shooter. In a good restaurant, you always try the wine first, in case it's not right."

"They try to trick you in a *mlungu* restaurant," sulked Shooter.

"It's not about being tricked, it's about checking whether the wine's faulty. Never mind. When is dinner served, please? I'm quite hungry."

"The dinner comes just now," said Shooter.

"Excellent. Where shall I sit? Just here?"

"Yes, yes. Sit down. Drink the wine."

"I will." I lowered myself into a frayed canvas chair and lifted the bottle, giving Shooter an encouraging smile. "Would you like some?"

"No, I am on duty," said Shooter. He disappeared back into reception.

I glanced at my beer-drinking friend, who was now snoozing gently on the bench, and poured a full glass. I spent half an hour working my way through the bottle, my stomach grumbles increasing in volume until they matched those of the refrigerator. When I was down to the final glass, I decided it was time to chase up dinner.

As I rose, I heard the sound of women's laughter. Shooter, face beaming, entered the room, followed by two young women wearing extremely short, figure-hugging dresses, one bright yellow, the other neon pink. I bid the women good evening and raised my glass. They found this extremely amusing and collapsed in a fit of giggles.

"You need more wine!" beamed Shooter, pointing at my empty bottle.

"Yes, I do now, thank you," I replied. "I thought you said dinner was coming?"

"Yes, dinner is ready just now," agreed Shooter. "These ladies are eating with us."

"Good. I'm starving," I said.

"I will bring some drinks," said Shooter, darting out of the room and returning with a bottle of Amarula Cream and another bottle of Meerlust Rubicon. The women sat down at the table and poured themselves glasses of the thick, caramel-coloured liqueur.

"This is Zola and this is Nomi," said Shooter.

"Hello Zola. Hello Nomi. Are you going to a party?"

The women whooped with laughter and fell into each other's arms. Well, this is an easy crowd, I thought to myself.

"They are going to a big party, yes," said Shooter, grinning and placing the Rubicon before me.

I had worked my way through half the second bottle before the hunger gnawing at my insides began to overwhelm me. I made my way, slightly unsteadily, back into reception. Shooter stood with his headphones on, playing a one-man game of table football and nodding to the music. McGregor had propped open the front door and was staring outside, a cocktail stick between his teeth.

"Chaps, I'm about to pass out with hunger. Where's the food, please?"

Shooter removed his headphones. "You don't want talk to the ladies?" he asked.

"We've exhausted the conversation. I'd rather have dinner."

"Do you like the wine?"

"Yes, it's very nice. I've nearly finished it while waiting for my food."

"You drink a lot of wine," said McGregor.

"Yes, well, there's nothing else to do right now."

"I prefer whisky. Johnnie Walker," said McGregor, nodding.

"You have excellent taste. Which reminds me, where's my dinner, please?"

"They are cooking it now," said Shooter.

"Who's cooking it? I haven't seen any kitchens here."

"The ladies cook it," said Shooter, nodding.

"Look, when will it be ready?"

"Just now," said Shooter. "In one hour."

"What do you mean? Is it now or in an hour?" I considered going straight to bed, though I was concerned my stomach might turn on me in the night and start digesting my vital organs.

"Yes, just now, in an hour."

I started to suspect Shooter was taking the piss.

"Right, never mind." I decided a change of subject might take my mind off my imminent death by starvation. "What's wrong with the old man in the restaurant?"

"He has a bad back," said McGregor.

"Yes, I can see that."

"He comes here for medical treatment."

"Does he?" I was now quite certain they were taking the piss. But I was still slightly embarrassed following the wine tasting incident, so I resisted the urge to adopt an overtly sarcastic tone. "I assume room two is the medical facility?"

"Yes, room two," said Shooter, slapping at the football spindles.

"Well, I work for a charity," I said. "A community clinic is just the kind of thing we're looking to fund."

"You are a charity?" asked Shooter. "You said you were a wine man."

"You don't look like a charity," said McGregor.

"Well, I am actually. The charity is based in the United States. I work for their London office. They give money to good causes."

"Ah, you are here to save us!" exclaimed McGregor, removing his cocktail stick and jabbing it towards me.

"Praise the Lord!" called Shooter, grinning from ear to ear.

"Thank you, Jesus!" said McGregor, nodding earnestly.

"Yes, praise the Lord!" called Shooter, louder, sending the table football spindles whirling.

"Very funny," I muttered.

"Save us, *mlungu!*" roared McGregor.

"Yes, you must save us please, *mlungu!*" shouted Shooter.

McGregor suddenly raised his finger. "I know your name!" he said.

"What is his name?" said Shooter.

"It is *Mlungu* Moses!" declared McGregor.

"*Mlungu* Moses! Praise the Lord!" shouted Shooter.

"I see," I said. "It's a lovely name, thank you."

At that moment of peak hilarity, a woman appeared at the front door, balancing a huge, linen-covered tray on her head.

"Look, *mlungu*. Your food is here," said McGregor, nodding at the tray.

"Praise the Lord," I said. "It's a miracle."

At this, Shooter flung his arms into the air and literally screamed with laughter, while McGregor nodded and gave me a loud round of applause.

"I'll go back to the dining room and take my seat, shall I?"

The two women had by now dispatched an impressive proportion of the Amarula. They whispered and giggled to one another as I weaved my way back to the table. I topped up my glass and awaited my dinner's final approach.

The serving woman entered the room, turning sideways to allow the tray through the doorway. Shooter and McGregor followed. She stopped before me, swung the load from her head and landed it before me with a bang.

"Dinner for *Mlungu* Moses!" announced McGregor.

Chapter 9

Smiley

With a flick of the wrist, the woman whisked the linen from the tray and grinned. Shooter and McGregor stepped forward, also grinning. The women whooped and grinned. The old man appeared alongside me, bent double, his face too painted with a broad, tooth-filled grin.

But it was my dinner that wore the biggest smile of all.

"Good God above!" I gasped.

Staring back at me was a huge, aggressively roasted sheep's head. The wool had been burnt away, leaving its naked skin smooth and bronzed, its ears charred to a translucent crisp. The creature's lips had shrivelled in the heat, revealing a grotesque grin of bulging, peg-like teeth. The beast fixed me with its grey, fatty eyes, as if demanding to know why I was not joining in the atmosphere of celebration and good cheer.

"The famous smiley!" declared Shooter.

"Only the best for *Mlungu* Moses!" said McGregor.

"How utterly wonderful," I spluttered, attempting to wrestle my face into an expression of delight.

"You see why it is called smiley!" said Shooter, happily.

"Yes, I do," I said, peering at the revolting grimace of stained, herbivorous teeth. I shuddered.

The serving woman placed a large knife and a gently steaming plate before me. She made a cutting motion over the horrific creature and nodded, encouragingly.

"Go on!" said Shooter. "While it is hot!"

"Shouldn't it be ladies first?" I whimpered.

"No, *Mlungu* Moses first!" said McGregor. "Don't you like sheep?"

"Yes, I do. I'm just more used to eating the other bits."

I lifted the knife. What was the least revolting bit? An ear, perhaps? A piece of cheek? There was bound to be a bit of meat there. I poked the knife, gingerly, into the side of the beast's head. There was a crackle as the tip pierced the crisp skin.

The serving woman made an impatient tut and grabbed my wrist. She forced the knife deep into the creature's cheek until I felt it grate against bone, then twisted my hand and pushed it to and fro, until I'd sawed a chunk of flesh free. She released my wrist and made a guttural sound, which I interpreted as an order to get stuck in.

"Anyone else fancy a go?" I asked.

"Taste it!" urged Shooter.

I picked up the cheek and nibbled the edge. It was dry, and I picked up a faint aroma of blow-torched wool, but it was moderately palatable, the crispy skin complementing the softer meat quite nicely.

The woman took the knife and set to work on one of the crispy ears, separating it from the head after a few seconds of vigorous sawing. She placed the unfortunate appendage on my plate and pushed it towards me with the knifepoint.

"Oh, you are spoiling me," I said. "Don't forget the rest of the group."

"You will have the best bits!" said Shooter.

The woman placed her hand on the creature's jaw and pulled it open. She stuck the knife inside and started sawing at the tongue.

"Ooh, Jesus, please don't!" I pleaded, holding my hands to my mouth. "I've got quite enough already, thank you."

A portion of tongue was deposited on my plate, next to the ear.

"And the best bit!" called Shooter.

The woman plunged the knife into the creature's eye. I made a strange, involuntary noise, halfway between a raspberry and a whinnying horse. She gouged out a lump of glistening gel and presented it for inspection.

I was, I confess, quite lost for words. My stomach, however, decided this was the moment to make a stand, and began to churn in a manner that suggested the imminent expulsion of a pint of Stellenbosch's finest out of my mouth and over anything within a six-foot radius.

I clapped both hands over my face and swallowed hard, just managing to suppress the first retch of hot, bile-scented Cabernet. Grabbing my glass, I hurled a mouthful of wine down my throat, hoping it would stun my stomach into silence while I recovered my wits.

"Eat it! Eat it!" urged Shooter.

The woman pushed the knife into my hand, the fatty globule still impaled on the end. I turned my head away, lips pressed together, and found myself face to face with the old man, who was bent over so low that his head was at the same level as mine. He gazed at the eye, longingly.

"I have been very selfish!" I declared, suddenly inspired. "The best bit should go to the gentleman here. I have heard that eyes have great medicinal properties." I thrust the eye towards the old man and looked at Shooter. "Isn't that true?"

"Yes! It is good for you," agreed Shooter.

"Well, then! And, of course, this is a medical facility, is it not?"

I took the old man's hand and placed it next to the tip of my knife. He plucked off the sheep's eyeball and popped it in his mouth. I averted my gaze and took an assertive swig of wine to distract my stomach.

"There is another eye," said McGregor. "Give it to him."

The woman took the knife and inserted it into the other side of the sheep's head. Panicking, I snatched up the sheep's ear and stuffed it in my mouth.

"I'm full!" I gabbled, chomping on the foul piece of gristle.

A second later, I realised I had made a terrible mistake. The ear tasted like a pork scratching dipped in crude oil and cooked inside a burning overcoat. I could feel bristly hairs tickling the back of my throat, threatening to provoke my stomach into a renewed bout of reverse claret gargling. I pushed some sheep cheek into my mouth to improve the texture, took a swig of wine to aid lubrication, and chewed like a rabid hyena.

But the woman just smiled and presented me with my second knifepoint-mounted eyeball of the evening.

"Yubby, so yubby," I gagged, through a gob-full of half-chewed sheep cartilage, waving my arms in an attempt to ward off the approaching horror.

"You must eat the other one," urged Shooter.

"Bo! Blease!" I pleaded, pointing to my bulging mouth in what I hoped was a gesture of blissful satiety.

But the woman interpreted my gesture as a demand for another revolting morsel of sheep extremity and, quite taking me by surprise, thrust it towards my face. I flinched and my right hand knocked the blade, sending the eyeball flying from the tip.

My companions watched the airborne globule, open mouthed, as it described a high arc, nearly grazed the ceiling, then descended towards the neon pink dressed lady on the opposite side of the table. With the precision of a laser-guided smart bomb, the gelatinous projectile planted itself deep into the woman's heaving bosom.

There was a shriek and the tinkle of breaking glass as the woman discarded her Amarula Cream Liqueur and threw her hands in the air. Her companion whooped and pointed at her friend's chest. Everyone's eyes were on the little globe of fat, glistening like a pearl in the centre of a gigantic dark oyster. The woman looked down at her bosom and shrieked again. Her companion clapped and howled with laughter.

While the room was distracted, I took the opportunity to expel the half-chewed ear into my handkerchief. I added the sheep's tongue and slipped the gristly mess into my pocket.

"That is very lucky," beamed Shooter, peering at the errant eyeball.

"Madam, I do apologise," I announced, rising to my feet. "It was an accident."

"You must help her," said McGregor.

"Yes, of course," I said. "I'll pay for the dry cleaning, obviously."

The woman stood and approached me. I couldn't help noticing that her dress's ratio of material to exposed flesh was extremely low. I suppose that's one of the benefits of living in a hot country, I thought to myself. She stopped before me.

"Sit down," she ordered.

I did as I was told. The sheep's eye, nestling deep in its valley, stared at me.

"I really am terribly sorry," I mumbled.

"Take it out," she said.

"Really? You want me to just—"

"Take it out," she repeated, seizing my wrist and pulling my hand level with her chest.

I looked from Shooter to McGregor, then to the serving lady, the woman's companion and finally the old man. They were all watching me. None appeared to think it an unusual request.

"Right. Well, if you're sure. Here I come. I'll try to avoid any unnecessary contact."

I extended my thumb and finger and slowly moved my hand towards the slippery little sphere. The woman continued to hold my wrist but made no attempt to stop me. In fact, she moved closer until her breasts were inches from my face. I could smell her perfume, strong and spicy.

"This is rather delicate," I said, as my fingers brushed against her skin. "Apologies for any accidental, erm, embarrassment."

I pinched the eyeball lightly between finger and thumb. It was rubbery and slightly greasy. I extracted it from its fleshy clasp and held it aloft.

"There's the little blighter," I declared.

"Now, you eat it," she said.

"Oh, no, I'd rather not," I said, panic rising. "Why don't you have it? After all, it belongs to you now, really…"

I gestured towards her mouth with the eyeball, but the woman pushed my hand back towards my face.

"No, you eat it," she said, smiling.

"Honestly, I really don't want to."

"You must eat it," she insisted, moving so close that I was forced to lean back, lest my nose become wedged between her breasts. She pushed my hand harder towards my mouth. "Yes, eat it!"

The globule was now brushing my mouth and I closed my lips tight.

"Mmmm! Mmmm!" I insisted. But the woman, in a rather assertive invasion of my personal space, grabbed my jaw with her other hand and pressed my mouth open.

"Ow! Jaysus!" I wailed.

Then, like a vet dispensing worming tablets to a misbehaving farmyard beast, she pushed the jellied gobbet into my mouth, followed by two of her own fingers.

"Argh," I said, conscious that my stomach was unlikely to take this provocation lightly.

"It is nice," she declared, her fingers still in my mouth.

I swallowed the eyeball whole. It slimed down my throat and everyone cheered. My stomach, thankfully, remained paralysed, presumably through sheer shock.

The woman withdrew her fingers from my mouth and wiped them on my shirt, taking the opportunity to give my chest a rather gratuitous grope as she did so.

"Yes! This is very good," said Shooter. "Zola likes you. Now, we can all eat smiley."

The serving woman doled a stew of beans and *samp*, tender-boiled maize, onto the plates, and carved some meatier portions from the sheep's head. Shooter and McGregor pulled up seats, and all were soon tucking in, chattering away in a bewildering blend of Xhosa and English. The *samp* and beans were a welcome relief after the blowtorched sheep and my stomach began to settle down.

To be honest, the episode was all rather unpleasant and embarrassing. It reminded me of an incident at my primary school, when matron had forced me to eat semolina in front of the whole school. I've never eaten semolina since, and I'm pretty sure I wouldn't be consuming sheep's eyeball again either. Then again, I mused, this wasn't Le Gavroche, and who was I to make judgments about the eating culture in a township guesthouse? Perhaps it was a dawning recognition of my white privilege, but I sensed such thinking might be the thin end of a very racist wedge.

Within half an hour, the smiley had been reduced to a grinning skull. The two women blew me kisses goodnight, before disappearing off to a township nightclub. The serving woman stacked the pots and plates on her tray, hoisted the load onto her head, and departed. The old man crept to his bench, leaned back against the wall and was soon dozing. Just Shooter, McGregor and I were left round the table.

"So, *Mlungu* Moses, you enjoyed your meal?" said McGregor.

"Oh, very much," I replied. "I wouldn't want to eat it every day, though. Just Sundays and holy days."

"Ah, you are a religious man!" said McGregor.

"Well, the Lord is my shepherd," I said, pouring myself another glass of red, before wishing I'd picked a religious metaphor that didn't involve manhandling sheep.

"Which church do you go to?" asked Shooter.

"Church of England," I replied.

"No, but which church here?" insisted McGregor.

"Oh, any church will do," I said, beginning to wish I'd never mentioned the good Lord at all.

McGregor frowned. It suddenly occurred to me they might expect me to attend a township service. And, as a God-fearing Christian, drop a generous donation into the collection bucket, no doubt. Time to improvise, damn quick.

"I'll be attending the Cathedral in Cape Town for morning service, of course," I said. "In fact, my charity is based there. I have to report in every day, giving news of my good works."

"Ah, the Cathedral," said McGregor, nodding at Shooter. "Very beautiful."

"*Mlungu* church," said Shooter, nodding back.

"Indeed. Well gentlemen, it's been a long day and an exotic evening. I hope you'll forgive me if I retire."

86

"Yes, yes, you must go," said Shooter. "Have a wonderful night!" He pressed his hands together, as if in prayer, and grinned.

"Good night, *Mlungu* Moses. Pray for us!" said McGregor. The two men giggled.

"I will. Good night."

I left the room, taking my glass and the remainder of the bottle with me. The passageway was shrouded in darkness, and I could barely see the outline of my bedroom door. I checked for the marker pen numeral. There it was: room one. I turned the handle, giving the door a shove as Shooter had done that afternoon. It scraped open. Someone had switched on the bedside light, but the feeble bulb was barely up to the task of penetrating the grimy lampshade, so apart from a circle of light around the lamp's base, the rest of the room lay in a deep gloom. A faint smell of disinfectant hung in the air.

I pushed the door shut and waited for my eyes to adjust. I had the peculiar sensation that the room was smaller than I remembered, but I put it down to the darkness. In the shadow at the foot of the bed, I could just about see something hanging on the clothes rail. A hand-towel, I guessed. Holding my bottle and glass in one hand, I stepped forward and felt the fabric. I realised there were two pieces of material. The room was too dark to make out the colours, though I could just about perceive one was lighter than the other. The material was thin and synthetic, and appeared to be full of holes. Oh dear, I thought. The sooner I could organise lodgings in the Stellenbosch winelands, the better. I imagined washing the township dust off my body under a steaming massage shower, before wrapping myself in a thick towelling robe, and phoning room service for a goblet of Caperitif and tonic. I stared at the scraps of fabric. There was something familiar about them, but I couldn't think what.

I became aware of the outline of a large object resting upon the bed. Clearly, someone had placed my suitcase on top of the sheets. I tutted. Call me fussy, but I've always had an aversion to dirty, outdoor baggage on clean linen, particularly when it's been manhandled by several teams of sweating airport operatives and trailed through the township dirt. Didn't the staff have even the most basic training? I made a mental note to mention this to Mama Bisha in the morning.

Then, with a shock, I remembered my suitcase had been in my car when it was stolen. So, whose bag was this? I crept closer to the bed and peered at it. Incredibly, it appeared the bedsheet had been pulled right over the suitcase.

The bed moved and I jumped out of my skin. I scampered backwards and bumped my head against the bedroom wall.

"Come to bed," said a woman's voice.

Good God above, I thought. I'm in the wrong room! But I'd checked the room number, I was sure of it. Had I mistaken the scrawl on the door for a different number? Who was in the bed? Perhaps it was McGregor's wife. If he entered the room right now, I suspected he wouldn't be very happy. He was a big chap and I doubted I'd get the better of him in a close-quarters tumble. I had to get out of there. I flailed my way to the door, holding my wine aloft, only to blunder into the clothes rail and knock it over.

"What are you doing?" said the woman. She lifted the bedside lamp and tilted the base towards me. The room lightened and soft, brown shadows raced around the walls. Panicking, I attempted to right the clothes rail, but the flimsy bloody thing came apart in my hands, leaving me holding the hand towels while the rest clattered to the concrete floor. But they weren't towels. They were the neon pink and yellow dresses worn by my excitingly dressed female companions over dinner. And I realised there wasn't just one woman, but two women in the bed.

"I'm terribly sorry," I yelped. "Wrong room!"

"Why do you not come to bed?" demanded the woman holding the lamp. In the half-light, I wasn't sure whether it was the lady whose breasts had captured my airborne sheep's eyeball, or her friend. From her assertive tone, I suspected it was the former. She flung the sheet aside and the lamp sent a wash of light across the women's curves.

"I think one or two of us have made a terrible mistake," I said.

My initial panic, however, subsided. I was fairly sure neither of the women were McGregor's wife. In fact, I was quite surprised they weren't making more of a fuss. Perhaps it was the two bottles of Rubicon, but it took me a few seconds to process that they'd just ordered me, quite clearly, to join them in bed.

"You come in," said the first woman. It was definitely an order, not a question. I tried to recall their names. Shooter had introduced my eyeball-catching friend as Zola, and the other, if I remembered correctly, as Nomi. The woman placed the lamp back on the table, reached into the vase of rose petals, and withdrew one. She waved it at me and patted the empty sliver of mattress between them. It dawned on me that the little squares weren't rose petals at all. The second woman placed her hand on the breast of her friend and winked at me.

"I'm sorry, Zola, I'm afraid there's been a misunderstanding," I said.

Now, I wouldn't want you to think me a prude, but I do, in fact, hold myself to a strict moral code. When it comes to leaping into bed with strange women, I insist on all parties meeting two criteria. Firstly, unalloyed enthusiasm. In fairness to my two companions, that box appeared well and truly ticked, going by the speed with which my eyeball-catching friend tore open the prophylactic with her teeth and placed it upon her waggling tongue, not to mention the other woman's enthusiastic kneading of her partner's bosom, which she accompanied with a peculiar, ghostly panting.

But, secondly, I require sensual congress to be unsullied by matters mercantile. By which, I mean the exchange of cash, precious metals, gemstones, stocks and shares, tenancy agreements or any reciprocity of significant monetary value. I have, I confess, been subject to many such indecent proposals over the years. A young man of vigour, of course, should expect such attention from older persons, particularly from those of means. My issue with such agreements is not the transaction *per se* but the resentment kindled when the creditor requests payment. For nothing darkens a heart quicker than the realisation that affection comes at a price.

Unusually, this evening found me on the other side of the transaction. I'm not a man unaware of his own charms but it was pretty clear this situation was fishy. Someone with sloppier morals, of course, might well have shrugged and dived in, but this wasn't really my style. And, ethics aside, I have a sixth sense when it comes to sins of the flesh.

"No misunderstanding," giggled Zola, removing the rubber from her mouth and beckoning to my groin.

"Madams," I replied. "Your emphasis on prophylactic hygiene is most reassuring. You are a credit to your profession. I must, however, decline your kind offer. I will be asking the management to find me another room."

I tossed the women's clothing on to the bed and, with some effort, wrenched open the door.

"No! Come back!" called Nomi.

I stepped into the dark passageway, still holding my wine bottle and glass. Behind me, the bedsprings creaked, and I heard the sound of bare feet on the concrete floor. Clearly, my new roommates didn't intend to give up without a fight.

"You don't like us?" said Zola, wrapping a strong arm around my stomach and pressing herself against my back.

"It's not that…" I began, only to be blinded by an explosive flash of light. I staggered backwards into the bedroom and would have fallen against the hard floor if my roommate hadn't been there to catch me. We toppled on to the bed, Zola's body cushioning my fall. Both women whooped and the bedsprings creaked in alarm.

I felt wetness spreading across my chest. Christ, I thought, I've been shot! This is it. The end. What the hell had I been thinking, a white man blundering into a township for the night? What a sap. And here I would die, gunned down in a cheap brothel, expiring in the arms of a voluptuous lady of the night, my blood mixing with her sweat, cheap perfume and the juices from an overcooked sheep's eye.

There was another flash and, for a split-second, I saw Shooter's grinning face, the headphones around his neck, his gun pointed right at me. What a naïve fool I'd been. I'd assumed the name Shooter came from his love of football. God, I was an even bigger idiot than Troy Frittersley.

I felt something soft pressing against my cheek. A pillow, no doubt, to muffle my death screams.

"Another!" shouted Nomi, laughing.

My blood was now trickling over my neck. Strangely, it was cold, and smelled of Cabernet Sauvignon. Christ, I thought, my veins are literally running with claret. Perhaps I drink too much. Too late to worry about that now. Another flash and, in addition to Shooter's grin, I spotted what was, unmistakably, a breast hovering inches from my face.

"You are spilling your wine!" complained Zola, from beneath me. The bottle and glass, which I had clasped to my chest, were removed. I touched the wet patch on my shirt and brought my fingers to my nose. They smelt of Meerlust Rubicon, not blood. A torch flicked on, illuminating the room in ribs of harsh, white light.

"You are a bad man, *Mlungu* Moses!" said McGregor, pointing the torch at me.

Shooter, who was holding a small digital camera, and not a firearm, grinned and nodded.

"Very bad," agreed Nomi, with a giggle. She picked up the two slight items of clothing from the bed and threw one to Zola, who pushed me aside and pulled it over her head.

"What the bloody hell's going on?" I demanded, shading my eyes. "All I wanted was a bed for the night, but I find these women in my room. Then, you burst in, taking photographs, like some sort of township gestapo, without so much as knocking!"

"Yes, you are in trouble!" said Shooter.

"For what, exactly?" I demanded.

"Why you not like African women?" asked McGregor, pointing at the ladies, who had now wriggled back into their dresses. "Are you racist?"

"What do you mean?" I said. "I do like African women!"

"Why you not in bed then?" demanded McGregor.

"Because I'm tired, after a day of criminal victimisation. Which you appear determined to continue."

"Your church will not like this," said Shooter, shaking his head.

"I'm sure they'll have a low opinion of your establishment too," I replied. "As will the authorities."

"We will tell the church," insisted Shooter.

"You can tell who you bloody-well want. Just do it quietly. I'm tired and I want some sleep."

"We will take these pictures to the Cathedral in Cape Town," said McGregor, pointing at Shooter's camera. "Unless you pay us one thousand dollars."

"US Dollars," added Shooter.

"Go ahead," I said. "Show them to Desmond Tutu if you like."

"You have no shame!" said McGregor, frowning.

"Well, that makes five of us," I said, standing up. "Now, if you wouldn't mind, I'd like to get some sleep. I have a busy day tomorrow trying to find a worthy recipient of my charity's money. It's probably fair to say you won't make the shortlist, gentlemen."

Shooter's grin faded.

"These ladies, on the other hand, would make excellent candidates," I said, nodding to Zola and Nomi. The two women clicked out of the room on their high heels, not giving me a second glance.

"Goodnight, gentlemen," I said, placing my hand on the door.

Shooter and McGregor stepped back into the passageway, sulking. I shoved the door closed and dragged the bed frame against it. Hopefully, that would buy me enough time to wake up the neighbourhood with my blood-curdling screams if they returned and attempted to murder me.

Chapter 10

Proposition

To my astonishment, I awoke the next morning to find myself un-murdered. I wouldn't say I'd slept well, and I'd been forced to relieve myself into the empty wine bottle in the middle of the night, but aside from a slight hangover, I was still in one wholesome piece.

There was a gap between the wall and the overhanging roof, and a line of bright, reflected sunlight shone through, illuminating the room. A lizard clung to the plasterwork above the Three Ships whisky poster and observed me, beadily.

"Morning, old chap," I muttered.

The lizard's eyes widened and with a flick of its tail it darted off, vanishing into the cavity above the wall. I dressed, then turned each of my boots upside down and gave them a good shake, slapping the soles. The Cape Flats were home to a fine population of spiders, scorpions and snakes, and I suspected the creeping, scuttling and slithering population of those fair parts might consider my footwear a most attractive pair of lodgings.

Thankfully, my boots were resident-free, save a sprinkle of brown sand. I tied my laces, then dragged the bedframe, very slowly, away from the door, attempting to minimise the screeching of metal against concrete. My plan was to slip away unnoticed, but in this I failed completely. Upon opening the door, a manoeuvre that required me to place my foot against the frame and physically wrench it open, I found myself face-to-face with Shooter, wearing his headphones, a woolly hat and a wide grin.

"*Mlungu* Moses!" he beamed. "You slept well?"

"No, I didn't," I replied. "Your hospitality is very poor. Please call me a taxi. I have an appointment at the Ministry of Development. Followed, quite possibly, by the police."

"You have breakfast first?"

"No, thank you very much. I've had enough sheep's face for the moment." I attempted to move past Shooter, but he side-stepped and blocked my way.

"The smiley is all finished, *mlungu*."

"I'm very sorry to hear that. Now, if you don't mind, I'd like to leave."

"We can get you another?"

"No, thank you, there's no need for that. I'll be on my way now." I stepped around Shooter but he blocked my way again.

"You have to pay the bill," he said.

"I've paid already. Forty pounds, remember?"

"The wine is extra. And, the other things." Shooter nodded, meaningfully.

"What other things?"

"The ladies!" he grinned.

"I didn't order them, so I won't be paying," I said.

"You will pay," said McGregor, appearing behind Shooter.

This altered the balance of power somewhat. I glanced down the passageway but the security gate looked bolted and locked. I could probably have knocked over Shooter and done a runner, but McGregor was a different matter. I didn't fancy tangling with him at all. And this time, they might be armed with more than a cheap digital camera.

"Well, gentlemen. Let's go to reception and see the bill," I said.

"The bill is one thousand dollars," said McGregor.

"I see. Well, I'll be happy to pay American Express," I said.

"No cards, just cash," grinned Shooter.

"I don't have any cash."

"You give us your cards and PIN codes," said McGregor.

Well, I thought. It's good to know, finally, where we all stand. Turns out it's a standard money with menaces scam after all.

Wish they'd got to the point before I was forced to eat a sheep's eyeball. I suspected Shooter would take my cards and attempt to withdraw the money, while McGregor stood guard.

"I'd like to see Mama Bisha please," I said.

"She is not here," said McGregor. "Give us your cards."

"My cards are in my car, which has been stolen," I said.

McGregor took a step forward, a rather severe expression on his face.

"Ah, you mean these cards!" I said, swiftly removing my wallet. I tossed it to Shooter, who removed my MasterCard and American Express. "The PIN is one-three-five-seven," I said. "For both cards."

"Go back in the room," said McGregor, pushing me back inside my overnight cell. He pulled the door shut with a scrape and a bang.

Well, this is all working out very well, I thought. I wondered how long it would take Shooter to find the nearest ATM, type in my fictitious PIN and phone McGregor. I pushed the bed frame against the door once more. The nearest bank was probably in Somerset West, around five miles away. Half an hour, perhaps? And how long would it take McGregor to batter down the door and murder me? Five minutes? No pressure then. I stared up at the Three Ships whisky poster and noticed my little lizard pal was back, his beady eyes upon me.

"Any ideas, my reptilian friend?" I said.

The lizard rolled its eyes, turned and disappeared into the gap where the corrugated roof stood proud of the wall. I gazed at the line of invading sunlight for a few seconds, before reflecting that sometimes the answer to life's problems is simpler than you dared hope. I picked up a length of the broken clothes rail and prodded gently at the sloping metal roof where it overhung the wall. It creaked, and I pushed harder. Sure enough, the sheet yielded a little.

I turned to the bed and flipped off the mattress. The base was made up of broad, interlocking diamonds of wire mesh. As quietly as I could, I turned the bedframe upside down and propped it at a forty-five-degree angle against the wall. Digging the toes of my boots into the mesh, and using the bed's front legs to pull me up, I scaled the slope until my head touched the ceiling. I pushed my fingers into the cavity above the wall, praying there were no scorpions lurking inside the gap, and pulled myself even higher, until my shoulders were pressing hard against the corrugated panels. Slowly, I straightened my legs, increasing the pressure. The ceiling creaked, and I pushed harder. The bedframe began to make twanging noises of complaint. "Come on, you bugger," I muttered, praying the whole thing wouldn't collapse beneath me.

There was a metallic squeak, then a snap as the roof panel popped free, and my head and shoulders emerged into the blinding sunshine. I screwed my eyes shut and raised my hand to shade my face.

Squinting between my fingers, I became aware that I had a rather splendid view. Barely any buildings were over a single storey, so my vantage point, ten feet from the ground, gave me an uninterrupted view of the township. Before me, over a sea of glittering, tin-roofed shacks, lay Table Mountain, its crags glowing in the eastern sun. Not the famous flat-topped view, of course, snapped by thousands of sightseers every year from the glamorous centre of Cape Town. This was the irregular, crooked-topped, backside view. The township view. A kilometre-high wall of iron-hard sandstone, shielding downtown's glitter from a million hungry eyes. To the mountain's right lay Devil's Peak, guarding the approach to the city, its point swathed in wisps of cloud. The same distance behind me, the Boland Mountains rose beneath the morning sun, the first ripple in a series of peaks that led to the harsh, semi-desert of the Cape's interior. To the south, over the little bridge and a mile of densely packed shacks, False Bay sparkled blue and white.

My sightseeing was interrupted by a familiar rasping sound, the scrape of bedroom door against concrete floor. With a shock, I remembered I was still in life-threatening peril.

"What you doing?" shouted an angry-sounding McGregor from somewhere beneath me.

With a yelp, I hauled the lower half of my body up and out of the room, and the bed frame clattered to the floor below. I scrabbled along the edge of the building, the corrugated sheets squeaking and complaining under my weight.

"You are in trouble! Come back!" shouted McGregor.

I had no intention of complying. But what should I do? I peered over the edge. It was a manageable drop down to the sandy dirt below, but I suspected McGregor was already tearing out of the building, ready to head me off. I was at least a mile from the highway, in the midst of hostile territory, and my opponent had the benefit of local knowledge. If I tried to hide in someone's shack, I'd probably be bludgeoned to death, possibly eaten. For a second, it occurred to me that might be a borderline racist assumption, but this was no time for intellectual analysis. I was in fear for my life. I reached the corner of the building and gingerly rose to my feet. The road from which I had approached Mama Bisha's last night was visible a few yards away, behind a row of shacks.

"Fire!" I shouted.

A pair of young women, carrying bags of shopping, glanced over.

"Fire!" I shouted, louder.

A group of youths, comparing mobile phones, looked up.

"Over here! Help! Fire!" I repeated, waving my arms.

One of the youths spotted me and pointed.

"*Mlungu!*" someone shouted.

"Yes! There's a fire!"

A small rock sailed past my left ear, just grazing it. I lost my balance and, arms wheeling, fell backwards on to the roof, which buckled beneath me with an angry creak. I flung my arms out, grasping a ridge of corrugated metal in each hand, grimacing as I prepared to crash, arse-first, back into the bedroom below. But, to my relief, the roof held firm.

A chorus of laughter floated over from the road.

"There is no fire," called McGregor's voice. From the sound of it, he was somewhere outside the building. I strongly suspected he had been the source of the rock.

"Help! They're trying to murder me!" I shouted.

Another round of laughter. It was extremely clear to me that my only option was doing a runner – and fast. I crawled to the opposite side of the roof, keeping my weight as widely distributed as possible, and peered over the edge. I was above the patch of waste ground I'd crossed last night, the portable toilet standing at the rear, like a blue sentry box, behind the line of washing. Where should I run? I considered dashing into one of the litter-strewn passages between the shacks, but God knows where I'd have ended up. In a shebeen full of drunken gangsters, knowing my luck. I decided I'd take my chances in the reed-filled gully on the right-hand side. Hopefully, the vegetation would provide cover and I could creep away, before making a run for the highway down to Somerset West.

I swung my legs over the side, shuffled to the edge, and pushed myself clear. As I did so, the security gate below me flew open and a figure stepped over the line of sandbags. It was far too late to check my fall. My feet landed squarely on his shoulders, as if we were two acrobats who'd been practicing the manoeuvre for months.

"Sorry!" I shrieked, as I dropped into a crouch and clamped the man's head between my thighs.

An average man would have buckled under the weight of a strapping young chap crash-landing on his shoulders from a height of several feet. But McGregor, for indeed it was he, was a powerfully built man. He gave a grunt of pain and stumbled forward, grasping my ankles.

Given the choice, my preference would have been to leap off McGregor's shoulders and put as much distance between us as my legs permitted. But my freedom to choose was constrained by the vice-like grip of McGregor's hands, which were preventing me from doing anything but wheeling my arms around my head like a drunkard warding off a swarm of wasps. McGregor lurched on, and to prevent myself toppling backwards, I clapped my hands over his face. He shouted something angry and incomprehensible, possibly a reaction to his newly restricted vision, or possibly because one of my fingers had inserted itself some way up his nose.

"Let go of me!" I shouted.

But McGregor either didn't hear or didn't care. He staggered on, his momentum unstoppable. We blundered through the washing line, which tightened across my chest for a second before pinging loose from its moorings and enveloping McGregor from head to foot in bedsheets. McGregor released my ankles, gave a roar like an enraged mummy emerging from an Egyptian tomb, and collided, heavily, with the portable toilet. He embraced the cubicle in his linen-swaddled arms, while my hands scrabbled against the smooth plastic, attempting to find purchase. I managed to hook my fingers over the rim running around the top and pulled myself upwards, leaving me standing bolt upright upon McGregor's shoulders. I realised a long line of township women, waiting to fill their saucepans and buckets at the standpipe, were observing our performance, open mouthed.

"Morning!" I called.

The cubicle began to tip, slowly and sickeningly, away from us. As the peaks of the Boland Mountains came into view over the top of the teetering toilet, I realised the facility had passed the point of no return and had no intention of ever reverting to an upright position. I held on tightly to the roof and said a brief prayer as the cubicle crashed to the ground, sending me bouncing into the air and into a patch of damp, scrubby sand.

I scrambled to my feet, weighing up whether to drop to my knees and apologise profusely to McGregor or to simply sprint off down the nearest alley. But McGregor was nowhere to be seen. I span around in confusion, but the man appeared to have vanished into thin air. One of the women pointed at the cubicle. Then, I heard a low, echoing growl of distress, like a bear awakening from hibernation and finding someone has burgled his pantry. I peered over the fallen toilet into the roughly dug pit that lay beneath it. There was something moving down there in the shadows. A large, irregular blob decorated in splattered black-and-white camouflage. I became conscious of a deeply unpleasant smell and stepped away.

I suspected that McGregor's attitude towards me might have soured even further than it had during the exciting few seconds I'd spent balanced on his shoulders. I trotted back towards Mama Bisha's, reasoning that with Shooter and McGregor otherwise occupied, I could dash unhindered through the building and retrace my steps to the road, before flagging down a Cape Town-bound taxi.

I skipped over the line of sandbags and re-entered the building, jogging past my bedroom door, through the empty dining room and into reception. The front door lay before me, swaying slightly on its garden gate hinges. Escape!

"Your bill, Mr Hart."

I leapt in shock. Mama Bisha stood at the door of her little office, unsmiling, her eyes shining.

"You haven't paid your bill."

"I have actually," I said, slight panic rising in my throat. "Shooter took payment." I made a move towards the door.

"You are not leaving, Mr Hart."

I'm going to give it a bloody good try, I thought.

"Your evil bloody staff have taken my credit cards!" I shouted. "So I'd say we're about quits, wouldn't you?"

I took a couple more steps. I could feel the breeze from the gap between door and frame against my face.

"How far will you get without a car?"

So long as it's further than a large, angry man wrapped in a poo-splattered sheet and attempting to clamber out of a township crapping pit, I don't mind, I thought.

"Or without money?"

"I'll manage, Mrs Bisha," I replied.

I reached out to push the door, but at that very moment, someone charged through from the other side, sending me staggering backwards.

"You are a liar, *mlungu!*" shouted Shooter breathlessly, removing his headphones and pointing at me.

"This man stole my credit cards!" I turned to Mama Bisha. "I demand you call the police!"

"You gave them to me," said Shooter. "The machine ate them up. You should have given me the right number."

"What rubbish," I said. "I wonder who the police will believe."

"The police will believe me," said Mama Bisha, quite calmly. "The chief of police is a good customer of mine."

"Well, that's very cosy," I said, slightly deflated. I prepared to barge Shooter aside and make a run for it.

"I want to talk about money," she said.

"I've told you, your staff—"

"No. Your charity. You wish to invest in the township." Mama Bisha raised her eyebrows.

"You're suggesting we make a donation?" Can't fault the old girl for thinking big, I thought. It was a step up from stealing her clients' wallets, at any rate. But what did she expect me to do, write a business plan to sponsor a brothel?

"You have lost your money, Mr Hart."

"I've had my money stolen by your employee here, Mama Bisha."

"The money from your charity. You have been discussing this with Mr Maduma at the government office."

"I see," I said, as it dawned on me the entire country was probably conspiring against me. "You and Mr Maduma have cooked up this little extortion racket between you, haven't you? What do you expect me to do, pop down to the ATM and withdraw a million rand? I think I'll take my chances with the police, after all. I demand you call them."

I paused as I realised a figure had appeared at the doorway to the dining room, a very large one. He stood, rubbing his shoulder, his free hand balled into a fist. His clothes were splattered with dark stains and he stared at me with unalloyed hatred.

"Oh no," said Shooter, wrinkling his nose. "Somebody has shit their pants."

"Now I will put *you* in that hole," growled McGregor, taking a step towards me.

"It was an accident," I yelped, edging towards the door.

"You in trouble now, *mlungu!*" called Shooter, clutching his headphones to his chest.

"Stop!" said Mama Bisha. "McGregor. Mr Hart is our guest."

McGregor paused and frowned.

"I'm terribly sorry about earlier," I said, in a high voice.

"Go and wash yourself," ordered Mama Bisha.

McGregor glowered at me then turned, slowly, and disappeared into the back. I glanced at Mama Bisha.

"Well," I said, sidling closer to the door, "it's been lovely, but I have an appointment with Mr Maduma at the Ministry of Development."

"Mr Maduma is useless," said Mama Bisha.

"Yes, he might be a touch inefficient, but he is trying to help."

"He is useless," repeated Mama Bisha. "He cannot help you. He is paid to sit in that office and do nothing. You need a real contact at the Ministry in Cape Town."

"That's where I'll go then," I said, taking another step towards the door.

"Twelve months, Mr Hart."

"I'm sorry?"

"Twelve months before you see that money. If you are lucky."

"Thank you for your concern, Mama Bisha, but I have a fast track agreement with the authorities."

"My cousin works at the Ministry. He can help you find your money."

"That's very kind of you. What's his name, please?"

Mama Bisha smiled. "Good luck with your fast track, Mr Hart."

I pushed open the door and stepped over the line of sandbags.

"May God be with you, *Mlungu* Moses," whispered Shooter, and winked.

Chapter 11

Fast Track

The moment Mama Bisha's front door swung shut behind me, I broke into a run. My bowels twitched as I imagined Shooter aiming a gun at my back or, even worse, being intercepted by the richly perfumed and no doubt still very unhappy McGregor.

I reached the main road and was immediately surrounded by several men competing to offer me a lift. I chose the least murderous-looking character, an elderly gentleman blinking behind a pair of battered spectacles. He showed me into the back of an ancient Volkswagen with a cracked windscreen and drove me, at low speed, out of the township.

As Maduma's ramshackle office came into view, I ordered the driver to pull over. I felt the time-wasting Head of Sustainable Development deserved a few stern words, not to mention a question or two regarding his relationship with the township's least reputable guesthouse. I climbed out and approached the entrance. Someone had tethered a goat to the bars of the security gate with a length of rope. The creature ignored me, its attention focussed on cropping the tufts of weeds growing from the side of the building. I tested the gate, then pushed between the bars at the door behind, but both were locked. Of Mr Maduma, Charles the security guard, or anyone else, there was absolutely no sign. I walked around the back, but the window from which I had first conversed with Maduma was closed tight. I returned to the front and knocked on the door.

"Hello?" I shouted. "Mr Maduma? Charles?"

I rattled the security gate. But the place was deserted and silent, the only sound the sudden gallop of hooves against earth, right behind me. I barely had time to flinch before the goat butted

103

its head, extremely painfully, into my right kidney. I cursed and retreated backwards as fast as I could, slapping the creature around the head as it doggedly head-butted my groin, before I finally staggered beyond the attack radius permitted by its tether. I hurled a few choice insults at the animal, whereupon it bared its teeth and began to mewl in a highly unsettling manner. Rubbing my bruised organs, I limped back to the vehicle and continued my journey.

I'd assumed my driver's cautious pace was out of respect for the elderly car's suspension, but it became clear the man had no intention of speeding up, even after the township's potholes had made way for the tarmacked approach to the N2. To my mounting horror, we ambled down the slip road and joined the lunchtime traffic roaring along southern Africa's busiest highway, like a beach pony nosing its way beneath the rail and on to the final stretch of the Kentucky Derby. The driver meandered into the middle lane and made it his home, resting his forehead against the windscreen and blinking owlishly through his glasses. For the next sweat-drenched half-hour, and despite my increasingly heartfelt pleas from the back seat to step on the gas, we proceeded at what can only be described as a moderate jogging pace, as cars, minibuses and trucks swerved around us, hooting with rage.

After what felt like a lifetime of continuous near-death experiences, I spotted a sign for Somerset West Retail Park and screamed at the driver to take the turnoff. He complied, though so slowly that I was obliged to lean forward and give the steering wheel an extra quarter-turn anti-clockwise, as it became clear our angle of divergence from the highway was too modest. The car vibrated sickeningly as it traversed the gravel-filled reservation and our departure from the highway was saluted by a long horn-blast from an articulated lorry that had narrowly avoided mowing us down. Once inside the retail park, I spent several minutes persuading the driver that twenty British pounds was a superb fare for the service he had provided, and that he might want to invest the money in a visit to the optician.

I found an internet café and charged my phone sufficiently to wake it from the dead, whereupon it informed me I had seven voice messages. The first was from the Uitsig Helderberg Guesthouse, yesterday evening, asking when I intended to check in and warning that the front gate would be locked at midnight. At least I now knew where I was supposed to be staying. The second was from Troy Frittersley at Tears of Pity, asking how my trip was going. Pretty bloody piss-poorly, old bean, I thought to myself. The third was from Gatesave's ever-empathising Head of Message, demanding I call her, urgently. The fourth was from Blanchkopf, complaining I hadn't yet confirmed his price increases, and dropping vague threats about imminent reputational damage. The fifth was from Foyley, in Gatesave's wine department, warning me of unspecified but unpleasant developments back at Head Office, and the next was the Head of Message again, sounding even more frantic as she insisted that I call her immediately. The final voicemail was from the car rental company, saying my vehicle had been found embedded in the front window of a jewellery store in Camps Bay last night, and that this contravened the terms and conditions of hire.

I phoned the bank and ordered my replacement credit cards, which I was informed would take three working days to arrive. Then, I phoned Foyley.

"It's a nightmare here, Felix. People are getting fired all over the place. It's the drug tests. Turns out half the company either smokes, pops or snorts something they shouldn't. Old Marris says he doesn't care how many people he has to sack. Says he's 'cleaning the Augean stables' or something."

"Sounds like hell. Are you ok?"

"I had a pretty close shave. They ambushed me one morning next to the lifts and demanded a urine sample. Next thing I know, I'm called into an office by HR. They tell me it's come back positive, for cannabis."

"What did you do?"

"I said I'd been attacked at Notting Hill market, last weekend, and three locals held me down and blew marijuana smoke in my face until I puked."

"What, and they believed you?"

"They were suspicious. They said I'd have to give another sample, next month. I've had to stay off the grass ever since."

"Thinking on your feet, very good."

"Oh, and the Head of Message and Head of Compliance have both been round this morning, asking why you're not picking up calls. They seemed very agitated."

"Reception's a bit dodgy round here. I'll phone the Head of Message now. Keep me informed, Foyley."

"Will do, Felix. Good luck."

The Head of Message answered my call within one ring.

"Felix! Where the hell have you been?"

"I've been here, settling in."

"You're not paid to settle in, you idiot, you're paid to deliver results. Have you visited Blanchkopf yet?"

"No, I'm due to see him tomorrow. What's the problem?"

"The problem, Felix, in case you've forgotten, is that your dreadful supplier is sullying the reputation of our CEO and the entire Gatesave brand. A campaigns manager from that interfering bloody NGO phoned Marris's office yesterday, asking for details of our policy on paying minimum wage in developing countries. They've confirmed they're releasing their report next week, including a comparison of Marris's salary with that of a South African grape picker."

"Oh dear. You mentioned they might be planning that."

"Which is why you need to get on and deal with the situation, Felix. I've just come from a very unpleasant meeting with Marris himself, where he spelled out, very clearly, the career consequences of any embarrassing publicity. I said you had taken full responsibility for resolving the issue and were on the ground, right now, straightening things out."

"Yes, I'm on the case."

"And what about the Fairly Trod and Black Empowerment wines? Have you identified any suitable suppliers? And any progress with the Tears of Pity project? You're supposed to be arranging Gatesave branding over something worthy, like a crèche full of township babies."

"I'm on the case with all that too."

There was a sigh on the end of the line. "Felix, if you mess this up, don't bother coming home. Understand?"

"Right."

The Head of Message hung up. I phoned the Tears of Pity office and asked to be put through to Troy Frittersley.

"Felix, dear boy! How are you? Has Africa embraced you to her fertile bosom?"

I decided not to regale Troy with my recent experience of Africa's bosoms, fertile or otherwise.

"I'm experiencing a little local difficulty, Troy. The Khayelitsha office of the Ministry of Development appears to be unaware of your grant."

"Unaware? That can't be right. We followed the Ministry's instructions to the letter. Did you give them the bank transfer receipt? It has the account number on it."

"Yes, I showed it to the local Head of Sustainable Development, but there's some kind of communication issue. I've been advised to visit the Ministry itself, in Cape Town. I'm heading there this afternoon."

"I see. I'll ask our lawyers to make enquiries from our end too. I'm sure we'll get it straightened out. How's the accommodation?"

I was about to make a joke about portable toilet cubicles and standpipes making a change from en suite bathrooms, then I remembered I was supposed to be staying at the Uitsig Helderberg Guesthouse.

"Oh, very comfortable, thank you."

"Well, don't get too used to it, young man! Your reservation is only for three nights, remember?"

My heart sank. Both Tears of Pity and Gatesave, driven by misplaced empathy and wretched tight-fistedness respectively, had indeed conspired to limit my accommodation budget, for the duration of my sabbatical, to the nightly rate in a township hostel.

"Actually," I said, "I visited an old friend last night, from my township fundraising days. She runs a boarding house in Khayelitsha. She prepared a special meal for me and some local community leaders. I confess I ended up spending the night there, rather than returning to my hotel. There's something about a township welcome that makes it virtually impossible to leave."

"Oh bravo, Felix! A lesser man would have spent his first evening at some ludicrously overpriced spa, drinking fine wine and gorging on rare steak. But you chose to spend it with the community you intend to serve. Good for you!"

"Well, start as you mean to go on, that's my motto."

"I'm so pleased, Felix. Every time we speak, I know we've picked the right man. Listen, I'll instruct our lawyers to contact the Ministry of Development right away, so they're prepared for your visit this afternoon. Let's speak again tomorrow when we've got to the bottom of this pesky snag. In the meantime, good luck!"

The bank on the retail park refused to change my pounds into rand without a passport. I was saved, however, by a sprightly old English lady, who owned a holiday home in Gordon's Bay and had overheard my increasingly desperate pleas at the bureau de change. She agreed to swap a wad of rand for the contents of my money belt, at a rather disadvantageous rate, allowing me to purchase a phone charger, a small suitcase and some new clothes. Then, I took a taxi to Stellenbosch and checked in to the Uitsig Helderberg Guesthouse, a modest B&B with a fine view of the mountains. After I'd washed and changed, I asked reception to arrange a car to Cape Town.

An hour later I was in the centre of town, outside the Provincial Treasury building on Wale Street. My research had revealed that the Ministry of Development shared the same address as the Treasury but, upon entering the gleaming marble atrium and explaining my business, I was directed back outside and around the corner to a rather less glamorous entrance. After buzzing an intercom several times, I was granted entry to a scuffed waiting room, given a ticket and told to take a seat. Three hours later, after repeated enquiries and much strained smiling on my part, I was ordered into a tiny office, where the most bored woman this side of the Zambezi stared, dully, at my bank transfer receipt. On the desk between us, an acrylic block, engraved in gold capital letters, informed me I was in the presence of Phyllis Nokwe, Case Manager.

"I do not know what this is," said Phyllis Nokwe, her eyes nearly closed.

"It's a receipt for a money transfer to your department," I explained.

Mrs Nokwe remained silent.

"We transferred the money to you two weeks ago for a development project in Khayelitsha. I believe our lawyers called earlier?"

She stared at the receipt a while, then pointed to the top left corner.

"What is this Natwest? I do not know what that is."

"That's our bank, in London. Look, that doesn't matter. We transferred the funds to your mandated account, as requested. The reference is there, on the receipt. We were told we would receive access to our funds once I'd arrived. I'm supposed to receive a credit card and chequebook, from you. I need access to the funds, you see, so we can begin our good works."

Mrs Nokwe continued to stare at the receipt beneath hooded eyes. She nodded, once.

"Thank you, Mrs Nokwe. Do I receive the card and chequebook from you?"

She nodded again.

"Excellent."

I smiled encouragingly and waited for Mrs Nokwe to furnish me with further information, but she remained deep in thought.

"Mrs Nokwe?"

The woman's head moved forward, almost imperceptibly slowly at first, then faster, as gravity drew her sleeping head towards the surface of the desk. Finally, she came to a halt, her nose an inch from my bank receipt.

"Mrs Nokwe!"

She woke with a start and drew herself back to a sitting position. Her eyes widened in surprise as I came into focus.

"Did I lose you for a second there, Mrs Nokwe?" I asked. "Shall I recap?"

The woman looked down at the receipt and pushed it across the desk towards me.

"I do not know anything about this," she said. "You must speak to our banking department."

"Do you have a contact name please?"

"You will have to make an appointment. But next week. They are on a team building exercise in Durban."

"Are they really?" I said. "Well, that's wonderful. I'm sure they'll return refreshed and ready to hurl themselves into action on behalf of the customer."

Mrs Nokwe stared at me blankly. I retrieved my bank receipt and stood.

"It's only a slight exaggeration to say your approach to case management has been eye-opening, Mrs Nokwe. I shall return to my lodgings and pray for divine intervention."

Chapter 12

Blanchkopf

As I stepped out of the warm shower, enveloped myself in a soft white towel robe and gazed over the Cape's manicured vineyards, I reflected that the Uitsig Helderberg Guesthouse was a definite step-up from Mama Bisha's villainous township brothel. So, you might be surprised to hear I'd far rather have returned to that ruffian-staffed house of ill-repute than suffer my next appointment. Not just surprised, but astonished, for my rendezvous was at a grand old wine farm in the hamlet of Aasvoëlsfontein, on the southern side of Stellenbosch, a visit that in normal circumstances should imply no hardship at all.

But these circumstances were far from normal. And the wine farm in question was, of course, none other than Blanchkopf Wine Growers, the proprietor of which was one Mr Blanchkopf: grape grower, winemaker, bulk plonk exporter, rabid dog fancier and, quite possibly, slave owner and kitten strangler to boot.

I pointed out a sign marking the winery entrance and the taxi turned on to an unsurfaced, red dirt road. We bumped along, pale green vineyards in the first flush of spring leaf stretching away either side of the track. In the distance, ahead of us, a growing cloud of dust advertised the approach of a vehicle. The dark centre of the cloud grew as it neared, resolving itself into a tractor towing a trailer. My driver slowed and moved over to allow the vehicle room to pass, the taxi's wheels whispering as they brushed the grassy verge. But, as the distance between us shrunk to mere yards, it became clear the tractor had no intention of either slowing or compromising its total possession of the road. Cursing, my driver swerved off the track, vine branches swatting the windscreen and stones clanging against the vehicle's undercarriage. The tractor roared past, trailer bouncing behind it, spraying the car with grit and enveloping us in a cloud of red dust.

Quite sensibly, we remained stationary until the dust had cleared. Muttering to himself, the driver nosed the car back onto the track and sprayed the windscreen washer, sending rivulets of red mud trickling across the glass, as if we'd just suffered a gore-soaked collision with a careless antelope. After another couple of minutes, we reached the main farm gate. It opened, powered by some unseen hand, and on the other side, leaning against a pickup truck, was Blanchkopf.

"Good morning, Mr Blanchkopf," I called, as I stepped out of the car. "I must say, one of your farmworkers nearly ran us off the road back there."

Blanchkopf was a tall, broad man of around sixty, with silver hair and a bushy beard. He wore tight khaki shorts and a grey shirt, festooned with pockets. He considered my outstretched hand for a second, then grasped it, very firmly, and shook it.

"My wife. She was probably in a hurry."

"She certainly was."

"Get in the *bakkie*, we'll take a tour," he said, gesturing to the pickup.

Clearly, the niceties had been concluded, so I climbed in. As I pulled the door shut, I heard a commotion from the back seat. A large Rottweiler thrust its head next to mine and barked, savagely, into my ear.

"Jesus Christ!" I shouted, banging my head against the passenger window in an effort to save it from being torn from my neck.

"He is quite friendly so long as you are friendly back," said Blanchkopf, climbing into the driver's seat. "Shut up!" he shouted, pushing the dog's face back. The Rottweiler continued to bark, angrily, from the rear seat.

"Is anyone working in the vineyards today?" I asked.

"Shut up!" shouted Blanchkopf, even louder.

I trusted Blanchkopf was addressing the dog, but I remained silent anyway. He started the pickup and we trundled past the farm buildings towards a steep track leading up the hillside. As we passed the final building, out of the corner of my eye I saw a streak of brown fly from an open doorway. I turned to see a great barrel of a dog running right at the vehicle. It leapt into the air and hurled itself against my door, manic hatred in its eyes. The Rottweiler behind me leapt up and down, barking in excitement, while its unhinged colleague fixed me with a bloodshot eye and raked the window with its teeth, leaving strings of white saliva on the glass.

"Is he friendly too?" I asked, praying the rabid creature hadn't been taught how to open a car door.

"No, he is not. That's a Boerboel. He will tear your arms off. Even bit me the other day, the beast. Anyway, keeps the troublemakers away."

I placed my hand on the interior door handle and held it tightly. The Boerboel had now attached its jaws to the side mirror, which it was slowly tearing from its mounting. Every few seconds, a crimson eye would swivel away from the unfortunate car accessory and fix itself on me, leaving me in no doubt that the creature would rather be tearing a chunk out of something warm-blooded.

"Get off the *bakkie,* you stupid dog," shouted Blanchkopf, and stepped on the gas. The mastiff tumbled away from the pickup, tearing the outer casing from the wing mirror as it did so. It bounded after us and threw itself against my door a couple more times but gave up once we'd picked up speed and begun our ascent into the higher vineyards. I uncurled my sweating fingers from the door handle.

After a few minutes, the incline became gentler and then levelled out. Blanchkopf slowed and pulled over at a junction marking the boundary between three vineyards. We climbed out and surveyed the rolling hills below, the vine-lined slopes looking like neatly combed heads of green hair. Behind me, the pickup's suspension creaked and I saw, to my dismay, that Blanchkopf had left his door open and that the Rottweiler had decided to join us.

"They are spring pruning right now," said Blanchkopf.

Teams of vineyard workers bobbed up and down along the rows of vines, crouching to snip away last year's canes before moving on to the next spur. Their dark blue overalls contrasted with the brilliant green leaf, and the constellation of different-coloured bobble hats made the vineyard appear sprinkled with live confetti. Other workers moved like ants between the pickers, collecting the severed canes and delivering them to a trailer parked at the edge of the vineyard.

"A busy worker is a happy worker," said Blanchkopf.

I became aware of the Rottweiler's hot breath against my hand. I whipped it away and clasped my palms before me, like a novice monk. The Rottweiler snarled.

"Yes," I said, wondering how to broach the awkward subject of slavery without upsetting either man or beast. "As you know, there are a couple of outstanding issues arising from our recent audit."

"The only outstanding issue is the price you are paying," replied Blanchkopf. "You agreed to give me a fifty percent increase on both the Pinotage and the white blend."

The Rottweiler took up position in front of me and growled again, its jaws just a foot or so from my crotch.

"I didn't exactly agree that," I said, as delicately as possible. "By outstanding issues, I am referring to certain irregularities in your workers' terms and conditions."

"What irregularities? There is nothing irregular."

"Mr Blanchkopf, our audit suggested you may have contravened some of the regulations governing the agriculture sector's minimum wage."

The Rottweiler barked and I jumped.

"Shut up!" shouted Blanchkopf.

I took a small step backwards and the Rottweiler took a slightly larger one forward. I was fairly sure I could feel the creature's breath against my groin.

"And, some of the regulations around loans to employees," I squeaked.

"Sometimes our workers need a loan to get them to their next pay check. There is nothing wrong in that."

"The problem, Mr Blanchkopf—"

The Rottweiler suddenly leapt up, placed its front feet against my chest and barked into my face. I staggered backwards.

"Goodness, he's very friendly," I croaked, holding a forearm in front of my neck as a sacrificial limb.

"Don't show any fear," said Blanchkopf.

"Good dog," I whimpered.

"*Kom*, get off," ordered Blanchkopf, and with some effort yanked the creature away by its collar. It growled and padded to the edge of the track, where it began barking at the workers in the vineyard below.

"As I was saying," I said, trying to remember where we'd left the conversation.

"Do you think my people are unhappy?" demanded Blanchkopf.

"Well, I wouldn't know."

"Come, I will show you," said Blanchkopf, striding back to the pickup. Get in the *bakkie*."

Blanchkopf gunned the vehicle down the slope towards the workers, leaving the Rottweiler to sprint after us through the dust, barking wildly. As we reached the first group, Blanchkopf braked and wound down the window.

"Hey, you! *Kom hier*!"

A man in overalls and a colourful bobble hat approached sheepishly, a pair of secateurs in his hand.

"Are you happy, man?"

The worker peered past Blanchkopf at me, then back to his employer.

"Yes, boss."

"Are you paid enough?"

"Yes, boss."

"Ask them. Ask the others," ordered Blanchkopf, pointing down the row of vines.

The worker called out to his colleagues, who responded in a vaguely affirmative chorus. He glanced nervously up the road towards the rising volume of barking.

"You see?" said Blanchkopf. He stepped on the gas and drove further down the slope to the next group of workers.

"Hey, you! Are you happy?" he shouted at a pair of women kneeling before a vine.

"Ah yes, very happy," called back the women, in a reasonably believable but not overly enthusiastic tone.

Blanchkopf roared on, to the bottom of the slope, where workers were throwing piles of vine cuttings into the back of a trailer.

"Are you all happy, working here?" he shouted.

The workers nodded cautiously.

"Yes, I take your point," I said. "But I'm afraid we'll need slightly more rigorous evidence to convince my bosses back in London."

"They must come here then."

"I'm sure they'd love to, but—"

"Hey," shouted Blanchkopf to a man standing next to the tractor, who appeared to be some kind of supervisor. "You bring the men to the house for a *braai* when they finish, ok? My customer here has agreed a higher price, so we can increase the pay. Good news, yes?"

"Very good, boss," replied the foreman, without any obvious sign of excitement.

As Blanchkopf turned the pickup around, the Rottweiler caught up and circled us, barking furiously.

"Open the door, let him in," said Blanchkopf.

"What? My door? Is that wise?"

"Yes, your door," said Blanchkopf, leaning across me and pulling the handle. The door sprang open and the Rottweiler bounded on top of me and began barking into my face.

"Get in the back!" shouted Blanchkopf, and grabbed the beast's collar, dragging it off me and pushing its head between the front seats. With a growl of protest, the hound scrambled into the back, leaving several saucer-sized paw prints on my thighs and stomach.

"We will have a *lekker braai* with the workers tonight," said Blanchkopf, "and you will see how happy they are. But first, you will meet my wife."

Chapter 13

Mrs Blanchkopf

"Ach, shame!" declared Mrs Blanchkopf, observing the grubby paw-prints decorating my shirt and trousers. "Here, we must clean you up." She proceeded to brush the dirt from my thighs and stomach with vigorous slaps, leaving me slightly winded.

Mrs Blanchkopf was a lady of considerable build, as tall as her husband and in possession of a vast, womanly chest. Her blond hair was scraped back in a ponytail, making her strong features all the more fearsome. She wore a sleeveless military jacket adorned with large brass buttons, though only the lower two were fastened, for her assertive breasts, sheathed in a tight, white blouse, rendered any further attempts at enclosure utterly futile. Her stout thighs, squeezed into a pair of jodhpurs, looked hewn from granite.

I took a couple of steps back, ensuring I was comfortably outside Mrs Blanchkopf's groin slapping radius, and looked around. The reception room was decorated in a style best described as 'assertive safari'. Much of the space was filled with sturdy wooden furniture, polished to a high shine, and the skulls of various ex-antelopes dotted the walls. A six-foot-long elephant gun hung above the fireplace, while a stuffed giraffe's head, plus the first few feet of its once magnificent neck, stood mounted upon a wine barrel. It observed the room, dolefully, its carefree, tree-top nibbling days well and truly behind it.

"That's better," said Mrs Blanchkopf, inspecting my clothing. "Now, you will be hot after your tour of the estate. What would you like to drink?"

"A glass of white wine would be lovely, thank you."

"Wine? I was going to bring you some water or tea!"

"Oh, water would be fine too," I said, wondering whether I'd made some dreadful cultural transgression. It was late morning and I was on a wine estate, for God's sake, what on earth was I supposed to drink?

"Get him some wine," said Blanchkopf. "He is giving us our price increase, let him have some wine."

"Well, only if it's not too much trouble," I called after Mrs Blanchkopf. "I'm perfectly happy with a cup of tea too." I cursed, silently, remembering just too late that a cup of tea in the South African countryside implied a beaker of *rooibos*, a quite dreadful brew to which the entire nation was inexplicably addicted, and which, to me at least, tasted like a bucket of boiled weeds filtered through an old sock.

"No, no. You want wine, you shall have some wine," insisted Blanchkopf.

Mrs Blanchkopf returned with a bottle of estate Chardonnay. She twisted a T-bar corkscrew into the neck and yanked out the cork as effortlessly as if it had been a wad of cotton-wool. She slopped a generous measure into a glass and handed it to me, then poured a rather smaller measure for her husband.

"Well, cheers," I said.

"Your health," said Blanchkopf, rather menacingly, and took a tiny sip. I took a larger mouthful. The wine was warm and tasted like cheap vanilla ice cream mixed with salty pineapple concentrate. I swallowed and tried to avoid gagging.

"This is our reserve Chardonnay," said Blanchkopf. "Three years in new oak."

"Lovely," I said.

"Then why do you only buy our cheap wines?" demanded Mrs Blanchkopf.

"Well, the market is rather difficult for premium wines like this," I replied, slightly disconcerted by her sudden plunge into negotiation mode, "but by familiarising our customers with your value-orientated wines, we hope to encourage them to trade up in the years to come."

Mrs Blanchkopf scowled.

"Mr Hart is finally giving us our long overdue price request," said Blanchkopf, stroking his beard. "A fifty percent increase for the Pinotage and the white blend."

"About time," replied Mrs Blanchkopf, folding her arms beneath her commanding bosom.

"I'm sure we can negotiate something mutually beneficial," I replied, swirling my glass and pretending to take another sip.

"We have already negotiated and agreed," said Blanchkopf, setting down his glass on the table.

"That's not entirely true, Mr Blanchkopf. There's still the little matter of our audit report." I swirled the wine faster in the hope it might evaporate.

"We have talked about this," said Blanchkopf. "We have happy workers here. You have seen it with your own eyes."

"Nobody complains," said Mrs Blanchkopf. "When did we last hear anyone complain?"

"Not for a long time," agreed Blanchkopf. "Even in the old days, nearly nobody complained. We have always been a good, family employer. I still have the journals, showing what we paid, and it was a long way above the market rates. Wait here. I will bring them." Blanchkopf strode from the room.

"You know," said Mrs Blanchkopf, taking a step towards me and lowering her voice, "apartheid was not all that bad."

"Well, I'm sure you're right, Mrs Blanchkopf. Though I imagine it probably depends on who you ask."

Mrs Blanchkopf moved closer, the tips of her prominent chest perilously close to my own. I kept completely still, conscious that retreat might suggest weakness.

"It was not as bad as they all say," she insisted. She moved closer still. "Not as bad as the British treated us!"

Despite the warmth of that Stellenbosch morning, I could feel the heat radiating from Mrs Blanchkopf's body. I lifted the glass of foul, room-temperature Chardonnay to my lips, so my arm formed a barrier between us, lest she lunge at my neck in a fit of historical revisionism. I took a mouthful of wine, a much larger one than I had intended, and grimaced.

Mrs Blanchkopf's face hardened. I prayed she'd interpreted my expression as a twinge of colonial guilt, rather than a criticism of her Chardonnay.

"Well, the British certainly behaved rather badly at times," I conceded, once I'd swallowed.

"Then you must make amends," said Mrs Blanchkopf, staring me in the eye. Her chest had closed the gap between us, and I felt the touch of warm fabric against my arm.

"Come, look at this!" called Blanchkopf, striding into the room and waving a leather-bound file. Mrs Blanchkopf took a step back, still holding my eye. Her husband opened the journal and pointed to an entry in a page of numbers. "In 1964, my father was paying the workers two rand each per month, plus accommodation and food."

I peered at the lines of numbers and indecipherable Afrikaans script.

"I've no idea if that's good or not, Mr Blanchkopf."

"Do you know what the minimum wage was in 1964, Mr Hart?" said Blanchkopf, stabbing at the page with a fat, grubby fingernail.

"I don't, no."

"Zero!" declared Blanchkopf, triumphantly. "You did not have to pay them a penny! But my father did!"

"Well, that's very laudable. I'm pleased to hear it. But, I hope you don't mind me saying, zero wages seems rather a low bar to clear."

"It is the principle!" shouted Blanchkopf, snapping shut the journal and waving it in my face.

"Yes, I agree," I said, hoping my response was sufficiently vague. "Now, look Mr Blanchkopf. We have a mutual problem. This dreadful NGO is threatening to slander both my employer and you, just to create some tawdry publicity. To defend ourselves against this, we must demonstrate we are on the side of the angels. And that means auditable records, showing that you are paying above market rates, offering medical benefits, and allowing trade unions, that sort of thing."

"Trade unions?" said Mrs Blanchkopf, aghast. "Criminals! Communists! Like that awful man Gambu and his gang, who have been causing trouble outside good, law-abiding wineries for the past year."

"Oh, yes. Mr Gambu," said Blanchkopf. "A very nasty piece of work. He would slit all our throats in a second! He is even a winery owner himself, though I do not know how he came to own it. Corruption, no doubt. Of course, no-one will sell him any grapes."

"He sounds very unpleasant. But if you pay your workers a little more, perhaps this Gambu will leave you alone."

"I told you, when you pay us more, we can pay them more," said Blanchkopf, gesturing at the giraffe head.

"Mr Blanchkopf, I'm here to propose an idea, which will benefit us all. I think you should convert your winery to Fairly Trod status."

"Fairly Trod? Ach, I am not interested in all that! Interfering busybodies, checking everything, talking to people, poking about in things that do not concern them."

"Yes, well that's really the point, you see. We have to allow a little poking about, otherwise no-one will believe us. I trust you, of course," I said, hastily, pointing to Blanchkopf's journal, "but we live in suspicious times, and we must be beyond reproach."

"I don't like it," said Mrs Blanchkopf.

"Listen to me, Mr and Mrs Blanchkopf, we have to do this, for the good of our long-term relationship!" I recalled the Head of Message, warning me not to bother coming home if I messed things up. A trickle of sweat began to work its way down my back.

Blanchkopf narrowed his eyes. "Perhaps I will think about it. But who will pay for all the costs to do with this Fairly Trod work?"

"Well, we've talked about a fifty percent price increase already. I think that's—"

"No, you must pay for all the costs," interrupted Blanchkopf.

"And we want a ten-year contract," added Mrs Blanchkopf.

"I can't possibly sign up to anything like that," I said.

My plan, of course, was to get Blanchkopf Wine Growers converted to Fairly Trod status, which hopefully would spike the guns of that interfering NGO, then end the relationship as quickly as possible and run for the hills. Ten years! If I was still dealing with this pair of bastards in ten weeks, it would be too bloody long.

"Then forget it," said Blanchkopf. "You said long-term relationship. You don't mean it. Let this NGO publish their lies and drag you through the *kak*. That will teach you to treat people badly. I can always sell my wine to the Chinese. They don't demand audits or ask stupid questions."

I don't know whether it was the oppressive atmosphere or the warm wine going to my head, but I nearly lost my cool. I was all set to deliver some home truths about exactly who had been treating whom badly, together with a few choice observations on the quality of their aged Chardonnay, but then I caught sight of the giraffe observing the proceedings with his wide, sad eyes, and I realised there's always someone who's having a worse day. And so, I let my temper subside and gave the wine a weary swirl.

"I can't offer you a ten-year contract, Mrs Blanchkopf. My superiors would never sign it off. But we could do five years. And we'll give you your increase, plus we'll cover all the costs of conversion to Fairly Trod status."

Blanchkopf looked at his wife, who nodded. He grasped my hand in his iron grip.

"So, we have a deal. *Goed*! We shall have a *lekker braai* this evening!"

Chapter 14

Fairly Trod

We did indeed have a *lekker braai* that night. Blanchkopf built a great pile of seasoned vine wood over the fire pit behind the farmhouse and invited his entire workforce to the feast. Once the blazing logs had quietened to white-hot coals, a never-ending procession of steak, *boerewors,* chicken and rock lobster were delivered to the grill, sizzling and spitting their juices into the warm night air. As the evening progressed, the piles of chicken bones, lobster shells and empty *papsaks* of cheap bag-in-box wine grew larger, and the loudness of the workers' conversation and laughter grew too. Even Blanchkopf's dogs joined in the good cheer, the Rottweiler running around, barking and snatching sausages from the hands of the workers, while the Boerboel, chained to a ring in the farmhouse wall, snarled and grated its teeth against an old antelope hoof.

As I tucked into yet another whorl of spiced *boerewors* sausage, Blanchkopf rose to his feet and clanged a rock against an old mess tin until the crowd of workers fell silent. He then announced that everyone would be awarded a fifty percent salary increase, with immediate effect, thanks to the great deal that had been agreed between him and the Britisher wine buyer they saw before them. At this, there was a great whooping and cheering, the glowing coals illuminating a hundred grinning faces.

"Give us more money!" shouted a voice, and everyone laughed.

Blanchkopf tugged at my arm and I rose, unsteadily, having already availed myself of a couple of bottles of Blanchkopf's aged Cabernet, which was just about tolerable when drunk over ice.

"Yes, you shall have more money!" I called, waving a sausage at the assembled workers.

Everyone cheered again.

"Give us all your money!" called another voice from the darkness, to more laughter.

"You already took all my money!" I called back, good-naturedly.

"No, you still have more. Give it to us!" called someone else. There was slightly less laughter this time.

"Right, we've had enough fun," called Blanchkopf. "The *braai* is finishing now. Back to your homes."

Slowly, and somewhat unsteadily, the workers began to vanish into the darkness, taking any uneaten food and undrunk *papsaks* with them. I bade Blanchkopf farewell and made my way to the waiting taxi. Blanchkopf had insisted I sign a written contract after we'd shaken hands, promising him the price increase, minimum annual volumes, and a five-year supply period, which he'd banged out on an ancient typewriter using one finger. I had protested that a handshake should be quite good enough, and that my word was as good as my bond, but much to my chagrin and, frankly, quite wisely, he had insisted on putting it in writing.

I awoke the next morning, rather muddy headed, in the Uitsig Helderberg Guesthouse. It sounded as though a very large, angry bee had found its way into my room, before I realised my phone was vibrating merrily on the bedside table. I grasped it and, not daring to move my tender head, placed the handset against my upturned ear.

"Hello?"

"Ah, Felix, hello there."

It was Troy Frittersley, sounding rather downbeat.

"Hello Troy." I could feel the blood pumping in my head, rather painfully.

"Felix, I'm afraid we have a problem."

I waited a few seconds for Troy to continue. It occurred to me that this was my final morning in the Uitsig Helderberg, and that my ongoing accommodation budget was insufficient to cover anything grander than a jerry-built hovel.

"Are you there, Felix?"

"Yes," I grunted. I wondered what problem could possibly be worse than having committed to a five-year deal to buy overpriced wine from a supplier suspected of modern slavery.

"Our legal team can't seem to locate the funds, Felix. I don't know what the problem is, but the authorities over there are being most uncooperative. It's very vexing."

"Oh," I said. I wondered whether this meant I could come home.

"Yes, we're in a bit of a pickle."

"Can you send some more money?" The pounding in my head was starting to speed up. I made a vow to never again drink aged Cabernet Sauvignon, over ice, from a pint glass.

"I'm afraid that's rather difficult, Felix. The other trustees won't allow me to send any more funds. We have to track down the one million rand we've already sent. Gatesave have already asked for a progress report."

"Oh." The pounding in my head had accelerated to a drum roll and was threatening to become a single continuous roar of pain.

"Yes, you see, it's all rather tricky. I'm afraid there are no funds for you at all, right now. For accommodation or anything like that." Frittersley tailed off. "But I told the trustees you are very resourceful, and that I was sure you'd be able to—"

The phone slipped from my hand, slid over the pillow and clattered to the floor. I slowly extended an arm from beneath the duvet and dangled it downwards, but the bed was too high off the ground. I could hear Frittersley's voice, very faintly, calling "Felix? Are you there?" but there was little I could do. I slipped into a fretful slumber, dreaming of eyeballs on barbeques, and audit reports stained with peri-peri sauce.

The chamber maid ordered me out of bed at just after eleven, insisting it was check-out time. To my dismay, upon retrieving my phone from beneath the bed, I spotted several missed calls from the Head of Message. After a shower and a couple of strong coffees, I was feeling slightly more human, and I took a taxi to the centre of Stellenbosch, to the offices of the Fairly Trod Foundation, where I had an appointment with Mr Sonn,

Managing Director. Mr Sonn was a short, plump, bespectacled man, of mixed race, and as his secretary showed me into his office he leapt up and pumped my hand.

"Very good to meet you, Mr Hart, welcome! We have been trying to work more closely with Gatesave for several years now, but you have proved rather resistant to our approaches so far."

Sonn waved me to a seat and hopped back into his large, leather chair. "Thank you, Jackie, very kind," he said, as his secretary placed a cup of tea before each of us. I raised the cup to my lips and noted, with a hint of nausea, that it was *rooibos*. Sonn peered at me through his spectacles. "So, what brings you to the Fairly Trod Foundation, Mr Hart?"

"You have indeed been very persistent in promoting the Fairly Trod Foundation to us, Mr Sonn. But, as you know, Gatesave developed an in-house ethical benchmarking system some years ago, which we felt was more understandable to our customers."

"A slightly lower benchmark, though, if you will allow me to say so," said Mr Sonn, chuckling and kneading his hands.

"Differently calibrated, yes," I said. "But things change, and I would like to explore a trial of the Fairly Trod standard at one of our suppliers."

"Well, that's wonderful. We'd be delighted to work with you, of course. We already have twenty-five wineries certified as operating to Fairly Trod principles, and another ten working towards it. Who did you have in mind?"

"Blanchkopf Wine Growers."

Sonn's face broke into a grin and he slapped his hands on the table.

"Oh, very amusing, Mr Hart, very amusing. To be honest, I'm quite surprised Gatesave continue to do business with Mr Blanchkopf at all. One does hear some rather interesting things about his operation. But never mind, it's not right to gossip, and I'm sure you have your reasons." Sonn took a sip of tea. "Who are you really interested in bringing up to Fairly Trod standards?"

"Actually, Mr Sonn, I'm quite serious in wanting Blanchkopf Wine Growers to comply with Fairly Trod standards. They're our largest supplier and we feel they have the most to gain from upping their game, so to speak."

Sonn peered at me for a few seconds, then removed his glasses and wiped them with a tissue.

"Well, Mr Hart, I am… quite flabbergasted," he said. "I must say, large retailers like yourselves often come in for criticism for your practices, sometimes for understandable reasons. But, when you decide to put your mind to it, you really do make a difference."

"We feel there's an opportunity to do some real good here, Mr Sonn."

"Yes, there is indeed. A great deal of good." Sonn furrowed his brow. "Now, Mr Hart, I don't mean to teach you your own business, but you are aware that Fairly Trod certification requires member wineries to enforce a minimum wage across their supply chain, particularly in the vineyards?"

"Yes, I understand. That's one of the things we like about the Fairly Trod Foundation. You have a rigorous inspection regime in place to ensure compliance."

"We do, yes." Sonn's brow furrowed once more. "Forgive me, but the Fairly Trod minimum wage is significantly higher than the industry average. The effect on the price of the winery's grapes will be quite marked. I assume Blanchkopf Growers are supplying you with, how should I put it, cheap plonk?"

"Entry-point wine, Mr Sonn, that is correct."

"I don't know how much Blanchkopf pays his workers, but assuming he is paying the legal minimum," at this, Sonn gave me a knowing look, "the required increase is likely to be in the order of, let's see…"

"Fifty percent?"

"Well, yes, quite possibly, if not more. Plus, the other improvements in terms and conditions, such as medical checks, good quality accommodation for seasonal pickers, will push the price higher still. The winery's input costs will almost certainly double."

"It's the right thing to do," I said, through gritted teeth.

"But this is wonderful, quite wonderful," said Sonn. He broke off and dabbed his tissue to the corner of each eye. "This is an act of real selflessness. I take my hat off to you and your company. I really do." Sonn sniffed and dabbed his eyes again.

"It's just a bit of corporate social responsibility, Mr Sonn. Are you all right?"

Sonn waved his hand. "I'm sorry, don't mind me. You've made my day, that's all. My grandfather, you see, he worked on Blanchkopf's farm in the olden days. It was... it was not a nice place to work. To think that an organisation with that kind of history, and a retailer such as yourself, thousands of miles away, are willing to invest in the future of simple vineyard workers... well, I'm sorry, it's just a rather wonderful thing." Sonn dabbed at his eyes once more.

"Right, well, we're just happy to help," I said, feeling slightly guilty. I took a sip of tea, which made me feel even more wretched.

"Have you considered how long a transition period you wish to work to?" asked Sonn.

"How long does it usually take?"

"It really depends on the resilience and profitability of the winery. Not to mention the will to change. Most take a couple of years. Twelve months if you take a fast-track approach."

"How about by next week?"

"What? You're joking! But no, as I have learnt, you probably aren't joking, are you, Mr Hart?"

"No, I'm not. Gatesave are an agile company, Mr Sonn, despite our size. When we move, we do so at pace."

"Goodness me. Well, in theory, if Blanchkopf Growers are willing to make the investment in their workers' terms and conditions straight away, and if Gatesave are willing to pay the higher cost of goods, the only remaining step is to organise an inspection."

"Let's get going then. Mr Blanchkopf will be happy to cover the costs, please send all the invoices to him. Oh, and there's one other thing I thought you might be able to help with."

"Anything, Mr Hart. Fire away."

"There's a slight problem with the maintenance grant from the charity that's funding my sabbatical. It's held up in the local government machinery somewhere. I wondered whether you could fund a room in a modest guesthouse here in Stellenbosch for a couple of weeks? Or somewhere in Franschhoek, perhaps? You can send the invoice to Blanchkopf."

Sonn gave a nervous laugh and brought his palms together. "I'm terribly sorry, Mr Hart, that sounds a little outside of our *modus operandi*. We can only make payments to approved vendors, like our audit partners, or providers of workplace services."

"Surely you must have an accommodation budget for visiting colleagues or clients? It's all above board, I can assure you. I'm just a little stuck at the moment."

"I sympathise, really I do. But we have to account for every rand. Our own auditors are terrible sticklers for that type of thing. Goes with the territory, I suppose." Sonn gave another nervous laugh.

I left Sonn to organise his certification visits and draw up his exquisitely audited invoices, and placed a call to Blanchkopf, offering not just a fifty percent increase, but a doubling of the price at which I bought his wine, for the next twelve months, in exchange for him covering any additional costs incurred in the process of attaining Fairly Trod certification. Blanchkopf knew a good deal when he heard it and agreed.

"It's terribly important that you pass the Fairly Trod inspection, Mr Blanchkopf, do you understand? There's a clause in our terms and conditions that says we can sever any supplier relationship if the Gatesave brand is brought into disrepute."

"And if you break our contract, Mr Hart, I will invite that Scandinavian NGO into my home, tell them everything, and see to it that your evil company is embarrassed across the world. Then I will set my dogs on you."

It wasn't ideal. But I felt Blanchkopf and I had an understanding.

Chapter 15

Hemelhuis

It was time to touch base with head office and check the lie of the land.

"Felix! How are you?"

"I've been better, Foyley, I must say. How are things on the mothership?"

"Grim, Felix. Very grim. Marris has challenged every employee to come up with ways of saving money for the business. They've created a 'cost slasher' room, plastered with specially made posters detailing examples of excessive company expenditure over the past year, to inspire a cost-saving mindset. Actually, come to think of it, Felix, one of the posters is a montage of your airline tickets, showing all the business class flights you've taken over the past year to California, Australia and Chile. Anyway, they lock you inside the 'cost slasher' room all day, in silence, until you've come up with an original idea to save money. Some people have been in there for a week."

"Good lord. What did you think up?"

"I suggested we replace head office notebooks with left-over cardboard packaging."

"That's an idiotic idea."

"I know, but it was the best I could do. Most of the easy ideas have been taken. Funny thing is, they've actually adopted it. From now on, if you take notes in a meeting, you have to use cut up pieces of card salvaged from stores, like those little trays that hold tins of beans. I was awarded a golden kumquat for the idea."

"A golden kumquat?"

"Yeah, Herbert Marris awards them for the best money-saving ideas. You don't actually get anything, Marris just emails you a picture of a gold-coloured kumquat with a crossed-out pound sign on it."

"Congratulations. I bet you're popular around the office."

"Not as popular as the guy who suggested using out of date supermarket food in the head office canteen. He got a golden kumquat too. But people keep leaving decomposing fruit on his laptop keyboard and now he just sits at his desk and cries."

"You've made me feel a lot better, Foyley, thank you. It sounds even worse than my own situation, which is decidedly sub-optimal."

"Anything I can help with, Felix?"

"Yes please, a couple of things. Firstly, I need a price increase put through on the two wines we take from Blanchkopf Wine Growers. The prices have doubled with immediate effect."

"Doubled? I thought you were supposed to be our star negotiator?"

"There are big problems with the vintage this year, Foyley. Parasites in the vineyards. Can you update the prices on Masterdata then use my login to approve, please?"

"I would, but Marris has brought in new controls. All increases have to be signed off by a Director."

"Good grief. Never mind, just go and see the Head of Message or the Head of Compliance. Mention my name and tell them the increases are required due to special circumstances. They'll understand."

"I doubt it, Felix. Everyone's scared witless of Herbert Marris. He fired the Marketing Director last week. Word on the street is she tested positive for crystal meth."

"Doesn't surprise me. It explains last Easter's TV ad, at least."

"The one with the gay, fire-breathing rabbits on the moon?"

"Exactly. And I have another request please. I need you to book me some accommodation. A nice little guesthouse, preferably attached to a winery. I have a couple of suggestions."

"I'll stop you there, Felix. Not a hope. All travel and hotel expenditure goes through Marris's office now. And he isn't authorising anything. People are being told that if they want to travel, they should take a sleeping bag and bed down in a local branch of Gatesave overnight. As for international travel, no-one even dares ask."

"Fabulous. Forget it then. Look, the most important thing is to get those prices pushed through. Can I leave that with you?"

"I'll try, Felix."

"Good man. I'll recommend you for another golden kumquat."

I hung up and called the Head of Message.

"Why the hell don't you ever answer your phone, Felix? I've been trying to reach you all day!"

"I'm sorry. I'm in a developing country, the coverage isn't great."

"Well, I hope you're enjoying yourself. Because you can stay there permanently. The Scandinavian NGO's report is being published next week and they've been kind enough to give us a preview so we can provide a response. The report claims that your supplier, Blanchkopf, is breaking modern slavery laws. They're putting Herbert Marris's picture on the front of the report and calling him a beneficiary of slave labour. I have until the end of today to provide Gatesave's response. We're screwed."

"Well, you can tell the NGO that their information is utterly incorrect," I said, smugly. "Mr Blanchkopf is passionate about redressing the wrongs of the past and is planning to attain Fairly Trod status. The Fairly Trod Foundation are inspecting him next week."

The Head of Message was silent for a moment. Then I heard her voice, slightly muffled. "He says Blanchkopf is about to obtain Fairly Trod status."

"Impossible!" I recognised the Head of Compliance's voice. "You can't obtain Fairly Trod certification that quickly! Put him on the speaker."

"Felix, you're on speakerphone," said the Head of Message. "We have some questions for you." I heard a door slide shut.

"Felix," said the Head of Compliance, a quaver in his voice, "the NGO's report contains several witness statements from ex-employees of Blanchkopf Wine Growers. They're not pretty. One man claims to have been savaged by Blanchkopf's dogs."

"I've met the dogs, sir. They are a little frisky."

"A little frisky?" shouted the Head of Compliance. "The man needed stitches and a rabies injection!"

"Blanchkopf told me he had to fire a couple of employees for theft. They're probably disgruntled."

"He sounds like a bloody Nazi!" I could hear the Head of Compliance clawing at his head.

"He *was* a bit of a Nazi, but he's seen the light. He's on a journey. He's determined to make amends for the past."

"Oh, he's seen the light! The rapture! How wonderful!" The Head of Compliance was sounding a little fraught, so I remained silent.

"Listen, Felix," said the Head of Message. "Short of large-scale bribery, how on earth do you expect Blanchkopf to turn around his appalling business practices and pass a Fairly Trod inspection within three days?"

"Ah. Well, that brings me to the reason for my call. I need you to authorise a couple of price increases, please. They're a little steep, I'm afraid. My assistant, Foyley, has the details."

"Marris isn't accepting any price increases," said the Head of Compliance. "Not a single one."

"But you have to! It's the only way we can persuade Blanchkopf to comply with the Fairly Trod inspection!"

"Then you'll have to find another way then, won't you?" said the Head of Message.

"There is no other way! I've promised to stuff his mouth with gold."

There was a moment of silence. Then I heard the Head of Message's bangles clunk as she moved close to the speakerphone.

"Your supplier stands accused of breaking slavery laws, Felix. I don't think they're terribly keen on slavery in the new South Africa. In fact, these days, I believe it attracts extremely severe penalties."

"So? He's the slave owner, not me!"

"You've seen our audit report. And you're still doing business with him. That makes you complicit. Just remember that."

"That's not fair! I want to come home!"

"Make sure Blanchkopf passes that inspection," she said, quietly. "Or we'll throw you to the wolves."

I returned to the guesthouse to collect my suitcase, feeling thoroughly depressed.

"Oh, the police are looking for you, Mr Hart," said the receptionist, brightly. I froze. How the hell had they connected me to Blanchkopf already? Of course, it must have been that damned Scandinavian NGO.

"They searched your bag." She pointed to my little suitcase, lying in the corner. My blood ran cold. The padlock had been snipped off and the top was half-open. My underwear, I could see, had been vigorously rummaged.

"How very strange," I said, in a high voice. "Did they mention any particular reason?" Christ, I didn't have a passport, I couldn't even flee the country. I'd have to hitch-hike north through Namaqualand, then cross the desert border into Namibia under cover of darkness.

"They said your hire car was used in a smash and grab. This guesthouse is registered as your address."

I nearly fainted with relief.

"Oh, yes, of course! I forgot about that. My car was stolen."

"You forgot your car was stolen?" The receptionist stared at me, somewhat unsympathetically.

"I've had a lot on."

"They left this number." She placed a torn-off piece of notepaper on the counter. "Maybe you should contact them."

"I'll be sure to do that, as soon as I have a moment." I took the number and zipped up my case.

"Where are you going now?"

"I'm heading to…" I stopped, conscious I didn't really have a plan. My remaining wad of cash was looking decidedly thin and accommodation was now a pressing concern. I had a reasonable working relationship with at least a dozen wineries around Stellenbosch, but it wasn't really the done thing to just rock up and plead for a room for the night. And, anyway, I needed a longer-term solution. "I'm staying with my church outreach group, in Khayelitsha," I said.

The receptionist raised her eyebrows. She hadn't expected that.

"Did the police mention whether they recovered my passport?" I asked.

"I think you should call them before they catch up with you."

"Will do. Cheerio."

It was time for a spot of begging. First, I called the local chapter of the Worshipful Institute of the Minstrels of Wine, based in the University of Stellenbosch's Department of Viticulture and Oenology. One of the perks of being a Minstrel of Wine is the ability to take advantage of cut-price institute accommodation wherever a chapter is located, but the apologetic woman on reception explained that all the spare rooms in the halls of residence were filled with delegates to an international conference on vineyard fungal diseases.

Next, I scrolled through my contact list of South African wine suppliers, pondering who might be willing to spare me a bed for a couple of nights. I crossed off Blanchkopf straight away. I suspected it would be a toss-up between being shot on sight and waking in the small hours to find a rabid hound, or possibly Mrs Blanchkopf, making a midnight snack of my knackers. There was Wikus van Blerk, at Vinkwyn Wine Cellars, I knew he'd let me doss down on a bed of straw in his cellar, but he was based way out in Robertson, too far from my urgent business in Stellenbosch. Josette at Diemersdal Estate might have been an option, but she'd turned a little frosty of late, on account of me refusing her latest price increase. I considered calling and offering her a raise in exchange for a bunk in her farmhouse, then I remembered the Head of Compliance's warning that Marris had banned all price increases.

I scrolled through a few more wineries, all unsuitable due to location or bruised commercial relationships. Then I paused. Hemelhuis Wines. Yes, that would fit the bill. Hemelhuis was a magnificent property, perched on the Helshoogte Pass between Stellenbosch and Franschhoek. The location was ideal and the estate hosted an excellent restaurant and spa too. Hemelhuis was owned by Paris-Blois International, the gigantic luxury goods conglomerate, and I had a reasonable working relationship with Sandra, their European Sales Director. With a bit of luck, she'd be able to pull a few strings and swing a room for me.

"Sandra, it's Felix. I'm in Stellenbosch on business and I wondered if you could help me out."

"Felix. Lovely to hear from you. Slightly disappointing that you only ever call when you need a favour, though."

"I'm in a bit of a scrape, actually."

"Of course you are."

"Yes, you see I've lost my passport and credit cards and I don't have anywhere to stay tonight."

"Oh. How very prosaic. I thought you were going to say you'd been cornered by a regiment of Zulus after seducing the chief's daughter, or something."

"An impi."

"I beg your pardon?"

"A regiment of Zulus is called an impi."

"Is it really, Felix? That's fascinating. What do you actually want?"

"Well, I wondered whether your Hemelhuis Estate might have a spare room. Any chance you could make a call and—"

"I'm here."

"Sorry? You're where?"

"I'm *here* at Hemelhuis, right now. Our CEO flies in tomorrow for our annual conference. I'm organising it."

"That's great. I know it's a bit of a liberty, but I don't suppose—"

"You can stay for one night. But you'll have to get lost first thing in the morning. All the rooms are reserved for the Paris-Blois global executive team."

"Fantastic, thank you."

"You can taste the latest vintage with our winemaker this afternoon. Time you listed a couple more Hemelhuis wines at Gatesave, I think."

"Unfortunately, we're not conducting a range review right now. But I'll be sure to give the Hemelhuis range serious consideration when—"

"Don't patronise me, Felix. Do you want a bed for the night or not?"

"Ok, I'll taste the wines."

"Good. Oh, and we're having a bit of trouble at the entrance to the estate. There's a demonstration taking place, organised by a local agricultural trade union. They've been here all day. Quite a large crowd, a bit rowdy, but they're unlikely to cause a white foreigner any trouble."

A band of marauding trade unionists didn't sound much fun at all. Thoughts of a rare steak, relaxing sauna and soft, clean bed, however, conspired to overcome my misgivings.

"Right. I'll be over within the hour."

The journey from the centre of Stellenbosch to the start of the Helshoogte Pass took fifteen minutes. The road steepened and the driver slowed as we entered the first of the tight bends leading to the summit. The rolling vineyards unfolded beneath us and I gazed out of the back-seat window towards the Simonsberg Mountains, rising jagged from the green foothills like rusted iron teeth. The driver moved down a gear and pressed on the gas as we rounded the second corner. Suddenly, he stamped on the brake, bringing us to a hard stop. A line of stationary traffic snaked up to the top of the pass and several vehicles were in the process of turning around. A crowd appeared to be blocking the road a few hundred yards ahead, near the entrance to the Hemelhuis estate, and a line of black smoke rose into the cloudless sky.

"Ah, there is some trouble here," muttered my driver. "We cannot get past."

"Don't worry, I'll walk the rest of the way," I said. "What's happening up there?"

"That is Gambu," he replied.

I'd heard that name before. "Who's Gambu?"

"They call him The General. He is trade union guy. Revolutionary."

Of course, it was Blanchkopf who had mentioned him, just yesterday. I vaguely remembered his wife suggesting he was a violent cut-throat.

"What do they want?"

"Money!" said the driver and laughed. "Same as everyone!"

I handed the driver a one-hundred rand note, grabbed my little suitcase and climbed out. "Well, there's your share. Keep the change."

"Sir, be careful," he called, through the open window. "They are trouble."

I paused and considered hopping back in and directing the driver back into town but sleeping under a bush in Stellenbosch Botanical Gardens didn't have quite the same draw as a massage in Hemelhuis's spa. So I gritted my teeth and began my trudge up the road, as the backed-up line of vehicles attempted to turn around, accompanied by much grinding of gears and sounding of horns.

Near the top of the pass, fifty yards from the entrance to the Hemelhuis Estate, the road was blocked by a police pickup. Beyond it, a crowd of perhaps two hundred men, and a few women, had blocked the road with a row of tyres, a couple of which had been filled with rubbish and set on fire. The atmosphere seemed upbeat, almost carnival-like, and I could hear a group of people singing over the shouts and whistles. I approached the pickup, in which sat four bored-looking, black police officers.

"I'm staying at the winery," I said to the constable in the driver's seat. "Ok if I pass through?"

The driver shrugged and turned to the officer beside him, who shook his head.

"Thanks very much," I said, and continued on through the line of car tyres, holding my breath as the acrid smoke from a mixture of burning traffic cones and wooden pallets wafted around me.

"No, you must come back," called one of the officers. But none of them felt strongly enough to leave their vehicle, let alone pursue me, so I didn't break my stride.

I walked on, keeping to the far side of the road and passing behind the main body of the crowd, most of whom were facing Hemelhuis Estate's imposing entrance gate. A few men, however, sitting in the dust at the edge of the tarmac, began to call after me.

"Hey, *mlungu*! Where you going, *mlungu*?"

I picked up my pace. The singing grew louder, and I could see a line of men moving back and forth in front of the winery gate. I now had no choice but to negotiate my way through the main body of demonstrators.

"Apologies, excuse me," I called, cheerfully, as I ducked and side-stepped through the crowd, using my bag to nudge people gently aside. Most people moved readily enough, though it was clear they weren't expecting a white face to be working its way to the front.

"Hey, who are you?" called a voice. I raised my arm and waved. I felt a hand on my shoulder but shrugged it off and pressed on. "Who is that man?" called another voice. Someone grabbed at my bag, but I was able to tug it away and press further into the crowd. I was nearing the front and the singing now drowned out the rest of the noise. The tune, I realised, was familiar, though I couldn't quite place it. A simple rhythm, sung at the same pitch, except for the final couple of notes, which dipped down then up again. The front of the crowd hopped from one foot to the other in time to the music and I felt my own steps falling in time with the rhythm, as I eased myself among them. A few yards forward of the crowd, a line of men faced the main gate, dancing more energetically than the rest. They wore Asian-style bamboo hats, the type a Chinese peasant might wear in a paddy field, and many were swinging open bottles of wine around their heads. The line of dancing men directed their chant at the gate, after which the crowd would chorus the same line in reply.

The tune was very familiar. What were they singing? A nursery rhyme? It was in English, I was sure of it, but I couldn't make out the words.

Dum-a-doodle-dum da-da dum-a-doodle-dum.

I caught sight of a dozen wary-looking, black security guards lined up behind the winery gate. They certainly didn't look equipped to repulse an attack by two hundred enraged demonstrators.

Dum-a-doodle-dum da-da dum-a-doodle-dum.

Damn, what was that tune? It was catchy, that was for sure.

I was about to push through the front of the crowd and stride to the gate, when I realised my presence had become the cause of some excitement. The men around me were hooting with laughter and each nudged the shoulders of their neighbours to point me out. Within seconds it seemed the entire crowd had turned in on me. I was now completely surrounded by dancing men and women, all of whom were directing their rhythmical chant, with some glee, into my face, rather than toward the winery gate. The overall effect was mildly threatening and I considered diving beneath their feet and attempting to crawl to safety, but just then someone pushed me from behind. I staggered forward into the men in front, who laughed, grabbed me, turned me round and pushed me back. Before I knew it, I was being propelled from one side of the circle to the other, while the tune buzzed around my ears.

Dum-a-doodle-dum da-da dum-a-doodle-dum.

I had an uncomfortable feeling that this particular playground game might end in tears. And I couldn't imagine the police or security guards, outnumbered twenty-to-one, had much intention of intervening on my behalf. Well, I thought, when in Rome and all that. I threw my suitcase to the floor and began to dance energetically around it, flinging my fists in the air in revolutionary fervour. The crowd roared with laughter and arms were flung around my shoulders. Hands pointed to my feet, ordering me to dance with more enthusiasm, or perhaps more rhythm, and I leapt from side to side with even greater vigour. The singing was nearly deafening. I felt a forehead bump against my ear and heard an intake of breath before the line was repeated yet again.

"*Come and have a go if you think you're hard enough!*"

My jaw dropped, even as I pogoed from foot to foot. The legendary chant of second-tier football hooligans, infant schoolyard thugs and small-town, Saturday night piss-artists the length and breadth of England! But to hear this dismal tune sung at such volume, not to mention such a level of musical ability, at a rural trade union demonstration in the Cape winelands, was one of the more surreal experiences of my life.

The circle surrounding me began to open and I could see the line of dancers had turned from the gate to face us. And a bizarre troupe they were too. Not one of the men was under six foot in height and their black faces gurned and streamed with sweat. Each wore the blue overalls of a vineyard worker, accessorised with rubber boots and a conical rice-farmer's hat. Each carried a bottle of wine, the neck of which was attached to a metal chain looped around the dancer's neck. Some held their bottles, taking ostentatious swigs during pauses in the singing, others allowed them to hang free from their chain, where they swung around wildly. The sun was beating down quite viciously, and I admired the men's stamina. I suspected they were all completely bladdered.

The singing began to quieten, then stopped. It felt as though a powerful spell had been broken and I began to feel quite giddy. My neighbours dropped their arms from my shoulders and I realised I was panting from the exertion. Sweat ran down my forehead and stung my eyes. I removed my sunglasses and wiped my face. The crowd was now completely silent. I tried to focus, blinking and squinting under the blazing sun. Before me stood a vast, black shadow.

"You are on the wrong side of the gate, white man!"

Chapter 16

Gambu

The man stared down at me. He was a giant, bettering me by at least six inches. Like his dancing companions, he wore the blue overalls of a vineyard worker, but his were undone to the waist, revealing a red t-shirt decorated with a yellow hammer and sickle alongside a bunch of grapes. His vast stomach suggested a man not shy of demanding seconds, and his expression, beneath the red beret perched atop his huge, black dome of a head, suggested he didn't suffer fools at all.

"Hello," I said. "I'm Felix Hart. Sorry for stumbling into your demonstration." I extended my hand, but the man did not move.

"We do not shake the hands of our oppressors," the man boomed, raising his head so he could stare down at me more haughtily.

"Oh, well, I promise I'm not intending to oppress anyone. I'm just visiting the winery here." I made a vague gesture towards the Hemelhuis entrance. The estate security guards watched us, wide-eyed, their faces pressed against the bars.

"Do not lie. You have oppressed us for over five hundred years," said the man.

"Well, not personally," I said.

"He says not personally!" declared the man to the crowd, smiling. There was a smattering of laughter and a few shouts and whistles. He turned back to me, his face darkening. "But I say it *is* personal, white man. I take it personally that your corporation comes here, that you steal our land, take our profits, pay us a pittance, and then," he paused and raised his head to the crowd once more, "and then, you have the arrogance to come here and count your money in front of us!"

There were a few more shouts, none of which sounded particularly friendly. I'd definitely preferred it when they were singing and dancing. Maybe they'd start again soon.

"Where is your shame, white man? Where is your humility? Where is your dignity?" He aimed these questions at the crowd, so I suspected they were more rhetorical than genuine enquiry. Then, he looked down at me once more. "You are here to count your money, yes? Tell us, white man, how much money have you made?"

"Yes, tell us," shouted a voice behind me. "Tell us!" shouted more voices. "Give us your money!"

"Ah, I think there's been a mistake," I blabbered, giving a slightly desperate smile. I wondered whether I could sprint for the gate and shin up the twelve-foot-high bars before someone grabbed me or hurled a rock. It was worth a try. Then I spotted the rolls of razor wire looped along the top of the gate, presumably designed to deter exactly that type of activity, and decided against it.

"Yes, white man, there have been many mistakes," boomed the man.

"Look, I don't work for the winery. I'm nothing to do with Paris-Blois International. I'm a tourist. I'm only here for... for the food," I finished, lamely.

"He is only here for the food!" declared the man to the crowd. "But we are all here for the food, are we not, brothers and sisters?" The crowd shouted their agreement. I heard a couple of cries of "Yes, General!" I shivered a little. I hoped they wouldn't attempt to eat me.

"So, you want the same as us, white man. Mr Hart, you said your name was, yes?"

"Yes, that's me."

The man extended his hand and I shook it. I tried to avoid wincing too overtly. He had a grip like an industrial vice.

"I am Gambu. Welcome to our cause."

"My pleasure, General, I mean Mr Gambu." Thank God, I thought. I'm not sure how I got away with that, must be the Felix Hart charm.

144

"So, Mr Hart, now you are with us, you can make these people open the gates, so we may all eat together."

There were shouts of encouragement from behind me.

"Right. I'm not entirely sure—"

"What is the matter, Mr Hart? These men will let you in, I promise." He turned to the gate. The security guards shrank back a few inches. "This white man and his guests wish to enjoy your food," he called. "He is ordering you to open the gates." He placed a hand on my back and pushed me towards the entrance. "Mr Hart, tell them, so we may all eat together."

I lifted my bag and approached the gates, Gambu a couple of steps behind. I glanced back and saw the crowd were edging forward, led by the dancers, who swigged from the bottles of wine chained around their necks and leapt from foot to foot.

"Do you like our berserkers, Mr Hart? They are my praetorian guard."

"Yes, they're quite something," I said. I stopped before the gates. "Erm, would you mind letting me in, please?" I said to one of the security guards. He took a step back and shook his head, wide-eyed.

"Black man! My Xhosa brother!" shouted Gambu. "Listen to the white man! He is ordering you to open the gate!"

The man looked from Gambu to me, appalled.

"Look, this is a bit awkward, Mr Gambu," I said. "I think they're worried you're all going to rush in and—"

"There will be no rushing, Mr Hart. We have waited over five hundred years. We will walk in slowly. Why should we rush? Tell them again. They will listen to the white man."

"I wonder, would you mind awfully just opening the gates, please?" I said.

Unsurprisingly, none of the guards gave the slightest inclination they intended to do so.

"What is this?" said Gambu. "They do not obey the white man. This is a disgrace!" He took hold of the bars and shook the gates. "This white man orders you to open these gates!"

The guards took another couple of steps backwards. Gambu turned to me.

"They will not do as you ask, Mr Hart."

"No, it seems not."

"What is the point of a white man who cannot issue orders?"

"Perhaps, if I ask them to let just me in, I can go and speak to someone, and maybe they can provide you with some food, or something," I said, lamely.

"What I mean is," said Gambu, releasing the bars and taking a step towards me, "what is the point of the white man, when he can no longer issue orders?"

I had a feeling my relationship with Gambu was on a downward trajectory once more.

"No point!" shouted Gambu. He turned to the crowd, who had pressed to within a few yards of us. "There is no point in the white man!" There were whistles and shouts of "No, General!"

"Look," I gibbered, tears beginning to well in my eyes. "Leave me alone! I'm just a tourist, ok? I haven't stolen anyone's land or anyone's money. In fact, I've had *my* money stolen! I haven't even got anywhere to stay tonight."

The berserkers had moved in close now, the bottles of wine swinging from their neck chains.

"Last chance, Mr Hart. What is the point of you? What can you do for me and my fighters?"

I swallowed, hard. There was no escape. I was pressed up against the bars of the gate, surrounded by an impi of angry natives, and I hadn't even shagged the chief's daughter. My eyes came to rest on one of the berserker's bottles of wine, swinging from its chain. Close up, I could see the label wasn't real, just a white square with the word 'oppression' and a simple hand drawing of a Cape Dutch farmhouse. What had Blanchkopf mentioned about Gambu, apart from the savagery and throat-cutting? Of course, he'd said that he owned a winery!

"I can buy your wine!" I yelped.

"What?" said Gambu.

"I'm a wine buyer! A professional wine buyer. I work for a British supermarket, a very big one. We buy wine. I could buy your wine and sell it in the UK."

"Now that, white man, is a very creative proposition," said Gambu. "But it sounds like you are just saying it to get out of trouble."

"No, not at all! We want to sell more wines from black-owned businesses!"

"So, white guilt does exist! How touching!"

"It's not guilt. It's just… doing the right thing."

"The right thing! You are a most enlightened man, Mr Hart! I insist that you come and tour my winery, immediately."

"I'd be delighted," I said. My phone rang. It was Sandra. "Sorry, excuse me one second, Mr Gambu. It's, erm, this lot, calling me." I jerked my thumb at the gates.

"What the hell are you doing, Felix?" shouted Sandra, before I could even say hello.

"I'm talking to the demonstrators. What's the problem?"

"You've led them to the gate and it looks like you're inviting them to invade our property, you moron! I'm watching you on CCTV. You're going to get someone killed, probably yourself. What on earth are you playing at?"

"Look, everything's under control. Just a misunderstanding. I'm talking to The General, right now. I'll ask them to stand down, then you can open the gate and I can pop in."

"You have to be kidding me. We're not opening the gate until that demonstration has dispersed. You can go somewhere else for the night. We've called for more police support, so I suggest you make yourself scarce before they start a riot."

She hung up. This was a very bad development. It sounded like I'd be sleeping in Stellenbosch Botanical Gardens after all. And I didn't like the sound of being caught up in a riot, either.

"I'm free next week," I said to Gambu. "I'll be sure to drop by."

"No, no. I'm not having you running off and forgetting your promises, Mr Hart. You will come and visit right now.

We are nearly finished here." He turned back to the gate and addressed the cowering guards. "But we will be back tomorrow morning at sunrise, brothers," he called, and rattled the gate for good measure.

We were escorted to a shiny pickup by three of Gambu's cadres, all wearing hammer, sickle and grape t-shirts. One opened the rear door for Gambu and saluted, while the other two jumped into the front seats. I squeezed into the back alongside Gambu, who took up the vast majority of the space, leaving me pinned between the side of his stomach and the vehicle's door. As we crested the Helshoogte Pass and began our descent into Franschhoek, Gambu expounded upon his personal revolutionary theory, which was based upon Maoist-Leninist thought combined with Black Consciousness and Pan-Africanism. He explained that the dress of his followers was inspired by this blend of ideology, the Asian paddy-farmer's hats representing the struggle of Ho Chi Minh against imperialist forces, the blue grape-picker's overalls representing the rural worker's struggle, the rubber gumboots representing the parallel struggles of the miners. The bottles of wine chained around the necks of the berserkers symbolised historical oppression at the hands of vineyard owners, and their dancing represented the legacy of alcoholism among poorly paid rural workers.

"My berserkers drink red grape juice, not wine. I do not permit alcohol on our demonstrations. Our oppressors do not realise that, of course. It serves to make them just a little more wary."

All in all, it was a rather dense and intellectual half-hour and I might have dozed off if it hadn't been for Gambu's bulging stomach restricting my ability to breathe. To my relief, Gambu's views on England were relatively benign. On the one hand, unsurprisingly, he was scathing in his criticism of Britain's colonial history and the oppressive influence of Western-inspired, corporate neo-liberalism. On the other, it turned out Gambu had studied at Oxford, thanks to a Rhodes scholarship, and had developed a fondness for the city during his two years of study there, though this affection was confined strictly to the salt-of-the-earth townsfolk, and very much excluded his tutors and fellow students.

Despite the funds for his graduate studies originating from the less-than-fragrant fortune of Cecil Rhodes – Victorian arch-capitalist, imperialist and general native-harasser – Gambu revealed a liberated attitude to taking advantage of the late diamond magnate's money, describing the scholarship as reparations for the slavery of his forefathers. The city had also kindled in Gambu an unlikely enthusiasm for Oxford United Football Club, no doubt connected to his sympathy for the underdog and willingness to support causes others might have considered hopeless.

"The dignity of a supporter of a lower-league English football team is a magnificent thing," declared Gambu. "To sit in the rain on a freezing Saturday afternoon, to watch your team lose two-three in injury time to Leyton Orient, and be relegated from the league, and yet still support them, still turn up the following season, that is the essence of struggle, of solidarity. I count those Saturdays in the Oxford Mail Stand as pivotal to the galvanization of my revolutionary thought."

"Is that why your followers sing *Come and Have a Go*?" I asked.

"It is. But my favourite chant is *Swindon Town is Falling Down*. It drives the forces of oppression here mad. They think we are singing *Swellendam is Falling Down*. It prays on their psychoses, most pleasingly."

I smiled and nodded, despite having not the slightest clue what he was talking about.

Gambu explained that following the completion of his post-graduate degree in political science, he had returned to South Africa to take up a prominent position in the youth wing of the African National Congress. It wasn't absolutely clear how he had ended up in possession of a winery in Franschhoek, and I felt it better not to pry.

After a few more minutes ascending the side of the steep Franschhoek valley, we turned on to a driveway overgrown with weeds and approached a pair of farm buildings.

"What's the name of the winery?" I asked.

"It is called Gambu," replied Gambu.

"Great name," I said. "Nice and snappy. How much wine do you produce?"

Gambu ignored me. The driver parked in the shade of the larger building and the cadre leapt from the passenger seat to open Gambu's door. Gambu extricated himself from the vehicle while I rubbed my bruised ribs and climbed out after him. The view was rather wonderful, Franschhoek village laid out beneath us and the mountain peaks on the far side of the valley glowing orange in the late afternoon sun.

"Here, come and see." Gambu pulled open a sliding barn door and I followed him inside. A dozen stainless steel tanks lined the wall and I spotted a pair of German-made presses and a de-stemming machine at the far end. There was something strange about the building, though. Apart from a faint aroma of paint, it didn't smell like a winery. That's to say, it didn't smell of wine. Or of grapes. Or of anything in between. There were no stray fragments of leaf, no smears of dried grape skin, no puddles of water or wine from trailing hoses. I could see dust coating the gauge on the nearest tank, while the pallets stacked in the corner wore a blanket of cobwebs.

"Do you actually have any wine?" I said.

"Oppression has many manifestations," said Gambu, cryptically.

"I'm guessing you don't own any vineyards. Do you have any contracts with grape growers?"

"The grapes will come," said Gambu.

"Right. Well, please do let me know when they arrive. There's not a lot of business to be done if you don't have any wine."

"Tell me, how many wines from black-owned wineries do you sell at your supermarket?"

150

"Ah, well, we're working on it," I said, slightly sheepishly.

"None. What a surprise! So, is it also a surprise that I have no wine, when international business refuses to buy from me?"

"If your wine's good, you'll be able to sell it. I'm sure no-one's deliberately refusing to buy from you."

"Oh, but they are," said Gambu, bitterly. "I had a contract to supply our national airline. Suddenly, the business was whisked away. Another contract with a chain of liquor stores in the Eastern Cape. That too, suddenly withdrawn."

"Can't you use your political connections? Do a bit of networking, I mean. You're in the ANC, aren't you?"

"Not anymore," sniffed Gambu, waving his arm. "Sell-outs, who would rather suckle at the teat of white capital than uplift their own oppressed brothers. I have broken from them. We are building a new movement."

"Oh, I see. Does your new movement have a name?"

"We are on a branding journey," replied Gambu. "We are known as the Black Soil Movement, but we have been subjected to a foul and sustained attack by the white-controlled media, who persist in associating our name with puerile jokes." Gambu waved his finger at me. "That is a sign we have the establishment rattled, of course. Nevertheless, a rebranding might be required." Gambu raised his face to the ceiling, in search of inspiration. "Something like… Our Soil Movement."

"Arse Hole Movement?" I said, genuinely confused. "I don't think that's an improvement, to be honest."

"Our Soil!" shouted Gambu.

"Oh, I see. Apologies." My cheeks began to flush. "Black Soil is fine, I'm sure. Or, perhaps you could just use the initials B.S.? Actually, no, forget that."

Gambu's face hardened. "You see, that is the type of comment I would expect from an Englishman. You people raise ignorance to a high art. Why should we care what the initials spell in English? Barely one percent of this country speaks English as a first language. You might be interested to know that

Black Soil, when translated into isiXhosa, has the initials N.O."
Gambu smiled, triumphantly. "N.O. spells no, white man! No to
imperialism! No to capitalism! No to exploitation!"

"Yes, that's a pretty clear mission statement, I suppose.
Actually, last year, my employer found themselves in a similar
situation to you. We decided to stock a European long-life milk
brand in our Brazilian subsidiary. We shipped twenty containers
of a new product called 'Pinto Leche' into the country, but it was
only when we put it on sale that we realised it translated locally
as 'Little Penis Milk'."

Gambu appeared unimpressed with my attempt at empathy. I
decided to move the subject on.

"You know, Gatesave might be interested in selling your
wine, once you've secured a supply of grapes."

Gambu's eyes widened for a second, then he remembered
himself and dismissed my offer with a wave of his hand. "We
will see. Something we might discuss at a later date."

I confess the germ of an idea had begun to sprout in my mind.
True, it was a pretty half-baked idea, but I felt the raw ingredients
had just presented themselves.

"Come, I will show you our label designs," said Gambu. I
followed him to the smaller building and we entered a messy
office, dominated by an enormous leather chair. Gambu yanked
open a drawer and extracted a box file. He swept some papers
aside, opened the file and placed four wine labels before me.

"This is the brand I planned to sell to the liquor store chain,"
he said.

The labels were very similar, each illustrated with a silhouette
of Gambu's huge head, complete with beret, in a different shade.
The red version was branded Gambu Cabernet, the purple one
Gambu Shiraz, the yellow Gambu Chardonnay and the green
Gambu Sauvignon Blanc.

"Well, there's no doubting whose wines they are," I said.

"Strong branding is as important in wine as in politics."

"Do you have any others?"

"What's wrong with these?" said Gambu, sounding slightly hurt.

"They're great," I lied, "but I wondered whether your design team had come up with anything else. Always good to see an alternative angle."

Gambu paused for a second, then grinned. "Actually, I did challenge them to come up with something more powerful. But you will not like these designs. They are strictly for the enlightened end of the market."

Gambu withdrew a label and placed it before me. My eyes widened and, involuntarily, my hand reached out to touch it. The paper was a deep, dark black, almost startlingly intense, and it glistened dully, like an inky, ebony wax. Beneath my fingertips, I sensed the texture of velvet, but dotted with almost imperceptible ridges and bumps, as though a message, invisible to the eye, had been disguised within. Carved around the edge, in blood red, lay the outline of Africa, and inside that, also in red, the profile of a raised fist. Beneath, in gold block capitals, were stamped the words BLACK POWER PINOTAGE.

"That's strong," I said, stroking the label. "Very strong."

Gambu nodded. "Once the Gambu brand is established in the South African market, we will launch this label. At present, my black brothers prefer to drink Scotch and Cognac, manufactured by white-owned multi-nationals. But my vision is to convert my people to wines grown in their own earth. The soil of their birthright."

"Very nice." I ran my finger over the label's tactile surface once more and felt a prickle of excitement. There was profit to be made here, I could smell it.

"Of course, these are unsuitable for export markets. I imagine they would upset the thin-skinned natives of your own, self-satisfied country particularly badly."

"Some of them, perhaps. But you were a student at Oxford. Surely you recognise there's an appetite for this type of design among those with a certain… political outlook?"

"I spent my leisure time in solidarity with the working classes, in the pubs and on the terraces. I could not endure the self-satisfied whinnying of the privileged elite that populated my college."

"Well, I didn't go to university at all, but I'm damn sure there's a market for this brand."

Gambu snorted. "You don't understand. This isn't just a label. The proceeds from Black Power Pinotage go into a fighting fund to support the expropriation of white land, right here. This brand is literally designed to destroy white power!"

"Honestly, Mr Gambu," I said, "this is marketing gold. I promise you, I can definitely sell these wines in the UK. They'll lap it up."

"Are you making fun of me, white man?" Gambu took a step towards me, his earlier cordiality gone. I imagined him on the terraces at Oxford United, chanting at the visitors' stand. I glanced at his hands, twice the size of mine, now half-curled into fists. And, after the match, several pints down, I imagined him indulging in another, rather less attractive, English sporting tradition.

"I'm certainly not, Mr Gambu," I gulped. "I'm just saying I think you'll find there's more sympathy in the UK for your political position than you realise."

Gambu narrowed his eyes, then harrumphed. "We shall see. I am in negotiation, right now, with a couple of growers to secure a good supply of grapes."

"Dare I suggest, it's rather late to still be negotiating for grapes? It's spring and most of the contracts will have been done. I'm not sure you'll be able to obtain the quality or quantity of fruit you need."

Gambu frowned. But he knew I spoke the truth.

"You don't need grapes," I said. "You need finished wine." Gambu, still listening, replaced the labels in the box file. "And I might just have a source of wine for you."

"We have already tried to procure wine. The last vintage was short, and no-one is willing to sell." Gambu snapped the box file shut.

"I know someone who's in the market to sell. He wants to work with a black-owned business too."

"You wouldn't be trying to offload your suppliers' faulty old wine on me, would you?" Gambu stared down at me.

"No! Of course not!" I could feel my palms sweating and tried to keep the trembling from my voice. "It's excellent quality. I just wondered whether you had any... shall we say... particularly strict criteria governing where you buy your raw material?"

"Put it this way, white man," said Gambu, moving his enormous face uncomfortably close to mine. "I am a businessman, so I will make a considered decision. But if you try to set me up with one of those disgusting fascists from whom you source your cheap bulk wine, my berserkers will hunt you down like a colonial war criminal."

I laughed, rather hysterically. "Oh, perish the thought, Mr Gambu! That's not what I had in mind at all!"

Chapter 17

The Platinum Fox

"Sandra!" I shouted into the phone, as my taxi wound its way back up the dark Helshoogte Pass. "I'm heading to Hemelhuis right now, and if you don't let me in, I'll throw myself on your electric fence, and you'll be responsible for manslaughter!"

"Calm down, Felix. The demonstrators have gone. Just give your name to the guards at the gate and they'll let you in, so long as you're alone."

"Thank God. Thank you. I'll leave first thing, I promise."

"Yes, you will. Though not before you've had a chat with our head of security. You were seen leaving in a vehicle with Gambu earlier, which means you're either a revolutionary communist, or you've just survived a kidnap attempt."

"A bit of both, really. I'll be with you in half an hour."

"Make sure your driver approaches the gate slowly, Felix. Or you're liable to get shot."

I directed the taxi to stop just short of the estate entrance and approached the gate on foot, my arms raised. I called my name, a torch was shone in my face, and the gate hummed open, just a foot or so, before closing quickly behind me. I climbed into a golf cart, and a silent guard drove me the several hundred yards up a bright, tree-lined driveway, acres of lawn either side of me bathed silver beneath the floodlights.

A staff member walked me to my suite in a cottage behind the manor house. Preparations were being finalised for the CEO's visit, and it was made very clear that I was to stay put and not explore the rest of the estate. My bedroom boasted a four-poster bed, dressing table and chaise longue, and included an annex housing a desk and computer screen, in case the occupant felt inclined to do some work, which I most certainly did not. I took a long bath and dissolved the day's grime from my body, before room service delivered dinner, a fabulous Cape Malay curry accompanied by a pile of samosas, washed down with Hemelhuis's estate Pinot Noir. I sank into the soft mattress and slept like a baby.

I was woken by a six a.m. alarm call, reminding me of my early breakfast appointment with Sandra. I scooped the Paris-Blois branded toiletries into my bag and entered the rear of the manor house, from where a member of staff directed me to the dining room. The room was huge, large enough to seat two hundred, though the only diners were Sandra and a small, wiry man with a moustache, sitting together at a table in the corner.

"This is Mikey, our Head of Security," said Sandra. The man shook my hand briefly, without rising or smiling, and returned to buttering his slice of toast. Sandra, her blonde hair tied back in a ponytail, looked rather lovely in a pink linen blazer and trousers, but then she always did look rather lovely. "Sit down please, Felix."

"Any chance of a coffee and croissant?" I asked. Sandra nodded to a waiter, lurking silently in an alcove nearby, and he glided off to fetch my breakfast. There was an awkward pause. "Nice place you've got here," I said.

"Your friend Gambu is back," said the Head of Security. He had a clipped, Afrikaans accent. He didn't sound happy.

"Yes, he's quite a character," I said.

"He's a snake," said the Head of Security.

"I don't know him terribly well, to be honest."

"Then what were you doing with him yesterday?" He fixed me with a beady eye.

"He insisted I accompany him to his winery. I didn't have much choice."

"You're lucky his men didn't rob you or murder you."

"Yes, I suppose I was rather lucky."

The man glared at me in a way that suggested he'd be happy to see my luck run out extremely soon.

"Felix, this Gambu person is back outside our estate this morning with two hundred of his followers. More are arriving every minute. We've tried negotiating with him but it's not clear what he wants."

"He wants war, that's what he wants," said the Head of Security.

"I think he wants to overthrow capitalism and white supremacy," I said.

"Well, it's rather irritating that he wants to do it today. Our CEO flies in shortly and we're having our annual sales conference this afternoon."

"Yes, I think that might be the point."

"It's ironic, actually," said Sandra. "Hemelhuis pays better wages than any winery in the Cape. Even our cheapest wines fetch four times the market average. It's hardly in our interests to embarrass ourselves by offering our workforce poor terms and conditions."

The Head of Security's phone vibrated. He snatched it from the table.

"*Ja?*"

He listened for a few seconds, snapped a short instruction in Afrikaans and slapped the phone back down.

"They've started throwing stones at the guards. Police nowhere to be seen, as usual." He sighed. "We've locked down the perimeter. We'll have to cancel the conference."

We listened for a moment, as if expecting the sound of rioting to carry across the grounds. But we were too far from the front gate, the only noise the clatter of crockery from a distant kitchen. Then, I heard something else. A distant mechanical chatter. My eyes widened. Was that gunfire? Christ, I should have stayed in the bloody township.

"That's Jacobus." The Head of Security had heard it too. The sound increased in volume and I realised it wasn't a machine gun, but an approaching helicopter.

"He's not going to be happy," muttered Sandra. "Why didn't we hold the conference in Singapore? Or bloody Davos?"

It dawned on me that the approaching aircraft was carrying none other than Jacobus Cortland, the Chief Executive of Paris-Blois International, nicknamed the Platinum Fox due to his wealth, business acumen and magnificent head of silver hair.

"I'll let you break the news," said the Head of Security, grimacing.

"Maybe I could have a word with Gambu," I suggested. "I think he and I built up a bit of rapport yesterday."

The Head of Security snorted and Sandra gave me a disdainful look.

"Yes," she said, "maybe you could ask him to go and picket one of your dodgy own-label suppliers instead."

It was at that moment that I was struck by an idea so brazen, and so brilliant, that I was rendered momentarily speechless.

"Do you have Fairly Trod certification?" I asked, once I'd recovered.

"No, we don't tend to bother with virtue signalling," replied Sandra, rising to her feet. "We prefer to let our wine's quality do the talking. Anyway, if you'll excuse me, I have to find a venue for two hundred people at an hour's notice and manage a highly distressed CEO into the bargain. I'd tell you to get lost, but no-one's allowed to enter or leave the estate while there's trouble outside, so I'd be grateful if you could return to your room and stay put."

"No, I genuinely think I can help," I said. "Listen, Gambu needs to buy wine. If you agree to sell to him, this could diffuse the situation. You'd become partners."

"Why would we sell wine to that viper?" spat the Head of Security.

"Quite," said Sandra. "And we happen to need our wine for the Hemelhuis brand. We don't have any spare."

"You wouldn't need to sell him your own wine. I have a great source. He could supply it to you, then you could sell it on to Gambu."

"I don't think so, Felix. We have little interest in associating ourselves with one of your dodgy, barrel-scraping suppliers."

"No, they're a great supplier, I guarantee it. They're Fairly Trod certified. All you'd have to do is buy the wine in bulk and redirect it to Gambu's winery."

Sandra paused for a second, torn between my plan and the imminent arrival of the Platinum Fox.

"And, Gambu's winery is a black-owned company, so it would get you Black Empowerment Credits from the government too," I said.

Sandra frowned. "True, but why are you going to all this trouble? This isn't your problem. What are you getting out of this?"

"There's some bad blood between my supplier and Gambu." The helicopter was very close now. It sounded as though it was circling the estate, and the noise was beginning to drown out our conversation. "I need someone respectable as a fire break between the two parties," I said, raising my voice. "One of my suppliers has excess wine that I'm contracted to buy. And Gatesave want more black-empowerment suppliers on their books, for PR reasons."

The chop-chop of the rotor blades began to slow, and the engine's whine lowered. The Platinum Fox had landed.

Sandra wiped her palm across her forehead. "Christ Almighty. Ok, see what you can do. We want him and his gang of troublemakers away from the estate within the hour. Our delegates start arriving at ten. Don't make any stupid promises." She turned to the Head of Security. "Mikey, take him to the front gate, will you?"

The Head of Security glowered at me. "You're kidding?"

"Either take him to the gate or get rid of Gambu's thugs yourself." Sandra rose and strode to the door. "Better still," she called over her shoulder, "you can explain to Jacobus how you lost control of the estate and ruined his annual sales conference."

The journey to the front gate was a wordless one, the only sound the golf cart's high-pitched scream as the Head of Security propelled it angrily down the drive. I spotted the helicopter, its rotors now stationary, set down in a field to the side of the manor house, a knot of four people walking quickly towards the building. I recognised Sandra by her long blond ponytail, while another of the figures, much taller than the rest, was crowned with a halo of white.

We neared the gate. A dozen Hemelhuis security guards had taken cover behind trees, and a sprinkling of stones, cans and broken glass decorated the driveway. The Head of Security slowed as we approached the resting places of the furthest-flung pieces of rock. I saw the berserkers, in their paddy field farmer's hats, rattling the gate in time to their singing.

Who are ya? Who are ya?

I stepped out of the golf cart. The Head of Security executed a tight U-turn and drove fifty yards back up the drive, before parking up to watch. I turned back to the gate, just in time to spot a highly accurate, fist-sized lump of rubble descending upon my location. I made a quick side-step and the rock bounced off the driveway and rolled into the grass. A cheer went up from the berserkers.

"Cease fire!" I shouted.

Several more missiles were launched skywards from behind the gate. I took cover behind a nearby tree as they thumped to the ground around me.

Who are ya? Who are ya?

A half-brick bumped to a rest just a few feet from my refuge. I skipped from behind the tree and retrieved it, dashing back to cover as a couple of pebbles clattered into the branches above. Then, I leapt out and sent the lump flying towards the gate. It hit the metal struts high up, near the razor wire, and shattered with a splendidly loud clang, showering the berserkers with shrapnel. The chanting and gate rattling suddenly stopped.

"I'm here to see Gambu," I called. "I have a business proposal."

After a moment of silence, a voice boomed out.

"Where is our breakfast, white man? You said yesterday we would eat together."

The berserkers parted and Gambu's huge silhouette appeared behind the gate.

"I'm working on it," I shouted. "In the meantime, I have an excellent proposition for you."

"Do come and tell me," called Gambu.

"Do you promise not to throw any rocks?"

"You have two minutes, Mr Hart."

I approached the gate, broken glass and fragments of brick crunching beneath my feet. Gambu stared through the bars at me, red beret atop his massive head, each hand grasping a metal strut. He shook the gate gently.

"We meet again," he said. "But now you are our prisoner."

"Yes, good morning, Mr Gambu. I've been discussing you and your winery with my friends here at Hemelhuis. I have some excellent news."

"They are handing over this stolen land to us?" asked Gambu, eyebrows raised.

"No, not quite that."

"Then that is the end of our negotiation," he said, and released his grip on the gate.

"No, they want to sell you some bulk wine," I said, quickly. "Excellent quality wine, that you can bottle, under your brand. And that I will then buy from you, and sell at Gatesave."

Gambu paused. "Why would they do that?"

"They want the black empowerment brownie points," I said.

"Brownie points?" roared Gambu. "What the hell is that?"

"I do apologise!" I said, mortified. "That was a slip of the tongue. I meant like credits or gold stars. Businesses are awarded Black Empowerment Credits if they do a certain amount of trade with black-owned businesses, as you probably know."

"Yes, of course I'm aware of Black Empowerment Credits," snarled Gambu. "A pathetic fig leaf worn by white business to pander to our sell-out government. And you and your white friends call them brownie points!"

"No, no, no, that was a mistake, I apologise," I said, bright red. "Brownie points is a British expression, meaning an award for good deeds. Brownies are the small girl version of Scouts…" I tailed off, lamely.

"A fascist, colonialist, militarist youth movement," said Gambu.

"Yes, that's the one. Never joined them myself." There was an awkward pause as Gambu stared down at me. "I'll lay my cards out, Mr Gambu. Hemelhuis has lots of wine. It's good quality and has Fairly Trod certification, so it's all produced ethically. The growers are paid double the legal minimum."

"Twice nothing is still nothing," said Gambu, stone-faced.

"Hemelhuis want to sell to you and we, at Gatesave, want to buy from you. I urge you to take us up on the offer. All we ask in return is that your followers stop throwing rocks over Hemelhuis's gate. With immediate effect."

"I will consider it."

"I think they're hoping for an answer quite soon, actually."

"Tell your friends to provide me with a memorandum of understanding and we will stand down. And I want a written undertaking from Gatesave too."

"I'm sure that can be arranged. I'll email you a Gatesave contract right now."

By God, I thought, as the Head of Security transported me back to the manor house on the back of the golf cart, I'm wasted in supermarket retail. I should be an international diplomat. A United Nations trouble-shooter, perhaps.

"Let me get this straight," said Sandra. "We buy bulk wine from some supplier of yours, then sell it straight on to Gambu. But you don't want either party to know about the transaction because they don't get on?"

"Yes, that's the idea."

Five of us were seated round a table in a small office at the rear of the manor house. Sandra and the scowling Head of Security had been joined by a suited man, who introduced himself as a company attorney, and a young man in T-shirt and jeans, one of the Hemelhuis winemakers.

"I won't deny that selling to Gambu, and gaining a few more Black Empowerment Credits, would be useful for Hemelhuis," said Sandra. "We're a little behind on our Black Empowerment measures and the Minister for Social Justice wrote to our CEO last month, telling us to raise our game."

"I get that," said the winemaker. "But this whole business around the origin of the wine sounds weird. Who's the supplier?"

"It's Blanchkopf Wine Growers," I said.

"You're kidding. I've heard some bad stories about that guy! Wine's crap too."

"What kind of bad stories?" said Sandra, sharply.

"Look, forget all that, he's turned over a new leaf," I said. "He's got Fairly Trod certification. He wants to redress the wrongs of the past."

"He's old school," said the winemaker, "in a bad way. No wonder you don't want Gambu to know where the wine's from. Or for Blanchkopf to know where it's going."

"So," said Sandra, "suddenly the facts emerge. You're buying dodgy wine from an exploitative vineyard owner and selling it on to a radical black communist. And you want to place us in the middle of it."

"It's not dodgy wine. It's Fairly Trod."

"How the hell did Blanchkopf get Fairly Trod certification?" said the winemaker. "The guy treats his workers like crap. I'm surprised he pays them at all."

"Well, it's pending," I said. "The inspection is next week."

Sandra rolled her eyes.

"Look, it'll be fine. All Gambu wants is a memorandum of understanding, saying you're willing to sell him a couple of wines, in bulk. Gatesave are the ones committing to buy the bottled wine from him. And Blanchkopf's inspection is a formality, I promise."

"We won't touch the bulk wine if Blanchkopf fails the Fairly Trod inspection," said the winemaker. "Too much reputational risk. What sort of wine is it? What cultivars?"

"There are two wines. A light, Pinotage-based red and an entry-point white blend."

"Wow. Sounds really premium," said the winemaker, smirking.

"A memorandum isn't legally binding, is it?" asked Sandra.

"No. Not the way I write them," smiled the attorney.

"And Gambu promises to leave, immediately, as soon as he receives it?"

"That's what he said."

"And you're willing to list our Hemelhuis premium Chardonnay and Cabernet at Gatesave, with immediate effect, at the price we specify?"

"No, I never said that!" I said, genuinely outraged.

"But that's what you're going to do, isn't it?" said Sandra.

"I suppose," I muttered, recognising the balance of power wasn't entirely in my favour.

"Right. Let's get the memorandum written up and that rabble cleared from outside our estate," said Sandra. "Looks like the conference might be back on. A provisional well done, Felix."

"My pleasure," I said, feeling as though I'd been mugged at the last minute. "I do have just another little favour, please."

"What is it?" said Sandra, drumming her fingers on the desk.

"I need some transport please, to get to the British Consulate in Cape Town. I'm out of cash. I lost my credit cards and passport."

"Mikey, can you organise a car and driver for Felix, please? And issue him with a Paris-Blois charge card too, with a ten-thousand-rand limit."

The Head of Security scowled and nodded.

"That's a loan, by the way, Felix," said Sandra, "you can repay us when you receive your new credit cards."

"Super, thank you. Oh, and I'm having a little trouble with the police, too. My hire car was used in a robbery or something." I gave an apologetic smile.

Sandra sighed and looked at the Head of Security. "Mikey?"

"I'll make a couple of calls," he said, with undisguised irritation.

"Anything else, Felix?" asked Sandra. "An outstanding Interpol warrant, perhaps? An advanced venereal disease that needs immediate treatment?"

The winemaker sniggered.

"No, that should be everything, thank you."

As we left the office, I glanced through the open door to the boardroom opposite and glimpsed a tall, smartly dressed man seated cross-legged in a leather chair. He lifted a china cup to his lips, a perfectly coiffured mane of silver rising above his long, tanned face. His eyes met mine and held my gaze until I passed the doorway. It occurred to me that he may have been listening.

Chapter 18

Upliftment

After arranging my replacement travel documents, I directed my Hemelhuis chauffeur back to Stellenbosch. The Mercedes turned off the highway and bumped its way up Blanchkopf's driveway until we arrived at the farmhouse gate, which, after a few seconds, granted us entry. We were greeted by Blanchkopf's dogs, the Rottweiler snarling and hurling itself against the driver's door, while the Boerboel leapt onto the bonnet and attempted to rip the windscreen wipers from their mountings.

"*Dom Honde!*" bellowed Blanchkopf, striding from the farmhouse in a green flak jacket and tight shorts. He grasped the Boerboel by its collar, dragged it off the car and secured it to a metal ring embedded in the farmhouse wall, while it howled in fury and attempted to fasten its jaws around Blanchkopf's arm. The Rottweiler danced frenziedly around the car, leaping up at each window in turn and raking the glass with its front paws.

The driver activated the internal locks and shrank down in his seat.

"Don't worry," I said. "At least one of them is relatively friendly."

I lowered the tinted window a couple of inches and the Rottweiler attempted to insert its jaws into the gap.

"Hello, Mr Blanchkopf," I called.

"Oh, it's you," he said. "Why are you in a Hemelhuis car?"

"Once you've secured all your animals, Mr Blanchkopf, I will explain."

With both dogs safely chained to the wall, I joined Mr and Mrs Blanchkopf in their reception room, and declined their offers of *rooibos* and warm Chardonnay.

"How are the preparations for the Fairly Trod inspection going?" I asked, as the stuffed giraffe gazed down at me, mournfully.

Blanchkopf made a sulky face.

"Why should we make any preparations?" said Mrs Blanchkopf.

My stomach gave a lurch of alarm.

"What do you mean? The Fairly Trod Foundation are coming to inspect you next week!"

"We never agreed to this inspection. And it is not acceptable," she said, puffing out her chest. "These people, they want to see all the pay checks for every worker, monitor their breaks, check for this, check for that. Then they say they will return every month to check again! No, it is too much."

"We've discussed this, Mrs Blanchkopf. They have to check everything, that's how you get the certification!"

"They tell us to install fans in the accommodation block," said Blanchkopf. "This is ridiculous. We do not even have fans in our own house! It is a waste of money."

"You promised! I've given you a huge price increase to cover exactly this type of thing. We signed a contract!"

"We only said we would think about it," said Mrs Blanchkopf. "This is our business. Our farm. We will run it how we like."

"Look, I came to tell you that I'm planning an exciting joint venture with Hemelhuis Estate. We want to use your red and white wines in a new brand we're developing."

Blanchkopf frowned. "Hemelhuis is a very prestigious estate," he said.

"They are indeed, most prestigious. But they will only buy wine with Fairly Trod certification."

"We said no," snapped Mrs Blanchkopf. "It is the principle."

I looked to her husband, but Blanchkopf shook his head.

"Then we have a problem," I said, rising from my seat. "You have placed our entire relationship in jeopardy. I will have to inform our partners."

To be honest, I didn't have a bloody clue what to do. My cunning plan had stalled before it had even left the hanger, let alone taken flight. I'd failed to properly check the contract Blanchkopf had tapped out after the *braai* a couple of days ago, mainly because I'd been completely bladdered. No Fairly Trod inspection meant no wine for Hemelhuis or for Gambu. All I had was an ungrateful, sociopathic supplier of overpriced plonk, who was about to be exposed to the world as an unreconstructed slave master, leading to worldwide embarrassment for my employer, humiliation for my CEO, and my immediate firing and arrest. What was the penalty for slavery in South Africa these days? Death, probably.

I shook hands with the Blanchkopfs, nodded to the giraffe, and strode from the room in despair. Accompanied by a chorus of rabid howling from Blanchkopf's hounds, I climbed into the Mercedes and we trundled back down the driveway to the main road. I placed a desperate, optimistic call to the Tears of Pity office, praying their lawyers might have tracked down their elusive development grant, but Troy Frittersley, sounding very down in the dumps, confirmed that the million rand remained stubbornly absent without leave.

I was left with just one final, lunatic option to avoid imminent homelessness. I asked the driver to take me to a liquor store, where I used Sandra's charge card to purchase a case of beer, two bottles of Meerlust Rubicon and a bottle of Johnnie Walker Blue Label. I then directed him to the N2 highway. If my driver was surprised by my request for the Khayelitsha turnoff, he didn't show it. But when I urged him on, towards the heart of the township, he slowed, and as the paved road petered out into loose dirt and gravel, he pulled over.

"Sir, this is the wrong way," he said.

"No, I know where I'm going. I have an appointment a couple of miles down the road."

"No, there must be a mistake, sir. This is not safe."

"Please, driver. Continue."

But the man did not. The car shook slightly, as a township taxi tore past.

"I am not insured, sir."

"Would you like me to drive?"

The driver smiled with embarrassment. "Please, sir. We must go back. They will steal my car."

"Nonsense," I replied. "Everyone exaggerates the crime problem in the townships. I've never had any issues." Apart from theft, burglary, assault, blackmail, kidnapping, false imprisonment, aggressive pimping, attempted murder and the forced ingestion of a farm animal's eyeball, I mused, and that all in the space of around four hours.

The driver pulled out a mobile phone and made a call. He spoke very quietly but I overheard the words "he wants Khayelitsha" and "I don't know why". After a minute, he turned and handed me the phone.

"What the hell are you doing in the townships, man? Are you mad?" I recognised the dulcet tones of Hemelhuis's Head of Security.

"I have an appointment with a colleague," I said.

"You have two choices. Either you return to Hemelhuis with the car or you get out of the car. Which one are you going to do?"

"You've been very helpful," I replied, and handed the phone back to the driver.

I stepped out of the car, my little suitcase under one arm and the case of beer under the other. As another township taxi approached, I stepped forward into the road and raised my hand. The minibus skidded to a stop beside me. The driver's mate leaned out of the window.

"Where's the party, *mlungu*?" he shouted, eyeing my case of beer.

"Mama Bisha's," I replied.

The man laughed and slapped the outside of his door in joy.

"Get in, *mlungu*, and give me a beer!"

He reached back and grasped the handle, flinging the sliding passenger door open. I hopped in and the taxi accelerated away. I slid the door shut and handed the man a beer.

"And one for the driver, *mlungu*!"

I handed him a second bottle. The man opened them on the rim of the window and passed one to the driver, who took a long gulp.

"Anyone else?" I asked.

"Yes!" said a young man, gleefully, wearing what looked suspiciously like a school uniform.

"No!" shouted the elderly woman sitting behind him and slapped the back of his head. The youth's smile was replaced by a sulk.

I recognised my drop-off point next to the red *spaza* kiosk, presented the driver with a five-rand coin, gathered my belongings and leapt from the vehicle.

"Another beer, *mlungu*," said the driver's mate, reaching out and pulling two more bottles from the case. It seemed rude to refuse, so I decided against snatching them back. The taxi roared off in a cloud of dust.

I walked the final few hundred yards to Mama Bisha's, unmolested bar a few whistles and shouts of '*mlungu*!' I pushed the front door open and stepped inside.

"*Mlungu* Moses!" shouted Shooter, leaping to his feet. Before I could reply, his head turned to the dining room doorway, from which came the sound of a scraping chair. "Oooh, he has a score to settle, you must run, *mlungu*!"

Sure enough, the broad, scowling figure of McGregor strode through the doorway, fists balled.

"Wait! I've brought you a present!" I gabbled. I fell to one knee and tore the zip of my suitcase open. McGregor was almost upon me but, just in time, I leapt up and thrust the bottle of Johnnie Walker at him. McGregor stopped and transferred his scowl to the whisky.

"Ooo-eee! Blue Label!" declared Shooter, pointing to the bottle. "Super premium. Two thousand rand!"

"I'm very sorry about the toilet incident," I said. "Please accept my apologies."

McGregor took the bottle and examined it.

"It's genuine," I said.

"Maybe it is a fake," said Shooter. "*Mlungu* Moses is a criminal and a bad Christian."

"It's definitely real," I said. "And so are these." I withdrew the two bottles of wine. "To replace the ones I drank earlier this week. And I've brought you some beers for the fridge too."

"And what is my present?" said Shooter, peering at the motley collection of boxer shorts and t-shirts.

"I haven't brought you one," I said. "Only McGregor gets a present."

Shooter's face fell but McGregor smiled. "Maybe I will share it with you. Or maybe not."

"Is Mama Bisha here?" I asked.

"Welcome back, Mr Hart." Mama Bisha's tall figure stood framed in the office doorway, her eyes bright, like stars in a midnight sky. "How far did your fast track approach get you with our Ministry of Development?"

"Oh, hello Mama Bisha. I didn't see you there. I'm making progress, thank you. Though I do remember you saying you had a contact at the—"

"I know where your money is."

Of course she did. Those ice-cold eyes knew everything. She stepped into the room, closing the door behind her.

"Oh. Really? Well, any chance you could... give us a clue?"

"It is tied up in local government bureaucracy, Mr Hart." She picked up a neat pile of papers and tapped the edges against the countertop, ordering them even straighter.

"Any chance you could help, Mama Bisha? I'd be happy to make a small donation to your... hotel and health retreat."

"It will cost you more than half a case of beer and two bottles of wine, Mr Hart," she said, not bothering to look up from her paperwork.

"Right. I could buy you a new fridge, too? Your one doesn't work terribly well."

Mama Bisha lifted her gaze. "You are a development charity, yes? Working for upliftment in the townships?"

"Well, yes. That sort of thing."

"Then you will invest your money here. We are a black township business. You should be uplifting us."

"Ah, yes. I recall you alluding to something similar earlier this week. I'm sure we can find a way to compensate you adequately."

"No. Not a donation. You will partner with us. You will invest your money here at Mama Bisha's."

"Yes... that might be a little tricky. You see, there are certain criteria that must be met, in terms of the type of entity we can invest with. We have trustees, you see, who are quite strict on the optics of that type of thing. Transparency is key, you see. Transparency and governance, not to mention due diligence, and…"

My explanation petered out, partly because I had run out of corporate gobbledegook, partly because Mama Bisha's piercing glare was rather off-putting.

"You will find a way to make this work, Mr Hart. If you want to see your money."

"Yes, well, I'll make a couple of calls. See what we can do."

Mama Bisha continued to stare at me, her expression unchanged. Shooter began to whistle and spin the handles of the table football.

"Right then. I need to find a bed for the night. I would stay here but you don't take credit cards. Well, you take them, but you don't give them back."

"You can't stay. We are fully booked," said Shooter. "Saturday night." He gave one of the handles a vigorous spin. "Party night."

"Well, in that case, I'll be off. Do you mind if I use your toilet first?"

I took the general silence to mean I could.

"Thank you. I know where it is. I assume it's all up and running again after the, erm, accident?"

Avoiding McGregor's eye, I passed through the doorway to the dining room, walked down the short passage beyond and stepped through the rear security gate into the rubbish-strewn yard. Shading my eyes against the late afternoon sun, I picked my way through the debris, ducked between the sheets of bed linen rippling in the breeze, and approached the blue portable toilet, which had indeed been re-erected over the pit. A line of women and children, waiting to fill their pots and bottles at the standpipe, watched me tiptoe through the puddle surrounding the cubicle and step inside. Upon exiting, the seated youth called to me and extended his hand. I gave him a few coins, which he pocketed without a glance. Musing whether I had over-paid or not, I returned to the main building.

As I passed back through the dining room, I became aware of raised voices from reception. Not for the first time, I marvelled at how loudly the locals spoke to one another, as though every conversation was some kind of boasting match. To the uninitiated, even a casual conversation about the weather sounded as though a fight was about to break out.

"Don't be brave, big man!" shouted a voice.

I passed through the doorway and stopped. Three policemen stood in reception. In the centre of the room, a large black officer squared up to McGregor, whose eyes bulged with indignation. Mama Bisha stood beside them, like a referee, her arm on McGregor's shoulder, which I suspected was the only thing preventing McGregor from escalating the situation from a verbal joust into more of a contact sport. The second policeman, a smirking white man, leaned against the wall beside the front door, hands in pockets, while the third, who appeared to be of mixed race, stood with his back to me, just a couple of yards away. It struck me that the Khayelitsha police service appeared a most admirable model of racial integration.

"I said, don't be brave, big man!" shouted the black officer, again. I noticed he'd drawn a large truncheon, which, along with his entire arm, was vibrating with anger.

The white constable by the door suddenly caught sight of me. He stood up straight and his hands flew from his pockets. "Boss, boss, boss," he called, but the black officer was far too concerned with McGregor. The mixed-race policeman, though, following his white colleague's eyes, turned around and jumped in surprise. I noticed he was holding McGregor's bottle of Johnnie Walker.

"Sarge!" he shouted.

The black officer, who was indeed wearing three chevrons on each sleeve, snapped his head towards us. Upon seeing me, he literally leapt in the air, as though his truncheon had just administered a severe electric shock. His face switched from anger to utter astonishment.

"Who are you?" he demanded, looking from me to Mama Bisha, then back.

"Felix Hart, Department of International Development, attached to the British Consulate," I replied, striding towards him. "Delighted to meet you, officer."

I extended my hand and the sergeant, open-mouthed, raised his, before realising he was still holding his truncheon. We both stared at the baton for a second, then I grasped the end of it and gave it a polite shake.

"Good to see the forces of law and order are keeping Khayelitsha safe!" I declared.

"What... what are you doing here?"

"I'm working with your wonderful Ministry of Development, here in Cape Town," I replied. "We're funding a project. Very high profile. It would be good to see more of you and your fellow officers, actually. There will be lots of VIPs visiting soon."

"Do you... do you have ID?" said the sergeant, attempting to rearrange his features into a more law-enforcing expression.

"Of course!" I replied. "It's at the consulate in Cape Town. You can give me a lift back there, once I've finished. Unless you're busy, of course?" I glanced at his colleagues. "Actually, I'm glad you're here officers, you might be able to help me with something. I had my car stolen recently, while I was meeting the local Head of Sustainable Development. I'm sure you know all about it. It would be very useful to have an update."

"You can call the station, they will help," said the sergeant. He turned to the mixed-race constable. "Let's go."

The constable followed the sergeant towards the door. As he passed me, he glanced down at the bottle of Johnnie Walker he was holding. I held out my hand.

"That's my bottle actually. Though you're welcome to drop by for a drink when you're off duty."

The policeman ignored me and followed his colleagues outside.

As the front door stopped swinging, it occurred to me that the reception area was looking rather a mess. Papers and boxes littered the floor and Shooter stood in the corner, contemplating what appeared to be a dismembered chest of drawers. It was only when I spotted the spindles sticking out of the side that I realised it was the remnants of the table football.

"What happened here then?" I asked, joining Shooter before the sorry mess of splintered wood.

"Ah, they broke it," said Shooter, miserably. "Really broke it."

"The policemen?" I crouched and picked up the lower half of a goalkeeper. The game was utterly wrecked, every spindle either bent or broken, the remaining handles protruding from the woodwork at eccentric angles.

"Yes, they stamped on it."

I rose to my feet. "Well, that was a bit mean." The goalie's lower torso sat in my palm, a smooth U-shape running through the figure's chest where it had snapped clean off the spindle. I looked down to see if I could spot the man's upper half. A tiny drop of water splashed against the wood, near midfield, where a boot had punched through the pitch.

I glanced at Shooter and saw tears were running down his face.

"Oh dear," I said. "Look, don't worry. We can easily buy another one." I patted him lightly on the back.

"Yes, I will get another one," said Shooter, softly. "It doesn't matter."

"I'll look out for one in Cape Town. How about that?"

But Shooter just stared down at his wrecked game, the tears cascading over his cheeks. He wiped his chin and folded his arms.

I turned back to McGregor and handed him the dismembered goalkeeper. "Sorry about the Johnnie Walker." McGregor shrugged and walked over to Shooter. He placed a hand on his shoulder.

I was conscious of Mama Bisha's eyes on me.

"Hope you manage to clear up all the mess," I said. "We'll speak again soon, perhaps."

Mama Bisha nodded, just once.

"Yes, we shall."

Chapter 19

An Honourable Plan

I didn't feel like eating that evening. I retired to my room at the Uitsig Helderberg Guesthouse, my spirits rather low, and turned in for the night. The following morning, a courier arrived with my replacement credit cards, and I felt a sliver of my autonomy return. I'd have preferred to be spending someone else's money, of course, but given that my maintenance grant was tied up with Tears of Pity's missing funds, I would be obliged to pay my own way for now. I reserved another night at the guesthouse and, in an attempt to cheer myself up, booked a dinner table at one of the Cape's finest restaurants.

An hour before sunset, my taxi deposited me outside my destination, a famous winery on the hilly outskirts of Stellenbosch. I ascended the steps to the entrance and a door of black glass slid open, noiselessly. A blonde maître d' with a shining smile waved me through to the dining area. The view through the windows running the length of the room was sublime, the vineyards rolling into the distance like a swelling green sea, the mountains behind them glowing rust-red beneath the evening sun. Works of contemporary art lined the walls, beneath which the patrons whispered to one another over their meals, the hush pierced occasionally by the chime of cutlery against designer crockery. From the ceiling hung a great sculpture of multi-coloured glass serpents, each with a silver eye, which writhed around one another in frozen turmoil.

The food, of course, was magnificent, indisputably worthy of the constellation of gold stars that had been showered upon the restaurant by the world's great culinary guides. Delicate foams, infused with the essence of crustaceans teased from the Southern

Ocean. Medallions of antelope, cooked rare and dappled with reductions of black balsamic fruit. Confections of frozen cream, impaled by spikes of crystalline toffee and dusted with cinnamon. And, naturally, wines to complement every dish, livid with fruit, vanilla and spice, served at optimal temperature in razor-thin goblets. I ate every morsel and drank plenty, though the richness of the food gave me a thirst that the wine couldn't quench, and I finished each course increasingly parched and jaded.

As I drained my carafe of water, I considered the series of paintings suspended on the wall closest to my table. I've never claimed to be a great connoisseur of art, but I'm pretty sure I'm no philistine either. For every water lily and hay wain, there's a pile of soup tins and some old girl with her nose on the side of her face, and I'm happy to say I can recognise the merit in most of them. But, I confess, the daubs to which my attention had been drawn tested my powers of appreciation to the limit. For a start, they appeared to have been painted on strips of old, corrugated cardboard, perhaps ten feet tall by a couple wide, creased and curled up at the bottom. The subject of each canvas, or cardboard, was a pink-faced woman, head lolling to one side or the other, painted in bright, primary colours, in a style that could only be described as 'infant with attention deficit disorder'. Depending on the piece, the woman's limbs were variously flung up, down, or off to the side, while in one, the subject had thrust one arm down her top and another up her skirt. It was unclear, from her expression, whether the subject considered this a positive move or not, possibly insufficient time had passed to be sure. For a minute, I wondered whether the artwork really had been produced by a small child. Then I spotted the tiny white plaque beneath the central painting. I took a closer look. From the details, it was clear that not only was the artist not a child, but that they had advanced quite some way into middle age. The series was titled *Don't Judge Me*, and each piece was for sale, individually, for just over half a million rand.

I paid the bill, which was considerable, and returned to my guesthouse. Back in my room, I leaned over the bathroom sink and slurped noisily from the tap in an attempt to slake my thirst.

Then, I fell into a troubled sleep, where I dreamt I was dying of dehydration while queuing before the standpipe in Mama Bisha's yard, which gushed with delicious, sweet-smelling water. I reached the front of the line, my lips cracked and bleeding, only to find I had no receptacle in which to catch the liquid. I crouched and tried to place my lips against the stream, but my head had swollen so large that I couldn't fit it beneath the tap. The seated youth collecting the money began to shout at me, declaring that this was the most disgraceful behaviour he had seen in the township since the end of apartheid. Then, he beat the ground with a large stick and declared that I was permanently barred from drinking at his standpipe.

I awoke to the sound of the receptionist rapping on my door.

"It's midday, Mr Hart, and we need your room back. Can you come and pay your bill please?"

I showered, dressed and presented myself at the front desk. While the receptionist processed my payment, I scrolled through the past few days' emails. Lots of depressing directives from Herbert Marris, informing colleagues that the staff discount was to be discontinued, that they were forbidden from charging personal electronic devices at work, and that they had to bring their own cups to the office if they wished to drink company tap water. Gatesave didn't sound like the happiest ship to be sailing in, I must say.

"Thank you, Mr Hart. Your receipt."

It struck me that I had another, more meaningful transaction to make.

**

The doors of Cape Town's Provincial Treasury building slid open and Mama Bisha strode into the air-conditioned atrium, accompanied by a gust of warm street air. I rose to my feet. She wore a dark, high-necked dress, buttoned to the top, and looked as upright and respectable as the government's chief convent inspector.

"Good afternoon, Mama Bisha," I said. "Actually, we might have to go next door. When I was last here, they directed me round the corner to—"

"Our meeting is here," she said, catching the eye of the man behind reception. He rose and disappeared into a rear office. Within seconds, a door a few yards further down opened, and we were ushered into a meeting room, rather larger than the dismal office I'd experienced on my previous visit. A young African man rose to his feet and stepped out from behind his desk.

"Elliot. How nice to see you." Mama Bisha gave the man a chaste hug.

"All the arrangements have been made, Mama Bisha," said the young man. He indicated several sheets of paper arranged neatly upon the desk.

"Hello, I'm Felix Hart," I said, feeling a little left out. I extended a hand and the man shook it politely.

"Ah yes, you must be the minority business partner. Am I correct?"

He addressed the question to Mama Bisha and I was about to contradict him, but Mama Bisha said "Yes, that is correct. Mr Hart is our foreign minority partner." She turned to me. "Black Empowerment regulations stipulate that the local partner must own at least fifty-one percent of the business, as you know, Mr Hart."

I nodded and my mouth opened and closed a couple of times in confusion.

"The funds have been released to a government escrow account," explained the man. "Your joint venture has been incorporated and the paperwork for that is here... please sign here and here, Mr Hart, thank you very much, and here is the chequebook for the JV, under the name of Tears of Pity – rather a strange name, sir, but never mind. Both your signatures are required for any drawdown over five thousand rand. Here is the authorisation form for power of attorney by the bank over the escrow – sign here please, Mr Hart, thank you, and here again, very good, thank you, and date it here please, thank you. Here is the affidavit confirming your good faith regarding the source of funds, thank you, and initial here please, thank you, excellent. Well, that's most of the paperwork dealt with. We just need to photocopy your passport."

I wondered whether I should have employed a lawyer of my own to double check everything, but it all looked fairly kosher, what with the marble-clad atrium and the man's brisk efficiency, so I let it go.

"Here are two debit cards and a credit card for the JV bank account," said the man. Mama Bisha snatched them up and placed them in her handbag. I scanned the desk for the chequebook but it was nowhere to be seen. I suspected it had found its way to the same place as the cards.

"Thank you, Elliot," said Mama Bisha. The man smiled and began to consolidate the paperwork.

"Right. I suppose that means we're in business," I said.

"Yes," said Mama Bisha. "And now, we shall sign some cheques."

A township minibus sat idling outside the Provincial Treasury building and, as Mama Bisha stepped into the front passenger seat, I realised it was for our own private use. It felt quite a luxury being able to stretch out on the back seat, instead of sharing the vehicle with a dozen soiled gardeners, paint-splattered handymen and stout housewives wrestling with vast bags of shopping.

Half an hour later, the taxi left the N2 highway and headed into the heart of the township. To my surprise, the vehicle didn't stop beside the red *spaza* kiosk but continued another hundred yards or so before turning left, then left again, down a bumpy, litter-strewn track, the shacks pressing in close either side. I spotted a simple bridge ahead, over a narrow gully filled with reeds, and I realised it was the back entrance into the waste ground behind Mama Bisha's guesthouse. I recalled the bridge had previously been blocked with car tyres and barbed wire, but these had now disappeared. A flat-bed truck sat in the middle of the waste ground, a shiny white shipping container dangling from its arm crane. Slowly, the container was set down next to two more already in situ.

"What's all this?" I said.

"We are expanding," said Mama Bisha. "Six more rooms."

And so, Mama Bisha and I jointly signed our first Tears of Pity cheque, made payable to Western Cape Shipping Containers Pty Ltd. That was followed by a second, to Stellenbosch Bedroom Furniture Supplies, and a third, to Bellville Kitchen Fitters. An hour later, I was summoned to sign half-a-dozen more, for timber merchants, electrical appliance wholesalers, septic tank installers and linen cleaning contractors. For the rest of the day, a series of goods vehicles nosed their way into the patch of waste ground and unloaded their wares, supervised by McGregor, who now commanded a platoon of young workmen, sawing, hammering and drilling before a crowd of curious neighbours.

I retreated from the hubbub to the privacy of room number one, its damaged roof and faded décor looking rather sad in comparison with the newer sections of Mama Bisha's cash-fuelled refit. I lay on the bed and drew out my phone to check my emails, reflecting that all this industry provided a stark contrast with my own efforts over the past week, which even the kindest critic might describe as somewhat wanting.

I was pleased to see a note from Foyley saying he'd been contacted by Gambu's winery and asking me to confirm they were a legitimate new supplier. I replied, confirming they were, and was considering phoning him, to plead with him once more to do something about my lamentable accommodation situation, when I was interrupted by an incoming call.

"Good morning, Mr Hart. It's Mr Sonn from the Fairly Trod Foundation. We appear to have a little issue with your supplier, Blanchkopf Wine Growers."

"Oh, yes. I think I know what you mean. I meant to call you last week."

"Mr Blanchkopf appears unwilling to engage with our inspectors, Mr Hart. It seems he doesn't share your appetite to make the journey to Fairly Trod status."

"No. I'm going to have to work on it."

"Yes, indeed. It's just that I do recall you said you wanted to move quickly."

"I did say that, yes. I'm sorry. You'll just have to give me a little longer."

"I also received a call, this morning, from a Scandinavian NGO."

My blood froze. "Oh?" I squeaked.

"Yes, they were asking questions about Blanchkopf Wine Growers and whether they had obtained Fairly Trod status. Someone certainly appears to have given them that impression. They were quite assertive with their questioning. They mentioned both Gatesave and your own name."

"Argh," I croaked.

"We're usually quite transparent about that kind of thing but I thought I should check with you first before we answered their questions. Especially given Mr Blanchkopf's apparent resistance towards the whole thing. We're very anxious to make this all work, you see. The last thing we want is any embarrassment. You do understand my position?"

I recalled the Head of Message's warning that failure was likely to lead to my arrest and incarceration on charges of modern slavery. If I was forced to flee from the authorities, which seemed increasingly likely, my only options would be to hitch-hike in disguise to Mozambique, hide in a cave in the mountains of Lesotho, or cling to the undercarriage of a Europe-bound jumbo jet. Mind you, even if I made it back to the UK, I'd still be fired on the spot by Gatesave, and no doubt there'd be an international arrest warrant hanging over me until the end of my days. Perhaps I could stow away on a freighter bound for Buenos Aires and make a new life in Argentina. They were pretty lax towards war criminals and other undesirables over there, I'd heard. Though, of course, they might have tightened things up a bit recently.

"Mr Hart? Are you there?"

"Yes. Yes. I'm here, unfortunately."

"Look, Mr Hart. Please don't think I'm trying to teach you your job. But it's not uncommon for suppliers to need a bit of a

184

nudge when it comes to gaining Fairly Trod certification. There is quite an investment required."

"A bit of a nudge, yes. I'll be sure to try that."

"Well, a bit more than a nudge, perhaps. I don't mean to speak out of turn, but you might need to give them a good push. Turn the screws a little."

"Turn the screws?"

"Yes, you know. You're a big supermarket. You're the customer. I'm not suggesting you go in too heavy or anything. But you might need to give them a kick in the pants, if you'll excuse the expression. A big, hard kick in the you-know-whats." Sonn gave an apologetic laugh.

"Yes, you're probably right."

"Exactly! You're a big buyer, you know what I mean. Don't let him get away with it. He needs you more than you need him. Put your foot on his throat. If he doesn't budge, threaten to shut the bastard down!"

It suddenly dawned on me that Sonn was rather committed to the cause of social justice.

"Look, Mr Sonn, I'll see what I can do, I promise. It's not as if I can just round up a mob and blockade his property."

"Oh, no, no, no, forgive me Mr Hart, I'm not suggesting that at all!" cried Sonn. "I meant metaphorically, of course! I just want this to work out for all parties. These NGOs can really dig their claws in, you see, and people can become terribly worked up about this type of thing..."

But I was no longer listening to Sonn. It had just occurred to me that a mob was exactly what I needed. And I knew just the man to ask.

*****

"So, Mr Hart," boomed Gambu, clapping me on the back and leaving me slightly winded, "your head office has confirmed we are now set up as a Gatesave supplier."

"Yes, they're quite efficient when they want to be."

Gambu eased himself into his enormous office chair and removed the box file from his desk drawer.

"This is a great step forward for your company, Mr Hart. You are doing the right thing by people of colour, at last."

"Gatesave are delighted to be playing their part in the upliftment of Africa."

"And to think that Hemelhuis, the very belly of the beast of white monopoly capital, are begging to supply us with wine!"

"Well, you were kind enough to stop picketing their estate, for which they were very grateful. I think your angry dancing men were rather scaring off the tourists. I'm not sure these multi-nationals are quite as bad as you make out, you know."

"Oh, they are bad, believe me, Mr Hart. They only respond to violence, or threats of violence. That is because, just beneath the surface, they are machines of violence themselves. It is literally the only language they understand."

Gambu removed his huge beret and placed it at the side of the desk.

"Anyway, to business. We must confirm which of our labels you wish to use." He opened the box file.

"The Black Power Pinotage, definitely," I said, giving the label a little stroke. "Hemelhuis can supply a delicious Pinotage blend, ready for you to bottle."

"We have another label, called Reparations Red. Why not take that one too?"

"Sounds good, but I think we've already got red wine covered with the Pinotage. We need a white to complement it."

Gambu grunted. "These brands are wines of power, of intensity. My vision is that they should all be reds. Deep, dark reds, from the blackest grapes."

"Yes, I see where you're coming from. But fifty percent of sales in the UK are white wine. Pinot Grigio, Sauvignon Blanc, Chardonnay. You risk half the market missing your message if you only sell reds."

"Then take the Sauvignon Blanc," said Gambu, pointing to the green label sporting his beret-crowned silhouette.

"It… doesn't deliver quite the same message," I said, carefully. "We need a white equivalent of the Black Power Pinotage."

Gambu frowned.

"I don't mean White Power, obviously," I said, hastily. "I mean something… enlightened. Liberated."

"Woke," said Gambu.

"Woke White!" I shouted, rather startling Gambu. He scowled and I raised my hands. "Apologies. I became momentarily over-excited."

"Woke White?" Gambu screwed up his face. "I'm not interested in wishy-washy, hand-wringing liberals hitching their wagon to my proud, African brand."

"Hand-wringing liberals are a huge growth market, Mr Gambu. Can I suggest a lightweight blend? Riesling and Chenin Blanc, perhaps? Don't put Riesling on the label though, it might put people off. Too Germanic. Use the same raised fist design as the Black Power Pinotage, but in a different colour."

"That is not my vision for the brand."

"Please, Mr Gambu. I promise it will be a great success. If you need to set people straight on your brand values, you can do it via social media."

Gambu had over a hundred thousand Twitter followers. I'd scrolled through his feed, most of which was selfies of him demonstrating in beret and revolutionary t-shirt, fist raised skywards, interspersed with quotes from Ho Chi Minh, praise for the Venezuelan government, and occasional retweets from the account of Oxford United F.C.

"Very well. I shall make clear that any white people claiming affinity with the brand are parasites, appropriating black-owned culture."

"That should do the trick," I said.

Gambu rubbed his chin and stared at me. "Are you quite sure about all this? Most of your customers are white. They will take offence, surely?"

"No, I don't think so. They'll love it. You'll have white people competing to be the most woke."

"Interesting. The more I condemn the white man, the more they embrace my cause."

"White privilege is extremely resilient, Mr Gambu."

Gambu narrowed his eyes, then shrugged. "Very well, local market insight is your job, I suppose. We will try it." He shut the box file, replaced his beret and smoothed it into shape over his huge dome. "Now, I must go. I have to meet some squatter activists in Stellenbosch."

"Oh, there was one other thing I was hoping you could advise me on," I said.

Gambu waved me aside and marched to the door. "I don't have time. Ask yourself what Malcolm X would do."

"I would, but it's quite specific to the local viticultural scene," I said, dashing after him. "So, you're probably better placed than Malcolm X."

I trotted behind Gambu as he strode to the pickup, fumbling for my shades in the midday sun. A cadre snapped to attention and opened the rear door.

"It's about Blanchkopf Wine Growers."

Gambu paused and placed his hands on the vehicle's roof, his back to me. "What about him?"

"Well, we're trying to persuade him to improve his workers' pay and conditions. Convert the estate to Fairly Trod status."

Gambu turned and looked down at me. "I must say, your employer appears to be on quite a mission to subvert traditional capitalist orthodoxy. Why would you bother to do that?"

"We think that better-paid workers make more productive workers," I replied, weakly.

Gambu snorted. "And why should I concern myself with your commercial problems, Mr Hart? Problems, it is fair to say, entirely caused by your involvement with the most disgusting and exploitative end of the wine supply chain!"

"Well, I hope you don't mind me asking, but I wondered whether you could do a little demonstration down there, or something. At Blanchkopf's winery. I understand you've done so in the past."

Gambu's face darkened. "How dare you! You presume I'm your private mercenary army, to be deployed at the whim of your white monopoly capital masters when the natives are misbehaving?" Gambu climbed inside the pickup. "How impertinent! You disgust me, white man!"

The cadre moved to shut the door, but I leapt forward and prevented it from closing.

"Move away from The General," shouted the cadre, placing a hand on my shoulder. I shrugged him off and leaned inside the pickup. Gambu turned his head away and gazed out of the window.

"The trouble is, Mr Gambu, my employer is refusing to let me ship any more wine from anyone in South Africa until I have resolved this problem with Blanchkopf. So, I won't be able to progress our project with you and Hemelhuis until I've sorted it out. And Mr Blanchkopf is being very intransigent."

The cadre had now taken hold of my arm and was attempting to drag me away from the vehicle. I grabbed the inside roof handle with my free hand and clung on.

"Please, Mr Gambu, just a little demo," I gabbled, desperately, "nothing too severe. I don't want the place burnt down, or anyone murdered. Just tell Blanchkopf's workers that they won't receive their promised pay rise if Blanchkopf doesn't convert the estate to Fairly Trod status."

Gambu turned to me and smoothed his beret. "You had better not let me down, Mr Hart."

By now the driver had jumped out and dashed around the vehicle to join his colleague. After a couple more seconds of wrestling, the two men succeeded in wrenching my grip from the roof handle, whereupon they hurled me into the dirt.

"Thank you very much, Mr Gambu," I called, as the pickup roared away, enveloping me in a cloud of dust.

Chapter 20

Swindon Town

I awoke to the sound of hammering and the revving of an engine. I considered phoning reception and asking exactly how this racket fitted the description of a luxury guesthouse on the edge of paradise, then I realised that bright, early morning light was streaming through the gap between the wall and the corrugated metal ceiling. I realised where I was and, to my astonishment, felt my spirits rise.

I dragged open the bedroom door and headed to the dining room. It had been completely stripped of its decrepit furniture, except for a single bench on which sat four workmen wolfing down bowls of maize porridge. A large pot of the same sputtered away in the corner atop a gas stove. Realising I was ravenous, I served myself a bowl, stirred in some sugar, and gobbled it down. Feeling a little stronger, I proceeded to reception, which had also been stripped of its broken fixtures and was looking markedly brighter. Two men stood balanced on a scaffolding platform installing a new skylight, supervised by Shooter.

"We are getting a new football table, *mlungu*," beamed Shooter.

"That is excellent news."

Imbued with a sense of positivity and righteousness, I decided to call Blanchkopf and appeal to his fiercely hidden sense of fairness regarding the upliftment of his workforce. I brought up the number and took a deep breath. At first, I thought one of Blanchkopf's dogs had answered. There was a chorus of barking and howling, accompanied by jeering, crashing and the bizarre sound of an African male choir singing a nursery rhyme.

"Hello?" I said.

"*Wie is dit?*" shouted Blanchkopf.

"It's me, Mr Blanchkopf. Felix Hart, from Gatesave. What's going on over there?"

"We are under attack, man. It is the Africans! They have finally come for us. But we will die defending ourselves, I swear it!"

There was the sound of smashing glass and a man screaming.

"Goodness me, it sounds rather fraught over there. Is there anything I can do?"

"*Ja*! Bite his *bollokke* off!" shouted Blanchkopf.

"Are you addressing me or one of your dogs, Mr Blanchkopf?"

"I am addressing my wife!"

"Right. Sounds like she's getting stuck in."

"It is Gambu's gang. Communists! They are causing trouble with my workers. They have forced them out on strike, damn them."

Bless you, Gambu, you Marxist lunatic, I thought. You've come through for me.

"Oh dear. Does that mean you're unable to supply us with wine?"

Blanchkopf remained silent. In the background, men jeered and dogs howled.

"Mr Blanchkopf? I had a call from the Fairly Trod Foundation yesterday. They said the Scandinavian NGO had been in touch and was asking questions."

"What questions?"

"The NGO were asking whether Blanchkopf Wine Growers intended to achieve Fairly Trod status. The Foundation told them that you were originally, but now you'd changed your mind. Which means the workers wouldn't be receiving their wage increase."

"That is not true! You have committed to the price increase!"

"Yes, clearly the Fairly Trod people have got the wrong end of the stick, which is very frustrating. It sounds like the NGO is going to embarrass us all, despite our efforts to do the right thing. Unfortunately, that means the whole deal's off."

"Hart, you cannot back out of our deal! I have it in writing!"

"But with no workers, you have no wine. Failure to supply is a breach of contract, Mr Blanchkopf. Well, this is all very disappointing. I will have to find a new source of wine for our venture with Hemelhuis. I don't suppose you could recommend anyone?"

Blanchkopf shouted a series of earthy words in both English and Afrikaans.

"The thing is, Mr Blanchkopf, if you hadn't retreated from our agreement to convert to Fairly Trod status, none of this would have happened."

Blanchkopf didn't reply.

"It may not be too late, of course. Though I understand your wife was very clear she'd made her mind up."

There was a strangled growl. I wondered whether Blanchkopf had handed the phone to one of his dogs.

"Mr Blanchkopf? Are you all right? I'm in the neighbourhood, as it happens. Perhaps I could pop over and try to straighten all this out? I could speak to this Gambu person and assure them of our joint commitment to Fairly Trod principles."

There was a further period of silence.

"Mr Blanchkopf? Are you there?"

"We will probably be dead by the time you arrive."

"Well, try to hold on, I won't be long."

As I stuffed my phone back in my pocket, I realised Mama Bisha was observing me from the doorway of her office.

"Mama Bisha, I need to use your driver please. Urgent business, to do with the charity."

Mama Bisha considered my request. "You have one hour."

"Thank you!" I called, as I dashed back through the dining room and out of the back door, skipping over the row of sandbags. The minibus was parked next to the gully, the driver dozing in the front seat.

"Stellenbosch please, my man," I said, leaping in beside him. "Top speed."

We tore out of the township, joined the N2, then took the junction north to Stellenbosch. A few minutes later, I pointed out the turnoff for Blanchkopf Wine Growers. A dozen serious-looking men in blue overalls and red t-shirts, sporting the yellow hammer, sickle and grapes of Gambu's Black Soil Movement, stood guard at the turnoff. Two trucks, which looked as though they'd been refused entry to the estate, were parked on the opposite side of the road. I climbed into the rear and lay on the floor, squeezing myself beneath the first row of passenger seats.

"Keep going as far as you can up the drive," I called. "Say you're here for The General."

The driver pulled up next to Gambu's cadres and they exchanged a few words of Xhosa. I heard the crunch of rubber boots against gravel as the men walked around the vehicle, but I was well concealed. The taxi bumped onto Blanchkopf's long drive and trundled towards the farmhouse. I wriggled out from under the seats and re-joined the driver in the front.

"But they will see you, *mlungu*," said the driver.

"Don't worry. I'm good friends with The General."

Still, I kept my head down as we approached the main group of demonstrators at Blanchkopf's gate. Unlike the tall, razor wire-topped entrance to Hemelhuis's estate, Blanchkopf's wooden gate was a mere five feet high, but no-one had attempted to gain entry. The reason for this became clear as I slipped from the taxi and crept closer. Blanchkopf's dogs were in paroxysms of rage, the Rottweiler leaping into the air and snapping at anyone who came close, while the Boerboel had thrust half its body through a gap in the gate and was chewing its way through one of the wooden braces.

Gambu stood a few yards from the gate, megaphone in hand, surrounded by his berserkers in their paddy-farmer hats.

"Fair trade or no trade!" he shouted.

"Fair trade or no trade!" shouted the crowd.

I realised I'd been spotted.

"Hey, *mlungu*!" shouted a man. "Who are you?" He began to approach me, somewhat aggressively, but a colleague, one of the berserkers, caught his arm and whispered something into his ear. The man stepped back. But I'd been brought to the crowd's attention and they turned to watch.

I jogged back to the taxi. "I need you to move towards the gate, please. I'm climbing on top." I placed a foot on the passenger seat and pulled myself on to the taxi's roof.

"Hey, what you doing?" shouted the driver.

I knelt down and knocked on the windscreen. "I need to be high up, so they can see me. Drive forward, please."

The driver did as I asked. I stayed kneeling, keeping a tight grip on the ridge at the front of the roof, until the vehicle's grille was within a few inches of the gate. The Boerboel howled with rage and transferred its jaws from the wooden brace to the taxi's Toyota badge.

"Ahoy, Mr Blanchkopf," I called.

A khaki-clad figure wearing a bush hat leapt from the farmhouse door, shotgun in hand. Blanchkopf was clearly prepared for total war, his face streaked with camouflage paint and the front pockets of his flak jacket bulging with ammunition.

"It's only me, Mr Blanchkopf," I said, waving my arms. The figure raised the weapon and aimed it. The realisation that he intended to shoot, and that the flak jacket wasn't bulging with ammunition but with a heaving bosom, struck me at approximately the same time. I dropped flat on the taxi's roof as the shotgun discharged and lead pellets tore through the overhanging leaves.

"Mrs Blanchkopf, cease fire!" I screamed. "I'm white, for God's sake!"

"You brought these people here!" she shouted.

"Don't be ridiculous!" I called. "Do they look like the kind of people I would associate with?"

"You see!" boomed Gambu, through his megaphone, "the white man's solidarity fractures in the face of our resistance!"

It's the white woman's solidarity I'm more worried about, I thought, as I slowly raised my head from the minibus roof. Mrs

Blanchkopf reloaded her shotgun. I cupped my hands around my mouth, so I could be heard over the jeering crowd.

"If you shoot me, Mrs Blanchkopf, my employer will consider it a breach of contract," I called.

"Get these people away from our farm," she yelled.

"Where is Mr Blanchkopf? Have you shot him?"

"I am here," boomed Blanchkopf, emerging from the farmhouse with his elephant gun. The crowd suddenly quietened, and a few people ducked or took cover behind nearby trees.

"I'm sure there's no need for heavy artillery, Mr Blanchkopf. We don't want a massacre, do we?"

It was worryingly unclear from Blanchkopf's expression whether he was pro- or anti- massacre.

"Why are you lying on the roof of that township taxi?" he said, shading his eyes.

"I'm sheltering from your wife. Please will you allow me to negotiate with the gentlemen besieging your estate?"

There was no response. Keeping a wary eye on the Blanchkopfs, I stood up on the taxi's roof.

"We capitulate unconditionally to your demands," I called to Gambu over the crowd. "I can confirm this estate will convert to Fairly Trod status by the end of the week."

"And you will triple the pay of your workers," called Gambu, through the megaphone. The crowd cheered.

"I think you mean double," I called, my bowels twitching in alarm.

"No, I mean triple. For centuries this estate has oppressed its workers. Now they shall be the best-paid grape pickers in the Cape, thanks to the struggle spearheaded by the Black Soil Movement!"

The crowd cheered again. Even from a distance of fifty yards, I could see the Blanchkopfs scowling. And, rather unfairly, it appeared to be in my direction.

"Very well," I called. "But I must confirm this agreement in writing with the owners. Can you let us through please, gentlemen?"

Gambu waved his arm and his followers fell back. After a few seconds, the gate began to open. Realising that the dogs were no longer penned inside the yard, a buzz of apprehension rose from the crowd. I decided to remain firmly on top of the minibus. I lay on my belly and knocked on the windscreen.

"Forward driver, please. And slowly."

The taxi crept into the yard, the Rottweiler leaping up at the driver's window and the Boerboel gurgling with fury as it attempted to complete the separation of the Toyota badge from the front grille. We came to a stop in front of the Blanchkopfs, the wife scowling through her camouflage paint-streaked face, finger on the trigger of her shotgun, while her husband grimaced through his beard, his knuckles white as he clenched the barrel of his elephant gun, the weapon's butt between his feet and the muzzle pointed skywards, as if he were about to begin an angry pole dance.

"Good morning, Mr and Mrs Blanchkopf. Please would you lock up your animals and weapons, then we can get down to business."

Once Blanchkopf had cajoled the dogs into a stable and secured the door, I clambered down from the taxi's roof.

"Now, I really do need you to promise, this time, that you're committed to achieving Fairly Trod certification. The inspector is due to visit the day after tomorrow. Everything rides on their evaluation."

"This whole thing does not sit well in my pants," sulked Blanchkopf.

"And you have agreed yet another idiotic price increase!" cried Mrs Blanchkopf.

"Well, that only happened because you told the Fairly Trod Foundation to get lost," I said. "It's either another price increase or no money at all. That Gambu person has your workers out on strike."

"They know he lies but they are scared of him," growled Blanchkopf. "They would be perfectly happy if he was not here."

"Well, he is here," I replied. "So, let's get that salary increase and the agreement to meet Fairly Trod standards down in writing, shall we? He won't go until you do."

A nursery rhyme, voiced by an African revolutionary male choir, floated from beyond the gate.

Swindon Town is falling down, falling down, falling down!

"Listen to them!" hissed Blanchkopf. "It's the Swellendam song. They want to push us out of our own country!"

"Are you sure that's what they're saying?"

"Of course it is! Swellendam is falling down! Listen!"

Swindon Town is falling down, goodbye Swindon!

"They know Swellendam has historical significance to our culture," said Mrs Blanchkopf, shaking her head, "and those savages want to destroy it!"

"I'm pretty sure they're just winding you up," I said. "Anyway, the sooner we reach an agreement, the sooner they'll go."

Blanchkopf took his elephant gun inside, hung it over the fireplace, and sat down at his typewriter. Tongue between teeth, and with a single forefinger, he spent ten minutes banging out a declaration committing to Fairly Trod principles and further increasing the salary of his workers. He handed me the sheet with a scowl and I dashed to the gate, where Gambu snatched it from me, read it silently, then held it above his head.

"Victory! Dignity! Solidarity!" he boomed, and the crowd cheered.

"Right, well, thank you very much for your cooperation," I began, but Gambu had already turned away and was striding towards his pickup, surrounded by a ring of cadres.

"Yes, victory!" called a demonstrator standing nearby. He grinned at me triumphantly and shook his fist in the air.

It's a start, old bean, I thought. I nodded to him, gave a grim smile, and raised my own fist in solidarity. The man's grin faded and he stared at me as if I were mad.

Chapter 21

Lubrication

"By George, Felix, you did it!" sang Troy Frittersley down the phone.

"Oh, it was quite straightforward in the end," I replied. "Just needed a little perseverance."

"To be honest, I was worried we'd lost Gatesave's donation. My fellow trustees were kicking up a bit of a stink. Lots of talk of weak governance, even corruption."

"It's important not to make cultural assumptions," I said.

"Quite so, Felix, quite so. And tell me more about this project you have identified in Khayelitsha."

"Well, it's a kind of community hub," I said, moving my legs aside to make way for a pair of workmen delivering a brand-new football table.

"Sounds wonderfully promising! Tell me, do they have literacy classes, music, life skills, that type of thing?"

Another pair of workmen edged past, struggling under the weight of a pink-painted bed frame.

"There's a strong emphasis on health education," I said.

"Of course, that's very important," agreed Frittersley. "Now, Felix, I'm going to need all sorts of boring paperwork from you, I'm afraid. Our trustees have become terribly strict about that sort of thing after our little scare with the original grant. They won't release any more funds until we've seen evidence of the project. They want to arrange a visit by a third-party auditing body."

"Oh dear," I said, my heart sinking. "Do we have to? It will only slow us down."

"I'm afraid so Felix, I do apologise. I can imagine how frustrating it must be when you just want to get stuck in and start doing some good."

"Exactly," I said, miserably.

"Hey, *mlungu*, stop the chat, Mama Bisha wants you," called Shooter, next to my ear.

"Yes, all right, Shooter, thank you," I said, clapping my hand over the phone.

"Sorry, I didn't quite catch that, Felix," said Frittersley.

"Oh, that was one of the doctors. The matron wants to see me about medical supplies."

"Goodness, of course, and here's me taking up your time with idle talk! You must get on. I'll be in touch. And if you could email a few pictures, that would be very useful. The trustees are dying to see the project."

"Will do, Troy. Cheerio."

The door to Mama Bisha's office was slightly ajar, but before I reached it she stepped out and closed it behind her.

"Further works are required," she said, pointing at four cheques on the countertop, awaiting my signature.

"Who's the lucky recipient of our latest spending spree, then?" I asked. "A prophylactic manufacturing plant? A Malaysian rubber plantation?"

"We need to improve the sanitary facilities," replied Mama Bisha, her bright, unsmiling eyes focussed on mine. "The drainage is unsatisfactory."

"Yes, I imagine there might be an awkward queue outside that portable toilet once you've filled your new rooms."

"Sign the cheques please."

"I was wondering when I might receive my allowance," I said. "I'm supposed to receive a salary from that charitable grant you're plundering."

"You have free accommodation and food."

Mama Bisha had indeed granted me the use of bedroom number one, scene of my abortive threesome the previous week.

I'd made use of it for two nights now, having no other option or source of funds, and last night I'd managed a reasonably uninterrupted night's sleep, despite the ceiling having a somewhat semi-detached relationship with the rest of the building.

"Yes, the kitchen staff know how to cook up a good stew, no complaints there. But a little pocket money wouldn't go astray. I was hoping you might lend me one of those credit cards, given that I helped set it all up."

"I am not convinced you will use it responsibly."

"Don't be ridiculous!" I said. "Of course I'll use it responsibly. I'm not some reckless spendthrift!"

Mama Bisha raised her eyebrows. I paused, musing that this wasn't entirely true. No matter, it was the principle of the thing.

"Look," I said. "I really need an allowance. I have to travel into Stellenbosch, for a start. I have business there, connected with the charity."

"All our expenditure must be accounted for by your people in London, Mr Hart. Am I correct?"

"Possibly," I said, shrugging.

"Definitely, I would say. Your charity does not trust us. They will check every rand we spend. That is why I have kept all the receipts." Mama Bisha tapped her middle finger, just once, on a thick pile of invoices held together by a bulldog clip. "If you travel down to Somerset West and spend a thousand rand on a rich man's meal at Waterkloof, your charity will cut off any further funding."

"Don't worry about it. You can leave me to handle all that."

"Like you handled the missing money at the Ministry of Development?"

I reddened slightly. "I'm not entirely incompetent, Mama Bisha."

"I did not say you were. I just said you must work for your money. Because then we can account for the expenditure. We can put it through the books as an employee's salary."

"Oh, I see. Well, I hope you're not expecting me to clean the toilets."

"No, you're not qualified."

"My thoughts exactly."

"We want you to work front of house."

"What, like a bouncer?"

"No, Mr Hart. Our security is taken care of. I want you to run the bar."

"Mama Bisha, that's a job I can do! I accept."

I signed the cheques and Mama Bisha handed me the credit card. As I grasped it, she held it tight for an extra second, raised her head and fixed me with those cold, bright eyes.

"Remember, we must account for all expenditure."

I nodded, dashed to the minibus taxi and directed the driver to an upmarket wine merchant in Stellenbosch. I ordered a dozen cases of beer, a selection of fine spirits, including a bottle of Johnnie Walker Blue Label, and a couple of litres of Amarula liqueur. Then, I set to work on the wine list, for I was determined that Mama Bisha's guesthouse should be as respected for its beverage selection as for its wider menu of delights. The ecstatic manager scurried back and forth from his stockroom, bringing piles of empty boxes, while I skipped around the store, plucking bottles from the shelves and filling the cases as fast as he could supply them. Pinot Noirs from Elgin, Chenins from Swartland, Syrahs from Tulbagh, Chardonnays from Hermanus. Hefty reds from the venerable estates of Stellenbosch, delicate whites from the cloud-kissed slopes of Constantia. Treacle-scented tawnies from the baking soils of Calitzdorp, ethereal fizzes conjured by the Cape's finest alchemists. In short, a wine list fit for an African emperor.

"That should do it," I said, nodding approvingly at the sea of boxes scattered around the store.

The manager directed an idle-looking assistant to pile up the cases next to the counter, then began ringing the wines through the till. While he was doing so, my attention was caught by an unusually labelled bottle on a high shelf in the corner. I walked over for a closer look. To my astonishment, the label sported an illustration of a roasted, grinning sheep's head, complete with bulging eyes.

"What's that?" I called, pointing up at the bottle.

"Oh, the Smiley Red. It's new. Made by one of the cool young guns up in the Swartland. It's artisanal, small batch stuff. Pretty funky. I like it but it's not to everyone's taste. Upsets the traditionalists."

"Does it go well with smiley? You know, an actual sheep's head?"

"I wouldn't know. I've never tried sheep's head. That's more of a township thing. But the wine is superb."

"I'll take two cases."

I stood on tiptoes and lifted down the remaining bottles. The manager put them through the till then continued with the rest of my purchases. When he'd rung through the final case, he clapped his hands together and rubbed them.

"Could you write out the invoice to say 'tonic water and ice' please?" I asked.

The man peered at the till screen. "That's a hell of a lot of tonic water."

"I'm buying for a health retreat. They're all very dehydrated."

The man gave a confused shrug and did as I asked. I was mildly alarmed when I saw the amount totalled forty-eight thousand rand, but I put it out of my mind and handed over the credit card with a nonchalant flourish. The card machine pondered deeply for a full minute, while patches of nervous sweat bloomed beneath my armpits. Then, it gave a merry chirp and a receipt spewed from the slit on top, spooling into a thick roll as the till itemised my loot.

"Would you like to open a business account, sir? We offer free delivery."

I completed the paperwork while the manager ordered the shop assistant to load my purchases into the taxi. Several dozen heavily laden and resentful trips later, the minibus was full. The manager looked over my completed form and his eyes widened.

"Your business is in Khayelitsha?"

"Yes, that's right."

"We don't deliver there. It's not safe."

"Good job we have our own transport then, isn't it?"

"Mama Bisha's. What kind of place is that? I haven't heard of it."

"It's amazing. I'd describe it as a kind of community hub-cum-guesthouse-cum-social club. Pretty famous locally."

"Is it?" He peered at the form. "There's no address. It just says T2-V2. Is that a place?"

"Yes. It's very up and coming."

"Well, you've got some great wines. Perhaps I should visit."

"You must! They've just had a refit. New investors. Big cash injection."

"I'll think about it."

"Please do. And spread the word. We've just been nominated for shebeen of the year. Anyway, great doing business with you. I'll be back soon. It won't take long to get through that little lot. They're a thirsty crowd in Khayelitsha."

The manager pumped my hand and waved us off. We drove at a sedate pace back to the township, the driver making a concerted effort to ensure the towers of wine piled jauntily upon every seat didn't topple over. We drew up outside the back of Mama Bisha's just as Shooter was emerging from the back gate. He spotted the piled-up boxes of liquor and pointed in delight.

"*Mlungu* Moses! How much wine did you buy?"

"Enough to get us off to a running start," I replied.

"You buy too much!" he grinned, shaking his head. "Mama Bisha will not be happy."

"I am Head Sommelier and Mama Bisha has given me full purchasing authority for the bar," I replied. "She'll be fine."

But Mama Bisha was not at all fine. I had carried roughly half the wine from the taxi to the newly furnished restaurant area and was working out where best to install a floor-to-ceiling wine rack when I became conscious of a tall, cold presence at the doorway.

"Ah, hello Mama Bisha. I propose we install a bar just here, to complement the new dining room furniture."

Mama Bisha considered the wall of wine boxes, which had already formed an impressively sized bar of their own, then turned her shining eyes upon me.

"So, I was right. You cannot be trusted with our money."

"This is an investment! You can't attract high quality punters without a good wine list."

"How much did this cost?"

"Less than you'd think, actually. The manager gave me a ten percent bulk discount."

Mama Bisha stepped towards me, her arm outstretched, palm upwards. Clearly, I had breached my credit limit.

"I asked, how much did this cost?"

"Forty-eight thousand rand," I said, breezily. I heard a snort of disbelief from just beyond the doorway and spotted a large figure watching me from reception. "Oh, hello McGregor," I called. "I've brought you a replacement bottle of Johnnie Walker."

But McGregor didn't reply. In fact, he was looking alarmingly stern.

"We needed that money for the drainage work," said Mama Bisha, her eyes boring into me.

"Drainage? That's a bit dull. We can't have spent all the money already."

"It is all accounted for." She considered the wall of wine once more. "You will return this tomorrow."

"But Mama Bisha!"

"The card."

I realised Mama Bisha's hand was still outstretched. With a heavy heart, I held out the Tears of Pity credit card. She snatched it from my hand.

"Our customers drink beer and whisky. Not wine. Do not make any more mistakes like this."

She turned and returned to reception. McGregor stared at me for a few seconds more, in a somewhat unfriendly manner, then pushed the door closed, leaving me alone once more with the finest wine selection ever assembled south of the Limpopo.

Chapter 22

Healing Hands

"Hey, *mlungu*!" whispered Shooter, poking his head from the rear passageway. "You must unload the taxi. We want it for shopping. Quickly."

I trudged outside and began transferring the remaining wine to the dining room, thoroughly depressed by the thought of having to load it all up again the following day.

"Ah, you did buy too much wine, *mlungu*. I told you!"

"Where are you going in the taxi?"

"We buy things for the ladies," beamed Shooter. "Nice clothes." He gestured towards the row of white shipping containers, which had given the patch of waste ground the feel of a United Nations emergency medical facility. Two workmen were installing a shop-front awning over the open doors of the first container and, just inside, I saw the old African man with the dodgy back, relaxing cheerfully on a sun lounger. I spotted movement further inside the container and realised he had company.

"Hey, Zola!" called Shooter and whistled.

To my surprise, one of the ladies I had encountered at Mama Bisha's last week emerged from the shipping container, wearing a short purple dress. She gave the old man a wave goodbye and picked her way over the uneven ground in her heels.

"Can I come?" I said. "I need to buy a couple of shirts."

"Ok, we all go shopping," said Shooter.

We set off, Shooter sitting in the front beside the driver, while Zola and I sat behind, a chaste empty seat between us. Every minute or so, Shooter would turn round, glance at me, wink at Zola, then both would dissolve into hysterics. Even the driver seemed to be in on the joke, his shoulders juddering as he chuckled away.

We turned off the highway and entered an underground car park beneath a huge indoor mall just outside Somerset West. The driver stayed with the vehicle while the three of us took the lift up to the mall, Shooter and the woman giggling incessantly.

"*Mlungu*, do you like Zola?" asked Shooter.

"She's very nice," I replied.

"So why don't you talk to her?"

"Hello Zola."

Zola and Shooter collapsed into giggles once more.

"What would you like to be when you grow up?" I asked.

"I am grown up!" she shouted.

"Yes. Of course you are. Apologies. Would you like to do something... different to this, one day?"

"Like clean the floor in white people's houses?" she said, glaring at me.

"Ok. No, perhaps not," I said, reddening a little.

"She wants to be a nurse," said Shooter.

"That's a laudable aspiration," I said, staring at the wall of the lift. Every inch of the interior, save the buttons and the dim yellow bulb overhead, was plated in dull, cross-hatched metal, as if we'd been imprisoned inside a giant biscuit tin. Somebody, presumably short of stature, had patiently scratched the word 'BEFOK' into the metal at waist height, each letter reinforced with careful, repeated strokes from a sharp implement.

The doors opened and the bright lights of the mall electrified the lift's interior, transforming it into dazzling silver. Immediately, I was struck by a fabulous idea. Following Zola and Shooter into a large department store, I made a beeline for the formal womenswear department.

"What is this, *mlungu*?" frowned Shooter, as I dumped a selection of white shirts and sober grey skirts into the trolley, on top of Zola's stockings, bras and other assorted scanties.

"Mama Bisha asked me to buy them," I said. Shooter peered at the clothes, suspiciously. "They are important, Shooter, I promise."

Zola returned from browsing the knickers fixture and dropped a selection of colourful thongs into the trolley. Shooter shrugged.

"Ok *mlungu*, but if she is angry, you will take them back, along with the wine."

"Don't worry, she'll be very pleased. I have a couple more things to buy. Meet you back at the taxi."

Checking the mall map, I located a novelty gift shop, a stationer's and an upmarket interior design store. I made my purchases and joined the others in the underground car park.

"What did you buy?" asked Shooter, eyeing my bags.

"You'll see," I replied, enjoying the feeling of being very slightly on the front foot once more.

On our return, Mama Bisha's had become an even greater hive of activity. Workmen were filling the cracks in the main building and most of the water marks had been obscured under a coat of paint. An air conditioning unit was being swung into position on the dining room roof while a gang of men dug a trench next to the portable toilet and others unloaded a heavy-duty hose from a pickup. The shipping containers had all been fitted with striped awnings, under which lay a selection of rattan patio furniture, accessorised with red cushions.

"We open tonight. Big party," said Shooter. "Ah, my new speakers are here," he grinned, pointing to two large boxes on the reception desk.

There was no sign of Mama Bisha and when I asked McGregor he dismissed me, saying she was busy with business. After the unfortunate miscommunication over my alcohol procurement policy, I'd wanted to get permission for my little plan, but the sun was now low in the sky and I was anxious to put it into action.

I placed my bags of supplies next to the nearest shipping container then headed back to the dining room and unpacked a few cases of wine. I took the empty cardboard boxes outside and, using a marker pen I'd purchased from the stationery store, labelled the wine boxes 'bandages', 'antiseptic', 'sterile gloves' and 'distilled water'. From the interior design store, I had procured paintbrushes and three tins of paint, of very particular colours; a bright red, pale blue and vivid green. I prised open the red and began painting a large, neat cross on the side of the white shipping container.

"*Mlungu* Moses! What are you doing?" shouted Shooter. He leapt up from the sofa lying beneath the awning of a nearby container and ran over.

"I'm securing our future revenue stream," I said, wiping away a red paint dribble with an old rag.

"Stop! You are making a mess! Mama Bisha will be very angry."

Shooter placed his hand on my arm, but I wheeled round and pointed the red paint-smeared brush at him.

"Don't interrupt a working artist!" I hissed. Shooter retreated, clutching his headphones to his chest. "I'm executing my master plan, ok? I'm doing this for Mama Bisha's sake. For all our sakes."

"You are crazy, *mlungu*." Shooter shook his head.

"Listen. I need Zola."

"Ah, yes! You like Zola!" he grinned. He glanced over to the farthest container, outside which lay two rattan armchairs. Zola was slumped in one, typing on her phone, and the old African man with the bad back snoozed in the other. "Hey, Zola!" shouted Shooter.

"Bring the old guy too."

Shooter stared at me, wide-eyed.

"I need them both!"

Shooter strode over to Zola and relayed my request, while I levered open the tins of green and blue paint. I unfolded the letter-headed Tears of Pity correspondence I'd been carrying around since my visit to the Ministry of Development and held it up against the shipping container. In the corner lay the Tears of Pity logo, a benevolent face crying blue tears on to the earth, out of which sprouted a lush, green bush. Selecting a paintbrush, I attempted to copy the logo on to the container. Unfortunately, oil painting is not one of my principal talents and, stepping back, I had to concede my rendering looked more like a deranged gorilla weeping over a stunted Christmas tree.

"Oh, that is a bad picture," said Zola, sauntering up behind me.

"Yes. Yes, it is," I sighed, soaking my rag in water and wiping the metal clean.

"Nomi is a good artist. I will find her."

A minute later, Zola returned with Nomi, who snorted at my efforts. She held out her hand and I surrendered the paintbrush. She took the Tears of Pity correspondence, considered the logo for a few seconds, closed one eye and began to paint. Within a few seconds, I could see she was reproducing the image beautifully – in fact, her version looked even better, perfectly capturing the dappy, weeping face gazing down from the heavens, like the good Lord himself watching the end of *Titanic* after a couple of bottles of Pinot Grigio. Beneath, a succulent bush leapt from the earth, bursting into life under His lachrymose irrigation.

"Brilliant!" I said, as Nomi added the final touches. "Now, Zola, I need you to wear this please."

I tore open the packaging of one of the outfits I'd bought from the novelty shop. The cardboard insert carried the title 'Naughty Nurse', and was illustrated with a cartoon medical professional, in short skirt and fishnet stockings, taking the pulse of an elderly male patient, whose flashing electrocardiograph appeared to be emitting steam.

"That is sexist," said Zola.

"Disgusting," added Nomi.

"Yes, it is. Apologies. I don't want you to wear those bits." I tossed aside the painful-looking fishnet stockings and the tiny, distinctly un-medical, nylon tunic. "I just need the accessories." I fished out the nurse's cap, badged with a red cross, and the fake fob watch. "Please can you change into one of these shirts and skirts?" I held up the clothing I'd purchased from the department store.

"What else do you want me to do?" sulked Zola.

"We need him too." I pointed over at the old man, still dozing in the rattan armchair.

"He is very drunk," said Nomi.

"That's great. He can just lie there."

Zola looked at me with disgust. "When are you going to pay?"

"What do you mean? I'm not paying anything. Look, I just need you to dress up and stand next to him so I can take a picture."

"He will try to escape without paying!" declared Shooter, pointing at me. "He has done that before!"

"I'm not doing anything for no money!" Zola folded her arms.

"Ok, I'll pay you, I promise. As soon as we get more money. Look, I need you to do this, then I'll be able to pay you."

"No money, no dressing up," said Zola.

"Oh God, all right!" I said, pulling the last of my cash from my pocket. To my dismay, I saw I had less than twenty rand, barely enough for a beer in a township shebeen. I suspected it wouldn't get a punter very far at Mama Bisha's either, unless a smack around the chops was your thing. "Is this enough as a down-payment?" I asked, holding out the entirety of my worldly cash reserves. Zola glanced at the crumpled notes and low-denomination coins, tutted and returned to her armchair.

"Mr Hart is explaining himself very poorly. But I think I understand his request."

Mama Bisha stepped from the rear door and approached the shipping container, raising her eyebrows as she inspected the new branding. Her dark eyes shone, reflecting the setting sun. I wondered how long she'd been watching us.

"*Mlungu* has gone crazy," said Shooter.

"No, he hasn't. Zola, this won't take long. Please change into those clothes, as Mr Hart has asked."

Zola nodded, rifled through the bag of shirts and skirts, and picked a pair that looked as though they might fit. She disappeared into the shipping container and emerged a couple of minutes later, looking like a slightly louche secretary. She placed the cap on her head, fitted the fake plastic fob watch to her shirt pocket, placed a hand on her hip and stuck her tongue out.

Nomi giggled, Shooter applauded and there were a couple of whoops of encouragement from the workmen on the roof but Mama Bisha held up her hand. "Wipe off your lipstick. And wear my shoes." She produced a tissue from an unseen pocket and stepped out of her black, low-heeled flats, her bare feet matching the dark, sandy soil. Zola kicked off her high heels, wiped her lips and slipped her feet into Mama Bisha's sensible shoes.

"Shooter, go and bring Uuka here," ordered Mama Bisha. Shooter jogged over to the comatose drunk, hooked his hands under the man's arms from behind and hoisted him to his feet. The man let out a groan. Shooter dragged him backwards across the dirt, glancing over his shoulder every few seconds to avoid piles of equipment or debris left by the workmen, his path recorded in the sand by the two parallel lines traced by the drunk's heels. Shooter deposited him on the rattan sofa where he emitted another groan and began to snore.

I handed Zola a small notebook and pen, which I'd purchased from the stationers, then arranged my cardboard boxes of fake medical supplies just inside the open container doors, orientating them so my fictional descriptions were visible.

"A little closer please," I said, withdrawing my phone and gesturing to Zola to move nearer the sofa. I took a few steps to the side, ensuring my shot would capture my red cross and Nomi's Tears of Pity logo, the pile of phoney medical supplies, Uuka the drunkard and Zola herself, resplendent in her jerry-built nurse's outfit.

Zola pouted and pushed out her chest.

"I need you to look more professional please," I called from behind my phone.

"I am professional," she shot back.

"Yes, I mean a medical professional."

"I am professional!" she shouted, even more fiercely.

"Imagine that you work hard tonight but you do not get paid," said Mama Bisha, sternly.

211

For a second, Zola's face morphed into a mask of frustration and anger. I tapped my phone's screen and gave a thumbs-up.

"Superb! That's a wrap. Thank you everybody."

I emailed the picture to Troy Frittersley and prayed to the gods that his most recent experience of a working medical facility was a TV repeat of *Carry on Doctor*.

Chapter 23

Off the Beaten Track

Mama Bisha's party started at around nine o'clock that evening. Shooter's speakers broadcasted *kwaito* tunes from the roof, and our newly equipped kitchen channelled its own rhythm; the clang of utensils against metal and the sizzle of fat against hot coals. Whether it was the hip-hop pulsing from the roof, or the mouth-watering aroma of grilled meat drifting across the township, the deserted space out back was suddenly full of shadows and murmuring.

That morning, the workmen had cut a serving hatch in the dining room wall, and through it I watched the crowd grow. The atmosphere, I observed, was distinctly muted. This may have had something to do with the male to female ratio, which was highly loaded in favour of the former. In fact, I suspected there were no more than a dozen women present, against a hundred or so men. The women lounged in pairs on the rattan sofas, sparkling like jewels in their neon and glitter dresses, while the men surrounded them, just out of touching range, the early arrivals occupying the spare furniture, the rest standing. Occasionally, one of the women would laugh and the sound would rise like a tinkling bell over the men's low murmuring.

I don't mean to boast, but I was at least as much an object of fascination as the women. It's probably unnecessary to point out that I was the only white person present, though I was taken aback by how much of a novelty this made me. When the fourth or fifth punter had done a double take as they approached the serving hatch, their face breaking into an astonished grin, accompanied by a cry of '*Mlungu!*' I wondered briefly whether the population of this part of Khayelitsha, like an uncontacted

Amazonian tribe, had perhaps never encountered a white man. The reality, of course, is that few white men dared venture so deep into the township, especially at night, and my bravery was rapidly making me something of a local celebrity.

"Can I interest you in a glass of unoaked Elgin Chardonnay?" I asked one man, as he pointed at me with both outstretched arms, a beaming smile on his face.

"What is that, *mlungu*?" he said, peering at the wine, before shaking his head. "No, I will have a beer."

None of the next dozen punters were Chardonnay fans either and I ended up drinking most of the bottle myself, dispensing only cold lager and the occasional glass of whisky to my rather undemanding customers.

"Ah, you do a very good job!" said Shooter, poking his head through the serving hatch, as I positioned a selection of lightly chilled Pinot Noir next to the Jameson's, in the hope of broadening my punters' repertoire.

"Can I interest you in a chilled red, Shooter? A Gamay, perhaps?" I brandished a bottle of Radford Dale Thirst, lightly misted with condensation after a half-hour in the fridge.

"I cannot drink when I am on duty. I will have some beer at the end."

"You should try the wine."

"Ah, poor *mlungu*. Nobody is drinking your *mlungu* wine! Ok, I will try it later."

"You'll like it, I promise."

"Yeah, ok." Shooter grinned. "Then you will take all the wine back to the shop tomorrow."

Shooter withdrew his head and I watched him skirt the crowd surrounding the closest shipping container. He sauntered to a dark area on the perimeter, which looked like the entrance to a passageway between two blocks of shacks, and conversed with a man, half obscured in the shadows, who I was sure was carrying a stout stick. After a minute, he walked on to the next passageway and spoke with another person, this time so concealed in shadow as to be invisible.

"Why are you here?" asked one of a pair of men as they stepped up to the serving hatch. Each held a paper plate loaded with chicken and sausages.

"I work here," I replied.

"You work for Mama Bisha?"

"Yes, she's the boss."

"Yeah, she is the boss," agreed the other man, nodding.

It occurred to me that I hadn't seen Mama Bisha all evening. She certainly wasn't sitting with any of the women, so far as I could see.

"Would you like some wine?"

The first man frowned and stuck out his bottom lip. I opened two bottles of beer and handed them over. The men returned to the circle surrounding my Red Cross shipping container, the Tears of Pity logo just visible in the glow from a jam jar lantern.

I'd lost sight of Shooter by now, so I turned my attention back to my wine inventory. Though it pained me to say so, I had misread the local market, very badly. As a professional wine buyer, that was a pretty significant misstep. I consoled myself with the thought that Gatesave were unlikely to hear about this particular episode of incompetence which, had I replicated it back at Head Office, would have resulted in a very black mark indeed, and quite possibly a demotion to buyer of wet wipes and moist toilet tissue.

"*Mlungu*!" called an excited voice. It was Shooter. He dashed up to the serving hatch and thrust his head and shoulders through, knocking over a bottle of beer I'd lined up for the next punter. He had an ecstatic smile on his face. "*Mlungu*! Your friends are here!"

"My friends?"

"Yes, your *mlungu* friends," beamed Shooter. He withdrew from the serving hatch and gestured across the open ground. I was conscious that the low buzz of conversation had quietened. Sure enough, a pair of white men, watched by the entire crowd, were picking their way, extremely self-consciously, past the shipping containers. The seated partygoers stood up and stared, and even the women climbed to their feet, no longer the centre of attention. One whistled and shouted something, at which the crowd roared with laughter.

I leaned out of the serving hatch for a better view. The men were in their mid-twenties and wore hiking clothes. One had a small backpack slung over his shoulder. Both looked hopelessly lost and very grim-faced. They headed straight for the dining room, which was understandable given that it was the only permanent-looking structure in sight. I was pretty sure I didn't recognise either of them, though it was difficult to tell in the low light.

Suddenly, one of them caught sight of me. He grabbed his companion's arm and pointed. They speed-walked over to my serving hatch, their relief palpable.

"Hey, how's it going? Is this Mama Bisha's?" The man was American.

"It certainly is," I replied, realising, to my surprise, that I was faintly annoyed to no longer be the only white man in Khayelitsha.

Shooter beamed at the men. "Welcome, welcome! I am Shooter!"

"This was such a bad idea," said the man with the backpack, quietly. He had a South African accent. "We're probably going to get killed." He glanced at Shooter, who was grinning like he'd won the lottery.

"Relax. We found it, didn't we?"

"You have indeed, gentlemen," I said. "Were you invited to the party?"

"No," said the South African.

"Sure we were!" said the American.

Behind the two men, Shooter gave me a clenched fist salute and wandered off into the crowd.

"I'm sure it's not a problem," I said. "I'm just interested to know how you found out about this place. It's a bit off the beaten track."

"Yeah man!" shouted the American. He struck his companion on the back and beamed.

I paused, weighing up the possibility that the men had escaped from some kind of secure medical facility.

"Sorry, man. I run a website called exactly that. Head Off the Beaten Track, dot com. Hotbeat dot com, for short."

"I see. Well, that would explain that, I suppose. Would you like a beer?"

"Do you have any wine?" The American peered past me into the dining room. "Sure you do! What a selection! That guy at the store was right, man."

I stood aside so the two men could view my wall of wine cases.

"That's quite impressive," said the South African. "Do people seriously drink much wine around here?"

"Oh yes," I said.

The two men turned to look at the crowd, most of whom had transferred their attention back to the women and food. Pretty much everyone was drinking beer, some held a bottle in each hand.

"The wines tend to be drunk on more formal occasions. Here, in the dining room."

"That's great. We're starving," said the American.

"You mentioned a guy at a store," I said. "Was it a wine merchant in Stellenbosch?"

"Yeah, that's the one! We were asking him for tips about unusual places to visit, for the website. He mentioned some guy had bought loads of fine wine for a place in Khayelitsha this morning, which is pretty unusual. We persuaded him to give us the address. Not that the address is much to go on, just a zip code or something. You know, you guys aren't on Google? I mean, the *roads* here aren't even on Google! It's just, like, an empty space. It's insane, man. This is *exactly* what Hotbeat dot com is all about!"

"Our cab would only take us as far as the highway turn-off," said the South African. "We had to pay a township taxi to take us further in, then do the rest on foot, asking directions. Took us an hour. I'm amazed we're still alive, bro."

"Well, here you are."

"Yeah!" said the American. "So, what's for dinner?"

"Well, there's a *braai* going in the kitchen, so there's roast chicken, sausages, that sort of thing."

"Oh," said the American, looking disappointed. "Isn't there any crazy township food or something? Like, what was that thing you were telling me about, the smiling sheep?"

"Smiley," said the South African.

"Yeah, do you have any of that?"

"I'm not sure. Let me check with the kitchen."

I poured the men two glasses of Radford Dale Thirst, then popped my head around the doorway cut in the dining room wall leading to our new kitchen.

Kuhle, the cook, was busy flipping chicken legs and sausages on the gas-fired grill, while her assistant dispensed them to the hungry punters queuing at the far door.

"Kuhle, do we have any smiley?"

"Go away, I am busy," she said, wiping her hands on her apron.

"Please, Kuhle. We have some VIP visitors."

"Why are they VIP?"

"Well, no, I don't mean VIP exactly," I said, flushing with embarrassment. "But they're from out of town. They want to try the smiley."

"There," she said, gesturing at the smaller of two refrigerators.

I crouched and opened the door. The top shelf was crammed with raw chicken legs but in the base lay a large object wrapped in newspaper, mottled with patches of grease. I unwrapped it, slowly. And there, staring up at me through its grey gel eyes, was the terrible smiley, shrivelled lips drawn back to reveal its obscene, peg-toothed grimace.

"Any chance you could pop it on the grill, please?"

"I am busy!" she shouted. "You do it!"

"Right." I lifted the smiley by its ears and placed it over the flames. It hissed as it touched the grill. The creature had been roasted once already at the township stall, so it only needed heating up.

The previous evening, I'd taken the opportunity of a quick walk around the neighbourhood and I'd stumbled across the local smiley butchers, looking like a cross between a village fete and an apocalyptic garden barbeque. A gang of tough-looking women sat on little stools amongst the ashes and debris, faces smeared with golden paste to protect their skin from the heat. They worked a production line, first cleaving open the raw sheep heads and removing the brains, then searing off the wool with metal rods heated in the embers. The heads were plunged into drums of boiling water for a few minutes, before being hoisted out, the raw red flesh now dulled to grey. Finally, they would be roasted over a fire pit fuelled with scavenged timber, where they would shrivel and crackle, the skin charring to a golden crisp. And, as the sheep heads completed their transformation from mere slaughterhouse offcuts to the township's most prized delicacy, their expressions would morph from mournful resignation to an ecstatic, bare-toothed grin.

I returned to the dining room. "You're in luck, gentlemen. One smiley, coming up. Why don't you come inside and take a seat?" I leaned through the hatch and pointed to the rear entrance.

"This is a weird place, man," said the South African, the passageway funnelling his voice quite clearly into the dining room.

"You should have seen it before the refit," I said cheerfully, as I waved the men to their seats.

"I think this is a really cool set up," said the American. "So, you're having a party. What's the occasion?"

The South African wandered over to the serving hatch and peered out. "What actually is this place? What are those shipping containers for? Bedrooms?"

"Exactly. It's a guesthouse. We're celebrating our refurbishment. We have some new investors."

"Did they steal the one with the red cross from the local hospital?"

"That's a medical facility for the local community, actually. Funded, very generously, by a British supermarket chain. People round here don't have private medical insurance, you know."

"Of course they don't, man," said the American. "You know, this place has a great vibe."

The South African frowned and took a seat.

"*Mlungu!*" screamed Kuhle, as a faint smell of burning wool reached my nostrils.

"One second, please." I dashed into the kitchen to find the smiley emitting smoke from its mouth. I grabbed a spatula and attempted to turn it over, but the creature had welded itself quite assertively to the grill. After a minute or so of frantic hacking, I managed to chisel it free, then by shoving the other end of the spatula in its mouth and tugging at the creature's searingly hot ears, I managed to flip the head upside down.

I returned to the dining room, blowing on my scalded fingers, to find a small crowd of partygoers clustered outside the serving hatch staring in at my guests, who were doing their best not to look nervous. I dispensed a few beers to the observers, then scanned my wall of wine boxes. Spotting the case I was looking for, I extracted a bottle of red.

"The perfect match for your smiley," I declared, presenting the wine to the table. The men peered at the label.

"Oh man! You've got a smiley wine! That's really cool."

I uncorked the bottle and poured the men a glass before heading back to the kitchen. I cajoled the sheep's head on to a large plate, right side up, while Kuhle urged me loudly to get out of her way. I placed the plate on a tray alongside the largest knife I could find and returned to the dining room.

"Holy shit, dude!" shouted the American, slopping a half-inch of wine out of his glass in shock. I advanced upon the table, my nose in the air like a Buckingham Palace butler. "That is friggin' awesome, man!"

"Your smiley, sir," I said, setting the creature down on the table.

"Have you tried this before?" the American asked his friend.

The South African shook his head and prodded the creature's cheek with his finger.

"Yes, that's the best bit," I said. "After the eyes, of course."

"The eyes! Oh, man! We've gotta try them."

"How's the wine?" I asked, wiping the table.

"Awesome, man. Hey, why don't you join us? Unless you're busy? I'm Josh. This is Glen." I shook hands with the two men.

"Don't mind if I do. I'll serve up the smiley first, though, while it's hot."

I began butchering the sheep's head and, though I say so myself, I made a pretty good job of it, carving several choice pieces of cheek and removing one of the creature's ears – the other looking rather too much like a blow-torched crisp – and depositing them on the men's plates. Then, I paused for effect.

"And now, the *pièce de résistance*."

I sensitively gouged out each eye with the tip of my knife, apologising to the creature under my breath, and deposited one on each man's plate.

"That's gross, bro," said the South African.

"It's an authentic dish of your fellow countrymen," I said.

The South African scowled.

"We've got to eat it, man," said the American. He lifted the eye, popped it in his mouth and began chewing. He screwed up his face and swallowed. "Not bad. Kind of meaty and salty and oily at the same time."

"Oh, hell," said the South African, and popped his in too, swallowing it whole. "Ok, not as bad as I thought."

"Grab a glass, man. Join us," said the American.

I stepped over to the bar and selected a goblet, holding it up before the open serving hatch to check it was clean. At that very moment, I saw the briefest of flashes, somewhere near the farthest container. It was followed, a split-second later, by a sharp crack. The crowd outside flinched and those seated jumped to their feet. Some appeared to flee from the source of the noise, while others

221

ran towards it. Shouting and whistles mixed with the *kwaito* still blaring from the roof.

"That was a gunshot," said the South African, rising to his feet.

I tried to make out what was happening, but it was impossible. Figures were running to and fro in the darkness, obscuring my view. I'm certain I saw McGregor's large, distinctive silhouette for a second, close to the source of the flash. He appeared to be holding a large stick. I saw him step forward and the stick arched through the air and down, but whether it was on to a person, wild animal or errant tent peg it was impossible to say.

"A firework," I said, turning back to the men. I raised my empty glass. "I'll take you up on that offer of wine now, if you don't mind?"

"I swear that was a gunshot," said the South African, striding over to the serving hatch.

"I promise you, it was a firework. A peony, from the look of it. Quite pretty, actually."

"Cool, I love fireworks," said the American. He rose and sauntered over.

The two men leaned out of the hatch, the American peering up at the sky, the South African scanning the crowd. But calm had returned and most of those standing had retaken their seats. I could see a knot of people congregated around the farthest container, but the source of their interest was obscured.

"Oh, did we miss it all?" asked the American.

"Yes. Just one firework, I'm afraid. They spent most of the budget on beer and chicken." I filled my glass with Smiley Red. "Your health, gentlemen." I could tell the South African wasn't entirely convinced, but after a last look around, both men retook their seats. We clinked glasses.

The men consumed their sheep's cheek while Josh, the American, held forth on the development of his website. It had begun as a guide to the wilds of Oregon, his home state, before taking in the Rockies, then the whole of North America, followed by South America and Asia. He was in South Africa to oversee the addition of a new continent to his empire, and Glen, his companion, was his point man for the region.

"Every guide to South Africa just covers Cape Town, the Winelands, the Garden Route, blah blah, maybe a bit of Joburg and Durban, plus the Kruger for safari. But that's it! It's boring, man. This is a vast country, there's so much more to be experienced. And that's what Hotbeat dot com is all about. Showing people where to head off the beaten track. The road less travelled, man."

Our glasses were empty.

"Fancy another?" I said, tapping the empty bottle.

"Yeah, sure, that wine is awesome, man. Tell us how much we owe at the end."

I opened another bottle of Smiley and poured us a refill.

"So, we've added some trails across the Drakensberg, a guide to Lesotho and loads of cool stuff in Mozambique. We've spent the past month researching the Great Karoo and further north into Bushmanland, so that's coming to the website soon."

"And now you're in Khayelitsha…"

"Yeah, well, here's the thing… since we launched the Africa section, we've been getting a lot of criticism on social for ignoring the urban areas. I mean, we're about going off the beaten track, so cities are kind of the opposite of that. And we're an American site, most of our users are English speakers and more into the wildlife and scenery side of things, you know, and I guess the urban parts of Africa aren't really what they're looking for. And we've been taking some flak for that, for not featuring diverse enough locations, which is fine, of course. So, you know, arrest me for being white, whatever." He held up his hands, then took another mouthful of wine. "So, anyway, we're trying to find some interesting urban stuff to mix in with Hotbeat's wilderness vibe. Nothing too dangerous though."

"Of course not."

"This kind of place is exactly what we're looking for, actually. Did you say there's, like, a medical centre or something here? Do they treat AIDS, that kind of thing?"

"Oh yes. They treat all sorts."

"That's so cool. And I love this smiley, man. The sheep and the wine. Such an awesome meal. Anyway, we should get the check now. What do we owe?"

"Oh, let's say a thousand rand. Is that ok?"

"Yeah man, no problem. Guess you prefer cash?"

"Yes please."

He peeled five notes from a wad and threw them on the table. I snatched them up and tucked them in my pocket.

"Can you do me a receipt?"

"No problem," I replied, congratulating myself for my foresight in buying several notebooks from the stationers to accessorise my fake nurse's uniforms. I rose and realised Shooter was leaning through the hatch.

"Business is good, *mlungu*!" he grinned, staring at the pocket in which I had stuffed the thousand rand.

"Yes, all good," I replied. "Everything ok with you?" For a moment, I worried that Shooter might be about to introduce a little urban edge to the proceedings, by brandishing a smoking pistol or a severed head at our guests. I stepped towards him, blocking the sightline between the serving hatch and the two men.

"Yes, the party is finished," said Shooter.

I peered over his shoulder. Sure enough, most of the crowd had disappeared and a pair of men were carrying the rattan furniture into one of the containers.

"Do you guys have a cab number or something?" called the American. "Uber doesn't seem to recognise where we are."

"Yes, we have a taxi," said Shooter, waving me aside. "You must pay him cash."

I wrote an itemised receipt for the sheep's head and two bottles of Smiley wine in my nurse's notebook, tore out the page and gave it to the American. I accompanied the two men to the minibus, stealing a glance towards the far container where the commotion had taken place earlier. To my relief, there were no blood-splattered corpses littering the floor, no-one impaled on a spike and no cadavers swinging by their neck from the electricity cables. The taxi driver was lying across the back seat of his vehicle, watching a video on his phone, but he scrambled into the driver's seat when he saw he had a fare.

I shook the two men's hands and wished them a safe journey home. "You're doing something really special here," said the American, as he climbed into the minibus. "I envy you, man."

Chapter 24

Generosity

Night sounds. The wilderness, pulsing with noise. I lay, face down in the earth, hearing the song wash over the savannah, as it had for millennia. As I listened and focussed, the chirp of bush crickets changed, slowly, into something more familiar. Something unnatural, urgent, unpleasant. A mobile phone, vibrating against the bedside table.

I flung out an arm, scrabbled around and located the handset. I brought it to my ear, yanking the recharging plug from the flimsy socket as I did so.

"Felix, dear boy! My Livingstone, my Carter, my Rhodes!"

"Oh. Morning Troy."

"I showed your photograph to the board of trustees yesterday. Oh, Felix. If the sadness and desperation of Africa could be summed up in one image, it would be yours."

I turned on to my back and made a feeble attempt to sit up. I noticed I was still wearing my clothes from the night before. I tried to work out whether I was hung-over or not. I didn't feel too wretched, but I could feel an oppressive fug clouding the inside of my skull, suggesting I'd had, at the minimum, a generous evening.

"But hope too, of course," continued Troy, his voice reverberating around my head.

I vaguely recalled insisting that Shooter share a bottle of red wine with me, once all the guests had departed. I had opened a bottle of Kanonkop Cabernet, an exquisite wine, oozing with luscious blackcurrant fruit, but Shooter had screwed up his face after one sip and poured himself a glass of whisky, leaving me to finish the bottle myself.

"And that brave nurse, that daughter of Africa! Her uniform spotless in the midst of the degradation. And her expression, defiant and resolute, in the face of despair."

I had harangued Shooter at length, telling him Mama Bisha should rebrand her guesthouse Smiley's, and that we should serve sheep's heads roasted over an open fire, every evening, for visiting Americans. Shooter, headphones on, gave me a thumbs-up and nodded encouragingly. After I'd banged on for a while, I realised he was nodding to the music and had been ignoring me for quite some time.

"And that poor, desperate old man, lying in agony beside her!" bleated Frittersley. "What a symbol of the neglect of a continent."

Suddenly, Shooter had removed his headphones, his attention drawn to the doorway behind me. There stood Mama Bisha, her expression that of an abbess realising a trainee nun had just broken wind in the middle of evening prayers. "I tell you, Mama Bisha, there's money in those there smileys!" I had shouted, hurling my earnings on to the table. What an idiot. I could have used that thousand rand. Why the hell hadn't I held on to it?

"What had befallen that poor wretch, Felix, the man lying on that couch? He looked at death's door!"

I had a faint recollection of rocking back on my chair in triumph as I pointed with both hands to the damp, crumpled notes, then the chair continuing to tip back, and me crashing on to the floor, as Shooter hooted with laughter.

"Felix? Are you there?"

"Yes, I'm here. Apologies Troy, I was just dwelling on how that's an everyday scene here at Tears of Pity Khayelitsha. We're truly an oasis of hope in a desert of despair."

The last thing I'd remembered was strong hands grasping my arms and dragging me backwards along the floor, McGregor's upside-down face wearing a distinctly irritated expression. "Don't hit me with your stick!" I'd cried.

I cringed. I suspected breakfast might be a little embarrassing.

"The sick man, Felix! What happened to him? Is he alive?"

"Yes, yes, Troy. He's alive. It was… an industrial accident. He was crushed beneath a poorly installed portable toilet cubicle. We've transferred him to the main hospital in Cape Town. He's expected to make a full recovery."

"Goodness. It looked horrific. All that blood!"

What the hell was Frittersley blethering on about? There hadn't been any blood, other than the old drunk's bloodshot eyes. It suddenly occurred to me that the patio furniture was accessorised with red cushions.

"Yes, it was a bit of a mess. Just another day in Khayelitsha."

"I don't doubt it, not for a second. By the way, the Tears of Pity branding on that repurposed shipping container is quite exquisite. The Board of Trustees were particularly complimentary. We've already asked our partners to use the same design on the favela schools we fund in Central America."

"Oh, that's good."

"Don't forget, your employer wants to see some Gatesave branding up too. After all, it's their money that's made it all possible."

"Yes, we're working on it." I decided to try my luck on the remuneration front, given my inability to loosen Mama Bisha's purse strings. "Troy, this is a little embarrassing, but I need your help with some funds."

"Felix, Felix. Don't worry. Your next tranche of funding is already on its way. You've assuaged any concerns our trustees may have had regarding financial governance."

"Oh, that's fantastic," I said, my heart sinking as I realised I was unlikely to see a penny of it.

"I know! And we're arranging the Tears of Pity audit visit for tomorrow."

"But you just said all concerns had been assuaged!" I said, sitting bolt upright.

"Our financial governance concerns have been put to rest, Felix. But we must ensure the medical facility itself is up to scratch. Especially if it's to carry Tears of Pity and Gatesave branding. You know, qualified staff, proper hygiene, that sort of thing."

"Oh," I said, miserably.

"I've asked the auditors to contact you directly, so you can arrange the details. They'll want to look at the infrastructure and speak to a couple of the staff. And please, you must send more pictures, showing those wonderful nurses. We're working up some publicity material. Preferably, without any distressed patients this time, if you could. I believe there are privacy issues around using images of unconscious people."

"I'll see what I can do."

"All these silly rules, Felix! It's a wonder that we men of action get anything done!"

"Quite."

"Well done. Keep it up!"

I dressed and dragged open the bedroom door. Mama Bisha, McGregor and Shooter were conferring in reception.

"Now look," I said, "before you all start having a go at me, I was only given one sausage and a small slice of sheep's cheek to eat last night. As a result, the wine may have gone very slightly to my head."

Mama Bisha turned her dark eyes on me, the centres sparkling like specks of diamond light.

"Good morning, Mr Hart. I spoke earlier to my cousin at the Ministry of Development. He tells me your charity is transferring more funds to our account."

I paused, slightly surprised that I wasn't in more trouble. McGregor watched me, somewhat unimpressed, while Shooter smirked. "Yes, that's right. I had a little word with them yesterday and explained we needed more working capital."

Was that a faint smile playing at the corner of Mama Bisha's mouth? If so, it was only for a second.

"Well done. You even managed to sell some expensive wine last night, which I would not have predicted."

"Well, I'm a wine professional. I understand these things."

"My driver tells me your guests were pleased with their meal. They took his number and some of their friends have already made arrangements to dine here tonight."

"Excellent. Looks like we're going to need more smileys," I said, rubbing my hands.

Mama Bisha removed a thin, neatly folded wad of notes from her pocket and handed them to me. Five orange-yellow banknotes, a leopard on one side, Nelson Mandela on the other. My payment from the American for last night's meal.

"Then you had better buy some."

"Don't spend it all on wine, *mlungu*," grinned Shooter.

And so passed a morning in the township's most entrepreneurial community hub. I procured half a dozen sheep's heads from the gold-faced women of the smiley stall, opting for a boiled finish so I could add my own roasted sheen back at Mama Bisha's that evening. I dug a fire pit outside the kitchen and dispatched a gang of feral children to source enough scrap metal to construct a grill over the top. Mama Bisha assigned me a pair of workmen and I supervised the construction of a proper bar next to the serving hatch. We even repurposed a spare chest of drawers into a wall-mounted wine rack.

I discovered Shooter and another man, presumably an electrician, unpacking CCTV equipment next to Mama Bisha's office. I recalled the brief episode of disorder that had erupted the previous night.

"For protection," said Shooter, indicating the TV monitors, cameras and rolls of cable lined up on the floor.

"Good thinking. There was some trouble last night, I think?"

"No, no trouble," said Shooter.

"Didn't someone fire a gun?"

"Ah yes. He was just drunk. It was nothing."

"It didn't sound like nothing. Was anyone hurt?"

"No. Just a hangover."

I wanted to enquire further but was interrupted by the high-pitched shouts of "*Mlungu!*" from my gang of infant procurement specialists, anxious to show me their latest haul. I returned to the back yard, inspected the pile of rusted barbeque accessories, oven utensils and miscellaneous plumbing equipment, filched from god knows where, and congratulated them on their initiative. I distributed a few coins to the gleeful waifs and ordered them to spend the rest of the day studying. They ignored me and retired to the bridge to hurl stones into the gully.

My phone buzzed. A local number.

"Hart, your boy is here."

Blanchkopf's insistence on getting straight to the point would have been admirable, if it weren't for the fact that his points were invariably mean, unpalatable and graceless. On this occasion, he'd managed to render himself utterly baffling too.

"Good afternoon Mr Blanchkopf, lovely to hear from you. I wasn't aware I had a boy. Would you care to elaborate?"

"Your boy, the inspector. He is here, outside my gate."

"Ah, the Fairly Trod inspector. When you say a boy, I assume you mean a young man? So long as he's not an actual infant, I'm sure he's capable of conducting the survey without my help."

"He won't get past the dogs."

"Have you tried locking them up?"

"Why should I? He's your boy, you must come and take care of it." And at that, Blanchkopf hung up.

Half an hour later, I was in a township taxi, bumping my way up the driveway of Blanchkopf Wine Growers. In the hope of softening the Blanchkopfs up, I'd swiped a couple of choice bottles from Mama Bisha's bar, which were now lying in a canvas holdall at my feet.

As we approached the gate, I spotted a car parked in the shade of a pine tree, the driver's door branded with the happy foot logo of the Fairly Trod Foundation. A young African man, wearing glasses, sat in the driver's seat, a wad of papers propped against the steering wheel. I gave him a cheery wave and he raised his hand in response, but our attention was diverted by a blood-curdling howl, accompanied by the crash of skull against wood.

"Oh, this is very bad," muttered my driver, as the Boerboel hurled itself wildly and repeatedly against the gate. "He will try to eat my taxi again."

"Don't worry," I replied, "he's not getting through that gate."

I climbed out, holdall in hand, and approached the Fairly Trod vehicle. The Boerboel's gurgling snarls were now joined by the more assertive barks of the Rottweiler, which leapt up and down energetically behind the gate. As the creature's head appeared repeatedly above the gate's top bar, I was rewarded with a slightly different snapshot of its bared fangs, as though it were modelling for a feature in *Canine Dentistry Monthly*.

The man lowered the window a few inches, his eyes on the frenzied hounds.

"Hello, I'm Felix Hart. I'm here to assist with the inspection."

Behind me, I heard a click and a creak. The man looked past me to the gate and his eyes widened.

"I suggest your first job is to deal with them," he said.

I span round. To my horror, Blanchkopf's gate was swinging slowly open. My driver, clearly in no mood to invest in yet another radiator grille badge, was already half-way through a swift three-point turn. I dashed towards him, waving my holdall, but he roared past and accelerated back down the drive towards the highway, vanishing in seconds behind a great cloud of dust.

I ran back to the Fairly Trod vehicle and tugged at the rear door handle. It was locked.

"Let me in!" I squeaked, now tugging in vain at the driver's door, but the inspector shook his head and stabbed at a button on his armrest. The gap in the window hummed shut, leaving my own reflection overlaid on the man's face.

I became conscious the dogs were no longer howling. I turned, slowly, and there stood the Boerboel, head lowered, grinning at me through the open gateway, a great thread of drool dangling from its jaws. The Rottweiler stood a few paces behind, looking from me to its companion, as if it knew from experience not to come between its unhinged colleague and a defenceless supper.

For a moment neither creature moved, and I wondered whether they'd been trained not to step beyond the boundary of the gate. Perhaps they only attacked trespassers who physically entered the yard. Perhaps they were bigoted dogs and chose only to attack people of colour. Unfortunately for me, though encouragingly for the new South Africa, the Boerboel proved to be entirely free of racial prejudice. In slow motion, red eyes fixed on a point exactly coinciding with my neck, the creature leapt forward, jaws agape. With just a couple of bounds, it had covered half the distance between us, the thread of drool whipping around its head like a gooey lasso. I estimated I had approximately two seconds to execute a life-preserving plan. Running was hopeless, the creature would have caught me within ten yards. The pine tree's trunk was too broad to climb, and the roof of the inspector's car barely reached my shoulder.

There was only one thing for it. I plunged my hand into my holdall, yanked out one of the gifts and held it before me. As the Boerboel prepared to hurl itself at me, its eyes flicked from my neck to the object and its foaming jaws gaped wide in delight. I flung it in the air and leapt backwards, clasping the holdall to my chest. I landed on the car bonnet, the metal buckling beneath my backside with a distressed, metallic twang, and brought my knees up to my chin, in the ridiculously optimistic hope that I'd be able to fend the creature off with a double kick to the face. Through the gap between my knees, I watched the Boerboel launch itself skywards, catch my gift in its jaws, and crash back to earth, where, to my enormous relief, it began ripping it to pieces in a joyful frenzy.

Now, I've never thought of myself as a particularly thoughtful present giver, but my roasted smiley absolutely hit the sweet spot for that rabid brute. As the Boerboel tore the sheep's grinning jawbone from its skull, the half-crazed hound looked up at me, and I swear a little tear of gratitude fell from one of its livid red eyes. I reached into my holdall once more, withdrew a second smiley, and hurled it towards the Rottweiler, which had begun to trot towards me with a rather resentful frown on its face. It too pounced upon its present and began tearing it apart.

I turned to the inspector and knocked on the windscreen. The man stared back at me, open mouthed.

"I think we have some work to do. Quickly, before they finish lunch."

Chapter 25

Rapprochement

Before I could knock at Blanchkopf's farmhouse door, it swung open, revealing the man himself.

"Where are my dogs?" he demanded, looking over my shoulder. "What did you do to them?"

"They're enjoying their presents," I said. "I brought you and Mrs Blanchkopf a gift each and I didn't want them to feel left out." I reached into my holdall, withdrew a bottle of Hemelhuis's top Cabernet, and thrust it at him with what I hoped was a winning smile. "Once we've got this little visit out of the way, the next vintage of this wine might just contain some of your grapes."

Blanchkopf took the bottle and made a low throat-clearing noise, which I suspected was the closest I was likely to get to a thank you.

"What the hell is that boy doing?" said Blanchkopf, as the inspector, giving both feasting dogs an extremely wide berth, manoeuvred his vehicle to within a yard of the front door.

"He's probably a touch nervous of your dogs. He doesn't realise how friendly they are."

"They're not supposed to be friendly," growled Blanchkopf. "Dumb dogs."

The inspector lowered the window an inch. "I'm not proceeding with this visit while those animals are loose."

"I'm sure Mr Blanchkopf will secure them once they've finished their lunch, won't you Mr Blanchkopf?" I said, glancing back towards the gate to check the beasts were still occupied.

Blanchkopf scowled.

"Excellent. Let's proceed then, shall we?"

I smiled, encouragingly, and tugged at the handle, but the door was still locked. The inspector checked his side and rear-view mirrors carefully for approaching carnivores, then, with a click, released the central locking. He stepped out of the car and retrieved a briefcase from the passenger seat.

"I'm Felix Hart," I said, grasping the man's hand. "And this is Mr Blanchkopf."

Blanchkopf grunted and gave the man's hand a half-hearted shake.

"I am Joseph Kwenda."

"Kwenda is a Shona name," said Blanchkopf. "You are from Rhodesia?"

"From Zimbabwe, yes."

"Your country is a mess now, eh?"

"Yes, the situation is not good there."

"That was the British!" said Blanchkopf, addressing me. "They put Mugabe in, they trusted him, and now look. I blame you British for everything."

"Yes, apologies, I'm sure you're right." I glanced towards the gate. "Shall we get on with the visit?"

We filed into Blanchkopf's reception room, where Mrs Blanchkopf stood, hatchet-faced, next to a desk, guarding a pile of papers and a laptop. I withdrew a bottle of Hemelhuis's top Chardonnay from my holdall and presented it to her with a flourish. With the briefest of nods, Mrs Blanchkopf took it and strode to the corner of the room. She opened a low cupboard, which so far as I could see contained firewood, and placed the bottle inside. The stuffed giraffe watched us, morosely.

"That is a splendid firearm," said Kwenda, inspecting the elephant gun over the fireplace.

"It has been in my family for over a century," said Blanchkopf.

"When I was a child, I watched my father put down an injured bull elephant with a similar weapon," said Kwenda. "It had been wounded by poachers and was rampaging through the neighbouring farm."

"It takes a strong man to fire such a gun," said Blanchkopf.

"It takes a calm man, Mr Blanchkopf. If you miss, the elephant will not grant you a chance to reload."

Blanchkopf stroked his beard and nodded. "Does your father still work on the farm?"

"No. My father worked for the owner, who was driven off his land by Mugabe's thugs. My father was also forced to leave. He nearly lost his life."

Blanchkopf shook his head. "Gangsters!" He shot me a filthy look. For reasons of diplomacy, I transferred my attention to the giraffe.

"So, Mr Joseph Kwenda," said Blanchkopf. "Here you are, in the new South Africa. Let us pray this country does not meet the same fate. Now, this inspection. Where shall we start?"

"I would like to begin by looking at the payroll, if I may?"

Blanchkopf gestured to the desk and Kwenda took a seat. He spent the next hour crawling through the Blanchkopfs' paperwork, every so often asking for clarification on some point or other, then he asked Mrs Blanchkopf to fire up the laptop and locate some supporting correspondence, including the recent pricing agreements with Gatesave. At one point Kwenda asked me to confirm that I had indeed signed up to the new terms in Blanchkopf's contract, but otherwise I was pretty redundant to the proceedings, and I passed the time skimming idly through work emails on my phone. Mrs Blanchkopf brought me a cup of revolting *rooibos* tea, and the three of them disappeared for a tour of the accommodation block next door.

I waited a few minutes and poured the *rooibos* into the vase of flowers atop the desk, only realising after I had retaken my seat that the flowers were dried, and that the empty crystal vase now contained two inches of evil-looking yellowish liquid. I leapt up again, removed the dried flowers and attempted to pour the tea back into the cup, only to discover that the vase was not at all designed for decanting, and that the foetid liquid instead preferred to meander its way down the outside of the vase and splatter across the desk, nearby paperwork and the front of my trousers. I removed my handkerchief and wiped down the papers, which took on a light brown hue and began to curl, giving them the look of ancient parchments unearthed after centuries in the Blanchkopf family cellar.

I heard voices returning from the yard. I mopped up the remaining puddle as fast as I could, frantically wringing the tea back into my cup. The back door opened and I attempted to reinsert the bunch of flowers, but the stems were absurdly fragile and most of them snapped in half, the dried heads shedding their petals all over the desk like zombie confetti. Panicking, I jammed the shattered vegetation back into the vase, hoping no-one would notice, swept the crispy detritus littering the desk into my palm and tipped it on top. I retook my seat, just in the nick of time, as the three of them returned to the room.

Mrs Blanchkopf strode straight to the desk and lifted the vase.

"What has happened here?" she demanded.

Only three denuded flower heads now stood proud of the vase, the rest sat squashed at crazy, zig-zag angles inside the bowl, some of them upside down. The bottom of the vessel was coated in soggy brown potpourri where the dried petals had soaked up the *rooibos* dregs.

"Oh, apologies, I think I may have brushed against them earlier," I said. I lifted my cup and took an innocent sip of tea.

"Brushed against them? It looks like you tried to eat them."

The *rooibos*, in addition to being cold, now tasted quite spectacularly foul, as though a clod of sodden compost had been filtered through a mildewed horse blanket. I winced, swallowed and immediately gagged.

"Are you sick?" asked Mrs Blanchkopf.

"I think he has had an accident," said Blanchkopf, peering at my tea-stained groin. "The toilet is through there."

"Everything's fine, thank you," I spluttered, replacing the cup of filthy liquid on the desk.

"Shall I hit you on the back?" asked Mrs Blanchkopf, raising her hand.

"No, that's quite all right," I said, flinching and raising my own arm in defence.

"Joseph and I had a good discussion," said Blanchkopf. "We have a few things to fix, but nothing that is a big problem." Blanchkopf looked at Kwenda, who nodded.

"What sort of things? Anything that might affect the outcome of the inspection?" I asked, nervously.

"Nothing to concern you," said Blanchkopf.

"We are all done here," said Kwenda. "Thank you very much for your cooperation, Mr Blanchkopf. I will need to take this paperwork away with me for a short time, if you don't mind?"

"You must take what you need, Joseph," said Blanchkopf, gathering the paperwork into a neat pile. "But what has happened here?" he frowned, as he caught sight of the splattered, tea-stained sheets. I ignored Blanchkopf's question and turned away to focus on the giraffe, who I suspected was a past master at keeping secrets.

Kwenda placed the papers in his briefcase and Blanchkopf opened the front door for him, shaking his hand and clapping him on the back as he departed. I followed, carrying my empty holdall, Blanchkopf giving me an extremely brief handshake accompanied by a glare.

"Joseph, I wonder if you'd be kind enough to drop me off in Stellenbosch," I said, suspecting a request to be dropped in Khayelitsha might be a favour too far.

"That will be no problem," he said, climbing into the car.

I strolled around the front of the vehicle, noticing the bonnet now carried a rather severe dent following the impact of my backside. As Kwenda slammed the door, a spine-chilling howl filled the air, followed by the pounding of paws against dirt.

"Get in the car, you fool!" shouted Blanchkopf from the doorway.

I scampered to the passenger door, not daring to look over my shoulder, and prayed Kwenda had disengaged the central locking. I grasped the handle and pulled, but it flapped, uselessly.

"Open it!" I screamed, conscious the creature's thundering paws were barely yards behind me. Then, for a sickening second, the beat of canine feet against earth ceased.

I'd never previously given much thought to the hopes and dreams of a wildebeest, nor to those of a zebra or gazelle. But ever since that day, when watching one of those nature documentaries, I've felt a little pang of empathy for the herbivores of the Serengeti. While the camera focusses on the glamorous, pursuing carnivore, it's the victim I feel for, and if a litter of mewling cubs ends up missing out on their dinner of hideously butchered flesh, I for one remain intensely relaxed at the thought of them going hungry.

The Boerboel landed on me like a collapsing bridge, knocking me to the ground and wrenching my fingers from the useless handle. I barely had time for a squeal of anguish before the collision with the earth knocked the wind from my lungs. The beast sank its teeth into the back of my neck and stamped its paw on my head, pinning my face against the earth. My lips tasted the dust of Blanchkopf's yard. With one arm pinned beneath me, the fingers of my free hand scrabbled uselessly in the dirt as I attempted, pathetically, to pull myself beneath the car. The hound's hot breath poured over my neck and all I could hear was a horrible rasp from its throat as the creature gargled in delight at the thought of dispatching the latest in, presumably, a very long line of God's innocent creatures. I whimpered into the earth and prayed for divine intervention.

To my surprise, I felt the hound's jaws release their grip, and the paw lift from my head. Thank the Lord, I thought, Blanchkopf must have dragged the creature clear. I rolled on to my side and looked up to find the Boerboel's grinning snout just inches away and Blanchkopf nowhere in sight. I gave a whimpering howl of my own and flung my hands before my face in a miserable attempt at protection. Of course, the foul beast was just toying with its prey! For how long would it torment me before tearing out my throat? A few minutes? Hours? Days?

The Boerboel, eyes aflame, opened its jaws and lunged. I closed my eyes and wailed as the beast's teeth clamped shut just inches from my nose. I felt my arm being dragged away from my face, far too powerfully to resist. The creature growled and stopped pulling for a moment, then yanked again. I could feel a strap wrapped tightly, and painfully, around my forearm. I opened my eyes and realised I was still holding the canvas holdall. The Boerboel had its teeth embedded in the bag and appeared to be goading me into a game of tug-o-war.

"He likes you," called Blanchkopf. "You've spoilt him. Stupid soft dog!"

"Oh, how nice," I gibbered, rising to my knees. I gave the hound an encouraging smile and pulled the bag softly towards me. The Boerboel growled and launched itself backwards, pulling me on to my front and dragging me a yard through the dirt.

"You should let him have the bag," called Blanchkopf, "or he will tear your arm off."

"Will do," I called back, and frantically untangled the strap. The Boerboel ripped the holdall from my grip and began to shake it from side to side with murderous violence.

"Good dog!" I called, trying the car door again, to no avail. "Will you please unlock the door now?" I screamed, beating my fist against the car roof.

The central locking clicked and I dived inside, pulling the door shut behind me.

"You have now dented my roof, as well as the bonnet," said Kwenda.

"Well, perhaps you should open your bloody car door when someone's in life-threatening peril," I said. "Why don't you send the bill to Mr Blanchkopf? You all seem to get on quite well."

Kwenda performed a slow U-turn around the Boerboel, which had now torn the holdall into several pieces, and proceeded back down Blanchkopf's driveway.

"Would you consider that a successful visit?" I asked, still shaking.

"I cannot tell you at this stage, Mr Hart. I can tell you, however, that I once knew a man in Chegutu who caught rabies from an infected bat. It is a most unpleasant disease. If you find any puncture wounds, I strongly recommend you attend a hospital."

Upon arrival at Mama Bisha's, I immediately asked Shooter to inspect the back of my neck for rabid puncture wounds. Frustratingly, he approached my request rather flippantly, swearing that I was bleeding to death before his very eyes, and making a series of puerile jokes suggesting I had solicited carnal relations with the entire population of the Kruger National Park.

I asked Zola for help instead. She lent me a hand mirror, and I was able to stand with my back to her bedroom's full-length mirror and inspect my wounds. Despite Shooter whispering "Hey, leopard-shagger," through the shipping container door every few seconds, and Zola giggling uncontrollably, I established that, quite astonishingly, the Boerboel's teeth hadn't even grazed my skin. Kwenda had rather put the wind up me with his tale of his Chegutu friend being mauled by a vampire bat, before frothing his way into an early grave, so this came as quite a relief. I wondered, for a second, whether I might even have a guardian angel, but I swiftly dismissed the idea, deciding it would be a pretty twisted angel that chose to thrust me into the middle of a township slum and forced me to dice with death on a daily basis.

As the shadow of Table Mountain lengthened and crept across the township, I made preparations for the evening's entertainment. My infant scavenging squad had procured a large pile of scrap timber, and the pit I'd dug that morning now hosted a roaring fire. As the twilight deepened, a dozen Americans and Europeans drew up in a minibus taxi, their eyes wide with wonder at the sights and sounds of a genuine township. A handful of local women greeted among the group, hawking model animals fashioned from beads threaded on copper wire. As usual, each guest felt obliged to buy at least a couple of items, and the fire was soon surrounded by an audience of toy elephants, hippos and guinea fowl.

As the group supped on a crisp, Fairly Trod Sauvignon Blanc, I threw myself into the community spirit and expounded upon the good works being carried out at Mama Bisha's, from adult literacy classes to arts and crafts, leaving my description of the medical centre until last. I borrowed liberally from Troy Frittersley, throwing in plenty of 'defiant in the face of despair' and 'the neglect of a continent', which earned my speech a rousing round of applause.

Next, Kuhle – the cook – and her assistant carried a huge covered tray from the kitchen and presented it to the guests. Pausing a few seconds, for dramatic effect, I whipped away the linen, exposing half-a-dozen boiled sheep's heads and, my word, the squeals and whoops could have been heard in Johannesburg. I solemnly took each head and placed it over the fire pit, whereupon the creatures began to crackle and smoke. And, as Kuhle prodded and turned them, the lips slowly shrivelled until half a dozen smileys were grinning back at the goggling first-worlders.

Mama Bisha did not make an appearance. I'd passed through reception earlier, all had been quiet behind the office door, and I'd assumed she'd departed for the evening. But, as I refilled our guests' glasses, I noticed a faint glow behind the barred and curtained window facing the back yard. Perhaps she'd left a light on by accident. Or was she working late? I imagined the wads of invoices for building supplies, plumbing equipment and soft furnishings being interrogated, mercilessly, beneath those ice-cold eyes.

I paired the sheep heads with Smiley Red, of course. Then, as the flames danced in my guests' eyes, I let rip with the finest my township cellar had to offer: Restless River Chardonnay, Crystallum Pinot Noir and Lowerland Tannat. By the end of the evening, empty wine bottles and ragged sheep skulls littered the ground and my guests were sprawled on the rattan furniture, their gastronomic and cultural needs satiated. The flames dwindled, then the embers too gave up their glow. It was time for our diners to depart, to leave our township paradise, and return to their vanilla lives.

The guests rose and, arm-in-arm, began their tipsy stumble towards the waiting minibus. But the quiet was interrupted by a clang from the door of a shipping container. The guests turned, startled. A figure, holding his trousers closed with one hand, froze for a second beside the medical facility, then hurried into the night.

"Who was that?" asked a woman.

"Just a patient," I replied. "Please don't stare, we do try to respect their privacy." I ushered them on towards the taxi.

"Curious time to be discharging a patient!" brayed an Englishman. "It's one in the morning!"

"We're not a prison," I replied. This raised a few chortles, but my guests' curiosity had been dangerously roused. "Of course, we're not a formal hospital either, as you would understand the term. We empower our guests rather than confining them. Patients come and go at times that may seem unusual to Western sensibilities."

"Of course," said the woman.

"Why was he holding his trousers up like that?" asked the Englishman.

"For obvious reasons, we remove their belts when they check in," I replied. "Those of you who work in the medical sector will understand."

By the grace of God, no one challenged me on this, and the group began to board the minibus, clasping their township trinkets to their bosoms. As the taxi executed a neat U-turn, I waved them off, but all were engrossed in passionate discussion and only the driver waved back, a huge grin on his face. I suspected he'd earned more money in the past six hours than the whole previous month.

Chapter 26

Reconstruction

The next morning, I stripped the bedding from my bunk and carried it to the new washing block, a zinc-lined shed partitioned into two halves, one housing a row of shower and toilet cubicles, the other taken up by a laundry room containing a no-nonsense, mop-wielding matron. The old standpipe outside the entrance now looked like an oilfield drilling rig, a bouquet of hoses blooming from its top and snaking their way to each of the shipping containers. The shortest length of hose, just a couple of feet long, fulfilled the facility's original function, namely the dispensing of water to the community, though the competition for water pressure had somewhat throttled the flow, which was now more of an indifferent squirt as opposed to a gushing torrent. As a result, the queue for the standpipe was now rather longer than it had been, though the enthusiasm of the youth collecting payment appeared undimmed. I saw that another lad had set up a small stall nearby, selling second-hand bottles and a variety of laundry detergents, and I marvelled at the spontaneous entrepreneurship.

I handed my sheets to the matron and was surprised to receive my own demand for payment. "Ah, no, I'm a resident at Mama Bisha's," I explained, with a winning smile. But the matron made it abundantly clear that if I wanted my linen washed, I would be paying, however prestigious my accommodation status. I felt this was a mite exploitative and considered returning to reception to raise it with Mama Bisha but, given that my bedclothes were a week old and somewhat ripe, I conceded and handed over a ten rand note.

On my way back, I stopped to watch a gang of electricians, who, from the look of their unbranded vehicle and plain overalls, appeared non-affiliated with the state-owned electricity company. They had constructed a scaffolding ladder around the concrete pylon and were busy integrating the web of wiring surrounding Mama Bisha's campus with the rats' nest of cable suspended over the yard. I had a vision of the whole tangled mess collapsing upon me as I strolled beneath, frying me alive in an explosion of sparks, so I gave the whole shambles a very wide berth.

I passed through the dining room, which was full of paint-splattered workmen eating breakfast, and entered reception. Shooter and McGregor were standing just inside the door of Mama Bisha's office, their backs to me, and appeared to be watching something, intently. I crept up behind them and stood on tiptoes to peer over their shoulders. I glimpsed a set of TV monitors sitting inside a tall cupboard, presumably something to do with Shooter's security system. As I craned my neck for a better look, McGregor sensed my presence. He turned, scowling, and stepped in front of me, blocking my view.

"You do not have security clearance!" grinned Shooter, pulling the door shut behind him.

"Clearly not. Well, suit yourself. I have some confidential business of my own to see to."

I sank into one of the new sofas lining the reception area and pulled out my phone. The two men disappeared back inside Mama Bisha's office, this time closing the door. I scrolled, lazily, through the hundred or so emails I'd received over the past day. There was a clutch of depressing missives from the office of Herbert Marris, CEO, publicising the ever-more heroic efforts of the Gatesave workforce to lower costs, including a special mention for the marketing department, who had volunteered to remove their footwear and reduce wear on the head office carpet, and the heart-warming tale of a section manager in Chichester who had brought her own cats to work, in a low-budget attempt to resolve her store's vermin problem.

Among the dross, there were a couple of interesting messages. Sandra had sent me an invitation to a party and awards ceremony at Hemelhuis Estate, next month, to celebrate Paris-Blois's new ethical trading initiative. And there was a one-liner from Josh, the enthusiastic American, informing me his review of Mama Bisha's was now up on Hotbeat dot com. I followed the link he'd supplied and, sure enough, there was a glowing report of our humble guesthouse-cum-community hub, under the headline:

HotBeat.com Venue of the Year! Get a Smiley in your Face in the Gangsta's Paradise!

Reading through the breathless prose, you'd think he'd just discovered a branch of El Bulli in the ruins of Great Zimbabwe. It was all 'fearsome, animal cuisine dating back to the dawn of mankind', 'the southern sun surrendering to Africa's hypnotic rhythm' and 'follow the township drums, not your GPS'. I dropped Josh a thank you email and expressed my hope that the article would do its job of protecting Hotbeat dot com from further criticism that it was over-focussed on the interests of the white, western middle classes.

My phone buzzed. A local number, one I didn't recognise.

"Felix Hart speaking."

"You need to send me a car." A thick, Afrikaans accent.

"I'm sorry? Who's sending who a car? Who is this please?"

"This is Tears of Pity in Khayelitsha, yes?"

My heart gave a little skip of fear.

"Yes, that's me. I mean, that's us."

"I'm Swart. The auditor. You need to send me a car. I'm not driving into the township myself."

My stomach lurched. I doubted a proper auditor would need more than ten seconds at Mama Bisha's before we were properly rumbled. There would be no further Tears of Pity development grants and, doubtless, that would be the end of my sabbatical too, swiftly followed by my recall to London and some kind of career-ending disciplinary process. I couldn't see Troy Frittersley, however soft-headed he might be, tolerating the kind of shenanigans that went on at Mama Bisha's during the hours of darkness, and I was pretty sure Gatesave would have something to say about it too, given what a humourless puritan the CEO had turned out to be.

"Any chance we can put it off for a few days? The nurses are away on a training course this week and the facility is closed."

"The audit is today. Your London office has paid for it, so you'd better send me a car or it's your money wasted. And you'll fail the audit into the bargain."

"Right. No problem. I'll organise something."

"I want the car in an hour. And make sure it has air con. I don't want to breathe any more of that stinking township dust than I have to."

Swart provided me with his address, impressed upon me once more that he was a very busy man, and hung up. I suspected he might be a tough one to charm.

"Shooter, I need your help!" I called.

Mama Bisha's office door opened a few inches and Shooter's head popped through, a small screwdriver between his teeth. Behind him, I could see McGregor frowning at me.

"Shooter, we need some nurses! We need to dress up Zola again. One of the other girls too."

"They are women, not girls, leopard-shagger," said Shooter, pointing the screwdriver at me.

"Yes, apologies, of course they are. Look, we have a visitor, arriving very soon. An auditor. He's coming to check the medical facility. We need people dressed as nurses again."

Shooter looked at McGregor, who shrugged. Everyone knew that Zola's magnificent medical performance earlier in the week had triggered an avalanche of money. Who's to say what riches a whole hospital of nurses might deliver?

"You have the nurse clothes?" said Shooter.

"They're in my room. Can you get a couple of the ladies together, please?"

"Ok *mlungu*." Shooter handed the screwdriver to McGregor and disappeared into the dining room.

"*Mlungu* Moses," muttered McGregor, as he pushed the office door shut.

"Yes, that's my name," I said, striding after Shooter.

I dispatched a driver to pick up the auditor, then approached the Red Cross shipping container. I flung open the doors, crossing my fingers that the room would look enough like a simple medical facility to fool a self-important auditor in a hurry. My jaw dropped. The interior, it's fair to say, looked like a medical facility in the same way that Suleiman the Magnificent's harem looked like a Victorian soup kitchen for distressed lepers. In other words, it didn't look like one in the slightest.

I stood, goggling at the décor, from the distinctly un-clinical soft furnishings to the mind-blowingly inappropriate pictures adorning the walls. In the corner lay a shower cubicle, on which hung a sign, stating 'Washing Body Compulsory'. Then, as it dawned on me that time was very short indeed, I hurled myself into action.

First, I pulled down the crimson chiffon tacked to the ceiling and upper sections of the walls. I ripped the pink linen from the bed, removed the black silken pillowcases and piled them all in the centre of the floor, on top of the red, heart-shaped rug emblazoned with the phrase 'Just Do It'. I tossed the scarlet, lip-shaped velvet cushions onto the pile, rolled up the rug and, weighed down under a ton of immodest fabric, waddled to my room and dumped it in the corner. I pulled the white sheets and grey blanket from my own bunk, ran back to the shipping container and quickly made up the bed, hoping the auditor would overlook the poorly executed hospital corners, not to mention the red-painted bed frame.

I removed the framed prints from the walls, none of which, despite their focus on the female form, were likely to pass muster as a legitimate anatomical reference aid. One by one, I stacked them next to the door; the famous poster of the blonde tennis player scratching her buttock, another showing a more voluptuous black athlete doing the same, and a pair of exercising gymnasts who had forgotten their leotards. There was a print advertising the film *Piranha 3DD*, which appeared to have little to do with marine biology, while another poster, covered with scantily clad, afro-haired women, promoted the vintage Blaxploitation movie *Stud Brown*, together with the tagline 'He Packs the Biggest Rod in Town'.

Heart now pounding, I inspected the gold-sprayed, plinth-mounted mermaid lying atop the chest of drawers, wondering whether it might, by some miracle, pass as a legitimate piece of décor in a medical facility. But the mermaid's proportions rather betrayed the sculptor's enthusiasm for the female torso, on which he (one assumes it was a he) had lavished the vast majority of his plaster-of-Paris. The rest of the creature's body had received rather less attention, or perhaps had been subcontracted to a drunken apprentice, for the tail was absurdly short, as if a confused haddock was attempting to swim up her backside, while her face had received the least focus of all, her expression not so much an enchanting siren of the sea as a yodelling gnome with cataracts. With a great deal of heaving, I relocated the sculpture to the dining room.

I scanned the now rather bare, metal-sided room, and satisfied myself there were no further risqué objects on display. The shower cubicle and its bossy little sign, I felt, looked authentically hygienic. I rattled the wardrobe doors and the chest of drawers but, thankfully, all were locked. Finally, and rather out of breath, I stood on the bed and unscrewed the frilly crimson lampshade, leaving the room lit by just an austere, bare bulb.

The clinic facilities were now in order but, of our dedicated health care professionals, there was no sign. I dashed outside to find Shooter playing with his phone.

"Where are our nurses, Shooter? The auditor needs to see nurses!"

"They are working, *mlungu*," he shrugged, sliding his headphones around his neck.

"Working where? Can't they knock off early or something?"

At that moment, the door of a nearby shipping container creaked open and a furtive-looking man peeped out. Ignoring us, and satisfied there was no-one respectable around to compromise him, he scurried off and disappeared into a passageway between the shacks. A minute later, the same happened at the container next door.

"There, you see," said Shooter. "They are coming."

Finally, with me dancing a jig of panic, and a full two hours after he'd made his first phone call, Zola and Nomi stood sulking outside the medical facility in their sober nurses' skirts and blouses. Nomi, in particular, had done a magnificent job of squeezing herself into her uniform. To my shame, it was abundantly clear I had failed to cater for the fuller-figured medical professional.

"Ladies. Thank you for your help. And I do apologise, Nomi, for the poor fit of your shirt. You won't have to wear it for long. Now, we must be quick. This is very important. We have an inspector visiting. I need you both to do your best nurse impressions, just like you did last week, Zola."

I handed them their novelty nurse's hats, but decided against deploying the plastic timepieces which, close up, even a cross-eyed child could have spotted as fakes.

"I'll answer any questions the auditor asks, ok? In fact, it would be best if you could all pretend not to speak English."

"But I am an English lady," said Zola, curtseying, at which everyone, except me, laughed uproariously.

"Yes, of course you are," I said, smiling desperately. Despite my successes earlier in the week, I had a feeling things were beginning to slip from my grasp. I'd got away with passing off a dodgy nurse to gullible old Frittersley, but a live audit was another thing altogether. I realised I was sweating heavily.

"Madams, please! For the purposes of this trick... I mean... role-play... I need you to pretend to only speak Xhosa. Or, better still, Sesotho. Something he won't understand."

Of course, I was assuming that Swart, the auditor, wouldn't speak any African languages, other than his native Afrikaans. That was, potentially, a risky assumption. South African children, whatever their colour, were obliged to learn a black African language at school these days, an admirable policy begun back in the nineties to bring the country together. But, by the sound of his rough, cynical voice, I was guessing Swart was too old to have been schooled post-liberation. And I prayed that he hadn't, in a fit of Mandela-inspired national unity, flung himself into the study of his black compatriots' mother tongues. In fact, I mused, it would be jolly useful if he were blind, deaf and drunk too.

The two women folded their arms, which I decided to interpret as a qualified willingness to play along.

"Thank you, ladies. Much appreciated. Right, Shooter, we need to lock all the other containers. I'll say they're being disinfected or something."

"Some of them are occupied, *mlungu*."

"We won't be long. Just lock them for half an hour or so, until the auditor's gone."

"I think that is bad for health and safety."

"Health and safety? You're kidding me! *That's* a health and safety hazard!" I pointed at the great bolus of electrical cables, the size of a cow, hanging from the concrete pylon at the edge of the yard. "You're telling me you're worried about locking a shipping container for a few minutes?"

"There might be a fire."

Our safety discussion was interrupted by the sound of a minibus nosing its way over the little bridge.

"Oh Christ, he's here! Shooter, please go and hide somewhere. Make sure no-one bothers us. And ladies, try to act like busy, professional nurses. Look slightly annoyed and impatient. As if someone's been sick in your bedroom."

Zola bared her teeth and scowled, while Nomi shook her fist.

"Not that annoyed! Oh God, we're screwed."

A brief memory of my schooldays flashed before me. An examination, a very important one, for which I had done no preparation beyond stealing a revision book from the dormitory next door. Then staring, blankly, at the gobbledegook questions, cold sweat prickling my back, before writing, furiously, whatever came into my head.

I had failed the exam, miserably.

Chapter 27

Insurance

The taxi door slammed and a frowning, sandy-haired man strode towards us carrying a leather satchel. The driver, clearly expecting some kind of payment, scurried after him.

"Are you Hart?" he barked. I was relieved to see he was in his forties, meaning he was unlikely to have been schooled in any black African languages.

"Yes, hello, that's me! You must be Mr Swart. Ooh, Hart and Swart, that rhymes! That's a good omen."

Swart stared at me as if I was an idiot. In retrospect, it was a fair assumption.

"Let's get started, shall we? Get away from me, man!" This second remark was directed at the driver, who had caught up and was politely but firmly requesting remuneration for the taxi ride.

"Of course, Mr Swart, this way please." I pulled a hundred-rand note from my pocket and pressed it into the driver's hand. "*Enkosi*," I said. The driver threw a hateful look at Swart's back and returned to his vehicle.

"Right, Mr Swart. I would like to introduce you to Sister Zola and Sister Nomi. Sadly, they do not speak any English."

Zola and Nomi curtseyed. Swart's eyes bulged as he contemplated Nomi's ill-fitting blouse. "I thought you said the staff were away on a training course. And who ever heard of a nurse that didn't speak English? Where did they study?"

"Lesotho Nursing College, I think."

"You think? What are Sotho nurses doing in a Xhosa township?"

"Oh, we're one big melting pot here," I said, breezily. I placed a hand on his arm. "Here, please take a look at one of the rooms. I'm sure you'll find it all hygienic and in good order."

But Swart shrugged me off. He appeared to be in no hurry to look at the medical facility, or even to remove his eyes from Nomi. I hoped she wasn't feeling uncomfortable under his oppressive male gaze. I certainly was.

"*Molweni. Nivela phi? Uyaqonda?*" he said, in horribly fluent Xhosa. My heart sank. We were well and truly busted.

"*Ndiyaqonda,*" smiled Nomi. "*iBhayi.*"

The conversation, which was already pushing the limits of my very basic Xhosa, had so far involved an exchange of pleasantries and an enquiry as to where the ladies were from. I suspected we'd be in trouble if Swart decided to ask Nomi how to stem the flow of blood from an arterial wound, or her favourite hepatitis B vaccine.

"The sisters are very busy," I said, idiotically.

"*Ngaba ungumongikazi?*" asked Swart, ignoring me completely. I looked helplessly to Zola for a translation, then remembered she wasn't supposed to know any English.

"*Ndizakubonisa yonke into,*" replied Nomi, with a smile.

As my mouth flapped open and shut, Nomi took Swart's arm and steered him towards the medical facility. I followed them inside.

"What is this place?" asked Swart, frowning at the badly made bed. The bare bulb's reflection glowed from each of the dull steel walls, like a sun through smog.

"I know it's not exactly the Christiaan Barnard Memorial Hospital," I said, over Swart's shoulder, "but we're proud of our humble little facility, aren't we, sisters?"

Zola and Nomi, who were doing a significantly better job at remembering they were non-English-speaking than I was, remained silent. Swart stepped forward to the chest and tried each of the drawers.

"What's in here?"

"Oh, just medical supplies."

"Open it."

"It's locked."

"I know it's locked. I just tried to open it. Unlock it."

"Sorry, I don't have the key. Sorry." I squeezed my hands. "Would you like to see the toilets? They're new."

Swart turned to the women and smiled. "*Unaso isitshixo?*"

Zola nodded and produced a key from her pocket. Then, as I goggled in horror, she placed it in the keyhole at the top of the dresser and turned it.

"*Enkosi,*" said Swart and pulled open the top drawer. I leaned forward to see the contents for myself, then stepped back and closed my eyes, hoping that when I reopened them, I might find I had been mistaken. I heard Swart open the next drawer down, then the bottom one.

"These drawers are full of condoms," he said, finally. I opened my eyes to find Swart holding a fistful of prophylactics in front of my face.

"Yes," I croaked. "Sexual health is extremely important."

"And what is in the wardrobe?"

"More condoms, I think," I squeaked.

Swart beckoned to Zola who produced another key and inserted it. There was a sharp click and the wardrobe doors swung open. The four of us gazed inside.

The rack of clothes, in a low light, might have passed for a selection of protective industrial outfits, the type worn while handling corrosive chemicals, perhaps, or decontaminating a misbehaving nuclear reactor. But just an hour earlier, I had removed the frilly lamp shade, and the bare bulb above us illuminated the interior of the wardrobe very clearly indeed. Swart's jaw dropped. A row of crotchless leather pants gaped back at him, while beside them, a selection of black rubber shirts squeaked on their hangers. Even if the bulb had been dimmed, and the kinky clothes rail somehow overlooked, the wardrobe doors would have required some inspired explaining, for the inside of each was festooned with a range of dangling dildos, dongs and strap-ons, in an eye-watering variety of sizes.

In any case, my powers of inspired explanation had abandoned me. I turned and exited the shipping container, moving as quietly as possible so as not to disturb the magical silence that had descended upon the room. I trudged across the yard, passed through the rear entrance into Mama Bisha's, shut my bedroom door and lay down on the bare mattress. Then, I placed my hands over my face and gave a long, low moan, a tragic, heartfelt moo of defeat, for I knew that I'd run out of road.

The next stage, just hours from now, would be a phone call from Troy Frittersley, his voice quavering as he implored me to contradict the Tears of Pity audit sitting judgmentally in his inbox, begging me to reassure him that his flagship African community-hub-cum-medical-facility was indeed a wellspring of empathy and healing and not, in fact, a prefabricated township brothel specialising in cavity explorations of an altogether less wholesome nature.

After that, I would receive a call from the Head of Compliance, perhaps even the CEO himself, informing me that I had brought disgrace upon the good name of Gatesave Supermarkets, that my employment was terminated, my office possessions redistributed among my colleagues and my desk chopped up for firewood. Finally, penniless, I would be obliged to hitch-hike across Africa in an attempt to return home, be kidnapped by Tuareg tribesmen as I crossed the Sahara, sold into slavery, and forced to sweep up camel droppings under the desert sun for the rest of my days.

Whether I passed out in despair or simply dozed off I don't know, but I was woken by a knock at the door.

"Yes?"

The door scraped open a few inches and Shooter's grinning head poked round.

"*Mlungu*! Your audit went very well!"

"Yes, thank you, Shooter. Forgive me if I don't find it quite so funny."

"No, it went very well. Very well!"

"If you say so." It occurred to me that once the Tears of Pity funding dried up, my free lodgings were likely to evaporate too. I'd probably be sleeping rough before the week was out.

"No, you come and see." He beckoned me to rise.

"What, he's left a copy of the audit here?"

I followed Shooter into the dining room, where a local woman, wearing a t-shirt emblazoned 'Township Upliftment Experience', was delivering a lecture to a table of earnest-looking, young white people. "Good afternoon, Moses!" called the woman. I gave an embarrassed wave and hurried on through to reception.

Mama Bisha was standing at the front entrance, seeing off a visitor. I only saw the departing figure for a split second, but I could have sworn they were wearing a uniform. A blue shirt, matching trousers, a glimpse of an epaulette. The police? Mama Bisha was smiling, so it can't have been an unfriendly visit.

"Has there been any trouble?" I asked.

Mama Bisha closed the door. Her smile vanished. McGregor leaned against the reception desk, arms folded. I was about to repeat the question but Shooter turned to me, eyes shining, and began regaling me with the concluding minutes of our audit fiasco.

"So, I said to the man 'is the audit good?' and he said 'no, it is bad', and I said 'no, it must be good!' and he said 'no, it is bad, you are a bad hospital', so I said 'no, the audit is good!' and he said…"

"Yes, thank you Shooter, I get the idea. I'm sure you did your best. If the audit genuinely turns out well, I promise there's a career awaiting you at Gatesave as a senior negotiator."

I turned to Mama Bisha.

"I'm afraid we've hit a little obstacle."

"So I understand," she replied.

"More than little, actually. The game's up. We're busted. I may as well pack my bags and leave."

Mama Bisha nodded to McGregor, who opened the office door. He gestured inside.

"Go look!" urged Shooter.

"Look at what?"

Again, my question was ignored. I followed McGregor into the office. He opened the door of the tall cupboard, revealing four TV monitors on shelves, along with a laptop and a control panel. Each of the screens displayed the interior of a small bedroom and the word 'live' in the top corner. McGregor fiddled with the laptop. One of the screens went blank, then a new picture appeared of a room containing four people. Two of them were dressed as nurses. I realised with a shock that the other two were Swart the auditor and yours truly.

"You've put cameras in the rooms," I said. "To protect the women."

"Yes, *mlungu*, you are very clever," sighed McGregor. He tapped the laptop and the video moved into fast-forward, the four figures vibrating and bobbing to and fro. I watched Swart yank open the three drawers, top to bottom, and thrust a fist-full of rubber johnnies at me, then the wardrobe was unlocked and the doors flung open, then there was me turning and leaving, my defeated trudge transformed into a comedy waddle as I passed out of sight beneath the camera.

For a few seconds, the three remaining figures moved back and forth, as though dancing a secret jig, then Zola stepped forward and reached for something under the camera. The room darkened and I realised she'd pulled the doors of the shipping container closed. The camera was obviously positioned over the entrance. It must have been well concealed. I hadn't spotted it earlier when I was tearing down the décor. McGregor tapped the laptop and the video slowed to normal playback.

Following my departure, it became clear the audit agenda had changed, quite radically. Swart leapt out of his trousers and flung himself, face down, on the bed, while Zola and Nomi liberated themselves from their ill-fitting nurse's garments and each selected a phallus from the wardrobe.

Swart was a thorough man, an auditor to his core, in fact, and clearly intent on testing as many of the items inside the wardrobe as his schedule permitted. In this, he was ably facilitated by Zola and Nomi, who helped each other in and out of the various straps and buckles like a pair of kinky Houdinis.

After a minute, I turned away from the screen and stepped out of the office. To view any more, entertaining as it was, would have been voyeuristic. Mama Bisha watched me, unsmiling.

"Has Swart seen the video?" I said, slightly stunned.

"Yes, I showed him on my phone when he came out," said Shooter, triumphantly. "I said 'the audit must be good, or *mlungu* will be very angry!'"

"And what did he say?"

"He said some bad things about you, *mlungu*. Some very bad words."

"Yes… I can imagine."

"But not as many bad words as the police inspector, yesterday. He was very, very angry!"

"Police inspector? A hygiene auditor is one thing, but I am rather hoping you didn't involve me in your intimate negotiations with the local police chief…"

"Don't worry, of course you were not mentioned," said Mama Bisha. "And Shooter, I think Mr Hart has heard enough, we don't want to frighten him about things that don't concern him."

"So, this police inspector is now the star of his own little peep show, is he? Are you sure that's going to improve your relationship with the local constabulary? It didn't appear exactly tip-top last week."

"The police inspector's anger will be nothing compared to that of his wife, should she ever see the video," said Mama Bisha. "Or, for that matter, that of the inspector's father-in-law, a prominent local politician, whose temper is even greater than his wealth."

"No more bad visits from the police," said Shooter. "Just nice visits. And I think the audit will be good. I am very sure of this."

"Well, that's… extraordinarily fine news!"

I swear that, at that very moment, a shaft of sunlight pierced the window above and bathed me in a warm, golden glow. I closed my eyes and relaxed for what felt like the first time that month. Even my bowels appeared to be vibrating with relief, until I realised it was my phone buzzing in my back pocket.

"Hello?"

"Mr Hart, I have news of the inspection!" said the voice at the other end.

"Good Lord! Already? That's fast. I trust Mr Swart found our nurses up to scratch?" I winked at Shooter, who beamed.

"Nurses? Mr Hart, this is Mr Sonn, at the Fairly Trod Foundation. I'm calling with news of our visit, yesterday, to Blanchkopf Wine Growers."

Chapter 28

Empowerment

I confess my overwhelming morning at Mama Bisha's had pushed Blanchkopf and his problematic employee relations to the back of my mind. Conscious I was being watched by Mama Bisha and her management team, I returned to my bedroom for some privacy.

"Of course! Mr Sonn, how are you? How was the survey? Good news, I hope?" I clenched my buttocks, praying to the gods that by some miracle, the Fairly Trod inspector had believed the story of Blanchkopf transforming himself from an unreconstructed slave driver to a paragon of workers' rights.

"Well, there are a few areas that require improvement," said Mr Sonn. I closed my eyes. "But in the key areas of wages and working conditions, our inspector found clear evidence of an attempt at radical improvement. And we were impressed by Mr Blanchkopf's agreement to contribute a levy to the Fairly Trod Foundation for every bottle sold."

"Oh. That sounds encouraging. So… has he passed, or what?"

"We're willing to grant a provisional certification, Mr Hart, on the condition we revisit next month."

"Brilliant!" I shouted, allowing my buttocks to unclench.

"Yes, it is a quite remarkable turnaround. I never would have believed it, given that estate's reputation. You clearly found a way to motivate Mr Blanchkopf."

"Yes, well, I think he's seen which way the wind is blowing in the new South Africa."

"Indeed. Oh, and that NGO were in touch again. The woman who works there is quite assertive, I must say. I was delighted to be able to tell her that Blanchkopf has achieved Fairly Trod status. She was very suspicious, but I promised to send her a copy of the certificate. They want to visit the estate themselves, but Mr Blanchkopf won't permit it, apparently."

"Yes, the Blanchkopfs are very private people."

"I explained that was up to them to resolve with the estate. Perhaps you could have a word with Mr Blanchkopf yourself."

"I'll certainly try. Oh, and if I could ask another little favour of you, Mr Sonn, one of my other suppliers, Hemelhuis Estate, wishes to purchase some bulk wine from Mr Blanchkopf, but they'll only do business with wineries that have achieved Fairly Trod certification. May I put them in touch with you, so you can confirm Blanchkopf Wine Growers are now compliant?"

"No problem at all, Mr Hart."

I called Sandra immediately, informing her that Blanchkopf had achieved Fairly Trod status and that our plan to buy wine from him and sell it on to Gambu could now proceed.

"Very good, Felix. Your agreement with this Gambu character and his gang appears to have held up. He's not been seen outside the estate gates since last week. My CEO is most impressed with your negotiating skills."

"The Platinum Fox? I'm honoured."

"His name is Jacobus. He doesn't really like being called the Platinum Fox. Look, I'm back at our head office in Paris, and a little tied up right now. Would you mind calling Hemelhuis yourself and confirming that everything is in order? I'll drop the winemaker an email confirming that Jacobus and I are happy to proceed."

I did as Sandra asked and Hemelhuis Estate's winemaker agreed to begin the purchase of wine from Blanchkopf the following week, subject to confirmation from the Fairly Trod Foundation. Next, I placed a call to Gambu.

"Mr Gambu, I have wonderful news!"

"Pray, tell me! Has the global conspiracy of white monopoly capital been smashed beyond repair, and the yoke lifted from the shoulders of the oppressed?"

"Well, not entirely, but Hemelhuis Estate have just informed me they are willing to supply you with Fairly Trod bulk wine, from next week. They have a red and a white blend that are perfect for your Black Power Pinotage and Woke White. Gatesave will ship the wines from you as soon as you can bottle them. And, if you would be kind enough to courier a case of each wine to our head office in London, ahead of the shipment, we'll send samples to all the top wine influencers, so we can create a buzz."

"Let me check I have understood correctly, Mr Hart. You are telling me that your friends at a rapacious, Western multi-national, which stole the land from under the feet of my ancestors, are now willing to sell back to me the produce of that very land, mixed with my compatriots' blood and tears? And that, furthermore, your own company, an exemplar of mercenary capitalism, wishes to make money off the back of it?"

"Well, yes, that's one way of putting it. But we're all trying to make amends." My buttocks began to re-clench. "The wine's Fairly Trod, after all."

"Fairly Trod? Am I supposed to be grateful that the produce of my dispossessed ancestors' land carries this tawdry logo of white liberal tears?"

"Mr Gambu, that's a slightly pessimistic take on the situation," I said, as a trickle of desperate sweat crept from my armpit.

"I would say five hundred years of oppression is enough to cultivate the pessimist in the most generous of souls."

"My company are ever so keen to put your wonderful wine on our shelves," I pleaded.

"They may well be. I am merely disagreeing with your premise that this is wonderful news."

"Not wonderful, then. Just… adequate news?"

"Barely adequate."

"Adequate enough?" I squeaked.

"For now, adequate enough," said Gambu, and hung up.

With shaking fingers, I called the Head of Message.

"Felix!" she shouted. "For the love of God, where have you been? I've been trying to get hold of you all week!"

The Head of Message had indeed left several increasingly frantic messages, but I hadn't been able to face returning her calls.

"I have some good news! Blanchkopf Wine Growers have passed their Fairly Trod inspection."

"Thank Christ for that. Are you absolutely sure?"

"Yes, they're fully certified. Well, provisionally certified, but that's just a formality."

"It had better be a bloody formality, Felix, or God help you. Right. Fairly Trod means Blanchkopf is now paying his workers a higher rate, correct?"

"Yes, that's the idea. Quite a lot higher."

"Good. I'll be in touch with that NGO as soon as I've finished with you. We'll sue those do-gooders into the next century if they dare suggest we're complicit in oppressing the developing world."

"The Fairly Trod Foundation is sending the NGO a copy of Blanchkopf's certificate."

"Excellent. That's very helpful. Hopefully that's the immediate crisis averted. But we still need to distance ourselves from Blanchkopf. There's too much dodgy history between us, and that NGO is bound to dig something out eventually."

"Fear not. I have put together a plan to insulate ourselves from Blanchkopf completely. A firewall, you might call it."

"Is it legal?"

"Of course it is," I said, trying to sound offended. "I've arranged for Blanchkopf to sell their wine in bulk to another producer who is, in turn, selling it on to someone else, who will bottle it and sell it to us. And the bottler is a prominent Black Empowerment winery. So, we're turning the whole tricky situation into a good news story!"

"Sounds rather complicated. Isn't it expensive routing it through so many different parties? I assume they're all taking a cut?"

"There's a touch of inflation, yes, but everyone's holding hands to make it work. And the new branding is excellent, we can jack the price way higher."

"Ok, the Black Empowerment story is good. This sounds like a significant improvement on where we were two weeks ago. I hope this is watertight, Felix."

"I think we're fine. And, on a related subject, the Tears of Pity project is progressing excellently. We should have some bold Gatesave branding up over a worthy community facility very shortly. It's all coming together. I really can't think of any flaws at all."

"For your sake, let's hope so."

"I do need you to sign off a couple of new prices please, for the Black Empowerment wines. And a couple of new wines from Hemelhuis Estate too."

"Please tell me they're cheap wines, Felix. Under a fiver, preferably. Herbert Marris is on a crusade to bring our average basket cost down. He's declared war on premium prices."

"They do nudge up against the higher price tier, I must admit. Nearer a tenner than a fiver."

"Jesus Christ! Can't you negotiate the price down? I thought you were supposed to be a ruthless buyer."

"It's part of the plan. You have to pay more when things are Fairly Trod. We're empowering people, remember."

"Right," she said, through gritted teeth. "Leave it with me."

I tapped out an email to Foyley, telling him to place an order with Gambu's winery for a thousand cases each of Black Power Pinotage and Woke White. Then, I sent a message to Gambu himself, warning him the order was imminent, that time was of the essence, and reminding him to courier a case of each wine to Gatesave HQ, as soon as it was bottled, so Foyley could send samples to the most important British wine journalists and social media influencers.

"We saved you, *Mlungu* Moses," said Shooter, as I skipped back into reception. "You were supposed to save us, but we have saved you!"

"I would suggest that Zola and Nomi deserve a lot of the credit," said Mama Bisha.

"They certainly do, Mama Bisha. However, maybe the truth is that we have all saved each other. It's rather beautiful, actually. It gives one hope for the world. I think we should open a bottle of Champagne."

"No, you need to fix that room you messed up," said Mama Bisha. "And you can take your sheets back."

"Oh. Perhaps later then." I glanced through the office door at the video monitor. "Hang on… have my sheets been… used?"

"Yes," said McGregor, pulling the door closed.

"Oh. How utterly foul. I suppose I'd better take them to the laundry block."

"And the driver is not happy," said Shooter, stepping up to the new football table. "Everybody calls him all the time."

"What driver? Who calls him?"

"Everybody. All the *mlungu* call him. All the day and all night. They want to come here for smiley and wine. He cannot rest for one second, his phone is beep beep, beep beep, all the time. Even when he is with his wife!" Shooter grinned and whirled one of the spindles.

"Ah, I see. The driver that gave his number to our first *mlungu* – I mean the American and his friend, when he took them home."

"Yes. Now every *mlungu* calls him."

"Well, why don't you hire a receptionist?"

"We did," said Mama Bisha. "She is sitting over there." She pointed to a young woman behind the counter, speaking quietly into a hands-free mic.

"Oh, I see. Apologies, I assumed she was a… well, you know. A worker."

The woman finished her call and made a note in an office diary.

"Hey, how many bookings we got?" called Shooter.

"Twenty-eight."

"You better buy some more smileys, *Mlungu* Moses," said McGregor.

"What, we have bookings for twenty-eight people? Tonight?"

"Mama Bisha's Tuck Shop, how can I help?" said the young woman, lifting her pen once more.

"More than twenty-eight!" said Shooter, whirling a spindle with each hand. "We are on Facebook now. And Instagram."

"I like the new branding," I said. "But I'm going to need some help."

"Don't worry," said Mama Bisha, revealing a very slight smile. "We know you are a terrible cook. We have hired more kitchen staff. You will serve the wine."

"That's a job I can do."

"Yes, *mlungu*, that is your job!" grinned Shooter, propelling a ball into the goal mouth with a loud crack.

Serving wine wasn't my only job that day. To cater for the greater number of guests, we had to dig a more substantial fire pit, large enough to allow many smileys to be roasted simultaneously. My gang of little scavengers brought bricks and tiles to ring the pit, then I set them to work collecting the rubbish still strewn around the yard into a series of piles, ready for proper disposal. We procured more patio chairs from a furniture store in Somerset West and a pickup delivered several sacks of woodchips, which we raked over the ground to give a more aspirational texture to the grubby township earth. As we beautified our little patch, McGregor supervised a group of workmen installing a ten-foot-high chain-link fence along the two sides of the clearing that abutted the rows of shacks.

At sunset, I washed the dust and sweat from my body in the new shower block, changed, and prepared the bar for action. I was assigned one of the new serving staff, a young man called Langa, and I opened a few bottles to give him an educational wine tasting before the guests arrived. Earlier that day, I had visited the wine merchant in Stellenbosch, to procure more cases of Smiley Red, and the beaming manager assured me he had been telling every one of his customers that Mama Bisha's sported the finest wine list in Africa.

That evening, taxi after taxi nosed their way over the little bridge and disgorged their cargoes of blinking, slightly frightened-looking white people into the township gloom. Our newly recruited front of house staff greeted each group and directed them to the fire pit along a pathway studded with jam jar lanterns. Mama Bisha had ordered me to stand, well illuminated, beside the fire at the start of the evening, so our newly arrived guests would be reassured by the presence of a Caucasian. Her intuition was correct, for each group of guests would creep, warily, towards the flames, uncertain of the motives of their township guides, until one of them would catch sight of me and, with a cry of relief, draw my presence to the attention of their companions. I would give a cheery wave and the front of house staff would smile and point me out to the rest of the group, declaring, "You see, everything is fine!"

In contrast to the previous week, when a mere handful of saleswomen had hustled their homemade wares to our guests, dozens of stalls had now sprung up beside the main building, selling trinkets, drinks, bootleg DVDs and smuggled cigarettes. The guests haggled good-naturedly with the stallholders, giving the area the feel of an open-air souk, and their arms were soon full of elephants, hippos and penguins fashioned from township refuse. A team of traffic control operatives in high-vis vests managed the coming and going of minibuses across the narrow bridge in exchange for tips, while a gang of squeegee merchants, armed with a hose snaking back to the standpipe, did a roaring trade cleaning the parked taxis.

"Come and taste the Township Beer Experience!" called Shooter, gesturing towards a pair of local women stirring an oil drum over a fire fuelled with timber offcuts. A group of guests approached and peered into the fermenting brew.

"Looks kind of gross," said a woman. She sniffed the vapour rising from the bubbling soup. "Smells pretty gross too! It's sour."

"This is *umqombothi*," said one of the local women. "It is traditional African beer, made from maize and sorghum. This is my family business."

"Oh, I do apologise!" said the woman, mortified. "I'd love to try some."

A battered paint tin was lowered into the brew then lifted out. "Fifty rand each, please."

The guests handed over their money and passed the paint tin around, each sipping gingerly from the rim.

"Ooh, it's got bits in," said the woman.

"Actually, this reminds me of a Belgian Lambic beer," said her companion. He pursed his lips and looked thoughtful. "It has an arresting piquancy."

Once the twilight had faded to black, and the flames had quietened to white-hot coals, the guests were invited to take their seats around the fire pit. Kuhle, who now held the title of head chef, led her staff from the kitchen, each carrying a tray covered in white linen. They lined up before the guests and waited for the hubbub to fade. Then, the linen was whisked aside, revealing two-dozen boiled sheep heads in all their glory, drawing shrieks and gasps from the crowd. As the heads met the hot coals they sizzled and hissed, and slowly the skin glazed and tightened, lips shrank over teeth, until the smouldering smileys, rendered even more ghoulish in the embers' orange light, grinned dead-eyed at their audience, who squirmed and cooed in delicious horror.

Langa, my apprentice sommelier, moved among the group, filling glasses with Smiley Red. As he showed each guest the label, there were further exclamations, with some of the more excitable young women squealing and grabbing their partners. I had to reassure one nervous-looking man that it was indeed fine wine we were pouring and not fermented sheep's blood.

Once everyone's glass was full, I repeated my Frittersley-flavoured sermon on the importance of Mama Bisha's Tuck Shop as a community beacon, dedicated to the celebration of dignity, upliftment of the oppressed, and the kindling of hope in the midst of squalor. Energised by my audience, and perhaps lubricated by the Smiley Red, I poured even more passion into my speech than the night before, leaping up and down and swirling my glass in great arcs above my head, barely spilling a drop. When I had finished, the guests leapt to their feet and paid me the honour of a roaring, standing ovation. I bowed several times and, to my surprise, found my chest swelling with genuine, community-inspired pride. As the guests retook their seats, I looked about me to see whether Mama Bisha had witnessed my performance but, as usual, she'd done her twilight disappearing act.

Langa and I replenished our guests' glasses, and Kuhle reappeared with a long, thin blade. With a flourish, she began carving eyes and portions of tongue from the sizzling smileys and handing them out on the point of her knife. This, needless to say, raised a cacophony of screams, hoots and chatter that wouldn't have been out of place in the heart of the Congolese rain forest. Steak, sweetcorn, *boerewors* and stuffed peppers were added to the grill, to reassure those unsettled by the eyeball hors d'oeuvres, and the guests had gargled their way through a case of Smiley Red before they'd finished the first course.

Langa and I kept the wine flowing. He was a fast learner. Not only were our guests' glasses kept topped up, Langa had composed a poetic tasting note, based on my earlier training session, which he delivered as each new wine was poured. If you'd closed your eyes, and swapped the tin shacks of Khayelitsha for the Georgian splendour of Mayfair, you'd have sworn you'd just been served by the maître d' of Claridges.

New logs were placed on the embers and were soon enveloped in fresh yellow flames. Shooter appeared out of the gloom, carrying a short fence post and a square of plywood. He crouched next to the fire pit and hammered the post into the ground with a rock. He tied the plywood square to the post with a piece of wire and stood back to admire his work. Someone artistic, presumably Nomi, had painted the Facebook, Instagram and Twitter logos side by side on the sign. The three icons flickered seductively in the firelight. Beneath them, our newly christened social media presence was spelt out in neat lettering: @MamaBishasTuckShop.

"Don't forget to like us!" called Shooter, pointing at the sign with both hands. The guests, who had spent the evening taking gleeful selfies accessorised with sheep heads, tongues and eyeballs, promised they would.

Gazing over the fire, and beyond the ring of guests, my attention was caught by the line of shipping containers, fifty-or-so yards away, their exteriors faintly visible in the firelight. The doors of some stood ajar, a strip of soft red shining from the interior. I remembered the crimson lampshade I'd removed, then replaced, in the bedroom-cum-medical centre that morning. I rose and stepped a dozen paces beyond the circle of guests, keeping my back to the fire so I could see more clearly. A few of our customers, all unaccompanied men I guessed, had detached themselves from the group, shadows drawn to the stripes of rosy light. I saw a figure pause in front of a container, silhouetted for a moment between the doors, before slipping out of sight. A second later, the strip of red thinned and disappeared.

I turned back to the fire. The sweet, medicinal scent of marijuana joined the aroma of wood smoke, and I poured myself a glass of excellent Syrah. Shooter's social media sign flickered in the firelight and I decided to pay a visit to the Facebook page of Mama Bisha's Tuck Shop. I'd expected something amateurish, but the page was extremely well produced. The cover picture featured a group of attractive young people, black, white and mixed race, laughing together and enjoying a smiley-themed feast around the fire pit. Several posts had been published, including a link to Hotbeat dot com's glowing write-up, an arty photo of the sun setting behind the reeds in the gully, a township taxi driver posing in front of his gleaming minibus, and even a picture of me serving beers through the dining room hatch, taken from behind, thank goodness, so I remained anonymous, though clear enough for me to be identifiable as a white European. Several events were advertised, including the three-times-weekly 'Original Township Tour' and something called the 'Uprising Experience', which was scheduled for this Sunday. The page had already received several hundred likes and follows.

There were not, so far as I could see, any posts featuring phoney medical facilities, fake nurses in ill-fitting blouses, or shipping containers decorated with crimson lampshades and collections of strap-ons. Just as well, I mused. Given Facebook's reputation as a wholesome, lawabiding company, I suspect such content would have been judged a most scandalous contravention of their terms of use. It crossed my mind that I might be complicit in a rather unsavoury and exploitative conspiracy. But if I'd learnt anything over the past few weeks – and I felt I'd learnt a very great deal – it was to ask myself one simple question: who am I to judge?

Chapter 29

Uprising

Mama Bisha's Tuck Shop entertained thirty-two guests, one way or another, that Friday night. On Saturday, by midday, the young lady in reception had taken sixty reservations and we were forced to bump further enquiries into the following week. The biscuit tin full of banknotes, counted into piles by Mama Bisha and McGregor the next morning, told a profitable story, and it occurred to me that one of the benefits of hosting non-township folk in the middle of darkest Khayelitsha is that few are inclined to run off without paying.

McGregor doled out the money, some of it anyway, to the kitchen staff, laundry workers and car park attendants, then to a line of rather large, unsmiling young men who I suspected might be something to do with keeping the peace. Finally, McGregor handed me a small wad of cash – rather grudgingly, I thought – and his mood didn't improve when I held out my other hand and mewled, humorously, "Please sir, can I have some more?"

However, I was still somewhat scarred by Swart's audit and, given that I was merrily informing our guests each evening that Mama Bisha's Tuck Shop was a world-class medical facility, I felt we needed to convert one of the shipping containers into something that would fool all but the most rigorous and passionless of inspectors. Mama Bisha agreed, and I paid a visit to a medical wholesaler in Bellville, procuring a couple of authentic nurse's uniforms, a wall-mounted first aid kit and some genuine hospital supplies. We painted the interior of the original container white, replaced the posters of *Piranha 3DD* and *Stud Brown* with medical diagrams and an optician's eye chart, swapped the pink-framed double bed for a pair of sensible bunks, then paid a couple of rough-looking township folk to be photographed in bandages alongside Zola and Nomi, this time wearing genuine and properly measured uniforms.

I commissioned Nomi to paint a large sign sporting the Gatesave logo, under which she wrote 'Adding Value to Every Community'. We erected it over the standpipe and I took a picture of the queuing township residents, most of whom, rather sportingly, gave a cheery smile for the camera, not least the youth collecting payment, who gave a huge grin and a double thumbs-up.

I sent the pictures of the standpipe and the new medical facility to both the Head of Message and Troy Frittersley, with a note saying I'd received positive vibes from yesterday's audit, and that the community hub had been able to expand even further thanks to the generosity of Gatesave and Tears of Pity. I also mentioned that, in an attempt at genuine upliftment, we were attempting to make the facility self-funded through selling educational services to the white population.

Frittersley responded with a gushing email, signing off with ABSOLUTELY OUTSTANDING, SO PROUD, followed by an emoji of a tearful face, while the Head of Message replied with a one-liner, stating 'Useful, need more of this, bigger branding and more children next time please'.

Flush with cash, I hired a driver to take me into Somerset West to purchase some provisions. Several dozen men were hard at work in the yard, assembling more market stalls, and I noticed a wooden *spaza* kiosk had sprung up on the other side of the little bridge, selling soft drinks and ice cream. As I passed, I saw Nomi was busy painting a mural on the side of the stall. In one corner, a masked township youth stood, arm raised, poised to fling a rock. In the other, a policeman took cover behind a car as stones rained down from the heavens. Along the top, Nomi had painted 'Uprising Experience This Way', and an arrow pointing back towards Mama Bisha's.

On my return, later that afternoon, I was disconcerted to find a military coup in progress. Two vintage but fearsome-looking armoured vehicles were parked beside the bridge and a dozen armed men in army uniform milled around in front of a large crowd. I spotted Shooter talking to one of the soldiers and I leapt out to investigate.

"Ah *mlungu*! We need you to be a soldier!" said Shooter, as he caught sight of me.

"What in God's name is going on?" I said, staring up at the armoured vehicles. I was relieved to see the soldiers were carrying paintball guns rather than actual assault rifles.

"This is a Casspir," said Shooter, slapping the nearest vehicle's vast metal bumper.

"A Casspir Mark One," shouted a voice. A mixed-race man with a tiny moustache marched up to me, dressed in military fatigues. "But this does not have the original Bedford chassis. No! This has the Mercedes chassis." The moustachioed man advanced to within six inches of my face. "The Bedford chassis proved unsuitable for use in the South-West African theatre. They replaced the drive line and transfer box with Mercedes components, and the rest is history!"

"I see," I said, taking half a step back. The man appeared to have misidentified me as a counter-insurgency fanatic, and I was horribly conscious he was peppering my face with flecks of enthusiastic spittle.

"He knows his stuff," beamed Shooter, pointing at the man.

"But, what's it for?" I said, looking up at the monstrous vehicle. It looked like a cross between a school bus and a gigantic metal coffin. The chassis sat high above the ground, with enough clearance for a small child to toddle beneath.

"The correct question, when considering the Casspir, is what is it *not* for?" shouted the man, eyes gleaming. He took a step forward, so his face was inches from mine once more. "Long-range patrol, mine clearance, special operations, exfiltration, anti-terrorism, peacekeeping. You are looking at the father of all mine-resistant, ambush-protected vehicles!"

"That's wonderful," I said, removing a handkerchief and wiping my face. "I mean, why is it here?"

"For the Township Uprising Experience!" declared Shooter.

"I'm sorry, I still haven't got a clue what you're talking about."

"The V-shaped hull deflects the blast from mines or IEDs," shouted the moustachioed man. I nodded and, keeping my mouth tightly shut, began to move very slowly backwards, praying my retreat was gradual enough to be imperceptible.

"The genius is making the leaf-spring suspension and critical components *external* to the monocoque hull," declared the man, ecstatically. To my dismay, I realised his face was moving towards me at exactly the same rate I was retreating.

"That really is genius," I said, preparing to make a run for it, but I was interrupted by Shooter dumping a set of army fatigues and a metal helmet into my arms.

"You must change into these. You must have a weapon too." He handed me a paintball gun. "You will ride on this Casspir here, with the other soldiers. When the uprising begins, you will shoot at the freedom fighters."

"So, I'm one of the baddies?"

"Yes, *mlungu*, exactly! You are the baddies!"

"And these soldiers are all baddies too?"

"Yes, yes. We could not get real *mlungu*. These mixed-race people from Mitchell's Plain look nearly white. And they speak Afrikaans."

"Shooter, where did you get these vehicles from?"

"From the Apartheid Museum in Cape Town. This guy works there." He pointed at the moustachioed man who was now glaring at a small child swinging from the Casspir's radiator grille.

"What, and they let you borrow them?"

"They are closed on Sundays."

"Ok, *kom*," shouted the moustachioed man to the troops. "*Kom ons gaan*! *Maak gou*. Let's go, let's go! You, get changed, quick!"

I did as I was told, hopping into my army fatigues and handing my jeans and shirt to Shooter. The engines fired up and one of my platoon pulled me up into the back of the Casspir. I peered through the narrow, bullet-proof windows at the happy crowd, black and white, milling around the marketplace, eating ice creams and gawping at the armoured vehicles.

"Go up top," shouted the moustachioed man from the driver's seat, as the engines snarled. I climbed up through the roof hatch and perched alongside three of my fellow troopers in the open air, our paintball guns pointed skywards. The top of the Casspir must have been ten feet from the ground, so I had a superb view. I could see over the tall reeds in the gully alongside us, to the water tanks and solar panels on top of the shipping containers, then across mile upon mile of shacks, all the way to the Boland Mountains, the sea of glittering tin roofs peppered by thousands of wisps of smoke rising into the cloudless sky.

With a growl, the Casspir lurched forward and the crowd cheered and waved. We lumbered over the bridge onto the dirt track running parallel to the gully, and I held tight to the roof with my spare hand. The other Casspir followed behind, belching a trail of blue-grey exhaust. We picked up speed and I was soon enjoying the sensation of the wind ruffling my hair, shaking my gun at the smiling and laughing township children as we roared along the track.

"Where are we going?" I shouted to the soldier beside me.

"We wait at the Swartklip Road for further orders," my companion shouted back.

After ten minutes or so, we slowed, and I saw a tarmacked road ahead. We pulled off onto a rubbish-strewn patch of waste ground and the drivers performed a slow U-turn then pulled on the brakes. The moustachioed man's head popped out of the roof hatch.

"Listen up, men. There are terrorists on the road back to Khayelitsha. Put your helmets and safety glasses on. Shoot on sight."

I placed my steel helmet, which looked as though it dated back to the Boer War, upon my head and tied the strap under my chin, then donned my safety glasses.

"Check your weapons!"

One of my comrades aimed his gun at a nearby tree and pulled the trigger. There was a pop as the projectile was blown from the muzzle and, a split-second later, a plop as the trunk was decorated with a splatter of pink paint. I checked the hopper was properly connected to my gun and did the same, this time leaving a bright green splash on the bark.

"We're moving out," shouted Moustache from inside the vehicle. He revved the engine.

"Stay frosty, people," called one of the soldiers atop the other vehicle, which I'm fairly sure wasn't something you'd have heard shouted during an anti-ANC insurgency operation in the late 1970s, but still.

We rumbled back down the track, slower than before, staying extremely frosty. For the first quarter of a mile, scrub and waste ground lay left and right, with just a few isolated shacks among the piles of rubbish. Insufficient cover for an insurgent ambush, I guessed. But soon the track narrowed and the informal settlements crowded in on both sides.

"*Mlungu*!" shouted a voice from below. I saw a child waving at me.

"How will I know the terrorists?" I asked the trooper beside me.

"Because they're white," he replied, looking at me as if I was stupid.

"But I thought—"

"Free Nelson Mandela!" shouted an American accent. I spotted a young, slightly overweight white man hiding behind a shack a few yards ahead.

"There! Terrorists!" shouted my companion.

The man stepped out from behind the shack, grinning, and to my surprise hurled a brick at the Casspir. It glanced, harmlessly, off the angled front side of the vehicle, which I guessed had been designed precisely with that scenario in mind. Now empty handed, the man's face fell, and as he turned and attempted to find cover, we opened fire with our paintball guns. I'm pretty sure I hit him at least three times, whereas my companion emptied his entire magazine into the unfortunate chap. As the Casspir roared on, I glanced back to see him writhing in the dirt, wailing and holding his stomach, as the soldiers on the vehicle behind us peppered his body with multi-coloured pellets.

A second later, two more white men jumped from an alleyway and unleashed a volley of stones. This pair, at least, had the wit to carry more than one missile, though their aim was poor and most of the projectiles missed our vehicle completely, the others cracking harmlessly against the armoured steel of the world's most rugged anti-insurgency vehicle. We returned fire and one of the men took a paintball to the face, which splattered into his eyes and left him staggering into a rubbish-filled ditch at the side of the road. The other man searched frantically for a place to hide, but he'd strayed too far from the alleyway, so he turned and attempted to outrun the Casspir down the road. Even if he'd been wearing suitable footwear this would have been a questionable strategy, but the man had not chosen apparel designed for speed. As he flapped down the road in his flip-flops, the poor fellow took a dozen shots in the back, shrieking in pain as each pellet slammed into his soft body. The vehicle behind us slowed and the troops on top finished him off with a devastating volley, leaving him curled in a ball, screaming for mercy, his t-shirt splattered with every colour of the rainbow.

My companion shouted a warning. A large branch toppled across the road ahead, clearly intended to block our progress. A dozen white men and women jumped out and began hurling bricks and pieces of wood at us, not to mention a barrage of curses that would have made your hair curl. For a second I thought we might be in trouble, but the driver didn't even bother slowing the Casspir, we simply bumped nonchalantly over the branch, which splintered into pieces beneath us, while we machine-gunned the hapless stone-throwers either side of us.

"Shoot him in the bollocks!" shouted one of my comrades, pointing at a middle-aged white man shaking his fists and screaming "Freedom!" in an English accent. We scored several direct hits and the man toppled over backwards, flailing around like an upturned beetle, while the platoon on the vehicle behind riddled him with paint pellets. It suddenly occurred to me that none of the freedom fighters had been issued with protective equipment. Either Shooter had not been educated in the principles of public liability insurance, or he felt it was more important for his guests to gain an authentic experience of oppression at the hands of the authorities. Or, then again, perhaps he just wasn't bothered.

We encountered our final gang of terrorists a couple of minutes later, hiding in the reed-filled gully on the approach to Mama Bisha's. Unfortunately for them, we'd spotted their location a hundred yards away thanks to the Casspir's height, so we were already peppering them with luminous paint as they clambered out of the gully, many of them falling back in clutching their paint-splattered throats before they could fling a single stone.

All in all, it was a rather jolly way to spend the afternoon. The closest I'd come to getting hit was when a rock bounced up from the bullet-proof windscreen, but it had passed a foot or so over my head and I was happy to say none of our platoon suffered even a scratch. We parked next to the bridge and the crowd applauded as we climbed down from the Casspirs. I shook Moustache's hand and he set about organising the taxi washers to hose the vehicles down. After changing back into my civvies, I joined Shooter in the dining room and poured myself a glass of aged Chenin.

"*Mlungu*, did the people enjoy the Township Uprising Experience?"

"The soldiers enjoyed it, Shooter, though I'm not so sure about all the rioters. Everyone got stuck into their roles, though. It was very impressive."

"Ah, yes," grinned Shooter. "One of our guides gave them a lecture about the old days, under apartheid, all the terrible things that happened. She told them about the Soweto uprising and the children boycotting the schools. The children would throw stones at the police but then the police would break the bones of the children. It was very bad. I told them you were all ex-South

African police and you had done bad things to people in the townships in the old days."

"What? You said we were apartheid-era policemen?"

"Yes," nodded Shooter, enthusiastically. "They became very angry. One of the women was crying. She was from Australia."

"Apartheid ended in nineteen ninety-two. What do they think we are, time travellers?"

Shooter shrugged.

"How much did they pay for this experience?"

"A lot of money," said Shooter.

It became clear, within the hour, that not everyone had enjoyed the Uprising Experience as much as I had. The Australian woman, her hair matted with congealed paint, including luminous green from my own weapon, demanded the soldiers be brought before her so she could remonstrate with them and, presumably, set up her own war crimes court in Mama Bisha's dining room. Fortunately, my fellow veterans had already collected their wages from McGregor and were long gone, no doubt already swapping war stories over beers in a Mitchell's Plain shebeen. Moustache and the other driver had also departed, presumably wishing to return the sparkling clean vehicles to Cape Town Apartheid Museum before anyone noticed they were missing. And luckily, without my steel helmet, safety glasses and combat fatigues, I was no longer recognisable as one of Shooter's dogs of war. I sympathised with the woman and advised her to lodge a complaint with Mr Maduma at the Khayelitsha branch of the Ministry of Development. She declared that she would and stormed out.

More serious, though, was the case of the English gentleman carried into Mama Bisha's dining room on a stretcher fashioned from a rusty bed frame. It was clear his groin had absorbed an excess of incoming fire, for he was wailing in misery, his hands cradling his meat and two veg through his linen shorts.

"We're going to sue!" shouted the woman accompanying him, who I presumed was his wife. She was also peppered with multi-coloured splotches. "It's ridiculous! We were given no warning this event would be so dangerous!"

"Yes, fighting for your rights is very dangerous," agreed Shooter.

"Who the hell is in charge here?" shouted the woman. She caught sight of me, just as I was taking a generous swig of Chenin. "You! Are you in charge?"

I swallowed my wine and shook my head. "Not as such, no."

"Not as such?" screamed the woman. "My husband needs urgent medical attention! What are you going to do about it?"

"I own this establishment," said Mama Bisha, gliding into the dining room like the proprietor of a Victorian tearoom. "Take this injured gentleman to the medical facility please."

I realised Mama Bisha was addressing me.

"What? Oh, yes! Of course! We have a medical facility!" I said, excitedly.

The paint-splattered woman stared at me, as if I was soft in the head.

"Yes, the medical facility. Off we go!" I gestured to the stretcher bearers, who, so far as I could tell, were two good Samaritans from the township who'd decided carrying an overweight, paint-splattered, wailing white man two miles along a rough track on a bed frame was the Christian thing to do, and off we trundled to the red-cross-decorated shipping container. As I opened the door, I had a horrible premonition that it had been turned back into a rubber-themed dildo palace but, as the light streamed in, I saw the sensible bunks, medical diagrams and wall-mounted first aid box were all in place.

With a fair degree of effort, we managed to hump the moaning patient from his bedframe stretcher to the bunk. As we did so, one of the springs ripped open his trouser pocket, at which his wife, who was turning out to be extremely hard to please, declared "that's something else you can pay for!"

"There!" I declared, once we'd made the man comfortable. "Welcome to our humble medical facility. We live by the principle of never turning away any patient in need."

"Well? Who's going to treat him?" said the wife.

I must say, this completely stumped me. In all the excitement of being able to utilise our clinic to house a real patient, I'd failed to realise that we might be expected to conduct a genuine medical procedure.

"I am," said a voice from the door.

And there stood Sister Zola, clipboard in hand, in a perfectly fitted nurse's outfit, sensible shoes and the face of an angel. She stepped into the container and consulted her genuine nurse's fob watch.

"You must all leave," she declared.

"I'm not going anywhere!" said the wife.

"You will leave!" said Sister Zola.

"We must do what the Sister says," I said. "This is standard practice. We can't have germ-ridden spectators fouling our clinic. We get audited on that sort of thing."

The man's wife took a deep breath and stalked out. I gave the stretcher bearers a hundred rand each, noting that their Christian charity hadn't blinded them to recognising good fortune when it came knocking, and closed the shipping container doors behind me.

I don't know what type of medical procedure Sister Zola had in mind when she decided to pull medical rank over the rest of us. It took me ten minutes to return to the dining room, satisfy myself that Langa was doing a good job selling fine South African fizz to the patrons of our new Sunday farmers' market, which he was, make small-talk with a couple of blonde women from the southern suburbs – who would never have dreamt of visiting Khayelitsha in the past but wasn't this marvellous, so heartening to see the township uplifting itself without begging for handouts – fix myself a glass of fine Elgin Riesling from the bar, stroll into reception, spot McGregor and Shooter crowded around the door of Mama Bisha's office, and peer over their shoulders at the CCTV monitors inside the cupboard.

But within that brief period, it was clear that Sister Zola, bless her, had not only diagnosed the complaint and begun a course of treatment, she had also gained the trust, confidence and enthusiastic compliance of her patient.

I didn't need to watch the screen for more than a few seconds. I suspected the gentleman in question wouldn't need to either, once Shooter had emailed a choice ten-second clip to the address from which he'd registered his interest in the Uprising Experience, the second part of which was now in full, tumescent swing. And it seemed very unlikely too, that Mama Bisha's Tuck Shop would be obliged to compensate the man for his trousers, his hurt pride, or his allegedly damaged testicles, which, so far as I could see, had made a recovery worthy of a pilgrimage to Lourdes.

A few days later, Shooter informed me that not only had the gentleman in question dropped any intention to pursue a legal complaint, he had been so overwhelmed by the after-sales service administered by the staff of Mama Bisha's Tuck Shop that he made a quite eye-wateringly generous donation to the clinic, proving true the old retail adage that the best way to guarantee loyalty is through the prompt and creative resolution of a customer complaint.

Chapter 30

Deluge

As the month progressed, the warmth of spring made way for the fiercer heat of summer. But the Cape is a wild and unpredictable place, and wise seafarers know why the first explorers to round Cape Point christened the coast *Cabo das Tormentas*, the Cape of Storms. The winds whispered of trouble far out in the Southern Ocean, and Table Mountain, her iron-hard rock usually sharp against the sky, donned her tablecloth, a thick blanket of cloud smothering the vast, flat summit. This shroud, the nemesis of many an incautious hiker, cascaded in slow motion off the plateau's edge before evaporating, silently, into thin air, like a ghostly Niagara Falls.

My mission, it seemed, was more or less accomplished. Blanchkopf's wine was now being funnelled, via Hemelhuis, to the splendidly empowered Gambu, rendering Gatesave's problematic relationship with Blanchkopf so convoluted as to be virtually untraceable. Blanchkopf had passed his Fairly Trod inspection, which, so far as I could tell, had shut up that interfering Scandinavian NGO. And Gatesave now had an arsenal of inspiring, diversity-flavoured stories to counter any wobbly publicity, from the funding of a popular cross-community medical centre, to the sponsorship of a clean and nearly-free township water supply, not to mention the stocking of Gambu's exquisitely right-on wine brands, which would soon be appearing on Gatesave's shelves after their six-thousand mile journey from the Cape.

My old life seemed increasingly distant. Occasionally, I would think of London's dark, drizzling streets, of car tyres sluicing through puddles and damp paving stones reflecting the glow of the street lights above. Or I would have a flashback to the Gatesave office, hard neon strips and abrasive carpets, a sea of flickering screens and motionless heads. I checked my emails less and less frequently, scrolling quickly through the increasingly irrelevant list of missives until I reached the bottom of the inbox, selected all, and with a delicious feeling of relief, hit delete.

The warmer nights grew the fame of Mama Bisha's Tuck Shop. Every evening's smiley feast was a sell-out, with numbers strictly limited to two hundred per sitting. The township butcher relocated next door and received its supplies directly from the slaughterhouse in Grabouw. At the end of each night, punters would queue to purchase a take-away smiley to barbecue themselves, in front of their friends, though all would insist one simply *had* to experience the real thing at Mama Bisha's Tuck Shop, for a smiley, so the saying went, always tasted best in Khayelitsha, just as a fine wine tastes at its peak when consumed on its own *terroir*.

Fame had, by now, spread far beyond the cul-de-sac of southern Africa. A London-based celebrity chef, known for his embrace of 'nose-to-tail eating', flew to Cape Town just to dine at Mama Bisha's Tuck Shop, and wrote a gushing article declaring that the people of Khayelitsha had a great deal to teach the West about environmentally sustainable lifestyles, not to mention the art of grilling animal extremities.

Such articles, of course, were promptly posted to Mama Bisha's Facebook page, joining the long list of glowing write-ups on travel and lifestyle websites from Europe, the US and Australia. The Mama Bisha's Tuck Shop page now had tens of thousands of followers, and each post was accompanied by hundreds of comments, many boasting of inspiring evenings around the fire pit, friendships made and the kindness and humanity of the locals. True, a few comments were negative, petty sneers along the lines of 'No thanks, African food looks gross, don't wanna die lol'. But what can one expect on social media these days, when bullies and other inadequates infest every corner of the internet?

Just occasionally, a specific complaint would be posted from someone who claimed to have suffered a minor injury or other mishap at Mama Bisha's. There was the man who complained of broken ribs after being struck by an armoured car, another who allegedly nearly choked to death on a stray sheep's tooth, and a highly-strung woman who expressed outrage at the appearance of a cobra next to her young children one evening around the fire pit. But Mama Bisha's supporters outnumbered the trolls hundreds-to-one and their nit-picking moans were drowned in a cacophony of counter-comments and angry-face emojis, condemning any negative posters for their ignorance, small-mindedness and, invariably, their white privilege.

One evening, a group of awkward-looking white men, wearing ironed safari trousers and polo shirts, arrived in a chartered minibus for a Friday-night smiley feast. They asked to be served the finest South African wines and, of course, I obliged. Noting their varied accents, I asked where they were from. It turned out they were students at Harvard Business School, no less, on a month-long study trip to the Cape, to research small-scale start-ups in disadvantaged communities. They had heard about Mama Bisha's and wanted to see the phenomenon for themselves. Before I knew it, I was being interrogated on the cost price of raw sheep's heads, the cash flow benefits of skimming electricity from the municipal grid, whether the intangible equity of the Mama Bisha brand was greater than that of the fixed assets, and a host of other financial questions of a quite tedious nature. I answered them as best I could before beating a retreat to the bar and helping myself to a glass from their open bottle of Thelema Cabernet. They loosened up after a few more wines, and before the night was over, their dedication to the investigation of shareholder value had drawn them to the shipping containers and the strips of crimson light beckoning from within.

The following morning I woke to find a chill in the air. A low hum sounded from the gap between my bedroom wall and ceiling, as though someone was perched on the roof using an electric shaver. I realised the wind had picked up and was causing the roof panels to vibrate. I pulled up my blanket, reached for my phone and reluctantly scrolled through my emails. The only noteworthy message was from Sandra, reminding me of the jolly at Hemelhuis next week, the purpose of which was to celebrate Paris-Blois's newfound, vampire-squid-like embrace of corporate social responsibility. I replied, confirming it was in the diary, though the invitation sounded deathly dull, with its promise of an inspirational speech from the Platinum Fox, an address by some top nob politician from the ruling ANC party, then the presentation of something called the Inclusivity and Partnership Awards, which sounded about as enticing as a mung bean sandwich. The only positive was that there would be lots of free wine, decent food and, I hoped, some attractive fellow-global development professionals to chat up.

The buzzing of the roof panels began to irritate me. I pulled on my boots and headed out back. As I tramped over the woodchips towards the shower block, I lifted my face to the clear, blue sky. But the sun's warmth seemed feebler than usual and there was the unmistakable taste of dampness on the breeze blowing in from False Bay. Table Mountain, I saw, was wearing her tablecloth, and after my shower I stood for a while, fascinated, as I watched the clouds spilling slowly down the sheer sides, the tablecloth thickening and roiling before my eyes. The reeds in the gully hissed and I could hear the township's rubbish rattling along the alleyways between the shacks.

The wind rose, not as a gust but as if the intensity had been turned up on a dial and left at a higher setting. The discarded soda cans ringing their way along the track behind Mama Bisha's changed their tune from a quiet cymbal roll to a louder, staccato clanging, as the air lifted them and bounced them along the ground. I became aware of a soft, high-pitched whine, and it took me a minute of wandering between the containers, with plastic bags whipping around me, before I realised it was the wind racing through the great skein of electrical cables.

The wind increased again, maintaining its strength. Before my eyes, the sky was changing colour. The vivid blue paled and low tendrils of cloud tore in from the ocean, towing a white mist behind. Whorls of ash span from the fire pit and whipped around me, making my eyes smart. Everywhere the shacks registered loud displeasure, wooden planks slapping against one another, tin roofs banging against the walls beneath them, doors slammed shut, over and over.

Table Mountain had disappeared. I wheeled around, thinking I had become disorientated, but it had vanished, along with Devil's Peak and the rest of the range. A minute ago, it had been right there, millions of tons of rock towering a mile above the township, the next there was just a wall of white, a great diffusion covering the sky from horizon to horizon, without substance or measure. I looked across the little bridge, the reeds in the gully either side whipping back and forth, and out over the shacks towards False Bay. The banging of wood against wood was interspersed with more violent sounds now, the splintering of timber and the creak of metal bending against itself.

I closed my eyes then opened them, unable to comprehend what I was seeing. The shacks, just a few hundred yards away across the bridge, were vanishing before my eyes. They weren't being torn apart or lifted away by the wind, they were simply blinking out of existence, as though a grey force field was advancing steadily towards me, disintegrating everything in its path. I looked to the heavens. A gigantic, dark curtain, a thousand feet high, was moving slowly inland, its top cresting forward, like a tidal wave poised to crash over the township.

I heard a voice faintly on the wind.

"*Mlungu!*"

It was Shooter, standing at the rear entrance, beckoning to me. He was less than twenty yards away, but I could barely hear his voice over the scream of the wind. I felt a faint drizzle against my face.

"You will get wet, *mlungu!*"

As the storm front advanced to within a hundred yards of the bridge, swallowing all before it, I realised the sound was not just the wind, but of water hammering against metal. I saw the front's dark wall, drawing slowly, almost ponderously closer, consuming each row of dwellings. I felt the sound of the rain in my chest as it roared against the tin roofs, bouncing up in a furious spray before each shack was dissolved within the maelstrom.

And then, too late, I saw the stormfront was not moving slowly at all. It raced over the bridge as fast as a sprinting man and consumed me, the wood chips dancing into the air about my legs and the rain slapping my face, stinging and freezing. There was no sense of gradually getting wet. One second I was dry, the next I was completely drenched, rivulets cascading down my face, my trousers soaked through and cold fingers trickling into my boots. I turned and splashed my way to the rear door, the water already an inch deep. As I stepped inside, I realised why the entrance was guarded by a line of sandbags.

The storm thrashed the township all day. The puddles joined one another until the ground was one single unbroken expanse of dancing water whipped into ridges by the wind. The woodchips thrashed upon the surface like scum atop a bubbling stockpot until they thinned and dissipated, escaping one at a time through the chain-link fence or into the gully, perhaps to grace another patch of waste ground a mile from here, or to be swept out to sea and ride the currents east, across the Indian Ocean.

The water level rose, slowly, inexorably, a couple of inches each hour. More sandbags were deployed until the protective wall outside the front and back doors stood four layers high. The back-door security gate, clanging against its frame, was closed and bolted. A brown, evil-looking liquid oozed between the sandbags and crept beneath the front door, but the stout woman from the laundry block worked the entrance tirelessly with her mop and bucket, never giving the invading water the advantage.

I was handed a broom and told to keep the rain splattering through the rear gate at bay. Through the bars, I watched the dark waters eddy around the shipping containers, their doors sealed and lined with sandbags. Every few minutes, over the roar of the downpour, there would be a crashing and splintering as some structure collapsed under the onslaught of wind and rain. Larger and larger pieces of debris nosed their way into the yard; empty five-litre mineral water bottles, used drums of cooking oil, chunks of polystyrene, tree branches, pieces of timber trailing frayed orange rope, tangled masses of plastic sheeting pushed ahead of the wind like crumpled sail ships, finally doors and wooden panels, bent nails protruding from their edges, one even adorned with a coat hook around which was wrapped a sodden, unrecognisable clump of fabric. Unless my mind was playing tricks, and I was confused by the shrieking of the wind, I'm sure I heard human cries too, faint, as though from a ship far out at sea.

The storm had brought gloom to the middle of the day. By late afternoon the sky was black with not a solitary artificial light visible beyond the back door of Mama Bisha's. In the absence of anything to see or do, I returned to my room, positioned a few strategic pots and pans to collect drips, and opened a bottle of wine. I sent an email to Foyley, enquiring whether Gambu's wines had arrived safely in the UK – they were due to have gone on sale the previous Friday.

The end of the storm, late that evening, was as sudden as its beginning. The blanketing roar of rain, like a thousand drummers pounding every inch of the roof, slackened to a patter then stopped, the unnatural quiet leaving a phantom ringing in my ears. I rose from my bed and, by the time I'd reached the rear entrance, not only had the rain stopped but the sky had begun to clear. A cold half-moon shone a ghostly wash over the devastation, silver ripples lapping around the flotsam as it bobbed in the black water. Several shacks had collapsed or lost their roofs, leaving gaps in the line of dwellings, and sodden debris choked the length of the chain-link fence. The coils of razor wire gleamed in the moonlight, the blades studded with raindrops that shone like fairy lights. Occasionally, in the dark, people called to one another. Everywhere, the sound of water, dripping.

I spotted something moving, just a yard from my feet. A scorpion, scuttling along the line of sandbags, an escapee from the rising waters. I shivered. Only a matter of time before it found its way inside and made a home in one of my boots, or my bed. I reached for the broom and brushed the vicious little beast into the dark water.

Chapter 31

Propaganda

The floodwater took two days to subside, babbling through the gullies and down to the ocean or draining slowly into the sand. In its wake it left a foul-smelling mud, from which sprung a billion flies, which tormented the township every second of the day and night. I hung a sheet over the rear gate in a vain attempt to keep them at bay, then retreated to my room and barricaded myself inside with a bottle of wine and a fly swat, but the little blighters merrily buzzed their way in through the gaps in the roof and I was soon thrashing my weapon around near-constantly and spilling my Shiraz on the bed clothes.

I finally found some protection by cutting a pair of eyeholes in a pillowcase, placing it over my head and carefully taping my sunglasses to the outside. Khayelitsha was cut off from the outside world for those two days and I had little to do except play with my phone, watch the locals attempt to patch up their wrecked homes, and drink wine.

Other than a cryptic message from Foyley, suggesting I might want to read up on the PR reaction to my new wines, I'd received no emails of interest. I spent the morning watching a group of workmen, under McGregor's supervision, removing debris and dismantling the damaged shacks. A pickup dropped off more rolls of chain-link fence and the workmen, perched on stepladders, began hammering tall, metal posts into the earth and extending the fence to encompass the newly liberated ground.

Watching all this activity had made me hungry and I returned down the passageway to the empty dining room, where I opened a can of pilchards in tomato sauce. I was searching for a saucepan when I heard the sound of two men speaking quietly in fluent

English. I could tell it wasn't Shooter or McGregor. I walked into reception, but it was deserted. Then I realised the conversation was coming from Mama Bisha's office. The door was ajar.

Of course, I thought. It's the IT guys. These were Mama Bisha's latest recruits, a pair of studious-looking youths around eighteen years old. They'd joined us a couple of weeks ago and spent their entire working day locked inside the office, not even emerging for lunch. A sign stating 'Private, Staff Only' had been screwed to the door and, every so often, when no guests were passing through reception, Shooter or McGregor would let themselves in, taking care to close and lock the door behind them.

"Social media, *mlungu*!" Shooter had said, when I'd asked him what they were up to.

Today, with a plague of flies and half the township still inches deep in mud, we had no guests. But the youths had still turned up for work, squelching up to the front door in their gumboots, changing into their shoes once they'd stepped the other side of the sandbag barrier, before squirreling themselves away in the office.

I pushed the door and it opened, noiselessly. The youths were sitting at their laptops, surrounded by bottles of soda, packets of biltong and cans of fly repellent.

"What are you posting on Facebook today then, chaps?" I said, slipping inside. "Ten inspirational ways to repurpose a drowned goat?"

The youths looked up from their screens. "Uh, are you supposed to be in here?" one of them asked. "That whole pillowcase and shades look is very weird, by the way." He lifted his phone and took a photo.

"Yes, of course I am. I work here. I'm one of the founding partners, actually."

"Oh, you're the British guy," said the other youth. "Close the door on the way out, would you? You're letting the flies in."

My curiosity, however, was piqued. I glanced over my shoulder, checking no-one was around, then pushed the door closed and removed my pillowcase mask. I glanced at one of the laptop screens. Straight away, I recognised the image. It was the interior of one of the shipping containers.

"Are you definitely allowed in here?" said the first youth, half-closing his laptop. "McGregor said no-one was to come in except him or Shooter."

"Or Mama Bisha," said the other youth.

"Or me. That's the CCTV in the bedrooms," I said, pointing at the laptop. Don't worry, I know everything. I helped set it all up."

The first youth looked at me, doubtfully, but re-opened his laptop.

"You guys are doing great work," I said, stealing a glance at the other laptop, which was displaying someone's Facebook page. "God's work, in fact."

"That's funny, man," said the other youth. He switched his laptop display from Facebook to a CCTV image and zoomed in on the face of a gormless-looking white man standing in the middle of the room, stark naked except for his socks, while one of Mama Bisha's female workforce lounged on the bed wearing even less. He switched back to Facebook, scrolled down the feed and clicked on an image. A picture of the same man, this time clothed and holding a fishing rod, appeared on the screen. The youth tapped the keyboard once more and the image was replaced by a spreadsheet of names and contact details.

Now, I'm no coding genius, but it was becoming clear that Mama Bisha's social media strategy was a touch more ambitious than that of the average guesthouse.

"That's a lot of effort just to get a five-star review on Trip Advisor," I said.

"Man, he *is* funny," said the first youth, swiping through an Instagram feed on his phone. His eyes moved back and forth between the handset and the image on his laptop, a CCTV screenshot of a portly man, his face wearing a beatific smile and his lower half obscured by another member of Mama Bisha's hard-working nursing staff.

"Do you make the requests for donations too?" I asked, nonchalantly.

"We're just the research department. Mama Bisha deals with the money."

"Of course she does," I said.

I replaced the pillowcase over my head, adjusted it until I could see through my shaded eyeholes, and opened the door a crack, checking the coast was clear. I slipped out into reception and closed the door quietly behind me. Realising I was still very hungry, I returned to the dining room, heated up the pilchards in tomato sauce and attempted to spoon them under the pillowcase. With my other hand, I tried to waft away the considerable number of flies determined to hitch a ride on the journey from the saucepan to my mouth. The net result was a great deal of fishy tomato sauce covering my neck and my chin, and several flies buzzing around deliriously inside the pillowcase.

As I wandered back to the rear entrance, wiping my chin on the inside of the pillowcase and slapping my face in an attempt to knock out any feasting flies, my phone buzzed into life. It was the Head of Message.

"Hello, Felix speaking."

The next minute or so of conversation, if it can be called that, passed as something of a blur. In fact, I doubt more than a dozen words emanating from the Head of Message actually qualified as Queen's English. The tone was clear enough. It was, very clearly, one of disappointment, disapproval and considerable dismay. It wasn't an exaggeration, in fact, to say it was one of bile, venom and unhinged, spittle-flecked rage.

The Head of Message's response to my opening greeting was not so much a reply as a primal scream, as though the earth itself had opened up and hell's foulest denizens had sprung from its depths, snatched her first-born child, and spirited it away to the underworld. When I enquired, somewhat stunned, whether everything was alright, the scream was repeated, at a volume even more blood-curdling than before. From there, the conversation degenerated, and it was all I could do to hold the phone in my limp, sweating hand as a tirade of the most eye-widening and buttock-clenching curses was unleashed upon my innocent ears.

The call ended and, apart from the knowledge that my relationship with the Head of Message was now at a low ebb, I was none the wiser as to what I'd done wrong. I called Foyley, wondering whether his email, regarding the press reaction to my new wines, might somehow be connected to the Head of Message's meltdown.

"Oh, hi Felix. I'm afraid you're in rather deep doo-doo."

"What the hell am I supposed to have done? I've just been screamed at, by the Head of Message. I mean literally screamed at. Virtually no words, just screams."

"It's the new South African wines. Those Gambu ones."

"What about them? Did someone not like them? You sent out the samples to the press, like I asked?"

"Yeah, we sent out the samples."

"Well? Were they corked or something? What happened?"

"It's not the taste of the wines, Felix. It's the labels."

"What's wrong with the labels? They're great. I chose them myself."

"They've upset a few people."

"How? How have they upset people?"

"It made the front pages."

"Which front pages? What are you talking about?"

"Probably easier if you just Google it and read for yourself. Search for Gatesave wine. Or just Gatesave. Or just wine. I think they'll all return the same results. It's the number one trending topic on Twitter. Globally."

"Oh, blimey. How's the wine selling?"

"We sold out. Every single bottle."

"That's amazing! I expected it to take six months. That's good news, surely? We should be ordering more."

"No, I'm pretty sure we won't be doing that. I think you need to read the news, Felix."

I retired to my room, pulled out my phone and typed Gatesave into Google. Before I'd even finished typing the word, I was offered a selection of helpful phrases to aid my search, including 'Gatesave wine', 'Gatesave woke wine', 'Gatesave hates white people' and 'Gatesave black Nazi'.

Scanning down the list of results, a sickening feeling spread from my stomach to my bowels, and it dawned on me why the Head of Message had sounded so emotional.

Of all the headlines, the BBC's was probably the least sensational. Their website led with the relatively sober 'Woke wines cause controversy in the supermarket aisle'. Next, a right-leaning broadsheet had given the story a slightly spicier spin with 'Black liberationists target Middle England's palate.' One of the racier tabloids had run with 'Black hate wines target young white drinkers,' while a mid-market paper, chiefly known for its scepticism towards the benefits of multiculturalism, had led with 'Pour this racist filth down the sink!'

This last headline, which I assumed referred to my wines rather than the publication itself, was the most problematic, for, of all media outlets, that newspaper's readership overlapped most heavily with Gatesave's customer base. Furthermore, our media department focussed massive resources on gaining that newspaper's approval for every move Gatesave made, from the launch of a new flavour of crisp to our end-of-year financial results. I suspected I might have driven a wine-scented coach and horses through my employer's media strategy. I noted, with dismay, that the newspaper's main story was accompanied by an opinion piece entitled 'Why does Britain's largest supermarket chain hate white people so much?'

The Head of Message's hair-raising mood began to make a great deal of sense.

The subject of each story, of course, was the launch of Gambu's Black Power Pinotage and Woke White wines on to the shelves of Gatesave, and the subsequent reaction of the great British public. All the articles included the same picture of Gambu, beret on head, teeth bared, wagging his finger at the camera, which I recognised from the Black Soil Movement's own website. Gambu was described variously as the 'leader of a thuggish, black Marxist rent-a-mob', a 'blood-soaked, African revolutionary', and a 'fanatical hater of white civilization', all of which I was sure would bring a smile to his face, though one columnist, in an epithet I suspected would not please him at all, declared Gambu a 'pound-shop Idi Amin'.

A key aggravating factor in the coverage appeared to be Gambu himself. Over the past week he had clearly been stirring the pot with gusto. Several of his tweets were printed verbatim in the press, including "My wines are an act of resistance against White Privilege", "Black Power Pinotage is a well-overdue punch in the face for the pale, Prosecco-drinking classes" and "Women drinking Woke White yearn to be impregnated with our proud black seed", the last of which had caused quite the brouhaha. I noticed that Gambu now had over a million Twitter followers.

The respectable newspapers declared the wines a propaganda effort by 'woke guerrillas', using Soviet-era tactics to sow discord among the British population and Western civilization in general. The tabloid websites insisted the wine be banned for stirring up racial resentment, a demand which had already been made official policy by a far-right political party.

Many of the stories focussed on where the proceeds of the wine might end up. One newspaper suggested the profits would be funnelled to 'inner-city, underground music schools', at which youngsters were taught to set violent, subversive lyrics to Jamaican dance-hall tunes. Another was concerned that the monies might be used to construct boats to transport 'fit, young, predominantly male' African refugees across the English Channel, while another tabloid claimed to have evidence that the ultimate beneficiary was Jacob Zuma, 'the sex-crazed, kleptocrat king of Kwa-Zulu', and his sixty-nine wives.

The alleged reaction from the British public was also overwhelmingly negative. Once-loyal customers declared they would boycott Gatesave forever. Pensioners were reported as feeling unsafe walking the wine aisles of their local supermarket, in case black terrorists had set booby-traps among the Liebfraumilch. One concerned father had discovered his sixteen-year-old daughter drinking Woke White in her bedroom with a group of friends and had immediately evacuated her to the countryside where she could be protected from 'incursions by black Nazis'.

A famous left-leaning newspaper, which I'd hoped might approve of the wines, declared them a 'clumsy blunder into the sensitive arena of racial politics', suggesting such discourse had no place on a wine label and should be reserved for academia and properly educated activists.

Even the website of the British Communist Party took a negative position, declaring the wines 'bourgeois BS', and 'about as liberationist as the Victorian slave trade', which was either a very lucky, albeit cynical, guess or suggested the British Communist Party had an agent within my grape supply chain. In the cruellest cut, the Communist Party's wine critic (who knew?) declared Black Power Pinotage to be 'unbalanced, insipid, and lacking in structure', though I dismissed that as demonstrating just how out of touch the upper-middle-class palate was to the needs of the wine-drinking masses.

Finally, I noted that the Royal Institute of Advertising and Influencing had declared the launch of Black Power Pinotage and Woke White the worst piece of marketing in British retail history and had nominated Gatesave for their Tin Ear award, bestowed each year in honour of the most customer-alienating initiative in British commerce.

So, it was with some trepidation that I answered my phone for the second time that afternoon, not least because the incoming number was, once more, that of the Head of Message.

"Hello?" I said, holding the phone a few inches from my pillowcase-covered ear.

A few seconds passed before the Head of Message spoke.

"Felix." Her voice, this time, was low. It wavered, as though she was under great emotional strain.

"Yes, hello there."

A long, slow sigh.

"Felix. I intend to keep this brief. So just listen." Her bangles clanked and I heard the rustle of paper.

"Number one. You are in breach of your Gatesave employment contract and are suspended with immediate effect."

"Oh," I said, miserably. "What have I done wrong?"

"Tell me you're joking, Felix?" Her voice began to rise, and I wished I hadn't asked. "Every newspaper in the country is accusing us of inciting hatred against white people. Questions have been asked in the House of Commons. Herbert Marris has been forced to apologise on national television, which, I can assure you Felix, is not something that comes naturally to the man."

"So, a few newspapers have written a story. It's not my fault. It'll all be forgotten soon, surely?"

"No, it won't be forgotten soon, Felix! Local councils are threatening to cancel our alcohol licences! Red-faced men of a certain age have been marching into our stores and flinging bottles of wine onto the floor! The British Nazi Party have threatened to blow up head office!"

"I didn't know there was a British Nazi Party."

"There wasn't, until your wine came along!" she shouted, sounding worryingly volatile once more. "You've single-handedly resurrected the British extreme-right through your provocatively designed wine labels. Quite an achievement! I mean, seriously, well done."

"It wasn't my design."

"Shut up!" She paused and regained her composure. "Why is your voice muffled?"

I brought the phone closer to the pillowcase.

"Sorry, I'm wearing a hood. To keep the flies away."

"You'll need to wear a bloody hood when you're back here, Felix, because you're likely to be lynched if you show your face in public. Listen. Number two. You are ordered, and I mean explicitly ordered, not to speak to any member of the media, or anyone at all in fact, in a Gatesave capacity. Do you understand?"

I felt something tickling my cheek near the corner of my mouth. A malevolent fly was feasting on a stray smear of fishy sauce.

"Pess," I said, out of the side of my mouth, hoping to prevent the fly from crawling inside.

"Pardon? Can you hear me, Felix?"

"Pess. Palk to po-one," I said, keeping my lips as sealed as possible. The fly tiptoed up to my nostril. I snorted, hoping to blast it downwards and out of the pillowcase, but I only succeeded in displacing it nearer to my mouth.

"What is the matter with you, Felix? Why are you speaking strangely? I hope you're taking this seriously, for your own sake. Number three. You are required to attend a disciplinary hearing with the Head of People Needs, at Gatesave head office, next week. We will email you with—"

"Piss off!" I spat, as the fly tap-danced over my lips. I expelled a long raspberry in an attempt to blow it clear and slapped my face several times through the pillowcase with my spare hand. In the chaos, I dropped the phone, which bounced off the bed and clattered on to the concrete floor. I scrabbled around, taking a while to locate it due to my vision being obscured by my poorly aligned pillowcase eyeholes.

"No, you piss off!" I heard the Head of Message scream.

I found the handset and brought it back to my ear.

"No, I didn't mean you! I meant the fly! There was a fly trying to get in my mouth!" I wailed.

But the Head of Message had already hung up.

Chapter 32

Gentrification

Gatesave wishes to apologise to all its loyal customers for accidentally placing on sale a small number of bottles of an offensively labelled wine last week. This incident was the result of an unauthorised decision made by a junior member of the buying team, who is no longer employed by the company. As soon as the product was drawn to our attention, we removed it from sale, and we can assure our customers that this disappointing occurrence will never be repeated. Gatesave is passionate about treating all our customers and employees in a fair and inclusive manner, whatever their race, gender or sexual orientation.

The Head of People Needs emailed an hour later with the date and time of my disciplinary hearing. Foyley phoned with the details of my return flight which, to my surprise, was in business class, direct from Cape Town to London.

"They want you back as soon as possible, Felix. All the economy flights had sold out."

"Oh well. Silver linings and all that. It was good working with you, Foyley. Maybe you'll get my job."

"I doubt it. Herbert Marris has announced a restructure. Half the departmental heads are for the chop. Mind you, a lot of them have been fired already, thanks to the drug tests. They're taking hair samples now, to catch people who indulged over the past couple of years. Marris says once a degenerate, always a degenerate. And he doesn't want degenerates in his business."

"Bloody hell. Are you worried about getting caught?"

"I've shaved my hair. Lots of people have. Office looks like a cancer ward."

"Well, at least I won't have to shave mine. You said they're restructuring the wine department?"

"Yes. The wine team is to be consolidated into a new Ambient Packaged department, along with cereals, jams and long-life desserts."

"Long-life desserts, eh? How the mighty have fallen."

"I know. Lots of other personnel are being cut too. They're getting rid of the social media team. Herbert Marris says social media is a fad that's had its day. He was very unhappy about all the negative comments following Winegate."

"Winegate?"

"Yes, that's what everyone's calling it. The rest of the PR team are being fired too."

"I hope that's not my fault?"

"It is, I'm afraid."

"Oh, God. That's not going to improve my relationship with the Head of Message. Maybe I will wear a hood."

"Don't worry. It's the CEO everyone hates, not you. Irony is, everyone on social media is now slagging off Gatesave for apologising and withdrawing the wines. There's an online petition demanding we put Black Power Pinotage and Woke White back on sale, otherwise we'll be subject to another boycott. Can you believe bottles of Black Power Pinotage are selling for five hundred pounds on eBay?"

"Blimey. Don't suppose that gives me a reprieve, does it?"

"I doubt it. Anyway, nice working with you. Don't forget those bottles of fine wine I sent to your club when we had to clear out the storeroom. Think of them as a coming home present."

"Farewell, Foyley."

That weekend, the reborn sun chased away the last of the puddles and dried the township mud until it was firm enough to walk upon once more. The flies disappeared, the reeds stood thick and lush in the gulley and tiny pink flowers sprouted along the edges of the shipping containers. A truck dropped off new sacks of wood chips and teams of workmen raked them around the grounds, rendering the township earth aspirational once more.

The fire pit was re-dug, the sandbag walls lowered to one layer high, and the taxi-washing gang hosed the mud splatter from the containers. The market traders returned and built their stalls, the smiley ladies restocked their butchery, and the *umqombothi* brewers lit their fire and began fermenting a fresh drum of maize and sorghum. The boundary fence, now expanded to enclose the newly vacated land, was crowned with gleaming coils of razor wire.

And, as the sun set, Mama Bisha's guests returned, in even greater numbers than before. During the past flood-blighted week, the Facebook page had published several updates featuring heart-rending photographs of township residents beside their ruined shacks, accompanied by commentary describing how Mama Bisha's Tuck Shop had thrown open its doors to the community in their hour of need. One post, jaw-droppingly cynical even by my high standards, showed a sad-faced Sister Zola, wearing her nurse's uniform, dabbing the grubby cheeks of a tearful township waif.

There were a few light-hearted posts too, such as the picture of me, thankfully unrecognisable, in my pillowcase hood and sunglasses, captioned *'A big welcome to our recent guests from the Deep South. Their 1986 Rough Guide to Africa was a little out of date, but we always be educating...'* which I saw had been shared, to great amusement, over a hundred thousand times. Mama Bisha's Tuck Shop now had one million followers, every post applauded by countless thousands of comments, shares and likes, pouring love and appreciation upon the Mama Bisha brand in a blizzard of approval the multi-billion-pound Gatesave could only dream of.

That evening, the fire roared bright in the cool, night air, the corks of the Cape's finest wines popped like a mob of hiccuping meerkats and the herd of slowly roasting smileys grinned wider than ever. In the shadows further back, the doors of the shipping containers lay ajar, the strips of soft, red light drawing the easily led from their post-feast repose to more vigorous and misjudged adventures under the crimson lampshades of Mama Bisha's Tuck Shop.

I lay alone in my room, the only part of Mama Bisha's to have been spared refurbishment. As I reflected on my imminent return to face the firing squad, Shooter shoved open the door and popped his head around.

"*Mlungu*! Mama Bisha wants to see you."

I padded through the dining room into reception and knocked on the office door.

"Come."

Mama Bisha stood at the barred window, her back to me, watching the guests cavort around the fire pit. I could see the gleam of the CCTV monitors through the crack between the cupboard doors.

"We intend to upgrade your room tomorrow, Mr Hart."

"Oh, that's good news," I said. "It is a little shabby."

"Yes. We need it for our guests. This will be your last evening here."

She turned from the window and looked at me, the bright pinpoints of her eyes shining.

"Oh, I see. That's a shame. It's also a bit inconvenient, actually. I don't really have anywhere to go until my flight home on Tuesday. I don't suppose I could stay until—"

"McGregor will give you twenty thousand rand tomorrow morning. That should be enough I think?"

"Right. Yes, I suppose that will do. Is that it then? You don't need my help with any more Tears of Pity donations, or anything else?"

"We are self-funded now. The donation from Harvard Business School was particularly generous."

"Oh, very good. Well then, all the best with everything. I'm sure Langa will be able to run the bar himself. I've trained him well, if I do say so myself."

"You have trained him very well. You have been very effective, in fact, in many ways. Much to my surprise."

"Thank you. I've always considered myself highly adaptable."

"Indeed. But I believe it is time for you to return home. I trust you will remain a friend and ally of Mama Bisha's Tuck Shop?"

"Oh yes, very much so. I'll be sure to recommend you to nearly everyone I meet."

"Thank you, Mr Hart."

Mama Bisha turned back to the window. I stepped out of the office and closed the door behind me. Extracting a bottle of Smiley Red from behind the bar, I returned to my room to toast my final night at Mama Bisha's Tuck Shop.

The next morning, I was awoken by an almighty banging.

"Yes, yes," I called, wiping the sleep from my eyes. I realised I'd fallen asleep in my clothes and there was a red damp patch down the front of my shirt. I checked my phone. It was only seven o'clock. "Can you give me another hour or two please? I was told check out's at nine."

There was another bang and I realised the noise was coming from above. A roof panel peeled upwards and vanished, sending a wash of early morning sun into the room. A pair of workmen peered down through the gap and appeared mildly surprised to see me.

"Right, that's my wake-up call, is it?" I said, shading my eyes.

I stood, stretched, and tossed my possessions into the suitcase; a couple of creased shirts, a spare pair of trousers, a toothbrush, a phone charger and a corkscrew. Before I'd even zipped up the case, there was a wrenching and screeching as more panels were torn from the roof. I yanked open the door, hearing it grate over the concrete floor for the final time, to find another pair of workmen waiting outside.

"All yours, chaps. Sorry I finished the wine."

One of the men raised a power drill and began unscrewing the door from its hinges. I headed through to reception where McGregor and Shooter were waiting for me.

"*Mlungu* Moses! You have been evicted!" grinned Shooter.

"Yes, it appears you've gentrified me out of the neighbourhood."

McGregor handed me a bundle wrapped in a plastic bag. I opened it and peered inside. It contained a large wad of used notes, secured with a rubber band.

"It is all there," said McGregor.

"I'm sure it is. Well, thank you for your hospitality, gentlemen, it's been a pleasure."

I held out my hand. McGregor grinned and shook it, making sure to squeeze it rather unnecessarily hard. Shooter embraced me, slapping me on the back several times.

"*Mlungu* Moses, leopard-shagger, this is a very sad day. I will miss you. Peace."

"I will miss you too. Goodbye and good luck to you both."

I zipped the bag of cash into my case, gave a final wave of farewell and returned to the dining room, intending to leave by the back door.

"Good luck to you too, *mlungu*," called Shooter, "don't get robbed!"

The two men laughed, and it occurred to me that people are murdered in the townships for far, far less than twenty thousand rand. I glanced around to check no workmen were nearby, unzipped my case, and stuffed a fistful of cash into each trouser pocket, some into my boot, and a thick wad inside my jacket, leaving less than a third in the case. I trotted out of the back entrance and jogged to the idling taxis.

"Stellenbosch, please," I said, choosing the driver with the slenderest build.

The vehicle nosed over the little bridge and bumped along the rough track until it reached the main township road. I placed my case on the floor, out of sight, then locked the passenger doors, rolled up the windows, and glanced repeatedly over my shoulder to see if we were being followed. I didn't relax even when we reached the N2 highway, watching every car that drove up behind us, particularly those with a male driver and passenger, then breathing a sigh of relief as they overtook, rather than bumping into our rear in a pretend accident, and shooting and robbing me once we'd pulled over.

We took the Stellenbosch turn-off and I directed the driver to pull over at the first gas station. I paid him, walked into the store and watched through the window as he drove away. Then I darted out and took another taxi to my real destination, an upmarket guesthouse with twenty-four-hour security in the centre of Stellenbosch. I pre-paid my room in cash, locked the rest of the money in the safe and kept a low profile for the rest of the day, asking room service to launder my township-soiled clothes and taking dinner in my room.

I had just two nights left in South Africa before my flight home. Tomorrow, however, was the shindig at Hemelhuis. And whatever nonsense the Head of Message had told me about not communicating with anyone, I was damned if I was going to miss out on a party just because of a bunch of trumped up misconduct charges. In fact, given that I was about to be court martialled and officially drummed out of the regiment, I decided I may as well give myself a proper send off.

Chapter 33

Truth and Reconciliation

The party began at midday so, not wanting to miss out on a minute's drinking time, I arrived outside the Hemelhuis Estate's main gates at two minutes to twelve. My guesthouse had ordered me a Mercedes taxi, rather than a township minibus, so the gates opened without complaint, and we glided up the tree-lined drive to the manor house.

I skipped up the steps to the front entrance. The imposing double front doors, as thick and ancient as a galleon's timbers, lay wide open, secured against the whitewashed brick by black iron hooks. A footman nodded and waved me through. I strode into the entrance hall, three silent paces over the sisal mat, then loud, echoing footsteps against the boards, sounding like Black Rod banging his staff against the door of the Commons. The roof arched high overhead and the walls, wood-panelled from floor to ceiling, reeked of wealth and polish. An oil painting of a smiling Nelson Mandela gazed down from on high, while beneath him, framed pictures of moustachioed men sat stern and frozen in black-and-white.

"*Cap Classique*, sir?" asked a waiter, his tray of glasses dancing with freshly poured fizz.

I didn't decline. With a tilt of the head, the man indicated I should continue into the main reception room.

I realised I'd been in the room before. It was where I'd eaten breakfast with Sandra and the winery security man, when Gambu and his mob had been misbehaving outside the front gates. Last time, I'd been ushered through the back entrance, like a grubby tradesman. Now, quite rightly, I was a guest of honour. I drained my glass and lifted another from a passing waiter.

A low stage had been constructed along one side of the room, above which hung a sign boasting 'Paris-Blois: 100 years of inclusion and partnership'. Pink and black balloons hung in bunches from the walls, like great inflatable grapes, and waiters hovered around the perimeter with trays of hors d'oeuvres. A dozen or so people chatted earnestly in the centre of the room and I spotted Sandra among them, her blond ponytail moving from side to side as she laughed, inclusively, with her guests.

Gradually, the room filled up. I wandered around, making small talk at first, then, when I was three or four glasses down, I found myself becoming more passionate on the subject of inclusivity and partnership. I talked of my work in the townships, empowering previously disadvantaged communities, and of my lifelong devotion to upliftment and sustainable development. After another few glasses, I found myself stumbling over some of the longer words, particularly 'inclusivity', which I discovered becomes harder to pronounce the more you've drunk. My audience, however, didn't mind at all, no doubt mistaking my tipsy inarticulacy as over-passionate enthusiasm for all things inclusive.

And the crowd was nothing if not inclusive. In fact, the assembled guests were no less than an exemplar of the modern, free South Africa, rampant in its diversity, the rainbow nation made flesh. I chatted to men and women of colour, some black, some of mixed race, others of Indian heritage, and I didn't neglect the whites either, of course. All were articulate, intelligent and extremely well turned-out. I silently praised my foresight in having my clothes laundered the day before. If I had not, I might have brought a lingering whiff of the township into that glittering crowd. And that, I suspected, might not have been tolerated with the same grace my audience showed as I regaled them with my stories of rescuing homeless children from the surging floodwaters and nursing them back to health at my inclusive breast.

As I stretched out my arm to liberate some prawns from a passing waiter, my hand was knocked aside by a larger, more assertive limb.

"Excuse me," muttered a gruff voice. A fat fistful of fingers grasped a dozen battered shrimp and lifted them to the owner's bearded maw. I stepped back in shock, for it was none other than Blanchkopf. He, in turn, widened his eyes, dropping a couple of prawns in surprise.

"They've invited you, have they?" I blurted.

"And why shouldn't they?" growled Blanchkopf. "I do business with them, don't I?"

"Yes, I suppose," I said. There was an awkward silence. "Did you bring your dogs?"

Blanchkopf ignored my question. "I heard your British employer got into hot water selling some nasty black supremacist wine."

"Oh. That news made it down here, did it?"

"Yes, it did. It was a South African wine. Made by that Gambu animal." Blanchkopf stared at me. "Everybody knows his tanks were empty. So I wonder who sold him that wine."

I spotted a waiter carrying a tray of mini samosas.

"Excuse me, I just need to line my stomach," I said, and leapt away to intercept the waiter. I snatched a handful of curry-scented parcels, then ducked and scurried into the crowd.

Sweating, I popped up next to a group nearer the stage.

"Felix!" said Sandra. "There you are! Come, you must meet some of our Paris-Blois friends."

"Oh, hello," I said, joining the circle of guests.

"This is Luzuko, our head of sales in the Eastern Cape," said Sandra. A young black man in a slim-fit suit smiled and extended his hand.

"Sorry, I'm a bit messy," I said, revealing the four slightly oily samosas in my right palm. I extended my left hand and shook his, awkwardly.

"Looks like you are hungry," smiled the man, and the rest of the circle laughed.

"Yes, well, I've just arrived back from a long stay in Khayelitsha," I said, pleased to be able to turn the conversation to a subject I'd been milking all afternoon.

"How fascinating," said a woman to my right. As I turned to acknowledge her, my jaw dropped, and had there been a samosa in there, it would doubtlessly have tumbled clean out. The woman was spectacularly beautiful, her flawless, white face and sapphire eyes framed by shoulder-length hair which, in an act of spectacular self-confidence, she had dyed light blue with silver highlights.

"This is Heidi Vestergaard," said Sandra. "She works in sustainable development, just like you, Felix."

"Hi Heidi," I said, gazing at her pink, plump lips.

Heidi smiled, revealing the cutest little gap between her top front teeth. Of course she had a cute gap. I wondered whether she'd had orthodontics treatment as a child to widen it, for maximum cuteness. Her beauty was beginning to make me feel slightly dizzy, though the sparkling wine might have been a contributing factor.

"Who are you attached to?" asked Heidi.

"Oh, I'm single," I said, at which everyone laughed uproariously.

"Funny Felix!" said Sandra. "You're on a sabbatical from your employer, aren't you? Gatesave, the British supermarket chain."

"Oh, I've heard of you!" said Heidi, breaking into a wide and heart-breakingly gorgeous smile. "I want to talk to you. I need your help."

"I would be absolutely delighted," I said, suddenly conscious that I had bowed slightly.

"Heidi works for an NGO," said Sandra. "They've been researching labour practices in the Cape winelands."

"Blimey, another one!" I said.

"Oh?" said Heidi. "I wasn't aware anyone else was covering the same subject. Do you know who?"

"Oh, some Scandinavian troublemaker," I said, smirking charmingly.

"You work with Blanchkopf Wine Growers, don't you?" said Heidi, her smile suddenly looking a little more professional. "We've been trying to engage with them for a while, but we've not been able to gain access to the estate. I understand Gatesave are one of their biggest customers. So, you could help us with that, I think?"

"Oh God!" I said, as my face flushed red and my armpits began to weep. "Oh, God, yes, yes, of course! I suppose I'd be very happy to help."

Sandra, I realised, was enjoying my discomfort. This struck me as rather reckless. It was in no-one's interest to be discussing Blanchkopf openly at an event like this. I glanced around to see if he was within earshot.

"Mr Blanchkopf is here tonight," said Sandra. "Felix could introduce you, couldn't you, Felix?"

"Yes, I could." I felt sick. What the hell was Sandra playing at?

"Thank you," said Heidi. "I've heard a lot about this Mr Blanchkopf." She touched my arm and her beautiful lips became poutingly serious. "Not all of it good, though."

"Well, I don't do all that much business with him these days," I said, lamely.

"Why not? Is there a problem with him?" asked her lips. Christ, I was quite drunk. I wished I hadn't skipped breakfast.

"I think Jacobus is about to speak," said one of the group.

The crowd quietened and I thanked my lucky stars, as the Platinum Fox, CEO of Paris-Blois International, skipped effortlessly onto the stage, not a silver hair out of place. The room burst into applause, along with a few cheers and whistles contributed by the keener, or perhaps drunker, Paris-Blois employees. The Platinum Fox raised his hands and gestured for quiet, a charming, luxury-goods-CEO smile on his handsome, tanned face.

"Please, please, you are too kind!" he called, in an unplaceable, Euro-American accent. "Thank you, thank you. And welcome, friends, partners and team members, to Hemelhuis, the African jewel in the crown of Paris-Blois International!"

There was more clapping and a few more whoops.

"I want to start and finish with an inspirational story."

More applause. With a gnawing sense of foreboding, I began consuming the mini samosas that had been lubricating my right hand for the past ten minutes. The Platinum Fox purred on, eliciting smiles, nods and smatterings of applause from the crowd as he listed the ways in which Paris-Blois International was straining every sinew to bring social justice to the downtrodden of the world. I edged my way to the back of the room, where I harvested more party snacks from the hovering waiters and replenished my glass. I kept my eye on Heidi's location, which was relatively straightforward, given her blue hair, wondering whether I should rekindle our relationship once the speeches were over, or just do a runner.

The Platinum Fox invited his first guest on to the stage, a portly black man in an expensive suit and tie. He was introduced as the ruling ANC party's Minister for Social Justice, and he proceeded to give a turgid speech on the achievements delivered by his government over the past two decades. The only highlight was when he mentioned the picture of Nelson Mandela in the entrance hall, then looked up at the Paris-Blois banner declaring one hundred years of inclusion and partnership, and suggested the company could have moved slightly faster to embrace inclusion and partnership, particularly during the twenty-seven years Mandela had spent in prison. At that, the Platinum Fox nodded so vigorously that I thought his head might topple clean off, and he led the crowd in a round of applause of such volume and duration that I could see people's hands beginning to smart.

When the applause had subsided, the Platinum Fox reminded everyone that he intended to finish the speeches with a final, inspirational anecdote. I lifted another glass from a passing waiter and took a sip.

"Liar," whispered a deep voice behind me.

Oh dear, I thought. Not everyone's a fan of the ANC government, clearly.

"Liar," whispered the voice again, this time into my ear. I froze then turned, slowly, to find myself staring up into Gambu's enormous face. He had swapped his hammer, sickle and grape t-shirt for a dark suit and white, open-necked shirt, and he'd left his beret at home, but he certainly hadn't misplaced his terrifying, intimidating stare.

"A liar," he breathed, his vast stomach pressing against me.

"Hoo… hoo… me?" I squeaked. "Or the A… A… ANC?"

"You!" he said, his voice vibrating like a bass tuba. A couple of people glanced round.

"If you attack me, there are witnesses," I gibbered.

"Let all Africa be my witness!" he purred, his face like black thunder.

"Felix Hart!" called the Platinum Fox from the stage. "Where are you?"

"Here!" I shrieked, spinning round and slewing my glass of sparkling wine across several nearby guests.

Loud applause erupted and the Platinum Fox, catching sight of me, beamed and beckoned me up to the stage. With a backward glance at Gambu, who had clenched both fists and was pressing them to his chest, I tottered forward through the path cleared by the crowd. I climbed onto the stage and the applause increased. The Platinum Fox grasped my hand, which was now coated not only in samosa grease but also in sparkling wine, and pumped it, before releasing me, withdrawing a handkerchief and wiping his fingers. I also shook the hand of the Minister for Social Justice, who winced slightly as my oily hand slipped inside his.

"This man has done more to bring the people of South Africa together than perhaps anyone in the entire wine industry," said the Platinum Fox, waving his handkerchief at me. I glanced over at Gambu, staring at me, motionless, from the far corner, like a carved ebony giant. Then, sensing movement on the other side of the room, I saw Blanchkopf's bearded face and bared teeth moving forward through the crowd.

"No, no, not me!" I protested.

"So modest!" declared the Platinum Fox, his hair glittering under the spotlight. "But who would have dared think, even a few months ago, that two people, from the opposite sides of this country's tragic divide, could be brought together, united by the bonds of commerce?"

Blanchkopf was half-way to the stage and I suspected he wasn't going to stop when he reached the front. I glanced behind me at the sash windows, wondering if I could hurl myself through them and sprint for the front gate. A camera flashed and I turned back to the crowd. I caught sight of Sandra, smiling at me. It was a malicious smile, of course. It appeared I'd been set up, most horribly.

"We have no fewer than three Inclusivity and Partnership trophies to award this evening," beamed the Platinum Fox. "Each of the recipients has only just been told, so we must forgive their shock and surprise! And the irony of one of the winner's identities will not be lost on you, Minister, or your ANC colleagues, I'm sure!"

"Indeed not! Quite incredible!" chuckled the Minister for Social Justice. He gestured at Gambu standing at the back of the room and the crowd turned. Gambu's eyes closed in disgust. "That man over there once swore to destroy every trace of the white man in Africa! But what a journey of reconciliation he has travelled. It is worthy of Madiba himself! Now, he even does business with his former sworn enemy, a man against whom he was demonstrating just weeks ago!" The Minister pointed at Blanchkopf, who snarled at me as applause rippled through the crowd. "I don't know what Mr Gambu's more radical political colleagues think," continued the Minister, "but I salute his bravery and his change of heart. Thank you, sir, for embracing the new South Africa! And congratulations on your Inclusivity and Partnership Award. If you wish, there is a place in the ANC for you once more, my friend!"

At this, the crowd laughed and burst into applause. Gambu opened his eyes and glared at me. Then he raised his great fists above his head and banged them together, one atop the other, before turning and leaving the room. I prayed the gesture was a symbol of inclusivity and partnership, though given the expression on his face, I suspected that might have been wishful thinking.

Blanchkopf had now reached the front of the stage, his face puce. He raised his own fist and shook it. But before he could say anything, Heidi clasped his fist in her hand.

"I want to say something!" called Heidi, her voice high and clear. The crowd quietened. "Before he receives his award, I want to talk about this man here, this wonderful man."

For an exciting moment, I assumed she meant me, but Heidi placed her arm around Blanchkopf's shoulders. Blanchkopf's eyes nearly popped out of his face. I suspected he'd never seen a woman with blue hair before, and certainly not one who called him wonderful.

"This man once ran one of the most problematic farms in the whole of southern Africa!" she declared.

"Grrr," muttered Blanchkopf, completely unable to comprehend what was happening.

"But then, he embraced a new path and showed true leadership. Within weeks he had tripled the wages of his staff, gained Fairly Trod certification in record time, and helped create one of the fastest-selling wine brands in South African history. That is a beautiful thing, Mr Blanchkopf!"

She kissed Blanchkopf on his bearded cheek and embraced him. Blanchkopf's hands flapped around for a few seconds behind Heidi's back before she released him, grasped his arm and raised his hand in the air once more. The crowd applauded and cheered.

"I'm glad I left my wife at home," muttered Blanchkopf, once the applause had subsided, and the crowd erupted in laughter.

The Platinum Fox brandished a trophy of two clasped hands surrounded by a wreath of grapes. He sandwiched me between himself and the Minister for Social Justice, thrust the trophy into my hands and beamed. I smiled, just in time, and a camera flashed.

"Congratulations on your Paris-Blois Inclusivity and Partnership Award," called the Platinum Fox, over the applause.

He brought his face closer to my ear. "Well done. You can go now."

Well, that worked out reasonably well, I thought, basking in the sea of happy faces. In fact, I mused, while I'm up here I may as well take a picture of my own, given that it was unlikely anyone would be smiling at me back in England. It might even come in useful at my forthcoming show trial. I held up my phone, took a step backwards and was conscious, for a sickening second, that there was nothing solid beneath my foot. There was a cacophonous clatter of metal, and everything went dark.

Chapter 34

Exile

I awoke to find a black woman in a nurse's uniform fiddling with my bedsheets.

"What are you doing?" I yelped. "You can't blackmail me! I have nothing left to lose."

"Calm down please, Mr Hart, or you will burst your stitches," replied the woman.

I tried to focus on my surroundings and realised one of my eyes was obscured by fabric.

"Don't touch the dressing please."

"Where am I?"

"You are in Stellenbosch Medicentre, a private clinic. You had an accident yesterday."

"What happened? Was I attacked?"

"I believe you fell off a stage onto some lighting equipment. There was evidence alcohol might have been a contributing factor. You received a cut to your lower back and a bump to the head. You may have slight concussion. How do you feel?"

"My back's sore. And my head."

"How is your sight? Is it clear or blurred?"

I looked past the woman to the far wall, on which hung a reasonably un-blurred picture of Table Mountain, taken from the city centre. An armchair lay in the corner, occupied by a stuffed penguin. Next to me, on the bedside table, stood a bowl of fruit and a gold statue, of two clasped hands surrounded by a wreath of grapes, which I recognised as my Inclusivity and Partnership Award. There wasn't a medical diagram or wall-mounted first aid kit in sight.

"Are you sure this is a hospital?"

"It's a clinic, yes. I'm quite sure of that. I work here."

My eyes fell upon the wardrobe.

"Could you open the doors of that, please," I said, pointing. "I want to see what's inside."

"These are your clothes, Mr Hart," she said, opening the wardrobe doors.

A single, neatly ironed shirt and a pair of trousers hung from the rail.

"They're not my clothes."

"Your old clothes were ruined in the accident, Mr Hart. We had to cut them off you. Your friends from the winery supplied some new ones. They're covering the cost of your treatment too."

"So, I'm free to leave?"

"You're welcome to leave if you like. But you need to take it easy and let that cut heal. You shouldn't drive, exercise or sit upright for long periods."

"I have to fly home tomorrow."

"I wouldn't advise that. Unless you're flying business class, on one of those flat beds."

"Actually, I am."

"Well, lucky you. Try to keep your weight off the damaged area and no sudden movements."

Back at the guesthouse, I wrapped my Inclusivity and Partnership trophy in a spare shirt and zipped it, together with the stuffed penguin, into my suitcase. The nurse had explained, earlier that morning, as I limped through reception with the toy bird under my arm, that it was a purchasable item rather than a free gift, so I told her to add the cost to the medical bill. Given Paris-Blois's negligence in failing to fit safety rails around the rear of their stage, I felt a stuffed penguin was the least they owed me.

I phoned Troy Frittersley, informing him that I was being airlifted back to the UK following a knife injury incurred defending the Tears of Pity medical facility from an attack by drug-addled gangsters.

"Dear boy, how awful! It is I who is responsible!" he had cried, sounding genuinely heart-broken. "Oh, I will never forgive myself! Tell me, are your injuries life-changing?"

"Well, in a sense," I said, feeling slightly embarrassed at having made up such a cynical porky. "But it's nothing really. Just a flesh wound."

"Thank goodness! But what a shame! Two of our board of trustees are flying out next week to see your work. I wanted to join them but, sadly, I'm not permitted to fly these days. Deep vein thrombosis. Such a drag."

Lordy, I've dodged a bullet there, I thought.

"They're just back from two months in the Philippines," continued Troy. "We run a facility on the outskirts of Manila for fallen women."

"Well, I can guarantee they'll be welcomed with open arms in South Africa," I said.

"I'm sure you're right. So sorry your sabbatical had to be cut short. But thank goodness you're all right. I shall be contacting Gatesave and telling them what a magnificent job you've done. And don't you dare forget to come and see us at Tears of Pity HQ once you're fully mended."

"I will do. Thank you, Troy."

After a sustained assault upon the business lounge wine selection, I boarded the evening British Airways flight and settled into my club class seat. For a minute or so, I was overcome by a most peculiar sensation, an unsettling feeling that something vital was missing, that the world was somehow unbalanced. For the life of me I couldn't work out what was wrong until I realised, with a jolt, that I was surrounded entirely by white people. I was conscious I had gained an insight beyond the grasp of most of my fellow Anglo-Saxons, and I wondered whether this was how it felt to be a great mathematician or scientist, divining profound truths while lesser minds wandered ignorantly in the darkness. I reclined my seat and, as sleep overtook me, I reflected, with a forgivable twinge of smugness, that I had quite possibly achieved full wokeness.

On arrival in the UK, I'm afraid to say, my fellow countrymen appeared not to be living their best lives. At immigration, the official scowled at my temporary travel documents and inconvenienced me for nearly an hour with tiresome questions regarding my place of embarkation, why I was carrying only a small item of hand luggage, and what I had been up to in darkest Africa. He appeared unimpressed with my account of upliftment and empowerment in the townships, and spent a further ten minutes tapping, self-righteously, on his keyboard until I was finally nodded through. Whether it was the graze on my head, my ill-fitting shirt, my truculent attitude at immigration, or all three, I was targeted for further interrogation at customs, where a large, angry, uniformed woman and a small, even angrier, uniformed man demanded I empty my suitcase on a metal table and explain again why I was travelling so light after such a long period abroad.

My Inclusivity and Partnership Award was tapped, rattled and sniffed for hidden explosives, then my poor stuffed penguin was slit open with a disposable craft knife and the woman rummaged its innards most disrespectfully. After a few seconds of ferreting, her eyes lit up and she withdrew a roll of fabric. My heart stopped as she triumphantly unfolded it and I wondered, wildly, whether I was a patsy in a sophisticated plot by the Stellenbosch Medicentre to smuggle hard drugs into the UK.

The woman frowned. I peered at the unrolled rectangle of fabric, which stated in red block capitals: DANGER DEATH FIRE CHILDREN CHOKE and, beneath, MADE IN CHINA.

"That's not safe for importation into the country," said the small man, angrily.

"It's all yours," I replied. "Take it home for the kids."

The woman dropped the disembowelled penguin and my Inclusivity and Partnership Award back into the case and pushed it towards me. I zipped up my belongings and trudged to the Heathrow Express, thoroughly depressed to be home.

Upon arrival at Paddington station, I caught the tube to Leicester Square and walked the few hundred yards to Minstrels

Hall, home to the Worshipful Institute of the Minstrels of Wine. There, I took a shower, checked that the wines Foyley had rescued for me three months ago had arrived safely, and headed to the Salon de Dijon for the only speck of jollity on a dismal horizon, namely a long, wine-soaked lunch with my old chum Elmo, Head Drinks Buyer for Goedkoper, our CEO's former employer. Elmo had emailed me a few days ago, just after I'd received the news of my recall and imminent defenestration, informing me he was in London for a week, touring Kentish sparkling wine vineyards, so we'd set a date for lunch at Minstrels Hall.

"Let's drink something expensive, Elmo," I sighed. "My treat. I've got a few nice bottles in storage here. Tomorrow's my final day of employment by Gatesave."

"Yes, I read all about your Black Power wines. You got some crazy PR for that, I have to hand it to you."

"Unfortunately, the wrong kind of crazy. I've been summoned to a disciplinary hearing in the morning."

"You mean they're going to throw you under the bus? That sucks. People get upset about such stupid things. Will they definitely fire you?"

"Yes. I'm seeing the Head of People Needs in the morning. He's known as the Butcher of Gatesave. You don't get a meeting with the Butcher unless it's your final few minutes in the business."

"Sorry to hear that, man. At least you won't have to spend any more time working for Herbert Marris. I give thanks to your company every day for taking him off our hands."

"Yes, it sounds like absolute carnage at Head Office. Better off out, I suppose."

"Anyway, Felix, I have to say, that Black Power Pinotage was such a funky idea. The Woke White too. Everyone is talking about it. Goedkoper are going to stock both wines from next month. We'll just sell it in Amsterdam and Rotterdam, though. The cool places. Not in the conservative regions. Those guys are dicks."

"Great to hear someone's building on all my hard work."

"Yeah, seems like I probably owe you, man. Hey, I'll pay for lunch, how about that? Let's have a bottle of Puligny to start."

Elmo waved to the barman.

"Oh, I nearly forgot. I brought you something to make you laugh." Elmo extracted a slim magazine from his bag and placed it on the table. The publication was titled *Goedkoper Vandaag* and the cover was dominated by an enormous pyramid of confectionary tins, covered in tinsel, next to which stood an attractive woman, wearing a pair of Goedkoper-branded dungarees and a Santa hat.

"I assume this is your employer's in-house magazine, Elmo."

"Yes, exactly. All the staff receive a copy." Elmo tapped the date in the top corner. "From two Decembers ago."

The barman extracted the cork from a very pleasant-looking bottle of white Burgundy and poured Elmo a measure.

"I'm not sure I've spotted the joke," I said. "Unless there's something intrinsically amusing about a large pile of *stroopwafel*?"

"That's very good," said Elmo to the barman, who poured us each a large glass.

"Is this a special Dutch joke, invisible to English people?"

"No, no. Not the front cover. Here, look inside."

Elmo turned to the middle pages, where a queue of miserable-looking children waited in line for a present from Santa Claus. I was surprised to see this particular Santa was black, beardless and wore a white ruff and large gold earrings.

"What's going on here then?" I said, peering at the oddly attired Father Christmas. There was definitely something peculiar about him. "Is Santa wearing lipstick?"

"Yeah, he's wearing lipstick, man," said Elmo, grinning. He took a mouthful of Burgundy.

"Actually, is that a *white* person wearing black makeup? And lipstick? And… an afro wig?"

"Yeah, yeah. It's *Zwarte Piet*. Black Pete."

"Who the hell's Black Pete?"

"He's like Santa's African friend. He gives presents to the kids on St. Nicholas' Eve. Look, he's giving out sweets to the children in one of our stores."

"What? You're telling me that in the Netherlands, Santa has an African friend?"

"Yeah, *Sinterklaas* has an African friend. Actually, Black Pete's supposed to live in Spain. But he's definitely African."

I took a swig of the excellent Burgundy.

"And your company couldn't find a black person to play the part, so you got a white person to black up?"

"Yes, that's the tradition! It's supposed to be a white person who blacks up."

"Let me understand this. Santa has an African friend, who lives in Spain, but he pops over to Holland on Christmas Day to distribute presents?"

"On St Nicolas' Eve. The fifth of December."

"Ok, so he's an early bird. Santa has an African friend, called Pete, who lives in Spain, but he pops over to Holland on the fifth of December to distribute presents. And he's played by a white person wearing black makeup, lipstick and earrings. What's Santa doing while this is going on? Smoking crack?"

"I told you, it happens everywhere in the Netherlands. He's *Sinterklaas's* friend, and he helps him give out presents. What's wrong with that? It's a beautiful thing. Racial harmony."

"It's a nice story, Elmo, but I don't understand why it's a white person blacking up. Don't people get upset about that?"

"Not really. Well, a few people, more recently. Like I said, people get upset about stupid things."

"Do any black people get upset about it?"

"Actually, yes, come to think of it, some black people do. And a few woke white people. Which is why I want to sell your famous racial wines in Goedkoper."

"Ok, well, you learn something every day. Is that the funny thing you wanted to show me, to cheer me up? It's more funny-peculiar than funny-ha-ha, to be honest."

"Look at Black Pete!"

"I'm looking at him. He's weird. You wouldn't get away with that in England, I can guarantee you. People would go nuts."

"You're not looking closely enough." Elmo grinned and took another mouthful of Burgundy. I shrugged, but he nodded at the page, widening his eyes meaningfully.

"I don't know what you mean," I said, looking at the strange figure in his red velvet costume and gold hooped earrings. "He just looks like some middle-aged white guy in… wait… Holy Jesus Christ!" I physically spasmed in shock, knocking my wine and slopping some on to the magazine.

"Careful, man, that's an antique!" said Elmo, dabbing at the wet page with a napkin.

"It's Herbert Marris!" I yelped. "What in the name of God is he doing?"

"I told you, it's a tradition!" laughed Elmo. "The CEO dresses up as Black Pete every year and gives sweets to the kids in one of our stores. Pretty funny, yes?"

I stared at the blacked-up, lipsticked face. It was quite clearly Marris. You could see his mean eyes and grim little smile.

"What was he thinking?" I said, shaking my head, still in shock.

"Look, it's a big thing in the Netherlands," said Elmo. "Though Marris gave it his own little cost-saving twist. All those sweets he's handing out, they're out of date. Such a stingy son-of-a-bitch!"

"May I keep this, please?" I asked, placing my hands on the magazine. "Just for a day or so."

"You see, I knew you'd find it funny!"

Chapter 35

Empathy

"Yes? Who the hell is it?" shouted the Head of People Needs the next morning, as I tapped on his door.

I turned the handle and entered. The Butcher of Gatesave glowered at me across his desk, his fists resting on a pile of paperwork. Beside him sat a sad-looking secretary. For a second, her eyes met mine, before they dropped to her laptop.

"Oh, it's you. Sit down, Hart. This won't take long."

I closed the door behind me and rested my hands on the back of the empty chair.

"Sit down, I said!" I spotted a couple of half-healed scabs on the Butcher's knuckles. "Why are you shaking? Oh God, you're not going to faint, are you? Not another one. Emma, get him a bloody glass of water, will you?"

The secretary rose to her feet.

"No, I don't need water," I said, quietly.

"Well, sit down then, damn it! This won't take long. I've done thirty-six this bloody month already. Surprised there's anyone left in this business with that lunatic in charge."

"It must be very difficult," I said.

"Shut up, Hart, you sarcastic arse-hole! It is difficult, actually, since you mention it. The number of high calibre employees we've had to march off the premises, just because they tried a joint at a party six months ago, is bloody ridiculous. At least we're firing a genuine moron this time."

I moistened my lips.

"I have something interesting to show you."

"Do you, Hart, do you indeed? Well, I've got something even more interesting to show *you*. The termination of your contract, with immediate effect, due to gross idiocy."

"I think you'll want to see this."

"Hart, will you be quiet! You're only here because we're required to go through this rigmarole for legal reasons." The Butcher waved his hand at the secretary. She slid a piece of paper across the desk, avoiding eye contact.

"Now, I'm obliged to ask you whether you wish to appeal against this decision. And before you answer, let me make clear that if you do, it won't make the slightest difference, except to make me extremely bloody angry."

I removed Elmo's magazine from my jacket pocket, opened it at the centre pages, and placed it on the table, facing the Butcher.

"What the hell is this?"

I leaned over and placed my finger next to Black Pete's head.

"I'm very disappointed to inform you that our CEO is a terrible racist."

"Oh my God!" gasped the secretary and clapped her hand over her mouth.

The Butcher stared at the picture, his eyes bulging until I thought they would pop from their sockets. He opened his mouth and made a low rasping noise, which he repeated several times, until I realised he was asking me a question.

"Oh, it's from when he was CEO of Goedkoper, that Dutch supermarket chain. Apparently, he used to black up and visit stores, for a bit of a laugh."

I slowly removed my finger from the magazine. The Butcher continued to goggle at Black Pete.

"It's very disappointing, isn't it?" I said, hopefully.

The Butcher remained silent for a while, as though committing every pixel of the image to memory. Then, he raised his eyes and spoke, very slowly and deliberately.

"Who knows?"

"No-one, yet," I said. "But I'm sure there are copies. People are bound to find out."

"So, no-one has made a complaint?"

"No. But I'm thinking of making one. I'm very offended."

"I want a person of colour," he said, looking me right in the eye.

"You want what?"

"A person of colour!" said the Butcher, more loudly. "You're no good. It must be a person of colour who makes the complaint."

"Oh, must it?" I said, rather disappointed.

"Yes. It must. Preferably, someone senior."

"I can't actually think of any senior managers of colour," I said, racking my brains. "I'm sorry to say it, but I reckon Gatesave might have a diversity issue."

The Butcher reddened, quite alarmingly.

"Though I'm sure it's very difficult to find the right talent," I added.

"Find someone, Hart. Very quickly."

He pushed the magazine back at me.

"Very, very quickly."

I stuffed the magazine inside my jacket and tore out of the office. I knew exactly who I needed to speak to. I flew down the stairs and sprinted to the grocery trading department.

"Henry!" I panted, pulling up a chair next to the buyer for pasta, rice and oils. "How are you?"

I didn't know Henry terribly well, but he was well regarded as a solid and tenacious buyer. He was also a person of colour. The only person of colour, in fact, in the entire buying department.

"Hello Felix," said Henry. "What do you want?"

I ran my eyes over Henry's desk. It was the cleanest and tidiest desk I'd ever seen. His paperwork, neatly labelled with luminous post-its, sat in immaculate plastic wallets and his laptop looked as though it had been deep cleaned. The only sign of dust was a thin layer of shavings in the transparent base of his rotary pencil sharpener. A handful of perfectly aligned pieces of card were fastened to the pin board at the back of his desk; a map of the UK showing the locations of Gatesave's depots, a reference guide to different pasta shapes, and a bible quote printed against a picture of an Alpine lake:

"Be not quick in your spirit to become angry, for anger lodges in the heart of fools." Ecclesiastes 7:9

"Great quote," I said, pointing at the card.

"Oh. I didn't realise you were a fan of the Holy Bible, Felix."

"Well, I'm no expert. But I dabble occasionally. Anyway, I have something to discuss."

"What's your favourite passage?"

"Passage? Oh, I see. Well, some of the Exodus stuff, perhaps. Let My People Go, that sort of thing. Now, I need to raise a serious issue."

"Wow. You're an Old Testament guy, then."

"Yeah, pretty old school, that's me. Look, Henry, I need to show you something." I placed the magazine on the desk, turned to the centre pages and smoothed it flat. "I'm very sorry to expose you to this. It's rather unpleasant, I'm afraid." I pointed to Black Pete. "This is Herbert Marris, our CEO, wearing blackface makeup."

Henry looked at the picture.

"Why does this concern me, Felix?"

"Well, it's pretty offensive, wouldn't you say? Blacking up? That's one of the most offensive things you can do."

"I am offended, Felix."

"Great! I mean, not great at all. But I agree with you. You might want to make a complaint to HR as soon as possible. We need to nip this kind of thing in the bud."

"I'm offended by *you*, Felix, bringing something like this to me."

"Are you? Oh, sorry. I really didn't mean to offend." I began to break out in a cold sweat. "I do apologise for just springing this on you."

"I happen to agree with a lot of what Herbert Marris is doing around here. Dealing with degeneracy, for one thing."

I began to realise I'd made a terrible mistake.

"Well, yes, he's been very effective on the degenerates, can't fault him there. But I thought you might, you know…" I tailed off and looked down at Black Pete, smirking at the line of miserable children.

"Shame on you, Felix, for bringing this to me. Shame on you."

"Right. Sorry."

I gathered up the magazine and moved away from Henry as quickly as possible. I marched past the rows of desks, checking left and right for people of colour, but the entire department was populated by white people. I realised I needed to adopt a more systematic approach and search the building from bottom to top. I took the lift to the ground floor and pushed through the double doors leading to the Marketing department. More white faces, as far as the eye could see.

"Where are all the people of colour?" I wailed, in frustration.

"Oh God, spare me, please! I assume you've been sent down here deliberately, to torment me?" It was the Head of Message. She slumped low in her chair, looking thoroughly miserable. "What the hell are you still doing here, anyway? I thought they'd kicked you out."

"They're trying," I said.

"Not hard enough, clearly. Well, this is our last day too." She waved in the direction of a dozen downcast colleagues, who I recognised as the PR and Social Media team.

"Oh, yes. I forgot. Sorry everyone."

"Felix, I could say it doesn't matter, no harm done. Unfortunately, that would be a lie. It does matter, and you've done us incalculable harm. But, quite frankly, I can't even be bothered to despise you anymore. That sociopath upstairs has a total monopoly on my hatred."

"Our CEO thinks social media isn't important," said a young woman. "Such a basic idiot."

"Given what a tight-arse he is, you'd think at least he'd appreciate we're value for money," said another. "Free communication, to over three hundred thousand followers, at the push of a button. You can't get that from old media."

"Screw him," said the Head of Message. "I'm tempted to post a picture of him on Facebook with a Nazi armband drawn on."

I said nothing, because my tongue had become temporarily paralysed. I forced my shaking hand inside my jacket and withdrew the magazine.

"And a spunk stain on his trousers," said another, to laughter.

Not only was I unable to speak, my fingers had become fat and uncooperative. I fumbled the magazine, trying and failing to open it. I flung it down on a desk, licked my fingers and began turning through the pages.

"Shall we all just go down the pub, right now?" said the Head of Message.

I turned, frantically, past pictures of shelves packed with fruit liqueurs, a sea-going barge in front of a Goedkoper depot, a double-page spread on the workings of a *stroopwafel* factory…

"Good call," said her neighbour. "Farewell Gatesave, you bunch of muppets. Let's go." The team got to their feet.

I licked my fingers again, but my tongue was dry. I tore past a feature on Goedkoper truck drivers doing a charity fun run, a step-by-step guide on how to assemble a cardboard advocaat display unit, an interview with the smoked eel buyer. Show yourself, Black Pete, damn you! Show us your foul face!

At last, I arrived at the centre pages.

"This!" I whispered, my tongue slowly coming back to life. "This!"

"See you around, Felix," called the Head of Message, as she led her team to the exit. "Let's hope your next career move is slightly less catastrophic than your last."

"This!" I said, more loudly.

"This what?" she said, reaching the door and pulling it open.

"This! This must not stand!" I shouted, a tear rolling down my face. I held the magazine out before me, open at the centre pages, my hands shaking.

The Head of Message turned, half out of the door.

"Felix, what the hell are you on about? I need a drink and I've had enough of your nonsense for a bloody lifetime. What's that magazine?"

"Look!" I whispered, pointing at Black Pete. "It's him!"

The Head of Message sighed and walked slowly back to where I was standing. Her team followed. She peered at the outstretched picture.

"Who's him?" she said. Then, her eyes widened. "Oh. Oh, wow. Oh my God!"

She took the magazine from my hands and placed it on her desk, smoothing the centre pages flat. Her team crowded round.

"It's him. It's really him," said a woman. "He's literally blacked up."

"You can see in his eyes that he thinks it's a really great idea," said another.

There was a minute of silence, as everyone absorbed the wondrous tradition of Black Pete, Santa Claus's best African friend.

"It would be bad. If it got out," I croaked, finally.

"Yes, Felix," said the Head of Message, kissing me on the cheek and opening the lid of the scanner. "It would be very bad indeed."

Chapter 36

Colour-blind

"Well, Elmo," I said, placing the rather crumpled copy of *Goedkoper Vandaag* on the bar of the Salon de Dijon, "they say the only constant these days is change."

It was a month later and Elmo was in town for a few days on a fact-finding tour of London gin distilleries.

"Very true," said Elmo, holding a glass of rather marvellous Gevrey-Chambertin up to the light. "Though I'm fascinated to know how you saved your career. Your disciplinary meeting must have gone well, after all."

"Yes, the HR department saw sense in the end and issued me a royal pardon. The Inclusivity and Partnership Award I won for my charity work definitely helped. They've even put the trophy on display in reception."

"I'm guessing they haven't put the other trophies on display, the ones from that marketing body?"

Hot on the heels of Gatesave's Tin Ear nomination, the Royal Institute of Advertising and Influencing had felt obliged to create a new award, christened the 'Tinstagram', to celebrate the most disastrous social media posting of the year. The inaugural award, of course, was dedicated to Gatesave's CEO, and commemorated the moment when an anonymous Gatesave employee posted the photograph of Herbert Marris, dressed as Black Pete, simultaneously on Facebook, Twitter, Instagram and LinkedIn, accompanied by the caption:

We don't care about your colour! Merry 'Colour-Blind' Christmas to you all, black, white and anything in between! From Herbert Marris, CEO and influencer, and his happy Gatesave dwarfs.

The judges, in a unanimous decision, highlighted the 'almost maniacally insensitive wording' of the post, declaring the imagery 'an unsettling melange of Grimm, Gradgrind and Goebbels', and asserted the posting, overall, to be 'the most catastrophic use of social media by a corporate entity since the invention of the world wide web'.

"No, I don't think they'll be placing that particular trophy in the cabinet, Elmo. How are Black Power Pinotage and Woke White selling in Goedkoper?"

"Like *stroopwafel* at Christmas, Felix. It's super-crazy! Great profit margin too. By the way, I visited a branch of Gatesave yesterday, just doing a little retail research while I'm in town. I saw you guys are selling the wines again."

"Yes, Gatesave soon changed their mind on that one. You can't afford *not* to sell Black Power Pinotage and Woke White these days. It would be like not selling Prosecco. Gambu sent me a press release last week announcing that Black Power Pinotage is on track to become the biggest South African wine brand in the world. It's massive in the States. I believe New Marxism magazine have declared him Revolutionary of the Year."

"Man, I was watching that Gambu guy on CNN in the airport. He was speaking at some US college, arguing that all white people should be thrown out of Washington DC and it should be a black-only city, or something. All these white Americans were cheering him. They really love him over there. He should run for president."

"I'm pretty sure there's a rule about presidential candidates having to be born in the US, Elmo."

"Yes, but I bet he's made enough money to persuade Congress to change it. They like winners over there, Felix, not boring rules."

We paused as the barman topped up our glasses, and my mind strayed to Mama Bisha's Tuck Shop. I'd dropped in on Troy Frittersley the previous week, who'd informed me that the visit to Mama Bisha's by his Tears of Pity trustees had gone extremely well.

"They were overwhelmed, Felix! Overwhelmed, by the passion of the nursing staff. How I wish I could have joined them!"

"I'm sure it was an emotional experience, Troy."

"It takes a lot to move the Tears of Pity trustees, Felix, but my! On their return, they proposed we fund several new roles, immediately, to support the diversification of the Khayelitsha facility. Usually, they're the cautious ones and it's me who gets carried away, but no, they insisted!"

"What kind of roles? More nurses?"

"We've appointed a Head of Nursing Services, a Community Football Coach and an Artist in Residence. All the positions are already filled. The trustees were particularly impressed by the young lady taking up the Artist in Residence role. We're also creating a Head of Security – we can't risk any more unpleasant incidents like the one you suffered. Luckily, we've identified a suitable candidate for that role too."

"There's no shortage of talent out there, Troy, so long as you discard your unconscious bias."

"You see, Felix, that's why we sent you. You have a level of empathy and intuition that others can only dream of."

I was brought back to the present by the arrival of our *boeuf bourguignon*. Rich, meaty steam billowed from the dish, leaving a faint smear of condensation on my wine glass.

"Oh, nice work dealing with the NGO too," said Elmo. "Those guys can be real ball breakers."

The Scandinavian NGO had finally published their long-awaited report on the South African wine industry, written by the beautiful, blue-haired Heidi Vestergaard. But instead of the coruscating tale of exploitation and misery we'd feared, the report was titled 'A Rainbow Dawn in The Cape' and declared the industry to be making slow but steady progress towards social justice and upliftment. The joint venture between Gambu and Blanchkopf was highlighted as an exemplar of radical transformation, and the report's front page had a photograph of the two men shaking hands, slightly uncomfortably, surrounded by cheering black workers. Next to this picture of racial reconciliation lay a quote, in bold type, attributed to both Blanchkopf and Gambu:

"We embraced our fellow South Africans and together we faced down our real enemy: the rapacious British supermarkets!"

I felt the quote was needlessly combative, to be honest, particularly in the light of the tireless support I'd provided to all sides. It was a relief, however, to see everyone playing nicely at last. The report spoke coyly of Blanchkopf's 'long journey' to a 'social justice destination', and Heidi had wasted no opportunity to blow her own NGO's trumpet, rather over-enthusiastically in my opinion, bigging up their role in Blanchkopf Wine Growers' transformation into a model employer. Needless to say, there was no mention of yours truly, but I had become somewhat hardened by now in regards to being taken for granted.

The NGO's report even included an anecdote covering the aftermath of the Paris-Blois Inclusivity and Partnership Award ceremony, a development I had missed, of course, due to the shoddy, near-fatal workmanship of Hemelhuis's events staff. Heidi and Blanchkopf had apparently returned to Blanchkopf's farm after the party, with a photographer in tow, where he was hailed as a liberator and carried around the vineyards on the shoulders of his workers, who were ecstatic with joy following receipt of their newly tripled salaries. Going by the accompanying photographs, Blanchkopf appeared to have taken to his new role as champion of the downtrodden with gusto, and I have no doubt that being carried around his estate by cheering workers made a nice change from being pelted with rocks.

"Hey, you were right about Black Pete, Felix. Everyone went super-mad about Marris dressing up like that."

"I just have a feeling for that kind of thing, Elmo. Call it empathy."

Once the Head of Message had posted the photograph of Black Pete to Facebook, I'd reported straight back to the Butcher. He wordlessly tore up my termination letter and whispered that he'd personally strangle me with piano wire if he heard even the tiniest rumour that he might have had sight of the picture prior to it going public.

Word of the Black Pete posting reached Herbert Marris approximately twelve minutes after it appeared on Facebook. Eyewitness reports claim that he propelled himself downstairs, from the ninth to the ground floor, in under twenty seconds, and burst into the marketing department like an exploding gammon, screaming that the post should be deleted immediately. In the face of Marris's crimson-faced shrieking, the Head of Message calmly stated, over and over again, that the company appeared to have been hacked by an outside, malevolent entity who had also changed Gatesave's social media passwords, leaving them unable to remove the problematic post.

The marketing team were then forced to endure Marris describing, for exactly forty-two minutes, how he was going to destroy the careers of every single person in the room unless he was informed exactly who had posted the offending picture. But solidarity was maintained, and at minute forty-three, eyes strayed to the television screens hanging above the PR team's desks, as the BBC and Sky News channels began to describe, to their millions of viewers, the curious tradition of Black Pete and how this particular institution probably wasn't going to play terribly well outside the borders of the Netherlands.

By minute forty-four, Marris was reported to have fled to the underground car park beneath Gatesave's head office. But the CEO's private parking bay had been most inconveniently hemmed in by a delivery vehicle, rendering his car inaccessible, and forcing Marris to seek out the security office and disturb the crowd of drivers, guards and maintenance staff clustered around the television. As bad luck would have it, the vehicle's driver, a gentleman of Caribbean origin, turned out to have mislaid his keys, and despite Marris's forceful exhortations that this unacceptable situation had to be resolved – accompanied, I am led to believe, by the paddling of his angry hands against the wall – a solution remained frustratingly out of reach.

And so, Marris was obliged to flee into the rain-lashed London streets, where he scurried to-and-fro in the gutter, oblivious to the hooting traffic, flailing at occupied taxis as they splashed past, as though he might somehow oblige a driver to pull over, eject any passenger of a lesser status than Marris himself, and whisk him to a place of safety. Once it dawned on him that this strategy was failing, witnesses claim the Terror of Tadcaster raised his fists to the dark clouds above and gave an unholy wail, a bone-chilling warble that curdled the blood of those who heard it, the death-howl, you might say, of a Yorkshireman who has accidentally flushed his last penny down the lavatory. Then he vanished, forever, into the sodden gloom.

"You've been on one hell of a journey, Felix," said Elmo, taking a large mouthful of Burgundy.

"I have indeed," I said, as the barman refilled our glasses. "Who was it who said that revolutions always eat their own? Someone French, I think."

"Probably," shrugged Elmo. "Doesn't sound like something a Dutchman would say."

I raised my glass.

"I'd like to propose a toast. To African friends."

Elmo raised his glass. "To African friends."

The wine, I must say, was showing magnificently.

The End

About the Author

Peter Stafford-Bow was born into a drinking family in the north of England in the mid-1970s. A precocious, self-taught imbiber, he dropped out of university to pursue a career in alcohol. After managing several downmarket London wine merchants, he became a supermarket buyer, a role which kindled his life-long love of food, other people's hospitality, and general gadding about. After periods living in East Asia and South Africa, Stafford-Bow returned to the UK to pursue a literary career. He has written three successful novels; *Corkscrew*, *Brut Force* and *Firing Blancs*. He lives in London with his beer executive girlfriend, an extensive wine collection and his pet ferrets, Brett and Corky.

Book Club Tipple Tips

Many readers, I am told, have discovered the adventures of Felix Hart through the sociable medium of book clubs. My publisher asked that I provide a list of pointers for the attendees of such clubs, so that they might transform their solitary enjoyment of *Firing Blancs* into a garrulous, group activity. As a dutiful author who knows which side his baguette is buttered, I readily complied.

The result is a menu of fine South African wines, many of which Felix Hart savours at some point in *Firing Blancs*, to accompany your literary discussions. At the end, I have suggested the names of some reputable UK stockists. Apologies to my American, Canadian and Australian readers, who will have to find their own distributors, and may struggle to obtain some of these wines outside their larger, more cosmopolitan cities. Commiserations also to anyone residing in continental Europe under fifty-two degrees latitude (south of Berlin, Rotterdam etc), who won't have a chance in hell of procuring them. A final *désolé pour le derangement* to my French publisher, who informs me this addendum obliges her to place an alcohol health warning on the back cover (I suspect she'll replace this section with a list of French wines anyway), and to my Dubai-based importer, who tells me the following pages render this edition illegal in several Middle Eastern states. So be it.

You have vacuumed the carpet, lit a scented candle in the toilet, and removed anything by E L James from your shelves. The doorbell chimes and your book group assembles, socially distancing if disease or personal dislike deem it necessary. To start; a sparkling wine, naturally. Not Prosecco, I'm afraid. I know there's a lot of it about, but let's maintain standards. Usually, I would insist on Champagne. In the rainbow-nation spirit of this coda, however, I shall recommend a *Méthode Cap Classique* – that's South African for *méthode traditionnelle*, the same process used to create Champagne. Many wineries struggle to produce classy fizz in South Africa's challengingly warm climate, but **Colmant Brut Chardonnay** or **Graham Beck Blanc de Blancs**, both made from 100% Chardonnay, are fabulously crisp and elegant party-starters. Let the literary brouhaha begin!

Next, a still white. A good tip when selecting wine produced in a hot country (and most of South Africa is very warm indeed) is to look for the produce of its cooler regions. Cooler climate wines tend to be better balanced, which is wine-speak for beverages that don't taste like claggy, fruity soup. Elgin, around an hour's drive from Cape Town on the way to the whale-watching capital of Hermanus, is just such a region. Try a juicy Sauvignon Blanc from **Paul Cluver**, a plush, creamy Chardonnay from **Iona**, or a zippy, aromatic Riesling from **Spioenkop**. If you can track it down, I also recommend **Restless River Chardonnay**, from the cool, maritime Hemel-en-Aarde valley, though it's made in such small quantities that you may have to visit the winery to obtain it. What a hardship.

On to the reds. A lighter one to start. As well as Chardonnay, the Hemel-en-Aarde valley produces South Africa's finest Pinot Noir, and you can't go wrong with a cherry-scented, pepper-and-leather number from **Crystallum** or **Ataraxia**. Moving up the muscularity scale, it's worth considering the Swartland region, home to many of South Africa's most exciting young winemakers, and if you only drink one wine at your literary evening, it has to be the funky, palate-slapping **Smiley Red**. You thought I'd made that wine up, didn't you? On the contrary, great wine and great literature are the booziest of bedfellows, each embracing the other in palate-and-cortex-stimulating symbiosis. There are several **Smiley White** wines too, which are just as delicious. Other corking Swartland producers include **Intellego**, who make gorgeous Syrah-dominated blends, **David & Nadia**, who make fabulous Grenache, as well as Chenin Blanc, and **Testalonga** with their **Baby Bandito** range, which includes a lip-smacking, smoky, unfiltered Carignan.

Ok, now for the big red beasts. A hat-tip to **Meerlust Rubicon**, the wine rather liberally tasted by Felix on his arrival at Mama Bisha's. This now-iconic Stellenbosch wine is assembled from the classic red grapes of Bordeaux: Cab Sauvignon, Cab Franc, Merlot and Petit Verdot. You should probably serve it with hearty food, rather than on an empty stomach, as Felix discovered to his cost. Another recommendation is the heavenly **Lowerland Tolbos Tannat**, produced on a fiercely organic estate in the Northern Cape.

Sadly, at the time of writing, no winery has yet produced a Black Power Pinotage or Woke White. But you can convert your book club into your own Inclusivity and Partnership Award ceremony by purchasing wines from the following Fair Trade producers, who all happen to make great-tasting wine too. **Bosman Family Vineyards**, an old but highly progressive company, now owned by its workers. **Stellar Organics**, who are organic (yes, really!) and low-sulphur into the bargain. **Thokozani**, a worker-owned brand made on the forward-thinking Diemersfontein Estate in Wellington.

Regarding UK stockists, I would avoid the major supermarkets. Waitrose is ok, as is Booths, but the rest have pretty poor ranges these days, dominated by indistinguishable, industrially produced branded plonk and seasonal overspill from the global wine lake. Much better to visit an independent store, such as London's **Handford Wines, The Good Wine Shop**, **The Salusbury Winestore** or **Real Ale** (which also sells great wines). Outside the Big Smoke, try Birmingham's superb **Loki Wines**, **Cambridge Wine Merchants**, **The Oxford Wine Company,** or Malton's **Derventio Wines**. Or, order online from a distributor who supplies the better independent stores and restaurants, such as **Caves de Pyrène**, **Red Squirrel, Noble Fine Liquor** or **Indigo Wines**.

With a bit of luck, your book club will, by now, have degenerated into a bacchanalian orgy. I just hope no-one spills their Meerlust on the carpet. Bottoms Up!

Peter Stafford-Bow, April 2020

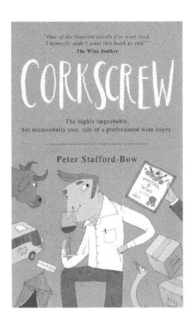

Felix, a tragic orphan, is expelled from school, cast onto the British high street, and forced to make his way in the cut-throat world of wine retail. Thanks to a positive mental attitude, he is soon forging a promising career, his sensual adventures taking him to the vineyards of Italy, South Africa, Bulgaria and Kent.

His path to the summit, however, is littered with obstacles. Petty office politics, psychotic managers and the British Board of Wine & Liquor prove challenging enough. But when Felix negotiates the world's biggest Asti Spumante deal, he is plunged into a vicious world of Mafiosi, people smuggling and ruthless multinationals.

Part thriller, part self-help manual and part drinking companion, Corkscrew is a coruscating critique of neo-liberal capitalism, religious intolerance and the perils of blind tasting.

"...one of the funniest novels I've ever read. I honestly didn't want this book to end."
Joey Casco, *The Wine Stalker*

Felix Hart, a wine buyer at the top of his game, finds himself compromised by a ruthless, multinational drinks corporation.

Forced to participate in a high-profile, corrupt wine tasting, Hart is drawn into a terrifying game of cat-and-mouse, pursued by blackmailers, assassins and organic wine fanatics.

The action moves from the Byzantine intrigue of the Minstrels of Wine to France's most glamorous chateaux, Hart relying on his quick wits, fine palate and a touch of muscle to stay ahead of his enemies. But he meets his match in Lily Tremaine, a beautiful and passionate sommelier, who disrupts his easy, pleasure-seeking life and turns his world upside down.

"It's an insane novel. It's clever… and brilliantly conceived."
Tamlyn Currin, *JancisRobinson.com*

Lightning Source UK Ltd.
Milton Keynes UK
UKHW040807150520
363228UK00003B/279